SONG OF WINDS

AN EAST OF THE SUN AND WEST OF THE MOON
RETELLING

THE SINGER TALES
BOOK 3

DEBORAH GRACE WHITE

LUMINANT PUBLICATIONS

SONG OF WINDS: AN EAST OF THE SUN AND WEST OF THE MOON RETELLING

By Deborah Grace White

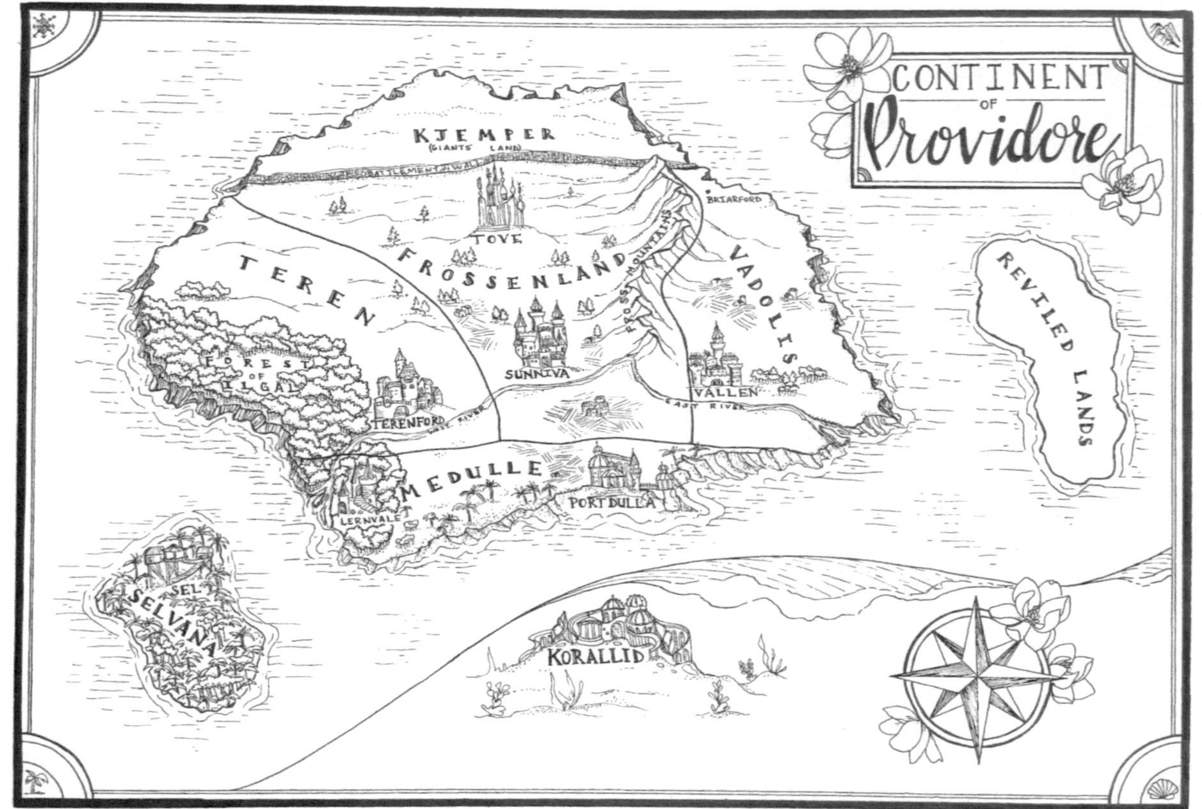

CONTINENT OF Providore
KJEMPER
(GIANTS' LAND)
BATTLEMENT WALL
TOVE
FROSSENLAND
BRIARFORD
VADOLIS
PROSS MOUNTAINS
TEREN
FOREST OF ILGAL
SUNNIVA
VALLEN
EAST RIVER
TERENFORD
WEST RIVER
MEDULLE
LERNVALE
PORT DULLA
REVILED LANDS
SEL SELVANA
KORALLID

PROLOGUE

Herleif

"All right, Your Highness, I'll take it from here."

Iver's command reached Prince Herleif's ears as the walls of the northern castle came into view between the tree trunks ahead. The building looked warm and comforting to Herleif, in spite of being mostly uninhabited. In point of fact, its secluded position nestled in the woods was a chief part of its charm. It was certainly a far cry from the chaotic bustle of his home in the kingdom's capital city of Sunniva.

Herleif grunted, trying to wave off the groundskeeper's helping hand. "I've got it, Iver, I can manage."

The look the older man sent him would have been more appropriately directed to an erring child than an eighteen-year-old crown prince.

"Just because you're built like a bear doesn't mean you can't let anyone help you, Your Highness," Iver scolded, undeterred by the fact that he had to look up into Herleif's face. "I'll take the catch to the kitchens, and you go freshen up."

Herleif grinned at the rebuke as he relinquished his burden. He had enormous respect for the shrewd and capable groundskeeper who watched over the mostly abandoned northern castle, but height wasn't on Iver's side. Herleif really was built like a bear, and it seemed absurd for the older man to carry the large deer carcass they'd brought back from their hunt just because Herleif was royal.

"You're as bad as your father," Iver grunted, as he heaved the deer across his shoulders. "Who ever heard of a king trotting up to visit the northern castle on the sly without even a guard to protect him?"

"We did bring two guards," Herleif corrected. "One's just in the town at present, buying supplies."

"I know that, Your Highness," said Iver patiently. "But two guards for a monarch and his heir?" He shook his head. "Bad form, if I may be so bold, especially up here, so close to the giants' realm."

Herleif laughed. "Oh, let us have our fun, Iver. It's not easy for royalty to get this much sport, you know. Sneaking off is our only option. And the giants surely aren't a concern, since they're stuck in their frozen, magic-less wasteland. They can't leave Kjemper. How would they get over Battlement Wall? There haven't been giants sighted in Frossenland since before I was born."

"Aye, because magic is scarce here, and the royals haven't been based in the north during that time," said Iver darkly. "So there's been nothing to attract them here. Giants are drawn to three things—magic, gold, and crowns. Don't become complacent, Your Highness. Just because they haven't crossed the wall in a long time doesn't necessarily mean they can't."

"Such doom and gloom," said Herleif lightly. He glanced around him as they left the tree line and started across the small castle grounds. There was a brutal chill in the air, in spite of it being the height of summer, and frost still clung to some of the undergrowth even so late in the morning. "I suppose I shouldn't be too glib with calling Kjemper a frozen magic-less wasteland, should I? Frossenland fits that description more each year. It's no wonder the capital was moved to Sunniva if the northern region has reached the point where this is the warmest it gets."

A frown creased Iver's forehead, and for a moment Herleif thought he'd offended the older man, who, after all, had made Frossenland's frigid north his home. But the groundskeeper didn't look upset.

"I don't know that the weather's changed," Iver mused. "It's becoming more barren, it's true, and it wasn't always so hard to find magic. Plus the quakes are much worse than they used to be. But I'm not sure it used to be any less frozen. The kingdom is called Frossenland for a reason, you know."

Herleif studied the other man curiously. "Are you sad that the capital moved? Tove used to be a thriving city, didn't it? It seems to be smaller each time I visit."

The groundskeeper shrugged. "I prefer the quiet, myself. It's not the people I miss, it's the magic. When I was a child, I could sing anytime I wanted, and get the magic to do all kinds of things. Now I can barely draw any to myself." He gave another shrug, causing the deer carcass to rise and fall. "Maybe my skill is declining."

"I doubt it's that." Herleif frowned. "Reports are consistent across the northern region—magic is much more rare than it used to be."

He gave the groundskeeper a sideways glance. He'd been curious before now about the man's choice of lifestyle, given that his rare capacity to sing—and in so doing, to wield the magic of the land—would open much more lucrative opportunities to him in the capital. Herleif couldn't imagine making the same choice. If he'd been born a singer, he would surely have wanted to put the skill to greatest use. He hadn't, of course—he couldn't so much as sing a note, and he knew it wasn't something you could learn.

"Have you ever considered moving to Sunniva yourself?" he asked delicately. "Or somewhere else further south, where the land is more fertile and the magic more plentiful?"

Iver extricated one hand from his load to scratch his chin. "People always speak of the two like they're connected," he muttered, more to himself than Herleif it seemed. "I'm not so sure that's the case."

Herleif raised an eyebrow. It was a strange opinion given how widely accepted it was across the continent of Providore that the more fertile the land, the more magic it exuded. It was a principle illustrated just as effectively by the barely manageable torrent of magic that flowed from the lush southwestern jungle as by the magic-scarce northern wastes.

"As for moving," Iver said, his voice louder now, "this is my home. My people have lived in these parts for generations." There was a moment of silence, then he sighed. "Truth is, my wife wants to move to Sunniva. Our eldest, Hagen, has inherited the singing ability, and she wants him to attend the academy there. But I can't imagine living anywhere else."

Herleif said nothing, recognizing that his opinion wasn't being sought. The castle was looming above them now, and Iver split off toward the kitchen with a promise to meet Herleif and his father inside shortly. Herleif watched him go with a tinge of guilt. Iver's wife would no doubt have her work cut out for her preparing the meal for them all that night. He and his father might get a thrill from making an unannounced visit to Tove without the hassle of a contingent of servants. But it would undoubtedly be more convenient for the tiny skeleton staff in the castle at Tove if they gave proper warning. At least he'd helped by catching the deer.

He let himself in through the side door that stood near the kitchens, hurrying to the room that had been hastily prepared for him. A shiver went over him as he went down the corridor.

Had it become draftier since he'd left that morning? He completed a quick wash and changed into fresh clothes before going in search of his father. It shouldn't be hard to find the king —only one small sitting room had been made inhabitable for their stay.

Herleif's first hint that something was amiss came as he approached the entranceway, through which he needed to pass to reach his destination. He could no longer doubt that the castle had grown draftier—the wind howling down the hall was much too strong for indoors. When he reached the entranceway, he drew up with a gasp. The enormous front door was flung wide, one half hanging off its hinges, the elaborate carving on the wood splintered and smashed. In a daze, Herleif looked around for a battering ram. What else could cause such destruction to the massive wooden structure?

Iver's warnings flashed through his mind, but it couldn't be giants. They hadn't breached Battlement Wall for decades. Surely they couldn't be here the one time he and his father made an unplanned visit.

Fear rising in him, Herleif sprinted across the stone floor, shouting for his father. To his horror, the doorway to the sitting room was marked by the unmoving form of the one guard who'd been with the king. The man was clearly dead.

Herleif threw himself over the body, emerging into the sitting room with his sword in his hand. A choking cry escaped him at the sight of his father's throat in the grip of an enormous woman. She was so huge, she was bent in a semi-crouch, although the ceiling was high. At full height, Herleif would guess her to be twice as tall as his father. Her proportions were all wrong as well, her arms and legs—as thick as tree trunks— too long for her stout body. Her head was more square than a human's, and her gray-ish skin looked rough, like the surface of a boulder. Her hair was dark and thick, pulled back in braids that resembled ropes. And with no sign of effort, she was holding King Eerikki so that his feet barely brushed the ground.

There could be no doubt what he was seeing. For the first time in his life, Herleif was looking at a giant.

"Let my father go!" he shouted, leaping toward the giant with his sword swinging.

She turned rapidly, dropping his father with a thud as she raised one booted foot. The thick leather of her shoe acted as a shield, and Herleif's thrust went awry.

"Father, did you say?" Her voice was deep and loud, but not as boorish as Herleif had expected. "You're the prince?"

Her eyes passed between Herleif and the king, who seemed to have been winded by his fall but was now scrambling to his feet.

"You're even better," she mused. "You're almost a respectable size, and you're young enough that you might still have some growing to do. You'll make my daughter a better husband."

Herleif's mouth fell open as he stared from his father to the giant. "A husband for your daughter?"

His father looked as bewildered as Herleif felt. "I've already told you, giant," the king snarled, "I already have a queen, and I would never—"

"Oh that's no matter," the giant said dismissively. "Human ceremonies mean nothing to us. But I've changed my mind now. You're too small."

Herleif tried to collect his scattered wits as her eyes moved to him. Although his father wasn't a small man by any means, it was true that Herleif already towered above him.

"Stay away from my son," said King Eerikki. "I won't allow you to—"

"As if you could stop me," the giant interrupted, scoffing. "Your son will do nicely. Bigger, stronger, with the status of a king." Her voice dropped to an irritated mutter. "A human king, which is still pathetic, but likely the best I can hope for."

"I'm not a king," said Herleif stupidly, still unable to comprehend what was happening. Why would this giant want him to marry her daughter? He'd always understood that giants despised humans as much as humans did them.

"That can be fixed easily enough," said the giant dismissively. Before Herleif had fully comprehended her words, her meaty fist shot out sideways. She didn't even take her eyes from Herleif as her fist connected with his father's head, taking the king completely by surprise. Without so much as a sound, King Eerikki crumpled to the floor.

"Father!" Herleif screamed, leaping over a footstool to reach the older man. He pulled his father's head into his lap, searching desperately for signs of life. Icy horror seized him at what he saw.

"You've killed him." The words came out the barest whisper, every part of Herleif's mind numb with disbelief.

"Yes, problem fixed, like I said," the giant told him impatiently. "You're king now."

"YOU KILLED HIM!" Herleif screamed, surging to his feet. He'd somehow lost hold of his sword in his scramble to his father, but he whipped a dagger from his belt, lunging toward the giant. There was nothing in his mind but death.

With a roar of irritation, the enormous woman's hands shot out, each one seizing one of Herleif's upper arms. She held him in an iron grip as he flailed, grief and fury making his vision spin.

"Enough of this nonsense," she screeched, her yellow eyes bulging with anger at the threats pouring from Herleif's mouth. "You will marry my daughter, and take her to your capital with you. She will rule there as a queen among you puny humans, and—"

"I would rather die!" Herleif screamed. "I would never in a thousand centuries marry any giant, let alone your vile beast of a daughter!"

"How dare you?" gasped the giant. "My daughter is beautiful beyond compare. Much stronger and more desirable than any pathetic human girl."

"I will marry a human girl," Herleif declared, his voice quivering with the strength of his emotions. "But not until after I've killed you."

She gave a disbelieving laugh. "Your insolence is unacceptable. Don't you know who you're speaking to? I am Grograna, Queen of Kjemper. You have been granted honor beyond compare to be offered the chance to wed my daughter, Princess Mundia."

At her words, Herleif's gaze flicked to her dark hair. He'd somehow missed the golden crown that glinted there. His arms still trapped against his sides, Herleif just spat on the hand that held him.

The giant's eyes narrowed in fury. "You need to be taught some manners, little king," she growled. "You think you can find a better bride than my daughter among the humans? I will make you so hideous no one will ever want to so much as look at you again, let alone marry you. Then we'll see who will yield."

"Even if another human never so much as looks at my face again," Herleif declared, "I will never marry your daughter."

A growl built in the giant's throat, and her grip tightened so much that Herleif wondered if she would crush him. But he was no stripling. He clenched his fists, putting all his strength into his arms. His muscles bulged as he strained outward, trying to break free of her hold. Just as he thought he would burst, the giant abruptly let go.

He fared better than his father had, managing to keep his feet as he landed. He raised his dagger again, but the giant already had something in her hand. He hadn't seen where she retrieved it from, but he could tell by the way the air crackled around it that the object was a powerful talisman. Where could she have gotten something so steeped in power in the magic-less northern wasteland?

Herleif dismissed the irrelevant thought, surging forward just as he heard a cry from the doorway. In the corner of his eye, he saw Iver come flying into the room just as the giant broke the object in her hand, and a rush of power sped toward Herleif.

A flare of impossibly bright light turned everything white as unimaginable pain assaulted Herleif. A low, throbbing hum told him that Iver had begun a desperate song, but Herleif could tell it was too late. The giant's vicious magic enveloped every inch of him, and he had no choice but to succumb.

FIVE YEARS LATER…

CHAPTER ONE

Adrienne

Adrienne sang softly to herself as she entered the chicken coop. She could feel the tentative strands of magic that seeped up from the earth, trying to respond to her song. She couldn't do much with them, and not just because the magic was so weak in this part of the kingdom. She simply didn't have the knowledge of songcraft.

But all that was about to change, she reminded herself. A shiver of excitement went over her as she knelt to check for eggs. Two weeks. Only two more weeks before she left for Sunniva to take up a place in the capital's Academy of Song. She could hardly believe it was really happening after eighteen years of dreaming.

"Come on, Henrietta," she scolded the nearest chicken, as she found the roost empty. "Nothing again? That's three days in a row. I know it's cold, but you need to at least try. We have to eat something, you know."

The hen gave no response to her reproach, but it did flap its wings in alarm as a tremor shook the ground. Adrienne clutched the nearest beam for support, waiting it out.

"That was a big one," she muttered, frowning. "Seems like they're getting worse."

She bit her lip, worry assailing her yet again at the thought of her family.

She hurried out of the chicken coop with the scant eggs she'd found. Her brother, Felman, was crossing the yard, and hailed her.

"Did you feel that one?" she asked before he could get a word out.

He nodded, his expression grave.

"I don't like it, Felman," she said distractedly. Unconsciously, her hand flew up to her neck to play with the simple necklace that had once belonged to her grandmother. "How will Mother manage once I'm gone, if the quakes are getting worse, and the hens aren't even laying? You and Kettil are both working so hard, and we can still barely feed ourselves. Let alone poor Revna, with three children already and her husband ill yet again."

"Don't worry about Revna," Felman said at this mention of their older sister. "We'll look after her and the children. We won't let anyone starve."

"Maybe I shouldn't be leaving," said Adrienne. "It's so much money. If we used it to live on instead of saving it up for a luxury I don't need—"

"It's not a luxury," Felman told her firmly. "Adrienne, you *must* learn your craft. This is bigger than just you. Our family hasn't seen a singer in generations. They're so rare in the north —you don't even realize how important you are. If you learn to use your gift, who knows how our fortunes might change?" His voice softened. "Besides which, you deserve it, Adrienne. You shouldn't have to waste your ability just because times are hard." He scowled. "And because our father is a useless layabout."

Adrienne sighed, but she didn't correct him. "Let's not bring him into this."

Before Felman could respond, another voice sounded across the yard. They both turned to see Kettil striding toward them, the look on his face proclaiming bad news.

"What is it?" Felman demanded when their brother reached them.

"It's Father," Kettil said, his voice tight.

"What about him?" Adrienne asked warily.

"He's just showed up," Kettil said. "He's in the house."

"What?" Dismay washed over Adrienne. Their father hadn't been near their town of Toveham for months. Why did he have to show up now, just as she was preparing to leave? It was terrible timing, after so many years of successfully hiding her ability from him. No one in the family knew what he'd do if he was aware of it, but none of them doubted that he'd find a way to use it for his own gain, without a thought for the good of Adrienne or the rest of the family.

"Don't panic, Adrienne," Felman told her sternly. "Just behave naturally. He doesn't know his timing is bad, and you haven't started packing or anything visible like that. He'll just think it's another visit. You know him. He'll breeze in, pretend he's come to check on his family like a dutiful husband and father, sniff around for any extra coin he can take with him, and be gone by the end of the week. In plenty of time for your journey to the capital."

Adrienne nodded. He was right. Her entire childhood had been riddled with such visits, and they didn't usually occasion fear. They'd all learned to look on their father's sporadic appearance as an irritation, but one that just had to be waited out. He never stayed for long. He couldn't, not without being hunted down by the many men in the village to whom he owed money.

Lifting the mostly empty basket higher up her arm, Adrienne followed her two brothers into the cottage. She recognized her father's presence the moment she entered, even before she saw his diminutive form stretched comfortably on a chair. The atmosphere was tense and unsettled, nothing like the usual cozy industry of the family. Adrienne's mother was kneading dough on the kitchen table, the crease between her brow telling Adrienne that she also felt anxious about the timing of her husband's visit.

"My, but it does a man's heart good to be home with his family," Adrienne's father said cheerily. "I've a deal to tell you, Estrid. I come bearing excellent news!"

"Do you?" Adrienne's mother sounded unimpressed.

"Yes, I've just learned of an incredible opportunity. A friend of mine has a venture starting up, and if I can come up with some coin to invest, we'll be sure to profit enormously. It could turn our fortunes around!"

"Could it?" His wife didn't turn from her task, her expression unmoving. "And have you come up with the coin?"

"Well, no," he acknowledged. "The trouble of it is, it costs so much for me to pay my way, while also supporting a family back home."

Adrienne heard a quiet snort from Kettil, but none of the children commented on this departure from reality.

"I wondered if you might have come by anything extra lately?"

The hopeful question sent another wave of tension around the room.

"I have nothing to spare, Svend," Adrienne's mother said tightly.

"Ah, that's a shame," her husband said. He waved to Revna's middle child, who'd been spending the morning under the care of her grandmother. "Come and sit on my knee, then. You're a bonny thing, aren't you?"

The little girl shook her head, backing into her grandmother's skirts.

Adrienne saw her father's brow darken with anger, and his eyes flicked to his wife. "What's wrong with the child?"

"Nothing's wrong with her," said Adrienne's mother, her voice crisp. "She's just shy around strangers. Most children are at her age."

"But I'm her own grandfather," scowled Adrienne's father. "She knows me."

"She doesn't, Father," said Adrienne patiently, moving into his line of sight. "It's been six months since your last visit, and she's only two years old. She doesn't remember that long ago."

"It's been three months at most," contradicted her father inaccurately, twisting in his chair to squint up at his younger daughter. "So you're still here, are you, Adrienne?" He cast an appraising eye over her person. "Shouldn't you be married by now? I'm sure Revna was by your age."

"You leave Adrienne alone," said his wife. "She's a good girl, and there's no haste for her to marry."

Adrienne could feel the tension thicken around the room, everyone trying not to make eye contact for fear their father would somehow read their thoughts about the different future planned for Adrienne. Not that she was against marrying. She would like to marry someone she cared for, like Revna had. But if that someone came from the capital, and had a more secure income that could help lift her family from poverty, so much the better. With any luck, her studies at the academy might bring her more than one type of opportunity.

"How old are you, Adrienne?" her father persisted, furrowing his brow in an effort of memory. "Seventeen?"

"Eighteen," she said, busying herself with unloading the eggs.

"Eighteen?" he repeated. "Well past time for marriage!" He

stood, peering over her shoulder. "What have you got there? Eggs, eh? Well, it's not quite the homecoming feast a man hopes for, but I'll take it. I'm famished."

He cast an expectant glance at his wife, who sighed and took the eggs from the bowl into which Adrienne had just placed them. She saw her brothers exchange angry glances. Those eggs would have lasted them two days, used sparingly as her mother knew how, and their father would undoubtedly guzzle them all in one sitting.

He's selfish, Adrienne thought, surprising herself by the passion in the thought. She'd always known her father wasn't someone to look up to, but somehow the contrast between what he should have been and what he was had become more painful as she watched her brothers grow into men.

"Now, let's look at you, Adrienne," her father said in a businesslike voice. He took her by the shoulders and turned her to face him, his eyes assessing her face and figure critically. "Stop fidgeting with that necklace," he said, pulling her hand down to better examine her. "My word, child, you've grown into a beauty! I never would have guessed it from such a little squab of a thing."

Adrienne kept her countenance with difficulty. She'd inherited her short stature from her father, although her pale hair and blue eyes came from her mother. In the last few years she'd begun to get attention from men in the village, none of which she welcomed. Even her mother always had a slightly anxious look in her eyes when she commented on Adrienne's beauty, as if she worried what would come of it.

"Truly, you're a sight for sore eyes!" Adrienne's father declared, still sounding surprised. "I don't know if you've changed since my last visit, or if I didn't look at you properly then, but you really have grown up. I never expected a daughter of mine to be so comely."

The compliment brought Adrienne no joy. A sick feeling of dread was pooling in her stomach. She didn't know what she feared exactly, just that nothing good could come of this conversation. Her father was looking at her with just the expression he'd worn when he came home two years before to find that they'd been given a loom by a generous neighbor. He'd taken it with him, claiming that he knew of a buyer who'd give him twice its value for it, and would send the proceeds home shortly. No one had even pretended to believe they'd see a single coin of it.

Her father released her, stepping back and rubbing his hands together as he cast a glance around the cottage.

"Why isn't there a fire in here? Can't a man warm himself after a long journey?"

"It's summer, Svend," said Adrienne's mother calmly. "We never have a fire in summer, except for cooking."

"We can't afford luxuries like that," Felman said, his voice tight.

Svend scowled at his eldest son. "What do you mean you can't afford it? I send gold home for my family, don't I? What do you squander that on?"

"Send gold home?" Kettil muttered. "Three years ago was the last time, by my count."

Their mother threw him a warning look, and he fell silent. Best not to provoke their father if they wanted him out of their hair.

"You forget how much it costs to maintain a home, Svend," she said placatingly. "I assure you, we do not squander money in this household."

Adrienne studied her mother's face in concern. Usually the older woman maintained her calm when her husband visited, but this time there was definitely something bothering her.

"Are you all right, Mamma?" she asked softly, sidling up alongside her mother where she was preparing the eggs.

"The savings," her mother murmured, the words barely audible even from right beside her. "They're in this room."

Adrienne's eyes widened. They usually kept their stash very well hidden. Never before had she known a moment's fear of her father finding it.

"I was retrieving some to go into the village and organize your transport when he arrived," her mother breathed. "I had to think quickly."

"Any hazelnuts to be found in this place?" Her father's cheerful voice cut across their conversation as he reached for a shelf above his head. "I'm very fond of them. We keep some up here, don't we?"

"No, we don't have any!" The panic in her mother's voice told Adrienne all she needed to know about the jar her father was reaching for. "Svend, there are no hazelnuts in—"

Adrienne's mother's voice cut off abruptly as her husband, distracted by her cry, accidentally sent the jar toppling. Everyone in the room froze in horror as it fell, smashing spectacularly against the hard earthen floor.

For a moment the scene was suspended, every eye on the mound of flour-covered coins, the golden metal glinting in the light that streamed through the window. Even Svend seemed too dazed to react, his mouth round with astonishment as he stared at the mess. Slowly, his comprehension caught up, and Adrienne saw anger spread across his features.

"What. Is. That?" Svend's voice was low and dangerous— Adrienne had never heard that note before. "You've been hiding coin from me, Estrid?" He turned on his wife. "You've been *stealing* from me?"

"Stealing?" Felman strode forward to stand beside his mother, his lean frame quivering with fury. "Not a coin of that is yours! We earned every mite—*we* did! Without a scrap of help from you!"

"I am your father!" Svend roared. "This is my family, and my home. It's right that you all do your part to provide for the family, and anything you earn belongs to me!"

"That's not true, Svend," their mother said boldly. "Felman and Kettil are both of age, and could be in their own homes. They're under no obligation to stay in my home and continue to help provide for me! Their earnings are not yours to claim!"

"Then why don't they go out and make their own way?" roared Svend. "Because they don't want to pay for their own food and lodgings, that's why. They continue to live under my roof, growing fat on my generosity, and you dare to tell me that I have no claim to—"

"Generosity?" Kettil's voice was incredulous as he joined his brother at his mother and sister's side. "You give us nothing! We stay because unlike you, we can't bear to see Mamma made destitute. You float in here, pretending to be surprised that we can't afford luxuries, acting like it's not your own debt that cripples us! If we didn't have to pay the interest for what you owe we'd be well able to provide for Mamma, and Revna's family, too."

"Watch it, boy," growled their father. "I won't tolerate being spoken to like that by my own son." He crouched down, scooping up a fistful of the coins. "This is a fortune here. Enough for my investment. Enough to—"

"Investment?" Felman was as angry as his brother. "We all know you'll invest it in your ale-fat belly and your love of the dice. I notice you didn't comment that it's enough to pay off your creditors. That thought never crossed your mind, did it?"

To Adrienne's surprise, her father's eyes narrowed in thought. "My creditors, eh?" He stroked his chin, his anger ebbing as some new—and likely disastrous—thought gripped his fickle mind. "That's not a bad thought, Felman. Not a bad thought at all."

"Use your own money to pay off your debts," Kettil interjected angrily. "That money is for Adrienne."

"Kettil." The warning from their mother came too late. Their father's brows had already drawn together in confusion, his gaze on his daughter.

"What do you mean for Adrienne?" He brandished a flour-covered fist of coins. "What's this money for, Estrid?"

His wife hesitated, and anger once again gripped his features. "Tell me," he commanded. "Now."

Still Adrienne's mother said nothing. Svend's brow grew stormier by the moment, and the dread in Adrienne's stomach was closer to nausea now. She couldn't bear it anymore. Her family had covered for her and protected her too much already.

"I'm a singer, Father," she said abruptly. "My power isn't very strong, and I'm not very skilled. But I can sing."

"A singer?" her father breathed, his face showing nothing but astonishment. "A singer in the family all this time, and I never knew?"

Adrienne nodded numbly. "We've all been saving for years so I can go to the capital and study at the Academy of Song. Don't you see, Father? There will be all kinds of opportunities there, and they say magic is much more plentiful further south. I know there are more singers there than there are in the north, but they're still rare enough that work should be easy to find for me, once I know how to use my skill. This could lift us all from debt and turn things around."

"It certainly could," her father mused. But his eyes were glazed over, and she had the impression he hadn't heard half of what she'd said. "This could change everything."

Everyone waited in tense silence as he followed some private thought down its course. Eventually, he gave a small nod, his expression pleased.

"She's to leave in two weeks, Svend," Adrienne's mother said hesitantly. "We need all of that money to cover her travel expenses, and the first year of tuition. Once she's there, she'll have to find other work to cover the subsequent years."

"What?" He turned his head, clearly still lost in his own thoughts. "No, no, all that academy nonsense would be a poor use of this unexpected boon."

Adrienne's heart sank. She wasn't sure if he was talking about the gold or her ability, but it made little difference. As she'd feared, he was going to ruin their years of planning and saving at the final moment.

"No, I have a much better plan," he said comfortably. "I'll take custody of this money," his voice darkened, "since clearly my own family can't be trusted. I'll put both it and Adrienne's talent to good use, you'll see. Put your trust in me."

"Our trust?" The words seemed to burst out of Felman. "None of us trust you with so much as a copper, let alone with anything to do with our futures! Stay away from our gold, and stay out of Adrienne's life. We won't let you make her suffer like Mamma's suffered because of you!"

The mood shifted again, their father going instantly from genial to furious. Before Adrienne could blink, he was up in his son's face, rage in his eyes.

"Get out," he breathed. "Get out of my house."

Felman opened his mouth to argue, but their mother gripped his arm. "Go, Felman," she told him, and Adrienne thought she could hear real fear behind the stern command. "We'll sort this out later."

Felman met his mother's eyes for a moment, then gave a curt nod. He strode from the cottage without a backward glance at their father, the door slamming behind him.

"How have you let him grow so ill-mannered, Estrid?" Adrienne's father demanded. But he didn't wait for a reply. His mind had already returned to whatever scheme he'd hatched. "It was a good idea of his about the creditors, though," he muttered. "We'll turn that to good account."

His eyes traveled to Adrienne, and her stomach clenched as he gave an absent nod.

"Yes, we'll turn it to very good account."

CHAPTER TWO

Adrienne

The next few days passed in tense misery for Adrienne. Her father showed no sign of departing. He'd disappeared to the tavern the night he found the coins, and returned more cheerful than ever, his breath reeking of ale. He assured them all his plans were well in motion, and life would soon be easy.

No one showed the smallest sign of enthusiasm at his claims. Kettil moved around the house with clipped, angry strides, saying little and leaving any room as soon as his father entered it. Felman had been banned from returning to the house by their mother, after his first three appearances had led to three furious rows with their father. He was now staying with Revna and her family in their nearby home.

Adrienne, meanwhile, went about her daily chores in a listless haze of disappointment, trying not to see the anxious look in her mother's eyes every time she looked at Adrienne.

She'd been so close. So very close. If only her father had delayed a few more weeks, she would have been safely settled in Sunniva, with her fees irretrievably paid to the academy. Instead, it was all over. All her dreams, all the family's hopes for the future. Her father would drink and gamble the money away as he always did, and nothing would ever change.

Adrienne's mother had come to her room the moment her father departed for the tavern that first night, rare tears escaping her as she apologized for the disastrous turn their plans had taken. But Adrienne didn't blame her mother for a moment. She only regretted that they hadn't spent the money as they went along rather than saving it for a purpose it would never serve. It could have made their lives considerably easier for years.

Four days after his arrival, Adrienne's father sat down to dinner with an air of excitement. When no one responded to his cryptic hints, he gave up trying to get them to ask what was happening.

"Well, it's tonight," he said, his eyes glinting. "It's all been arranged. I may be out late, so don't wait up for me. I may be out all night, in fact. Depends how things go." He rubbed his hands together. "But by tomorrow, we'll be flying high, just mark my words."

"What's tonight, Svend?" Adrienne's mother asked warily. "What are you talking about?"

"Felman's idea," her husband said happily. "I've sent a note to all my creditors, as he called them. They're all coming tonight, and we'll sort this thing out once and for all."

"What?" Adrienne stared at her father, unable to believe her ears. "You're actually going to use the money to pay your debts?"

Svend chuckled. "I certainly am, my child. That and more." He rubbed his hands together again. "That reminds me, Adrienne, I got you a gift. It's on your bed."

"A gift?" Adrienne repeated. "For me?"

He nodded, chivvying her with his hands. "Go on, child, hurry up."

Bewildered and suspicious, she rose from the table, pausing as a rumble swept through the room. At first she thought it was another tremor, but she quickly realized it was only thunder. Another summer storm must be coming. Making her way to her room, she found a new gown laid across her bed. It wasn't fancy, but it was considerably better quality than anything she owned. The deep blue fabric was thick and durable yet soft beneath her touch.

"I don't need a new gown, Father," she called over her shoulder. "The money would be much better spent on something practical."

"That is practical," her father assured her. "I can't have my little singer dressed in rags now, can I?"

Adrienne turned, meeting her mother's eyes through the doorway. She saw her own unease reflected back at her, but neither woman said anything.

"Well, go on, try it on," her father urged.

Reluctantly, Adrienne shut the door and did so. The dress was a good fit, and she had to admit it was both flattering and comfortable. But knowing it was a gift from her father—bought with the money her mother had so carefully saved for her training—made it sit uncomfortably. Her skin seemed to crawl at the touch of the costly fabric.

She moved out into the cottage's main room, squirming under her father's approving look.

"Excellent," he said. "You'll do very nicely, Adrienne. You'd best get your cloak since it's looking stormy. We'll leave as soon as I've finished eating."

"Leave?" Adrienne's mother asked sharply, as Adrienne glanced in dismay at the window, against which rain had begun to patter. "What do you mean?"

"Adrienne's coming to the meeting with me," Svend said comfortably. "She can act as a hostess of sorts."

"I don't want to come." Adrienne blurted the words out before she could stop herself.

Her father frowned at her. "Don't be disobliging, Adrienne. I didn't ask what you want. You're coming with me."

"If you need someone to act as hostess, I'll come," said Adrienne's mother quickly. "I can have my cloak on in a moment."

Svend threw back his head and laughed. "Bless you, Estrid, you wouldn't serve the purpose at all."

"What purpose?" she demanded, leaning toward Adrienne in a subtle protective gesture.

"Relax, Estrid, it's all under control," Svend told her impatiently. He gave Adrienne a meaningful look. "Are you ready?"

Adrienne looked between her mother and Kettil, unsure how to respond. "I suppose so," she said reluctantly. "But I'd truly rather stay home, Father."

"Don't be silly," he said dismissively. "Surely you're not afraid of a little weather? You'll be with me, it's not as though you'll be unsafe."

Adrienne bit back her words, long experience telling her that challenging her father only prolonged unpleasant interactions without achieving anything. She sent one last glance at her mother, who gave a tense nod, then she donned her threadbare cloak.

She pulled the garment nervously around her as she followed her father out into the gathering night. The rain was pelting down now, and she was soaked within moments.

"Where are we going?"

"To the tavern," her father grunted.

"The tavern?" Adrienne stared at him, water dripping steadily down her face. "I thought you said you called your creditors for a meeting. Is the tavern really the appropriate place for a business conversation?"

"I've hired a room," he said with dignity. "And I don't have to explain myself to you, Adrienne. Enough questions."

They walked the rest of the way in silence, Adrienne's hand

bunched nervously in the fabric of her new dress as her boots squelched through the mud. Thunder cracked around them just as a flash of lightning split the darkness. The storm was properly upon them, and it was shaping up to be a violent one. She had no idea where the evening would end, but she couldn't remember the last time she felt so vulnerable.

The stormy weather had turned the long summer day into darkness earlier than it ought to have, and the tavern was already busy. Even over the rain, the sound of raucous laughter and clinking flagons bled out into the night. Adrienne followed her father inside with a racing heart, unable even to appreciate the rush of warmth as she got out of the weather. She'd never been inside the building before, and she'd never wished to.

Life in Toveham was hard, and pleasures were few. For every person who was motivated by poverty to work harder and never waste a copper, there seemed to be two others who went the other way, spending their meager pay as if there would be no tomorrow.

Perhaps they drank to forget that there would be a tomorrow, and it would be no better than today, Adrienne reflected, as her eyes rested on the village notary drinking in a corner. He already looked halfway to inebriation.

"Through here, Adrienne."

Her father, who'd been engaged in a jovial greeting with the owner of the tavern, suddenly remembered her presence. He ushered her to a large table at which three men already waited. Calling it a hired room had been generous. It was more like an alcove. The noise of the tavern still surrounded them, and a dozen pairs of curious eyes rested on Adrienne as she slid into the seat her father indicated, shivering in her sopping clothes.

Her eyes darted around the space, taking in the unfamiliar scene. The room glowed from the light of many cheap tallow candles, their unpleasant odor mingling with smells of stale ale and the sweat of men who'd worked hard all day for the delight of having nothing to go home to. The ceiling was low, heavy wooden beams making the space feel dark and enclosed. Long wooden tables covered the floor, their benches draped with fur pelts that had worn through in many places. A serving girl was stoking the fire, ready with a quick retort for any of the men who crossed the line in their comments as they passed. The flames weren't yet strong enough to counteract the chill that emanated from the stone walls.

In spite of her nerves, Adrienne was fascinated by this glimpse into a world she would never have expected to see. She was certainly out of place. Other than the serving girl, she was the only woman in the room. Keenly aware of a number of observers—some of their expressions not at all to her taste—Adrienne withdrew her gaze from the somewhat gruesome row of animal's heads mounted on one wall and lowered her eyes to her lap.

"What've you called us out for, Svend?" demanded one of the men seated at the table. "Why've you had us bring proof of your debts? If you think to get them from us by some trick—"

"Who's the wench?" another cut across him, the slight slur in his speech suggesting he'd already been drinking freely.

"This is my daughter, Adrienne," said Adrienne's father. "And no trick. I told you it would all be settled tonight, and so it will be. Ah, here are some of the others."

Adrienne looked up, taking the opportunity to study the three already in attendance as they all looked to the door. What she saw made her uneasy. She'd been expecting a gathering of respectable tradesmen, perhaps a few of the less scrupulous vendors who'd made life particularly difficult for their family when they'd been late paying their father's interest. But neither the men at the table nor those approaching fit that description. They looked like cronies of her father's, men who worked the fields, or perhaps mined the nearby quarry. She could only think of one reason her father would owe them money, and her heart sank further.

Another hour had passed before any more mention was made of debts. Everyone was in good spirits, drinking freely as her father bought round after round. Adrienne could hardly bear to see the money for her first year at the academy being squandered for such a meaningless, revolting purpose, but she had no doubt her father had a plan in mind.

Sure enough, when there was a lull in the ribald conversation of the dozen or so men around the table, her father rose to his feet. Perhaps because of his lack of height, he still had to bang his flagon on the table repeatedly to get everyone's attention.

"Thank you all for coming," he roared, and half the tavern looked over at him. "I'm glad to be back among you." He gestured to Adrienne. "And my daughter is also delighted to meet your fine selves."

A few laughs went around the group, many pairs of eyes flicking to Adrienne. She felt color rising up her cheeks, and dropped her gaze again. The men had mostly been ignoring her, for which she was grateful, and she didn't appreciate her father reminding them of her most inappropriate presence. She had no idea why he'd thought it so important for her to come. This was clearly not a location or event where a hostess was necessary.

"Fine speaking, Svend, but we haven't forgotten how much money you owe us!" thundered someone from the back. "Time to pay up, or we'll send you home to your family with two of them coins over your eyes."

This pronouncement was greeted with a cheer, even Adrienne's father grinning.

"Not necessary, my friends," he started, but he'd lost his audience.

Adrienne looked up quickly, unnerved by the sudden hush that had fallen over the tavern. She followed the gaze of the man next to her to the doorway, and like everyone else, she stilled.

The figure framed against the stormy night behind was arresting, to say the least. He was the largest man Adrienne had ever seen, although it was impossible to tell how much of the bulk was created by the enormous fur pelt he wore draped around his shoulders. She could make out nothing of his features, even with the light of the fire glowing on him. He wore a hood so deep and low that his entire face was in shadow.

It wasn't just his size or his air of mystery. There was something commanding about his presence, something impossible to put into words. He'd made not a sound as he entered, and yet he'd instantly had the attention of every person in the tavern. Even the serving girl had stopped clearing tables, staring at the newcomer with a calculating glint in her eye.

Adrienne shivered, lowering her gaze again. For herself, she couldn't see the appeal in a man so enormous he was more like a beast.

"It's that fellow Bjørn," someone muttered audibly, and the spell was broken. Everyone began murmuring amongst themselves, many of them returning to their previous activities. But most people's eyes flicked regularly back to the man in the doorway, Adrienne noticed.

"Bjørn came," her father said, sounding a little dazed. "I sent him a note, but I admit I didn't really expect him."

Another of the men at the table gave a low whistle. "You owe money to that giant of a man?"

An angry murmur went around the table, and the man in question raised his hands in apology.

"Sorry, figure of speech," he said. "Where I come from down south people say it all the time."

"Well, up in the north, we don't make light of giants," growled another man. "So keep your trap shut unless you want it done for you."

Unsurprisingly, the first man took offense at this threat, and a lively argument broke out. Before Adrienne knew what was happening, several of the men were on their feet, the table in danger of tipping as they tried to solve their disagreement with fists instead of words.

"Friends, friends!" Her father's placating voice rose above the din as Adrienne dodged to the side to avoid a tipped tankard. "Let's not get distracted."

Adrienne looked up to see that the enormous man had approached, and now hovered within hearing range, his hooded face directed toward her father.

"I know you've all come hoping for repayment of debts," Svend continued. "But I also know there's something we all like better than any dull business transaction."

He reached into his pocket and pulled out several worn dice, throwing them dramatically onto the table. Although it was in no way a surprise, Adrienne still felt herself deflate. She'd known how her family's precious money would go.

A combination of cheers and laughter greeted the action, and others hastened to produce their own dice.

"Friends," Svend said, pulling a pouch from his fur coat. "I'll play you for my debts." He tipped the pouch upside down, coins spilling onto the ale-stained wooden table. Another pouch followed the first, and another.

Exclamations and comments came from all sides, as the drunken group jostled for a look. Out of the corner of her eye, Adrienne saw the enormous man in the fur pelt turn away, edging around a table toward the door. Clearly he wasn't interested in her father's games.

When it came to the other men at the table, however, her father's instinct seemed to have been accurate. "Where'd you get all that?" one demanded, already shaking his dice experimentally in his hand.

But another, apparently still more clear-headed than his fellows, objected.

"Even with all that, you don't have enough to pay what you owe all of us."

"I will once I win your gold," Adrienne's father said with a provocative grin.

The man shook his head. "Your faith in your luck is as legendary as your luck is bad, Svend," he said. "But you can't expect us to put our credit on the line when you don't have the funds to honor your losses."

"Ah, but I do," said Svend, his eyes gleaming. "I brought more than just gold with me, lads." He gestured to Adrienne, who stiffened. "Some of you are yet to get a good look at my daughter Adrienne, I think."

CHAPTER THREE

Adrienne

Every man turned to Adrienne, who squirmed under so many eyes studying her with unsavory interest.

"I don't follow," said the objector coldly.

"Don't you?" said another one with a ribald laugh. "She's as pretty a morsel as ever I've seen."

An icy rush went over Adrienne at the way the man was leering at her. She shrank back into herself, aware of how her wet clothes still clung to her form. Was this truly her father's plan? To willingly expose her to this kind of attention?

"There's more to her than that," said Svend with dignity. "She's a singer, and if my funds prove insufficient, I'll stake her hand in marriage. She's of marriageable age, and not yet spoken for. Think of the possibilities!"

"Father!" gasped Adrienne, pale with horror.

"Don't be foolish, Adrienne," her father murmured to her. "It won't be necessary. With this much gold at my back, and this many deep pockets, I can't lose. I'll make us a fortune by sunrise, see if I don't. Haven't you noticed how much they've all been drinking?"

"Father, please," Adrienne begged, her hand curling instinctively around her necklace. "Let me go home. If you won't need me, don't make me stay. Are you truly proposing to barter me like a coin?"

"No need to be vulgar," her father sniffed. He raised his voice, speaking to everyone now. "I won't have you thinking anything untoward, here. If you play for Adrienne's hand and win it, you take it." He nodded toward a nearby table. "The notary is here, ready to officiate any necessary ceremony."

Adrienne's eyes widened as the man in question raised a tankard, grinning toothlessly at her. Was this some terrible nightmare? It must be. How could her father tell her one minute that she was there as a prop, and wouldn't actually be bartered, then show evidence the next minute that he'd planned for the event of her being won by one of these leering strangers? To her alarm, she saw that even the enormous man had paused, his hidden face turned back toward the table as if the new inducement made him think better of his plan to take no part.

"Is she really a singer?" one man demanded. "Prove it."

"Go on, Adrienne," her father commanded her. "Sing."

"Father, please," Adrienne whispered. "I don't want to—"

"Sing," he said, his voice cold. If she humiliated him in front of all these men, he would not forgive it.

Swallowing, Adrienne opened her mouth. The only thing she could think of was a lullaby she'd heard as a child from a singer who made her living as a minstrel. It had been her unconscious attempts to imitate the sound that had made Adrienne's mother realize her daughter could sing. The melody came out thin and quavering, and Adrienne felt only the smallest stirring of magic from the frozen ground beneath her feet. Certainly not enough for her to shape to any useful purpose. But singing was rare enough in Toveham that everyone was clearly impressed. The mood of the group changed again, several men leaning forward in their chairs.

"I've yet to take a wife," one said, his breath unpleasant as he leaned toward her. "She's certainly pretty. I wouldn't mind the singing blood passing to my children."

An involuntary shudder went over Adrienne, but her father looked pleased.

"Not so hasty," he said. "You have to win my money from me first."

And just like that, the game commenced. Everyone taking part produced their own dice, and with a speed that Adrienne could barely follow, the men began to roll, obscuring their results zealously with their hands.

Indecipherable cries went around the table, clearly meaning something to the men, because they responded in kind, rolling again and again with a flurry of barely synchronized movement. Men dropped out, and money changed hands, the pile before her father gradually dwindling. He didn't seem to notice, his eyes alight with the thrill of the game and his dice rolling more rapidly than anyone's. Every now and then someone would call bluff on another player, with varying results. More than once, her father was caught out in a bluff, the pile of coins intended for the academy halving each time. Adrienne wanted to groan aloud. Why did he keep doing it? Why was he incapable of learning from his errors? In a less direct sense, her life and the lives of her family had always been tied to his heedless, selfish ways. But now her life was quite literally on the line, and she didn't think she could bear it.

The worst of it was, every time she thought her father must realize the hopelessness of his plan, he would rally, raking in a large enough win to make his eyes gleam once again. At one stage he had almost half the gold on the table, as well as several of the notes of credit. He sent Adrienne a drunken grin, as if inviting her to acknowledge that he'd been right.

Most of the time, he ignored her, however. He certainly

didn't look to her for a reaction shortly afterward, when he was called in a bluff and lost half his stash to the clear-headed man who'd objected that he hadn't brought enough gold.

A great deal of gold was on the table now, many of the men having produced more of their own once they'd lost their records of Svend's debt. To Adrienne's horror, several strangers had even joined in the excitement, jumping into the game from other tables, looking her over eagerly as they threw their gold onto the wooden surface. It was all like a nightmare from which she couldn't wake.

Time blurred, hours passing as the fortune of the game ebbed and flowed. Adrienne had finally dried out, but she still felt cold and miserable in spite of the close, warm room. At one stage her father had a particularly lucky win, and one of his more intoxicated opponents cried foul, claiming that Adrienne had used her magic to direct the dice.

A few of the men turned to her with outraged expressions, leaping to their feet. One even grabbed her by the arm, tugging angrily.

She gave a cry, and a sharp movement to the side drew her gaze. She saw with a jolt of alarm that it was the huge hooded man who was approaching the table. She hadn't realized that he'd stayed. He'd taken no part in the betting, and she'd assumed he'd slipped away hours before. Why was he still there? His head turned toward her, and she could have sworn she felt his eyes on her, but she couldn't tell for certain. His face was still completely obscured.

A sharp tug from the man who held her brought her attention away from the hooded stranger.

"Let her go!" roared her father, grabbing the offending player by the shirt. "Don't be a fool—you would have heard her singing if she used magic. Do you think you can cheat the rest of the players by stealing the prize from under their noses?"

That comment turned popular opinion against the man who'd grabbed Adrienne, and she was released. Soon after, her father lost massively, and no more accusations of foul play emerged. In fact, from that point, her father's luck ran worse and worse. Even without a proper understanding of the game, Adrienne could tell that he was losing badly, both from the pile in front of him and from his demeanor. She watched, trembling, as the cold-voiced man who'd first challenged her father on how much gold he'd brought slowly gathered the majority of the coins and notes on the table.

Another half an hour passed before the inevitable moment arrived. Her father bet wildly on a final hopeful throw, and his dice betrayed him. The last of the gold he'd accumulated was swept away, added to the pile in front of the man with the cold voice. Adrienne had noticed that this man hadn't been drinking much. For some reason, that made him more frightening than all the rest.

Her father turned to her with a growl. "Give me your necklace," he spat.

"My...?" Adrienne's hand flew to the simple chain at her throat. "It isn't worth anything, Father," she said miserably. "If it was we would have sold it years ago."

"I know it's not worth anything," he said impatiently. Reaching forward, he seized hold of it and tugged. The clasp gave way painfully, and the chain flew off her neck. Her father threw it onto the table in front of him. "For Adrienne's hand," he pronounced, picking his dice back up.

"Father!" Adrienne cried, gripping his arm. "You said you wouldn't need to—you said—"

"Quiet, girl!" Her father's words were slurred now, and she could tell there would be no reasoning with him. Her eyes flew around the table, looking for help, for some sign of sense and compassion in the men around her.

She found none. Many of them were in a stupor, and several of those still playing withdrew at the new stakes. Likely they already had wives, or else weren't interested in being saddled with one. She could only be grateful.

But others leaned forward more eagerly, their interest in the game reignited. Some who'd previously withdrawn even threw gold back on the table. One of those was the man who'd said he wanted his children to have singing blood. To Adrienne's horror, the hooded man moved forward, reaching out a hand imperiously to the closest inactive player.

"Lend me your dice." His voice was low and throaty, and it sent a shiver down Adrienne's spine.

The words were not a request, and the man in question hastened to hand over his dice. Adrienne thought the stranger —Bjørn, her father had called him—would sit down, but he didn't. He remained standing at the edge of the table, his face still hidden in shadow. The sheer size of him was alarming.

"In," he called in that rumbling voice, tossing a pouch onto the table. Coins spilled out, sending murmurs around the table.

"Think you can win the singer at the final hour, do you?" The cold-voiced man looked the huge stranger over with disfavor. "I'm not intimidated by your size. You'll walk away with nothing you haven't won in fair play."

The hooded man gave no reply, merely shaking his dice in a swift, confident movement. Play commenced again, the mood altogether different now. There were about five men still in, each of them playing seriously. Adrienne could tell by her father's growing agitation that it wasn't going well. The world seemed to spin around her, her gaze flying rapidly between the barely conscious notary and the players. Would she really walk out of this tavern the wife of some drunken stranger before the night was out?

The play rose and fell. Emboldened by the gain of a few

coins, her father tried another bluff. The cold-voiced man called it, and Adrienne watched in numb disbelief as her necklace—the symbol of her life, her future, her very self—slid across the table to the cold-voiced man's pile.

Her father didn't even look at her. With a roar, he stood, upending his stool and shoving his half-full tankard to the side. Ale spilled across the table, and Adrienne didn't even flinch as it dripped slowly into her lap. What could it possibly matter now?

Her head turned unconsciously at a sharp slapping noise. The hooded man had slammed his enormous hand down on three of his own dice, trapping them in position. Two more were in his other fist, and his voice rumbled out once again.

"Pair's secret, all in."

The words meant nothing to her, but murmurs once again passed around the table. With one exception, each other player laid his dice down, pocketing his remaining coins with a shake of the head. The cold-voiced man, however, studied the stranger thoughtfully. He had slapped his hand over his own three dice immediately upon hearing the call, and he was now looking between the stranger's hoard—which still amounted to a sizable pile of gold—and his own. In addition to Adrienne's necklace, he now had every one of her father's notes of debt.

Somewhere behind her fear for her immediate situation, Adrienne understood the catastrophe of this fact. The man who won all those notes would be owed all her father's debts—and would have proof to hold over her family's heads forever. At worst, he could throw them out on the street as he took their home and everything they owned in a futile attempt to pay it all back. At best, he could make their lives a misery as he hounded them for the payments.

In short, the value of his pile was much greater than his opponent's. But on the other hand, the hooded man's pile held more actual gold.

"Accepted," the cold-voiced man said.

The stranger gave a curt nod, then began to shake his pair of dice. The next moment, both men had thrown two dice on the table, everyone leaning forward eagerly to see how they landed.

Adrienne stared between the four dice, the markings conveying nothing to her. Slowly, both men lifted their hands from the three dice they'd already thrown, and every pair of eyes flitted between the results.

The man next to Adrienne gave a low whistle, leaning back in his chair. "Well, that's decisive," he said.

Adrienne wanted to scream her frustration, to demand to be told the outcome. It was *her* life being decided, and she still had no idea who'd won. But her mouth wouldn't open, every muscle of her body frozen.

For a moment the cold-voiced man was equally still, then, with an abrupt movement, he shoved his pile forward. Without a glance at anyone, he collected his dice and his cloak and elbowed his way through the crowd and out the door into the driving rain.

Adrienne turned slowly, her eyes landing on the huge stranger. His hooded face was turned toward her as well. When he spoke, his voice was quiet, but his words still carried across the tavern with perfect clarity.

"Your name is Adrienne?"

She swallowed, trying desperately to keep her dignity. "Yes," she said, lifting her chin.

It was impossible to read the stranger's thoughts with his face hidden from her, but his movements were smooth and steady as he rose to his feet and held out his hand.

"Well, Adrienne?" he asked. "Will you come with me?"

Again his throaty voice sent a shiver over her, a confusing tumult of emotions accompanying it. Adrienne's heart was pounding ferociously, and she couldn't seem to tear her eyes from that enormous, calloused hand outstretched to her. With an effort, she forced her gaze upward to rest on the dark shadow that hid the man's face, her answer rising to her lips almost without thought.

"Yes."

CHAPTER FOUR

Herleif

Herleif said nothing as the girl placed her hand in his. His own fingers dwarfed her slim ones. His pulse was thundering in his ears, but in spite of the strength of the emotion that had him in its grip, he was utterly incapable of articulating what he felt. He had barely a coherent thought in his mind, other than relief that the heinous spectacle was over.

He glanced around the room, wondering whether the notary had succumbed to his intoxication yet. Would it be better if he had? Could Herleif just return the girl to her family? But that was no solution. He'd seen more than enough of the head of her family to know how little safety she'd find in her home. Besides which, he'd entered the game with the stakes clearly laid out. By entering play, he'd accepted the terms—that if he won the girl's hand, he was bound to take it. The requirement on his honor was absolute.

The notary stood, apparently having followed the play more closely than Herleif had thought, in spite of his condition. His gait was wobbly as he moved toward the pair, but his words were clear.

"I take it I'm called upon to offer my services," he said, in an ingratiating voice that made Herleif's lip curl with distaste.

"It seems so," Herleif replied.

The notary cleared his throat. "Are you, sir, of full age and sound mind?"

"I am." Herleif's voice, so little used these days, came out as a scratchy rumble.

The notary turned to Adrienne. "And do you have the requisite authority from your parents to marry without the customary period of notice?"

"I..." The girl seemed to be trying to speak, but nothing more than a whisper came out. Her hand trembled a little in Herleif's, but she didn't try to withdraw it. She turned uncertainly to her father.

Svend, sniveling worm that he was, started to protest. "As to that, well, there are matters to discuss. If Bjørn is to marry my daughter and gain permanent benefit from her abilities, he ought to pay a substantial bride price. I'm owed that much, surely."

"*You* are owed?" Herleif repeated the words in an ominous growl. Reaching onto the table behind him, he scooped up a handful of the notes outlining Svend's debt, all of which he'd just won. He crushed it in his hand as he raised it to the level of Svend's eyes. Which wasn't very high. "I believe the situation is the reverse, in fact."

Svend seemed to quiver before him, a flash of fear replacing the greed in his eyes.

"You staked her and he won her, Svend, all fair and clean," said one of the other men from behind them. "You can't refuse to pay now."

"Honor," said another severely, and the cry was taken up around the group.

"Honor."

"Honor!"

Svend looked between Herleif and his daughter—who in spite of her evident distress held his eye with a boldness Herleif had to admire—then turned furiously to the notary.

"Yes, fine, I give my permission," he said, the words clipped and bitter.

"Very well, let us begin," the notary said pompously.

Svend ignored him, his glare bent on his daughter. "I little dreamed how you'd betray me, Adrienne."

"*Me* betray *you*?"

Herleif noted with approval that the girl quivered with anger as she spoke the words. He'd begun to wonder if she knew how to feel the emotion, given how poised she'd remained throughout the whole humiliating debacle.

"You were set against my plan from the start," Svend spat. "You brought me bad luck with your presence and your dour predictions. If you hadn't been here, I would have won everything."

Herleif had expected more anger in response to this outrageous declaration, but the girl surprised him. She swelled with tension for only a moment before deflating in apparent resignation.

"Don't expect a welcome in my home, either of you," Svend added furiously. "Neither of you will enter my sight again if you value your lives."

With a final growl, he pushed past them, slinking out into the night without another word.

Herleif felt the girl slump further beside him, and he gave his own head a little shake. Svend truly wasn't even going to stay to watch his daughter safely married to this near-stranger to whom he'd lost her like a coin? What a pathetic excuse for a man and father.

"Not here," Herleif told the notary, pausing to scoop all his winnings into the pockets of his enormous cloak. He leaned his head toward the fireplace on the other side of the tavern. "Over there." He didn't intend to be married in front of a crowd of leering drunkards.

Married! You can't get married! You can't take a wife! The voice screamed at him from somewhere in the depths of his rage-fueled mind, but he ignored it. If he was going to listen to that warning, he needed to have done it before he threw his dice into the game, not after the play was over. There was nothing to do now but deal with the consequences, or he would be the one to be shamed by all the witnesses for his lack of honor.

"Very good, sir, but we do need two witnesses," the notary informed him.

Herleif scanned the crowd, pointing to two men who were so drunk they barely seemed aware of their surroundings. They would be lucky to even remember all this in the morning. "You two," he said curtly. "Come."

He spoke as one might speak to a dog, and they came with just the same blind obedience. A minute later, the five of them stood by the fireplace, Herleif once again holding the girl's small, cold hand in his. He knew many pairs of fascinated eyes were still fixed on them, but hopefully they wouldn't be able to hear the words of the hasty ceremony. In particular, the one part he'd prefer no one to catch.

Sure enough, the girl beside him started visibly when Herleif gave his name for the exchange of vows. She'd obviously heard her father call him Bjørn. What did she think at hearing his true name? Did she connect him with the prince who had supposedly died in these parts five years previously? Unlikely, but he was still glad not to have shared the information with a tavern full of indiscreet men.

He half expected her to protest when it was her turn, but she repeated her vows in a voice that was steady, if whisper-quiet.

Herleif barely took any of it in himself. It all felt surreal, impossible to comprehend. Almost before he'd really grasped it was happening, the thing was done.

Thankfully, the notary gave no awkward suggestions that Herleif kiss his new wife. A bitter laugh almost escaped him at the thought. That would have been something of a problem.

The notary produced a battered book, into which he scrawled some details Herleif could barely read, so unsteady was the man's hand. Extracting a crumpled piece of parchment from his pocket, he copied the information onto it, before offering both it and the book to the newlyweds to sign. Herleif watched out of the corner of his eye as his new wife wrote her name in a clear, strong hand. She was literate, then. That was something.

To his relief, the notary didn't even read over what they'd written. The man might check it in the morning, but Herleif wouldn't be at all surprised if he didn't. He was clearly not the most conscientious example of his kind. Herleif was half surprised the notary didn't accidentally set fire to either the parchment or the book in applying his seal. But there was no mishap, and a moment later, the man smoothed out the parchment with the details of their union and handed it to Herleif. With a slightly slurred goodbye, he staggered out the door, his book clamped under one arm.

A glance back at the table showed that most of Svend's group had dispersed as well. It was late now, very late. Herleif wasn't sure of the time, but he would guess there were only a few hours before dawn. He would have to hurry if he wanted to reach home before the sun rose.

Tugging his hood down to ensure it still covered his face, he turned to the silent girl beside him. "Is there anything else you need to collect?"

She shook her head. "Nothing."

For a moment he regarded her in silence. He would once have been unable to comprehend the idea of having so little, but now it didn't even seem strange to him. At least her gown was warm.

"Are you ready?" he asked her.

She nodded, and Herleif turned for the door. He pulled his hood down again as he strode into the night, but he needn't have worried. In the rage of the storm, the darkness was nearly absolute, no moonlight sneaking through the clouds. It was gusty, but he would be unlucky indeed if a flash of lightning came at the exact moment the wind flapped his hood from his face.

He strode through the deserted streets, his new wife hurrying behind him. *His new wife.* He couldn't seem to make his mind believe the description applied to the girl following him, and he decided not to try. There would be time enough for panic when the sun had risen. In spite of how rarely he'd been there in recent years, he knew the town well, and he led the way straight to the small store where he'd gotten supplies previously.

"Do you live here, over the shop?" the girl asked nervously. He should really try to remember her name better. Adrienne, she'd said.

"No." His answer was curt. "We need to get you a warmer cloak. It's not a short distance to my home, and you'll freeze in this storm in what you're wearing."

"Oh." She seemed taken aback, and Herleif wondered fleetingly what was in her mind. "I think...I think they're closed."

"They won't be in a minute," Herleif said. He raised a fist and pounded on the door. The thunderous knocking was muffled by the sounds of the storm, but after a minute of persistence, he heard movement within the building.

"What do you want?" someone shouted through the door. "It's hours until dawn! We're not open!"

"Then make an exception," Herleif growled.

A face appeared at the small window next to the door, and Herleif saw the man's eyes widen at the sight of his bulk. After a moment's hesitation, the owner of the shop fiddled with the lock, and the door creaked open.

"This is not how we usually do business," he muttered without conviction, skittering out of the way as Herleif strode over the threshold.

"I need a warm cloak," Herleif said.

The man cast an eye over his dripping fur pelt. "I, uh, I don't know if we have anything large enough to—"

"Not for me," Herleif said impatiently. "For my wife."

He gestured behind him, and the shopkeeper's eyes widened yet again as they rested on his companion.

"Aren't you Estrid's girl?" he asked, bewildered. "Adrienne, isn't it?"

"Yes." Her voice came out faint, and she cleared her throat. "Yes, that's right."

The man's eyes flew between the two of them, and Herleif could almost hear his mind repeating the word wife. What tale was his imagination constructing to explain her appearance in his shop at this hour, married to a man whose name the shopkeeper didn't even know? Nothing more outrageous than the truth.

Sudden comprehension grew in the shopkeeper's eyes, and his mouth set in a thin line. "Your father back in town, is he?"

"Yes." Adrienne's voice was noticeably harder, and Herleif felt another rumble of anger pass over him.

"The cloak?" he prompted the shopkeeper, and the man bustled into motion.

"Yes, for her size, we can manage," he said. He glanced at Adrienne calculatingly. "Perhaps one of the larger children's ones."

Adrienne gave a long-suffering sigh, and something that was almost like a smile lifted one side of Herleif's lips. They were certainly an odd pair, her petite form contrasted against his bulk. If she'd been standing rather than sitting when he first saw her, he would have had difficulty believing that she was of age. But in spite of her short stature, her features and figure were that of a woman, not a child.

"Choose whichever one you like," he told her curtly, eager to be off.

Adrienne cast an uncertain look at him, then moved toward the cloaks the shopkeeper had indicated. She selected the nearest one, and Herleif frowned. It was neither thick nor pretty. Surely she couldn't want that one.

"That's not warm enough," he told her. He saw her bite her lip, and added, "I meant it when I said choose whichever you like. Don't consider the cost." His voice darkened. "I'm returning home a richer man than I left it."

Even in the darkness of the shop he could see the way her cheeks flushed, and he regretted his words. His sarcasm had been targeted only at the tawdry nature of the game in which he'd won so much gold, but he realized belatedly that it may have sounded like a scathing reference to their hasty marriage.

Whatever embarrassment she might feel, Adrienne took him at his word and selected a much more appropriate cloak. Herleif paid the stated sum as she pulled it around her shoulders, then turned and took stock of her. The purple fabric was thick and soft. A leaf pattern was cut from the section that draped across her torso, and the rest of it fell around her in voluminous folds. It was much more suitable than the worn garment she'd had over her dress before.

"Time for us to be gone," he said by way of acknowledging her choice.

She nodded, then turned to thank the shopkeeper.

"Is there anything else I can do for you, child?" the man asked anxiously.

Herleif turned away, not wishing to hear whatever polite and inaccurate reassurances she would give. A moment later, she followed him out into the rain.

"I'm afraid we'll have to walk," he told her gruffly.

"I didn't expect any different," she assured him.

With a curt nod, he set off, trying to shorten his strides to allow her to keep up. It would be a much longer journey than it had been for him alone, and he felt unease creep over him. What would happen if they didn't make it home before dawn?

They passed quickly through the small town of Toveham, ducking under eaves as often as possible. When they reached the outskirts of the town they weren't as lucky, and both were thoroughly soaked by the time they crossed the small area of scrub that separated the village from the bulk of the abandoned city.

It was hard to believe, as they wove between dilapidated buildings and jumped over cracks in the cobblestones where weeds had forced their way through, that Tove had once been the capital of Frossenland. Herleif could feel the tension growing in the girl beside him the further they traveled into the labyrinth of crumbling stone.

"You don't live inside the abandoned city, do you?" she asked, a hint of nervousness coming through with the words.

"No." Herleif shook his head.

"You live beyond it?"

He paused. "Yes."

She said no more, but he could tell that she wasn't satisfied. And no wonder. She must be terrified, and he had no idea how to reassure her, or if he should even try. The panic he'd fought back in the tavern was beginning to cloud his mind.

What had he done?

CHAPTER FIVE

Herleif

The question continued to circle in Herleif's mind as he led Adrienne through the empty cobblestoned streets. What had he done? How had he let this happen?

He'd been so cautious all this time. In five years he could count on one hand the number of times he'd sought out the company of other humans. The occasion about two years earlier, when he'd allowed himself to get drawn into a game of chance with Svend and his unsavory cronies, was certainly the most regrettable of those instances. But even that was nothing to what he'd done tonight. He'd known all along that the one thing he could never contemplate was getting married. So how did he find himself with a silent young woman striding along beside him, both wife and stranger?

But he knew how. He'd been astonished a few days before to visit the town and discover a message waiting for him at the posting house. He'd never received mail there before, and had been surprised Svend had even thought to inquire for him there. It was rare for him to visit the village—the timing had been so remarkable, he'd ignored his better judgment and gone to the tavern on the appointed night. It had been a moment of weakness, born out of the deep ache of his loneliness. The gold Svend owed him also would have been welcome, of course.

He certainly hadn't intended to acquire a wife. He'd simply been incapable of doing nothing when he saw Svend offer up his daughter in a sordid bargain to pay his shameful debts. Herleif had fully intended to leave when he grasped the nature of Svend's offer to "repay" his debts, but then Svend had revealed the reason for his daughter's presence. What could Herleif have done? To leave then, careless of her fate, would have made him little better than her father's lecherous friends. He'd lingered, hoping that her father's luck would turn or the game would end before things reached a desperate pass.

When Svend had actually offered the girl up—ripping the necklace from her throat as if she were another coin to toss on the pile—Herleif had barely been aware of the decision to act. He'd found himself in the game before he knew what he was about, his only thought to save her both from the drunken players leering at her and from the coldly calculating man who was clearly hoping to acquire her. Herleif knew that man by reputation from his other sporadic visits to Toveham. He could only hope Adrienne knew nothing of him, as he could see no benefit in her knowing the fate she'd so narrowly avoided. Her father couldn't possibly be ignorant of the man's reputation, which made his willingness to stake his daughter even more vile.

As they finally left the city, Herleif cast a glance at the girl beside him. The rain had finally begun to slacken, and he could see her clearly in the faint moonlight. She was flagging in her weariness, but she'd made no complaint. It was unthinkable to imagine her tied to one of those drunkards. It was unthinkable for her to be tied to him as well, of course. Much worse in many ways. But at least she needn't fear him forcing himself on her.

He almost let out a laugh at the thought, although there was no mirth in his heart to lighten his bitterness. He pulled his eyes from her quickly, suddenly pained at the sight of her exquisite features. She was certainly beautiful, that couldn't be denied. He'd rarely seen a face so appealing.

Her eyes flew suddenly to him, their expression so penetrating that he felt a flash of alarm. But a surreptitious check assured him that his hood was in place. The night was deep. She would be able to see nothing of his features.

Adrienne lowered her eyes quickly, and Herleif was assailed with the memory of when her gaze first fell on him, back in the tavern. Fear had been written plainly across her face then, and also when he'd joined the game at last. Was she feeling it now? Was that what she was trying to hide with her averted face?

The thought was unbearable.

"Are you afraid?" The question slipped out before he could assess its wisdom. To his surprise, Adrienne looked up without hesitation, her eyes searching his hooded form seriously.

"No."

The word was calm and convincing, and Herleif felt himself relax. A moment later, a frown crossed his features, however. Surely she was afraid. She must be. Nothing else would make sense.

As if reading his thoughts, Adrienne gave a sudden smile. It was the first he'd seen on her face, and his breath actually caught in his throat at the effect it had on her already beautiful features.

"I was afraid," she acknowledged unprompted. "When you threw your dice into the game, back at the tavern." She gave him a smile that was half appealing, half shy. "You're just so enormous."

Herleif said nothing, his mind a tangled web of reactions. After a minute of walking in silence, another question slipped out without permission.

"Then why did you agree to come with me when I asked?"

Adrienne's expression was thoughtful as she tried in vain to peer at his face. "I agreed *because* you asked."

Her voice was soft and clear, and once again Herleif was unable to think of a reply, even as the simple words sent a dull ache through his heart. She confounded him at every turn.

"I believe this is yours," he said, suddenly remembering the necklace in his pocket and drawing it out.

She stopped moving, and he came to a stop also, holding it out to her. For a long moment she just stared at it, and Herleif waited.

"Thank you," she said at last, her voice a little choked as she took it. The clasp was broken, of course, so she didn't put it on. She just wound it around her hand, clutching it so tightly her knuckles went white. Her face unreadable, she cast a glance back the way they'd come.

"You're thinking of your home." Herleif's words weren't a question, and Adrienne didn't give a reply.

"Are there others there who might be in danger from your father?" he asked curtly.

She bit her lip. "I don't think they're in danger of anything imminent. For all his faults, my father isn't given to violence. And my family can look after themselves. But they'll be… worried, when he returns without me."

Herleif made no comment on what was clearly a gross understatement. At least the poor girl had someone who cared about her.

"Do you wish to visit your home?"

Her lovely face hardened. "Not while my father is there."

"Would he make good on his threat to harm you if you returned?" Herleif pressed.

She gave a helpless shrug. "I don't know. Normally he'd calm down once he was sober again, but..." She sighed. "He was very angry. I don't know what he'll do."

"Well, he won't harm you," Herleif told her. "For better or worse, you're under my protection now, and I won't allow that to happen."

Adrienne said nothing, eyeing his enormous form thoughtfully. It was impossible to tell what she thought of his words, or his integrity. He wouldn't blame her if she was skeptical. How could she be expected to trust a word he said? After a moment, Adrienne turned away from him, her eyes searching the path ahead where it disappeared into the trees.

"Where are we going?" She sounded nervous again. "Isn't this the forest that surrounds the old castle?"

"It is," Herleif confirmed.

She cast an alarmed glance at him. "But is it safe?"

"You'll be safe if you're with me," he replied.

Adrienne fell silent, her expression twisting in a way he couldn't decipher. His answer had been unpleasant to her, but he didn't know why.

Probably because he was a total stranger whom she'd just effectively been forced to marry.

"I thought nobody came this way," she said at last. "I thought everyone knew to avoid these woods."

"Why is that?" Herleif asked calmly. He knew the answer, of course, but he thought it would be interesting to hear it from her. It might also be useful to know what version of events she believed.

"Well, people claim the castle itself is under an enchantment," she said. "But I don't put any stock by that."

"Why not?" Herleif pressed. "I thought you were a singer."

"I am," she acknowledged. "But even I know very little about magic. Most people in the town know even less. I doubt anyone could recognize an enchantment if they encountered one. It's just the sort of legend that would grow around the place given its grim history and the very tangible danger."

"What grim history?"

She cast him a look of surprise. "You don't know it? You must. The former king, King Eerikki, and his son were killed there." She snuck another look at him. "His name was Prince Herleif. Were...were you named for him?"

Herleif paused. "Yes." It was sort of true, he justified silently. One could argue that he was named for himself.

For another minute they walked in silence, Herleif uncomfortably aware that Adrienne's eyes barely left his hooded face.

"Are you going to lower your hood and show me your face?" she asked abruptly.

Again he paused. "No."

Again his answer was met with silence, and he could sense her wariness returning. But there was definitely a hint of suspicion on her features as well. She was clearly no fool.

"So what's the tangible danger you mentioned?" he asked, trying to turn the conversation.

She let out a breath, apparently accepting the redirection. "The bear."

"Bear?" Herleif wasn't sure he quite succeeded in keeping his voice casual.

Adrienne nodded. "Yes, the giant white bear which killed the king and prince and still haunts these woods, defending its territory. They say the beast actually forced its way through the doors into the castle itself when it attacked the royals."

"Do they?" Herleif asked mildly. "That's a strong bear."

"Well, it is supposed to be enormous," Adrienne said with a touch of defensiveness. "And it haunts the woods still, keeping anyone away from the castle. My own brother swears he saw it once, when he was hunting on the outskirts of the woods."

"Fortunate that he wasn't eaten," Herleif commented.

Adrienne nodded in fervent agreement. "He was very lucky, I think. Probably because he got out of there in a hurry rather than challenging the bear's territory."

"Probably." Herleif felt his lips twitch.

"Have you ever seen it?" she asked tentatively.

Herleif paused, unsure how to answer the question. "Should we take a rest?" he asked instead.

"How much further is it?" Adrienne cast a look around them at the dark, dripping forest. "I thought we must be almost there."

"Another half an hour's walk," said Herleif. "At least at the pace your legs can manage."

"My apologies for slowing you down." Adrienne didn't sound apologetic. She sounded put out, and again Herleif smiled. At least she seemed to be getting over her initial fear.

Hopefully his next action didn't reignite it. He didn't feel any need or desire for a rest, but he'd just remembered something crucial. And he wasn't sure he could afford to wait until they reached the castle. Already he could hear the first stirrings of birdsong in the trees. Dawn would be upon them before long.

He led her to an overhanging rock, just large enough for her to fit under. He would have no hope. Adrienne sat in the relatively dry patch he indicated, but Herleif continued to hover awkwardly above her.

"You can...you can lie down if you need to."

She gave him a bemused look. "I'm all right," she said. "If it's only half an hour further, I'd rather rest when we arrive."

Herleif cleared his throat, wincing with discomfort under his hood. "Can you please?" he asked. "To humor me?"

He saw a muscle in Adrienne's leg jump as she continued to stare at him, as if some instinct was telling her to run away. But after a painful moment, she lowered herself onto the bracken, her eyes never leaving his form.

She looked so small and vulnerable stretched out below him, and Herleif hastened to sit on the wet earth himself, trying to narrow the gap. After an agonized moment in which he tried in vain to think of a way around it, he lowered himself to a horizontal position as well.

He could feel Adrienne stiffen beside him, and saw in the corner of his eyes that she'd looked quickly away. He didn't look at her, either, keeping his face averted to ensure his hood was still covering it. His arm lay along the ground mere inches from her slender one, no part of them touching.

Seconds crawled by in painful silence. How long would be long enough? Was a mere moment sufficient?

A glance around showed the darkness lightening. A mere moment would have to be enough, because it was all he had to spare.

"Come on," he said gruffly, hastening to his feet. "That's enough rest. We should keep moving."

Adrienne followed more slowly, her movements self-conscious as she brushed pine needles from her hair and her new cloak.

She asked him no questions, but all her tension and uncertainty had returned. For maybe ten minutes they walked in uncomfortable silence, covering the ground more quickly than Herleif had expected.

"Tell me more about this bear," Herleif said, desperate to reclaim the ease of conversation they'd had before his strange behavior.

"Um..." Adrienne was clearly still struggling to regain her earlier equilibrium. "They say its attack on the king gave it a taste for humans, and it's become very aggressive. It will attack people as soon as it sees them."

"Like your brother?" Herleif asked dryly.

"Well...he was lucky," Adrienne reminded him.

"Clearly," said Herleif. "So how many villagers have been mauled to death by this bear?"

Adrienne's forehead wrinkled, the expression endearing in the gray light of the pre-dawn. "Do you know...I can't actually think of any specific person I've heard of being killed by the bear. Just lots of close calls."

"And yet it has a reputation for being vicious," Herleif commented.

She shrugged. "I suppose the deaths came early on after it killed the king, and everyone's learned to be more cautious since then. I did tell you that no one comes into these woods anymore." The birdsong was all around them now, and the trees were beginning to thin. Adrienne looked curiously around at the lightening forest. "Do you live near the old castle? You must have seen the bear, then. Rumor is that the castle is still there, even filled with all the finery of the old days, because the bear stops anyone from getting in and plundering it."

"Such an industrious bear," Herleif muttered.

"What?"

"Nothing," he said. With the word, they stepped out of the trees, and the castle came into sight. Herleif tried to look at it with fresh eyes. It was grim and gray in the growing light. He could imagine it would look imposing even without the local legends surrounding it. A glance at Adrienne's face suggested that his assessment was accurate.

"The castle," she whispered. "Why are we here? Did you bring me because I told you the stories? I didn't mean I wanted to see it. I'd rather just go straight to wherever you—"

"I have to leave you now," Herleif cut into her babbling, the words coming out in jumbled haste. The sun was surely moments from rising, and there was no time to waste. "I'm truly sorry to leave you alone, but it can't be helped. If you go inside, you'll find it's comfortable, if not very warm."

"Inside the castle?" Adrienne repeated, clearly horrified. "Alone?"

"I'm sorry," Herleif repeated, already stepping away toward the tree line. The sun was rising, and he could feel the magic starting to work. "Try to sleep. I'll be back at nightfall with some food."

"At nightfall?" Adrienne gasped. She lunged toward him, taking him completely by surprise when she gripped his arm. Her touch was warm and overpowering, and for a moment he forgot why it was imperative that he get out of her sight with all speed. "Please, Herleif," she said, and his heart seemed to stop at the sound of his name. "Please don't leave me alone in this place."

"Adrienne, you must let me go," he said desperately. "I'm sorry, but I—"

Too late. The words cut off in a grunt as familiar pain assaulted him. He tried frantically to stumble between the trees, but he'd lost all power of motion. Adrienne's hand was ripped from his arm as the magic brought him to his knees, his vision exploding in stars, and agony overcoming his awareness.

CHAPTER SIX

Adrienne

"Herleif?" Adrienne threw herself forward, alarm racing over her as she stared at the writhing form on the ground. "Herleif, are you hurt? What's happening?"

A strange sensation swirled through the air, centered on Herleif's hunched figure. Adrienne couldn't put words to it, but it felt wild and dangerous, and it took all her willpower to move toward it instead of backing away.

She knelt beside him, reaching out a tentative hand. What was wrong with him? And what would happen to her if he died and left her in this otherworldly place? Forget dying, even if he just left her there alone as he'd been about to do, she'd be in trouble. He'd seemed very sure of his path through the woods, but she had absolutely no idea how to find her way back out. And she didn't relish the idea of exploring the abandoned castle, even in the daylight now creeping through the trees.

"Herleif?" she tried again, laying a hand on the fur pelt that covered his shoulder. With a startling motion, he jerked his arm back, throwing her off with what could only be described as a roar.

Fear filling her, Adrienne stumbled backward, her eyes riveted to her strange new husband's form. Before her gaze, it was changing. She'd thought Herleif large before, but he was growing even bigger. The fur pelt over his shoulders seemed to expand, fusing together and covering his whole form. He gave another roar of pain as his body hunched further, even while his kneeling form rose above the height of her head. The feeling in the air was so sharp now she could almost taste it. She didn't understand what she was seeing, but some kind of magic was definitely at work.

At last Herleif's hood fell back, but Adrienne caught no glimpse of the human face she was so desperately curious to see. Instead, she found herself gazing up into the eyes of a gargantuan white bear two times her own height.

Adrienne fell back, gripped by terror too intense to even scream. The bear took an experimental step toward her, and her frozen body burst into motion. She turned toward the trees, sprinting with an energy she hadn't thought her sleep-deprived body had possessed. She raised her arms to ward off branches as her new cloak caught in the undergrowth. She'd barely gone twenty paces when her boot became hooked on a stone, and she fell heavily to the forest floor.

With a choking sob, she pushed herself to her feet, ignoring the blood already beginning to ooze from her scratches. She expected to be torn to shreds at any moment, but a glance over her shoulder showed no sign of the bear pursuing her. In fact, there was no sound of any movement except her own.

Trembling, Adrienne crept a few paces back the way she'd come, peering between the trunks. There stood the white bear still, in the clearing beside the abandoned castle. Herleif's hooded cloak lay beside it on the grass, the pockets bulging with the coins her family had saved for her education, along with everything else that had been staked at the tavern.

Was it a trap? Was he—it—the creature hoping she'd come back for the gold, and make easy prey of herself?

As she watched, the bear turned away, loping across the clearing and into the trees in an entirely different direction. Still trembling, Adrienne watched it disappear. What did she do now? The sun had properly risen, and exhaustion tugged at every muscle. But she couldn't sleep, not while she was alone in the forest with the murderous bear.

She struck off into the trees at random, heading away from the bear's path. She didn't run now, just hurried as quickly as a walk would allow. Birds sang all around her, and animals skittered through the undergrowth. If not for the eerie castle behind her, and the horrifying transformation she'd witnessed, it would have been a beautiful, serene wood. Not at all the dark and dangerous place she'd imagined this forest to be.

When she'd been stumbling along for about ten minutes, she realized the risk she was taking. She had no idea where she was, and if she got lost among the trees, she might never find her way out again. But then, it wasn't such a huge forest. Even if she came out on the wrong side of it, she'd surely be able to skirt around its edge until she found her way back to the abandoned capital and the town of Toveham beyond.

And then what? Would she trot home with her head hung low? Anger rippled through her, providing a welcome relief to the fear. She'd meant what she said to Herleif. She didn't want to go home as long as her father was there. Besides, she couldn't just leave. She'd bound herself to Herleif, and honor required her to remain faithful to that vow.

Of course, she'd made the vow before learning that the hooded man her father called Bjørn was in fact the giant white bear that terrorized the castle woods.

A shudder went over her at the memory of what she'd just witnessed. It was tempting to think she'd dreamed it, or somehow misunderstood the testimony of her eyes. But tired as she was, she wasn't delusional. Herleif hadn't run away from the bear, or been eaten by it. He'd *turned into* the bear. The bear was him.

Her husband.

A low moan escaped Adrienne, and her steps faltered. What had she gotten herself into? She'd thought she wanted to go to the academy so she could explore her magic, but this was a level of magic she wanted nothing to do with. And she'd gone and shackled herself to it for life.

Not that she could really carry the blame for that, she reminded herself, her father's face swimming before her mind. But another image joined it—that of the hooded figure with whom she'd trekked through the woods. She might not have known what Herleif was when they said their vows, but he'd known. Where was his honor to bind her to him in ignorance?

The word made her pause. *Honor*, the men had chanted at her father in the tavern, even the most inebriated of them scorning him for the suggestion of backing out of his own gamble. Once he'd entered the game, Herleif had been equally bound. So why did he enter at all?

The trees thinned ahead, and Adrienne hurried forward eagerly. Had she made it out of the woods already? But when she pushed through the last few branches, she found herself looking once again at the castle. With a shudder, she plunged back between the trunks, wondering how she'd gotten so turned around. After having the same experience five more times, however, she was forced to conclude that her sense of direction wasn't the issue. A lingering impression that she hadn't pinpointed earlier finally broke through to her consciousness on her final entry into the clearing. It was a fainter version of what she'd felt when Herleif had turned into the bear. It must be magic. She was so inexperienced in her craft that she hadn't identified it at first, but as a singer she could feel magic. And it was magic that was herding her back toward the castle no matter how far she tried to run from it.

Fear rippled over her as she looked up at the structure. Moss covered the base of the outer walls, and she could see a few broken windowpanes. But on the whole, it was in better repair than she would have expected. In the full light of the morning it was actually quite picturesque. She might even have said beautiful, if the whole scene wasn't tainted by the fact that she was magically prevented from leaving.

Adrienne's eyes darted across the clearing to where Herleif's cloak still lay crumpled on the grass. There was no sign of the bear, but that didn't mean much. The forest surrounding the castle was thick enough that he could be watching from a stone's throw away, and she wouldn't see him.

Exhaustion pulled at her, the night of high emotion and no rest taking its inevitable toll. Unless she counted the one-minute lie down in the forest on the way to the castle, of course. A shudder went down her frame. Up until Herleif turned into an enormous bear before her eyes, that request of his had been the strangest moment of their time together. What was its meaning? He'd been so insistent that she lie down, but then he'd seemed as uncomfortable as she was. She didn't know whether to be relieved that he hadn't been expecting anything more or alarmed at what his mysterious purpose might be.

She rubbed a hand over her eyes, trying to clear her blurring vision. She couldn't keep going indefinitely. Her stomach was tight and empty as well, but sleep was the more immediate need. What had Herleif said? That she should go inside the castle and try to sleep. He'd claimed it would be comfortable, and that he'd return at nightfall with food. He must have meant that he'd return as a human. She had the distinct impression he hadn't intended for her to witness his transformation.

It was possible he was lying, of course. Maybe he had no intention of returning, and had simply been trying to get her at ease so he could attack her in his bear form. But much as her instinct was to fear the enormous creature Herleif had become, her logic told her that made no sense. He'd surely had opportunity to attack her when she first ran from him, and he hadn't tried anything of the kind. She remembered his dry tone when they'd been discussing the bear. He'd been the one to point out that in spite of the terrifying rumors about the creature, she couldn't point to a single time someone had actually been injured by the bear.

Other than the infamous occasion, of course. She'd only been thirteen at the time, but she remembered clearly the pandemonium that had struck the town when the castle groundskeeper's wife and son had run screaming into Tove, declaring that an enormous white bear had killed not only their husband and father, but the king and crown prince as well. Felman had been in the town at the time, and had heard the story firsthand. According to him, their tale had been clear and credible, in spite of their great distress. The groundskeeper's son had gone into the castle in search of his father and had found his father dead beside the king. With his own eyes he'd seen the bear bent over the groundskeeper's body, the man's blood on its snout. The bear had turned on the boy and chased him out of the castle.

When the royal guard who'd been in Tove at the time had gathered a small group to go back to the castle, they'd encountered the bear again. They recounted that the creature—its white fur still smeared with blood—had chased them from the woods as they struggled with their burden. The guard claimed to have dealt the creature a fatal blow with his spear, and at first the townspeople were reassured. That was before the sightings began, of course.

On that terrible day, Adrienne and her sister had run into the town to watch the commotion, as had most of her peers. She could still remember seeing the three bodies borne down the main street—the king, the groundskeeper, and another guard. The prince had already been carried off by the creature, and his body couldn't be recovered.

A memory stirred, a random comment she'd overheard when she and Revna had been pressed into the crowd of goggling villagers who watched the procession pass. A woman she didn't know had commented to a companion that the bear probably went for the prince because he was so large in stature. More meat for the creature. Adrienne had found the placid observation a little gruesome at the time, but now it struck her for a different reason.

The prince had been called Herleif, and apparently he'd been a large man, even at eighteen. And he'd last been seen at this very castle, where he'd supposedly been killed along with his father, although his body had never been found.

Adrienne wasn't an imbecile. She knew how to put these pieces together, incomprehensible as the completed picture might be. Herleif wasn't named for the prince, he was the prince.

She'd just married the supposedly dead crown prince of Frossenland in a hasty ceremony in a tavern, the outcome of a bet.

It was simply too impossible to believe, and yet the coincidences required to make it untrue were even more absurd.

Also, there was the other little detail. The one where he was actually a giant skulking bear.

Abruptly the reality broke upon Adrienne that she had very little to lose at this point. Pushing aside her lingering fear of the place, she strode across the clearing toward the castle's enormous double doors. She cast a dispassionate glance over the carved wood. She could see a splintered section on one of the surfaces, but if the doors had been forced from their hinges by an enraged bear—her enraged bear, she supposed she should say—then it had been passably repaired since then.

The doors didn't seem inclined to budge, but a moment's investigation uncovered a smaller door set just around the corner from the main entrance. It was unlatched, and opened at the first attempt. Adrienne slipped into a stone entranceway, a shiver going over her that had nothing to do with nerves this time. Herleif hadn't been wrong when he said it wouldn't be warm inside. Chill permeated from the stone walls, the long rug under Adrienne's feet worn and threadbare. She needed to find somewhere to sleep, and this drafty entranceway wouldn't serve the purpose.

Glancing around, she saw that the rug was noticeably more worn in one direction than in the other. She followed this dubious trail, every sense on the alert for the unknown. She tried to reach out with her extra capacity, searching for signs of dangerous magic. Nothing came to her awareness.

Thinking it might help, she began to sing softly. She felt the magic stirring glacially beneath her feet, but it wasn't enough for any defined purpose she knew. The sound warmed her slightly, though, making the abandoned dwelling seem less eerie. At least she couldn't sense any sinister power speeding toward her.

As she wandered, she glanced into room after room. Everything was swathed in fabric, dust covering all surfaces in a thick layer. She could see that the rumors hadn't been entirely accurate. Although there were plenty of dust-covered, silver candlesticks and sculptures, some surfaces definitely looked like they'd once housed treasures which were no longer there. She could even see paintings that had fallen from their positions on the walls, their frames missing. The theft hadn't been recent, however, by the look of the undis-turbed dust.

The extra-threadbare track down the rug led her up a stair-case and down several corridors before it reached a room where the door stood ajar. Peering in, Adrienne felt her heart lurch nervously. This room wasn't covered or dusty. It was a handsome bedroom, and although the surfaces couldn't be called gleam-ing, it lacked the abandoned feel of the rest of the castle. It was definitely lived in, and there was only one candidate for its inhabitant. This must be Herleif's bedroom. She was no authority on these matters, but looking at the size of the hand-some, canopied bed, it seemed like a bedroom fit for a prince.

Adrienne ducked back out, checking the nearby rooms for any other beds that were in a fit condition to be slept in. But the rest had clearly not been touched in years, and she didn't feel equal to the task of making them habitable. Not in her current state.

She drew in a breath, telling herself not to be squeamish. Herleif had told her to try to sleep, and there was nothing else for it. She let herself back into his room, shivering once again at the chill in the air. Heavy curtains were drawn over the windows, so that very little light permeated the space. Adrienne didn't worry about any of these details. She just kicked off her boots and slipped into the bed, glad to feel the weight of multiple blankets and fur pelts on top of her.

Ruthlessly pushing everything but her need for sleep from her mind, she closed her eyes, and let herself drift.

CHAPTER SEVEN

Adrienne

When Adrienne awoke, it was to utter disorientation. Her first impression was of warmth, and a more comfortable mattress than she'd ever slept on before. Keeping her eyes shut, she kicked one stockinged foot to the side, expecting to encounter the edge of the bed. But her leg extended fully without any sign of the mattress ending. The new territory was cold on her foot, and she quickly withdrew back to her original position.

Fighting a lingering sense of alarm, she opened one eye. A wedge of orange light fell on a huge canopy above her, the wooden beam a dark mahogany. Thick curtains draped down from the frame, and dust motes floated through the air.

The castle.

She sat up quickly, pulling the blankets around her. She was alone in the room, as she had been when she'd gone to sleep. She slipped her boots back on, hurrying to pull back the heavy curtains over the windows. Light streamed in, mellow with the warmth of afternoon. She'd slept for some time, then, but not all day.

Her need for rest was now satisfied enough to make her

hunger painfully prominent. She hadn't eaten since the dinner she'd shared with her family, at which her father had announced his horrifying plan. Almost an entire day had passed since then. She wandered back out into the corridor, wondering how hard the kitchens would be to find.

In the end, it took her half an hour of wandering empty hallways to find them, and doing so brought no relief. They were cold and silent, clearly not in use. However Herleif ate, he didn't prepare his food in there. Adrienne tried not to think about the likely answer for how he ate.

By the time the sun went down, Adrienne had explored much of the castle, and was so hungry that she would almost have welcomed raw fish, or whatever bears ate on a brisk summer evening. With no source of light in the castle, and no way to build a fire, the abandoned halls became eerier as the sunlight faded. Darkness found her sitting on the front steps of her new home, a thick blanket from Herleif's bed wrapped around her as she scanned the tree line apprehensively. The summer storm had blown itself out, and although everything glistened with moisture, no rain fell on her bare head.

As expected, mere minutes after the last light disappeared from the sky, a large figure stepped into the clearing. Large for a human, that was. Herleif was considerably smaller than he had been when Adrienne had last seen him. And considerably less furry.

She remained sitting, studying him critically. He'd donned the hooded cloak again, and his face was obscured. But something in the way he held himself communicated his tension and uncertainty. He seemed to be waiting for something.

Adrienne's eyes traveled down to Herleif's hands, and she saw that he gripped a bundle. Rising hopefully to her feet, she gestured for him to come to her. He responded at once, striding across the darkening clearing with a gait that she now noticed was reminiscent of an ambling bear, even in human form. How much time did he spend on all fours, covered with fur?

"You've returned," she said, when he came to a stop about three feet from her.

"I said I would." Herleif's voice was deep and calm, but Adrienne thought she sensed a hint of wariness. He was likely expecting a rebuff, as well he should.

"You're not a bear anymore."

Unsurprisingly, he didn't respond.

"Why did you marry me?" Adrienne asked abruptly.

Herleif shifted slightly, his body language impossible to read. "A moment of weakness, I suppose."

Ouch. Trying to pretend the curt answer didn't sting, Adrienne lifted her head. She'd been much too meek throughout the whole process so far, and it was time to be more direct. When your new husband turned to a bear in front of your face, the need for stepping daintily was surely past.

"Are you going to harm me?"

Her husband started visibly, one strong hand lifting slightly before dropping back to his side. "I will never harm you," he said in that deep, reverberating voice. "I told you last night that you'll be safe so long as you're with me, and I meant it."

"Hm." Adrienne considered him, not convinced. He seemed sincere, as much as she could judge from a stranger. But even if he spoke honestly, his idea of what would harm her might differ from her own.

"Are you hoping to benefit from my singing ability?" Adrienne asked. "Because you should know, I have little strength and no training. And as you must know, the magic in this part of the country is so scarce there's not much even experienced singers can do with it."

"How disappointing," Herleif said. "You should have made full disclosure of your lack of skill before I married you."

For a moment Adrienne swelled with indignation, then her mind caught up with the change in his tone. It was so difficult to read him without being able to see his face, but she realized suddenly that he was teasing her. Somehow it made her like him ten times better.

"Yes, our marriage does seem to be plagued with a lack of disclosure," she commented lightly. She wondered if she was going mad. She'd been afraid when she first laid eyes on Herleif, and even more so when he entered the game to gamble for her hand. Why was she *less* afraid now, when she'd actually seen him transform into a giant, savage beast?

"I didn't consider any benefits from your singing ability at all when I married you," Herleif said, the words abrupt, and this time obviously sincere. "Although of course I wouldn't object to benefiting from them."

Adrienne nodded slowly, wishing her craft was more use to her.

"What's in the bundle?" she asked, trying to redirect her mind as much as the conversation. "Did you bring food?"

The hooded head nodded. "You must be starving."

"I am." She sniffed hopefully. "What did you bring?"

"Fish," Herleif said, his tone apologetic. "And some berries. You can eat those at once." He extracted a large maple leaf, unfolding it to show a pile of blackberries.

Adrienne snatched the leaf from him with more eagerness than dignity, downing the berries in a few bites. The juice was sweet and refreshing, in addition to the welcome offering for her stomach.

"Thank you," she said.

Herleif didn't respond, and Adrienne wished again that she could read his face.

"What's wrong?" she asked when the silence stretched out. "Did I say something I shouldn't have?"

"No," he said. "I just didn't expect thanks. You would be justified in recriminations instead. I should have thought to provide food for you before..."

"Before you turned into an enormous bear," Adrienne finished for him.

He twitched slightly, but gave no answer.

"Does that happen often?" she asked.

Silence.

Adrienne pushed on, undeterred. She'd had plenty of time to think through what she'd seen during the hours since she woke. "It didn't escape my notice that you changed at sunrise, and reappeared at sunset. Do you spend your days as a bear and your nights as a man?"

Still no answer.

Adrienne sighed. "What's the point in keeping secrets, Herleif? I'm married to you, aren't I? We're stuck with each other, for better or worse. Isn't that what we vowed?"

She saw a muscle in Herleif's arm jump, but it was another long minute before his deep voice rumbled across the space between them.

"It is."

"So let's not draw this out," Adrienne said crisply. "You're the prince, aren't you?"

He didn't speak, and Adrienne narrowed her eyes in annoyance. "I'm not a fool, Herleif. The prince was last seen here, supposedly killed by a huge white bear. Your name is Herleif, and you've just turned into a bear. You're Crown Prince Herleif, and clearly whatever killed your father didn't kill you." A horrifying thought occurred to her, and she blurted out the next question before she could think it through. "Did *you* kill your father?"

"No!"

The passion in Herleif's reply caused Adrienne to recoil

slightly. She'd succeeded in rousing his emotion for the first time, but she took no satisfaction from it. She hadn't intended to call him a murderer—she'd been thinking that he might have no control in his bear form, and might have killed his father and the others in that state. But she thought it best not to explain her ill-mannered question further.

"I'm sorry," she said instead, her voice small.

She bit her lip as she considered the matter. Clearly he'd enjoyed some level of control twelve hours earlier, when he'd refrained from chasing her through the woods.

"But you *are* the crown prince," she mused. "It's the only explanation that makes sense." She paused as a thought occurred to her. "I suppose you're the king now, actually. Or you're supposed to be."

Herleif had gone back to being frustratingly unresponsive, although she could see the tension in his posture.

"Hold on…" Adrienne's eyes widened. "Does that mean that technically I'm now…" She gave her head a sharp shake. "No. Noooo no no. I'm not going to think about that. That's just too —" Another shake of the head. "No."

A frown creased her forehead. "Do your family know you're alive? They can't know, surely. I remember when you supposedly died, there was such a hubbub over your sister being named queen as only a child. Although everyone still refers to her as Princess Runa. I understand your mother is acting as regent until Princess Runa comes of age. How old is the princess now?"

"Eleven." The word seemed to slip out of Herleif's mouth without thought, and Adrienne let out a breath. He clearly wasn't going to confirm it in words, but as far as she was concerned, she had her answer about his identity.

"Is that why you've been hiding your face?" Adrienne asked hopefully. "To conceal your identity? You needn't have—I wouldn't have known you just by sight. Now that I've figured it out, will you let me see you?"

Herleif let out a long sigh, his answer clear even before he spoke. "No."

Adrienne ran a hand over her face, weariness creeping back over her in spite of her hours of sleep.

"Where's the fish you mentioned?" she asked.

Herleif hefted the bundle. "In here. But I'm afraid I don't really know how to prepare and cook it so it's fit to be eaten by, you know…"

"A human?" Adrienne supplied. "I can cook. I might need help starting a fire, though."

"No fire." Herleif's voice was suddenly sharp, and Adrienne flinched. When he spoke again, his voice was gruff, but no longer angry. "No fires in the castle."

"Well, I can't cook it without a fire," Adrienne pointed out. "And I won't eat it raw. I'm not yet hungry enough for that."

Herleif lifted a broad hand, slipping it under the hood to rub his neck. "I suppose I see your point. If there's to be a fire in the kitchen, it must remain in that room only. And I won't come in."

"If you insist," said Adrienne. She was a little surprised to find herself disappointed. Perhaps it was natural after the lonely afternoon she'd spent wandering the halls, but still, it must be further sign of her madness to be craving the company of this bizarre half-bear stranger she'd been all but sold to.

"Wait here," Herleif told her curtly, dumping the bundle beside her.

Adrienne pulled her knees up against her chest, watching as Herleif strode toward the trees again, the darkness swallowing him up before he reached the edge of the clearing. He returned a short time later with an armful of wood, striding straight past her into the castle.

Scrambling to her feet, Adrienne snatched up the fish and

followed him as he retraced her earlier steps to the kitchen. She thought he would go inside, but instead he deposited the wood by the door.

"The fire stays in the kitchen," he repeated gruffly. "Understand?"

Adrienne nodded, some of her nervousness returning.

The hooded head gave a nod as well. He hesitated for a moment, as if unsure what else to say, then swept down the corridor.

Adrienne watched him go for a moment, then turned to the kitchen. Apparently Herleif had been lurking in this castle as some kind of bear-man for five years. His mysteries could wait an hour while she had some dinner.

Herleif hadn't brought her much wood, and she had no difficulty getting it into one of the kitchen's smaller fireplaces. But actually lighting the fire was a different matter. She'd told Herleif she might need help, and she was a little miffed that he hadn't offered. She'd helped make the fire in her own house plenty of times, of course, just not alone.

She glanced around the abandoned kitchen. The place was going to need a lot of work to be properly functional again. But for now, one simple fire would do.

Adrienne stacked the wood, looking around for some flint. A search through the cupboards yielded some kindling but no flint, and she resigned herself to the much less effective method of rubbing the wood together. Ten minutes of effort soon convinced her that she wasn't going to get the fire lit without assistance.

But she had no assistance, she thought, as she threw the wood down in frustration. She was powerless.

The thought made her pause. She wasn't powerless. She had access to power, little as she might know how to use it. No doubt for a properly trained singer, lighting a small fire would be a simple matter.

Adrienne picked the wood back up, placing it against one of the larger logs and rubbing it rapidly between her hands. As she worked, she began to sing softly. She could feel magic stir in the earth, down deep beneath her feet. She focused her mind on it, trying to coax it up within her reach. A thin tendril seeped through the floor, wrapping itself around her. It would have to do.

Clumsily, by guesswork, she directed her song, making up words about light and warmth. She willed the power to go back out from her, to enter the wood. A spark leaped from the stick in her hand, and the thinnest trail of smoke rose up. Encouraged, Adrienne doubled her efforts, singing happily to the fledgling flame. Soon, she was able to light the kindling, and had the satisfaction of seeing flames licking the wood she'd carefully stacked.

Gutting the fish was a more familiar task, and Adrienne made short work of it while the fire grew. Herleif had caught three large fish somewhere—Adrienne tried not to dwell on the teeth and claw marks that marred the catch. By the time the fish was prepared, the fire was ready to receive it. She didn't worry about seasoning. She was hungry enough that it wouldn't matter. And she doubted Herleif would be picky, given his usual method of eating.

Unused though the kitchen was, it was well stocked with crockery and other items of that nature. As in the rest of the castle, there were places where items seemed to have been taken, but nothing had been touched in the recent past. Adrienne soon had two plates out with matching silverware, and she slid the fish onto them as cleanly as she could. Some potatoes would have been nice with it, but she supposed that wouldn't be easy for a bear to acquire.

Holding a plate in each hand, she pushed her way through the door back into the corridor.

"Herleif?" she called uncertainly. There was no sign of him, and no reply greeted her ears. Pursing her lips, Adrienne continued down the corridor, making for one of the dining halls she'd discovered in her wanderings. It was on the smaller side, and had shown signs of recent use. The table hadn't been covered in cloth at any rate.

The room was dark and deserted, and it was tempting to use her magic to light a fire in the hearth there as well. But remembering Herleif's sternness, she refrained. Setting the plates on the table, she turned regretfully away from the tantalizing meal and returned to the corridor. Unable to think of anywhere else to look, she made her way to the bedroom where she'd slept most of the day away. It was deserted.

Frustrated, Adrienne was about to go back out when she noticed that she'd left the curtain open. It probably wouldn't make much difference in the already cold room, but it went against the grain to invite the frigid night air to seep through the glass unchecked. She strode across the room to pull the curtain closed, but a glance through the window stopped her in her tracks.

The sky was as clear as it had been stormy the night before, and moonlight was slanting down into the clearing that housed the castle. A lone figure stood on the grass below, his back to the building and his head raised to the sky. Herleif's posture spoke so clearly of loneliness that Adrienne's breath caught in her throat. She couldn't see his face, of course, but she could tell even in the silvery light that his hair was as pale as her own. A fleeting desire to run a hand over it darted through her, and she pulled back from the window, embarrassed. Closing the curtain, she hurried back through the castle to the entranceway.

Herleif must have heard her open the front door, because when she stepped out into the night, his hood was back on.

"Didn't you hear me calling for you?" she asked, trying not to sound too sulky. "The food will be cold by now."

"Why didn't you eat it?" Herleif asked blankly.

Adrienne stared at him. "Because I was waiting for you, of course."

The silence stretched out once again, and Adrienne's impatience grew with it. The relief of the berries had worn off.

"You prepared some for me as well?" Herleif asked finally. He sounded utterly confused.

"Well...yes." Adrienne was beginning to feel foolish. "Can you not eat human food anymore or something?"

"No, I can." But still Herleif didn't move.

"Well, come on then," Adrienne prompted him, turning back to the castle. She didn't wait to see if he would follow, making her way straight to the dining hall. Thin moonlight slanted through a window, but it was barely enough to see her plate. She'd laid the places across from each other, and when she seated herself, she heard another chair scrape across the dusty floor. In the darkness she had no hope of seeing Herleif's face, but she could make out his hulking form.

Adrienne tucked right into the food, pleased to find that some warmth still lingered. It was nothing fancy, but in her hunger it was one of the best meals she'd ever prepared. She was halfway through hers when she looked up to realize that Herleif hadn't begun to eat.

"What's wrong?" she asked, a little self-conscious. "Was I supposed to use the gold plates?"

Her joke failed to hit the mark, as Herleif remained silent.

Disheartened, she added, "It's not a culinary masterpiece, but—"

"I have no doubt it's excellent," he cut her off quickly. His voice turned a little dry. "And there are no gold plates in this castle. But are you sure you won't want all of it? You must be hungry...I truly wasn't expecting you to cook for me."

Adrienne gave a light laugh, her spirits much higher now she had something in her stomach. "It's a fairly common wifely duty, isn't it?" She shook her head. "I am hungry, but even I don't need this much all to myself. Besides, it would feel strange to eat alone. I've never cooked for just myself in my life."

"You cooked for your father?" Herleif asked, his head tilted a little to the side.

Adrienne snorted. "Only if I absolutely couldn't avoid it." She sensed his confusion, and added, "My father has played very little role in my life, actually. For as long as I can remember, he's showed up only sporadically. When he needed money, basically. My mother is the one who did all the work, and raised us on her own."

There was a moment of silence. "I feel that it would be polite to commiserate with you on what sounds like a difficult situation," Herleif said. "But having met your father, I'm more inclined to congratulate you on having him absent so often."

This time Adrienne's laugh came out slightly brittle. "You're not wrong."

"You said your mother raised 'us'," Herleif said. "You have siblings?"

Adrienne nodded. "My sister Revna is the oldest. She's already married with three of her own children. My brother Felman is next, then my other brother Kettil. I'm the youngest."

"What are they like? Are your brothers like your father?"

"Of course not," said Adrienne sharply. "None of us can stand the way he behaves when he's with us. My siblings and mother are nothing like him—they're all as hardworking as they are kind." She thought of Felman, and smiled reluctantly. "If a little pigheaded at times."

It was hard to tell in the darkness, but Adrienne thought Herleif nodded. He finally took a bite of the fish, letting out a small sigh.

"This is good," he said. "It's a long time since I had cooked food."

"Well, get used to it, because I don't intend to eat raw anything," Adrienne said crisply.

She thought she heard the ghost of a chuckle. "Does your family live in Toveham?" Herleif pressed after another minute of eating.

"On the outskirts of town, to the east," said Adrienne, fishing out a bone from her mouthful. It was harder in the dark. Definitely a strange experience to eat without light to see by. "Are you sure we can't light a candle or something?" she asked hopefully.

"No candles." Herleif's voice was terse, the space between them suddenly full of tension. "No lanterns, no fire outside of the kitchen."

Adrienne fell silent, half chastened, half impatient. "Were you injured in the attack that killed your father?" she asked after a moment.

"Why would you ask that?" Herleif sounded suspicious.

"Just wondering if your face is disfigured or something," Adrienne commented daringly.

Herleif made an impatient noise in his throat. "My face is not hidden out of vanity."

Adrienne said nothing, but she felt marginally encouraged. At least he'd acknowledged aloud that he was intentionally hiding his face. Her meal finished, she rose to her feet. Without a word, she leaned across the table and took Herleif's plate, carrying both to the kitchen. Without water there wasn't much she could do to clean up the mess she'd left from cooking, so she decided to leave it for the morning. She was weary enough to sleep, in spite of the hours of rest she'd had earlier in the day.

The dining hall was empty when she returned, and she continued straight on to the castle's one occupied bedroom. The chill seemed to seep out of the stone around her as she traversed the corridors. Now that night had truly fallen, the lack of a fire had become a real problem. She could only imagine that in winter the castle would be uninhabitable without heat. Surely Herleif's strictures against fire wouldn't last that long.

It made Adrienne squirm to think of being here alone with her strange new husband for enough months to reach winter. But she had no reason to expect anything different. They were married now, after all. She would have to adjust to her new reality.

She'd reached the bedroom now, and she hesitated. The door stood open, but of course no light issued from inside. Adrienne swallowed as she stepped over the threshold. She could tell with that indefinable extra sense that she wasn't alone. Herleif was in the room.

"Herleif?" she asked softly.

"Yes, I'm here." The voice came from the far side of the space, and Adrienne searched the shadows fruitlessly.

"I gather this is your bedroom, since it's the only one in the castle that's set up for use," Adrienne commented.

"It is," Herleif confirmed.

She bit her lip, her heart thrumming unsteadily. "I suppose it's mine now, too."

There was a pause during which Herleif's presence seemed to pulse tangibly in her senses out of the darkness.

"I suppose so."

Telling herself to be brave, Adrienne moved forward into the room, running her hands nervously down the skirts of the costly new gown her father had purchased for her. At some point she would really need to find some more attire, but for the moment it looked like she would be sleeping in her clothes again.

As her eyes adjusted to the darkness of the space, she noted that Herleif was hovering by the window, well back from the enormous bed. Adrienne moved to the far side of the bed from his position, sitting down on the covers with awkward stiffness. Since he was the one who'd thrown his dice in for the prize of marrying her, she thought it should be up to him to speak first in this situation. But still he remained silent.

"It's cold, isn't it?" she said awkwardly. "I don't suppose you have a fire in here at night?"

"No fires," Herleif said, his tone uncompromising.

Adrienne sighed, not surprised. "Would you prefer me to sleep in a different room?" she asked. "I'm sure we could make another one suitable, but it would be an easier task in daylight."

"No," said Herleif quickly. "We should both sleep here."

"All right," said Adrienne, still awkward. She remained sitting on the bed for the longest minute of her life, waiting for Herleif to move or speak. He did neither.

"I don't know what you expect me to say," Adrienne burst out, unable to stand the tension any longer. "You seem to be waiting on me, but do you think I know how to navigate this situation? A day ago I was home with my family, with no intention or expectation of getting married! You're the one who entered that game with the hope of winning a bride!"

"Our marriage was no more planned by me than by you," said Herleif quickly. "My actions were the impulse of the moment—I didn't go to that tavern looking for a wife."

"Well, you acquired one," said Adrienne crisply. "So now it's up to you to deal with that situation."

"I know it is," said Herleif calmly. He drew an audible breath. "I need to sleep here. And—and so do you." The words were determined in spite of his clear discomfort. "But I don't wish to make you uneasy. I can return once you're sleeping if you prefer. I can even leave before you wake."

"Is that what you would prefer?" Adrienne asked, her voice coming out small.

"What I prefer is immaterial," said Herleif with a touch of impatience. She heard his steps as he moved away from the window. "I should speak more plainly. That worthless notary may have been satisfied by the circumstances last night, but I wasn't. I don't consider you to have entered this marriage of your own will, not truly. We're bound together now, and that can't be helped. But I don't expect anything of you, any more than I've offered you the full confidence a true wife could be entitled to expect." His voice was low and serious. "I won't force so much as a kiss on you, Adrienne."

Adrienne lowered her gaze, unable to bear the intensity of his regard, even without his face visible. She was overwhelmed by the strange tangle of emotions produced by his words. She was most definitely relieved, but there were other feelings, too.

"I don't know whether to trust you," she whispered.

Herleif's reply was curt, and she could almost hear him nod. "That's understandable," he acknowledged. "I don't expect you to give trust until it's earned." He hesitated. "But I also can't give all that you might wish or expect."

Adrienne nodded, her eyes still on her lap. "I understand." It was far from true, of course. The various mysteries of her husband's strange situation remained completely beyond her understanding.

Herleif turned to leave, but Adrienne wasn't done. "And I did marry you of my own will," she said. She could almost feel his skepticism, and she hastened on. "I was in a terrible position, I don't deny it. But no one forced me. I made my own choice."

Herleif paused in the doorway, still silent. Then, without word or gesture, he swept from the room.

CHAPTER EIGHT

Herleif

Herleif strode from the castle, his mind swirling with a barrage of conflicting thoughts. How had he gotten himself into this mess? How had he gotten Adrienne into it?

Better this than letting her be shackled to that monster in the tavern, he tried to assure himself.

But it was hard to hold on to that conviction when he remembered the raw vulnerability in her whispered words. *I don't know whether to trust you.*

Of course she didn't, and he didn't blame her for it. At least she would see with time that he meant it when he said he wouldn't harm her.

But even that thought brought little relief to the turmoil inside him. He was painfully aware of how easily he could harm her, without wanting to or even meaning to. One slip, and she would pay the price.

No.

If it came to that, he would have to yield. Doing so would be bitter indeed, but it would be more honorable than allowing the innocent girl currently perched nervously on his bed to bear the cost of his curse.

The night air stung Herleif's face as he crossed the clearing. It was certainly cold for summer. No doubt the girl's family had a fire to warm them at this moment, and a place for her by the hearth. If he could send her home, he would. But little as she knew it, that option would bring a worse fate on her than the one she currently faced.

Herleif paused among the trees, his face turned up to the stars obscured above. He rarely spent the night hours out in the forest. But it felt good to have the fresh night air on his human skin. The last twenty-four hours he'd felt submerged in a dream, and he needed to wake up to the situation he now found himself in. He had a wife, and superficial as their union might be, it was recognized by both the law and the magic. Certain responsibilities came with that.

And in addition to questions of responsibility, his heart was still moved by the same compassion that had caused him to so rashly intervene on Adrienne's behalf in the tavern. She was as vulnerable now as she'd been then, and as in need of a friend. He wanted her life with him to be more than tolerable. He wanted to make her comfortable.

With that aim in mind, he strode into the trees. He'd slept several hours during the day in his bear form, so he wasn't desperate for rest. He would forage for enough food to cover more than one meal this time.

It was a few hours before he returned to the castle. The night was as clear as the previous one had been wild, and stars spangled the sky above when he crossed the clearing. He made his way into the kitchen, noting the last few embers in the hearth. He would have to be very careful if Adrienne was going to need a fire in there regularly.

In depositing his load, Herleif discovered the signs of Adrienne's cooking. A moment's thought explained why she hadn't cleaned up. He retrieved a large bucket and made his way back into the night, heading for the well which stood not far from the kitchen's outside door. After several trips, he'd filled the large tank the cook used to use, back when the kitchen was presided over by a cook.

Once the kitchen was in order, his next mission took him to rooms he hadn't touched in years. He felt a pang as he entered the chamber where his parents used to sleep when the whole family traveled to Tove during Herleif's childhood. He knew that giving Adrienne her own room wasn't a viable option, but there were other things among his mother's discarded items that might prove useful for his new wife.

His wife.

It was impossible to comprehend, and he pushed the thought aside. Having raided the wardrobe, he made his way at last back to his own room, laden with gowns that smelled musty but would be serviceable nevertheless, as well as several other items.

He paused in the doorway, his eyes trying to pierce the darkness. He'd made sure the curtains were closed earlier, and Adrienne had dutifully left them as she found them. The room was very cold—he could only hope she was warm enough under the mound of blankets he always slept under. Come to think of it, he was cold himself, and longing for sleep. She would surely be warm to lie beside—he'd never before gotten into a bed that someone else had warmed already for him.

He turned that thought aside quickly, knowing how dangerous it was for him to dwell on such matters. But however wary he felt, there was no help for it. He had to sleep beside her. He deposited his burden on top of a chest at the foot of the bed, then felt his way to the writing desk that stood against a window on the far side of the room. The ink in the well had long since dried, but he found a piece of parchment and a length of lead. As best he could in the darkness, he scratched out a note before turning back to the bed.

He could see the still form occupying one side of the vast mattress. Adrienne's breathing was slow and steady, and he was fairly certain she was genuinely sleeping. Trying not to disturb her, he divested himself of his thick fur pelt and boots, slipping beneath the blankets on the other side. The bed was so huge, she was a full arm's length away. Turning onto his side, Herleif could almost imagine that he was alone in the bed as usual.

No. He couldn't imagine that. Her presence was tangible. Awareness of the petite stranger stretched out beside him filled every corner of his mind. He had no idea how Adrienne had fared—for Herleif, at least, it was a slow and uneasy descent into sleep.

Herleif woke abruptly in the still hour before dawn. The final shudder of a quake in the earth told him what had broken his sleep. He frowned into the darkness. The tremors were far too frequent these days.

Still, he could thank the quake for one thing—it had woken him in time to keep his promise to Adrienne. He would be gone before she awoke.

He glanced over at her. Outside the sky would be showing the first hint of gray, but in the curtained room, all was dark. He was unable to make out her face—thankfully, given she would be equally unable to see his if she woke first—but he could see her form huddled under the blankets. A strand of fair hair streamed back across the pillow, and Herleif was gripped by a sudden, foolish desire to touch it and see if it felt as soft as it looked. Mastering the impulse, he slid out of bed, once again donning his boots. He could already feel the first tingles. Dawn must be near, which meant his transformation was minutes away. He'd better hurry if he wanted to be clear of the castle in time.

He'd only just reached the tree line when it started. Pain rushed over him, as intense as that first time. No matter how many times he experienced it, he was never quite ready for it, it came so suddenly.

His conversation with Adrienne regarding his supposed death turned his mind unwillingly back to the moment he'd been cursed. As he felt his limbs extend and his fur sprout, he heard again in his mind the chaos of those terrible first moments. He could hear the giant queen's growl in his ears, and see poor Iver bursting through the doorway.

Don't give in, Iver had warned him, the words sung as he tried to pull magic into them. *Don't stop fighting her.* His song had become low and furious, no words discernible for a moment. Then he'd looked at Herleif again, sweat beading on his brow as he sang another warning. *I have softened this curse all I can with the magic I can reach. But your own determination fights for you as surely as my magic could. Do not give in. You must outlast her.*

Herleif wrenched his mind from these memories with an effort, not eager to relive the moment that had followed, when the giant queen had fallen on Iver and thrown him across the room with as much strength as Herleif had in his bear form. More than one good man had died that day, and in his lower moments, Herleif had wished he could have been one of them.

No. That same determination that Iver had sworn by rose once again in Herleif. He wouldn't give in. He wouldn't let his enemy win, either by his surrender or his death. He had obligations to his family and kingdom, and one day he would be free to fulfill them. And in the meantime, he had a more immediate obligation to the wife he'd taken.

Of course, he reflected sadly, as he ambled deeper into the forest, his massive paws sinking into the mud, there wasn't much he could do for her during the hours of daylight. Her reaction the previous dawn had made her feelings on enormous bears as companions fairly clear.

With very little to do, Herleif wandered the forest for most of the morning, thinking of ways he could make Adrienne's lot easier. His mind was as clear in bear form as it was in human form, just with an additional layer of animal instinct. It helped him hunt for food, and avoid dangers his human senses would likely not have detected. Not that the latter ability was especially important in his case. There wasn't much that was dangerous in the woods aside from himself. They didn't even get wolves in these parts. Reindeer were the largest creatures he usually saw, and they were no threat to him.

He didn't even encounter humans anymore—as Adrienne had said, the people of Toveham knew to avoid these particular woods. Herleif had no specific memory of the encounter with Adrienne's brother, but it must have been a few years before. It had been a particularly tough winter, and a number of the townsfolk had become desperate enough to venture into the forbidden woods in search of food. Herleif had avoided them wherever possible.

He was therefore incredibly surprised to hear a human voice when he approached the boundary of his territory.

"I tell you there's magic around here. This method of detection never lies."

"There's no magic in these parts," responded another voice tersely. "At least, not enough to bother with. Can we go back to the village now?"

The second voice was as high as the first, and Herleif

suddenly realized they weren't humans at all. In his astonishment, he momentarily forgot about his form, and he lumbered forward curiously. Sure enough, two elves came into sight, their skin almost as pale as snow, and their emerald eyes glinting through the tree trunks.

Herleif had forgotten, however, that elves had vastly superior hearing to humans. He thought he'd moved silently, but one elf's head shot up, and he gripped his companion's arm.

"Did you hear that? What's—" To Herleif's dismay, the elf's eyes latched right on to the sliver of him that was visible between the trees. "Is that a BEAR?"

The other elf let out a squeak, and the two of them practically tumbled over one another in their haste to flee.

Herleif settled back on his haunches, letting out a huff. He should have been more subtle—he had to remember that he couldn't camouflage as well as he thought in the snow-less summer. Now he would get no more answers.

Even as he thought it, his enhanced ears caught the words of one of the fleeing elves.

"Did you feel it? Magic pouring off the creature! I don't know what's afoot here, but that's no magic I want to..." The voice trailed off as they passed out of hearing range, and Herleif turned thoughtfully away.

The rest of the day passed interminably, Herleif's thoughts back at the castle with Adrienne. Only when the sun finally began to set did he allow his padding paws to follow the direction of those thoughts. He was surprised by his own eagerness. The thought of company, of having someone to come home to, was almost painfully welcome. He'd been consumed by guilt since he brought Adrienne back to the castle, but when he spotted her through the last of the trees, once again awaiting him on the castle steps, he allowed himself to feel the tiniest shoot of another emotion as well.

He would almost have called it happiness.

Like the elves, Adrienne surprised him with her sharp sight. He'd thought himself still hidden by the trees, but she shot to her feet, her eyes fixed on his position.

"You can come out," she called calmly. "As you are, I mean. You don't have to wait for the sun to go down."

Herleif paused, not sure whether he trusted either himself or her enough to take advantage of the invitation. After a moment, however, he found himself slipping between the trunks, moving with careful slowness as he emerged into the clearing.

CHAPTER NINE

Adrienne

Adrienne considered Herleif thoughtfully. He was a bear, that much was indisputable. Now that she wasn't screaming and running, however, she could see that he was far from an ordinary bear. There was the size, of course. That she'd observed the previous day. But there was also the way he held himself. There was simply no shrouding the human intelligence in his bearing.

Not to mention the eyes. Even in the fading light of sunset, they were arresting. They were somewhere between blue and gray, and they watched her with a calm, steady regard that no bear could ever manage. In fact, they were more human than bear in shape as well, and it was frankly unnerving. Although of course she was grateful that he kept his human mind even in his bear form.

"Is it safe for me to come closer?" she asked.

The bear dipped its head in one slow nod.

Adrienne moved forward onto the grass, wondering how much time she had. It had been evident the night before that the change wasn't something Herleif could control. The sun would soon be below the horizon, and she assumed that he would then turn back into an aloof man.

She came to a stop about a foot away from the bear. Herleif was holding himself rigidly, watching her as warily as if she were the dangerous beast and he the prey. Daringly, Adrienne lifted a hand, extending it toward him. The bear's ear twitched, its front paws shifting uneasily on the grass of the clearing.

"May I?" Adrienne asked.

Again, more slowly this time, the bear nodded. Adrienne laid her hand against the side of his vast head, feeling the way the muscles jumped under her touch. She shifted forward, walking around his bulk as she ran a hand down his shoulder and side.

"You're not as soft as you look," she informed him solemnly. "Quite coarse, actually."

The bear gave an audible huff.

Grinning a little, Adrienne dug her fingers in further, surprised to find a second layer of fur under the first.

"Actually, you get softer as I go deeper," she commented. She leaned back to catch his eye as he swiveled his enormous head. "Is that symbolic of your personality, Herleif? Will you lighten up as I dig?"

The bear gave no reply, perhaps taken aback by her cheeky banter. She was a little surprised herself. But a day of solitude had given her ample time for thinking, and she was less inclined than ever to be afraid of Herleif.

In fact, her dominant reaction to him was curiosity. She was grateful for his forbearance the night before, but it also left her bewildered. If he didn't marry her either in hopes of benefiting from her singing ability or in order to seek the usual comforts and companionship of a wife, then why had he done it? What did he stand to gain? The fact that he seemed to expect nothing of her made her more inclined to discover what she could do to make his strange situation more bearable.

Unfortunate choice of words.

The fur under her fingers began to ripple, and the bear pulled sharply away from her. Grasping the reason, Adrienne retreated quickly to the castle steps, her eyes fixed on Herleif's enormous form. The bear hunched in on itself, a growl escaping as its whole body began to shake and undulate. The fur receded as the figure shrank, and without Adrienne quite seeing how it happened, she was suddenly looking at a man, down on one knee with his back to her and his head hunched right over. He was fully clothed right down to his boots, presumably wearing what he'd been in when he changed into a bear. The sun had set now, but there was enough lingering light for her to see his unkempt mane of pale hair. Then two strong hands came up and pulled the hood of his cloak up, and she was denied even that glimpse of her husband's appearance.

"Are you all right?" she asked softly, when Herleif didn't rise.

He stood, his voice coming out gruff as he replied. "I'm fine. Are you well?"

"Of course," Adrienne said lightly. "I've had a very easy day compared to you. At least, I assume." She gave Herleif a strained smile as he turned around. It was so difficult to tell how she was being received without his facial expressions to guide her. "I found your note."

"You didn't ring for me, did you?" Herleif asked quickly. "I didn't hear anything."

"No, I didn't," Adrienne assured him. She drew the silver bell from her pocket. "I was confused when you said to ring for you if I needed anything, though. Is this bell a talisman? I couldn't sense magic on it."

Herleif shook his head. "It's not a talisman. But bears have excellent hearing. And I suspect mine is increased even beyond that of a normal bear."

"Interesting," said Adrienne brightly. She stood to the side. "Why don't you come inside where it's marginally warmer, and we can talk more easily? I'm very curious to know what life is like as a bear."

Herleif grunted as he strode past her, his hood low over his face as always. "It's not very interesting, to be honest."

"Not to you, maybe, but I haven't had five years to get used to it," Adrienne said with the hint of a laugh. "At any rate, dinner is ready, so we can discuss it while we eat."

"You cooked for me again?" Herleif asked over his shoulder.

"Of course," said Adrienne. "I found the food you left in the kitchen. You must have been up half the night gathering all that." She studied his back curiously as he walked. "You cleaned up my mess from last night as well. I didn't expect that."

"It seemed the least I could do," Herleif said in his deep, rumbling voice.

Adrienne considered him in silence. He certainly wasn't what she would have expected from either a husband or a prince.

They once again ate their meal in darkness, Adrienne shivering a little from the chill. She'd donned the warmest of the new gowns Herleif had left for her, but she was going to need something thicker if she truly wasn't allowed a fire.

"So what did you do today?" she asked, as she felt around her plate with a fork, trying to figure out if she'd finished all her food. "Anything interesting?"

"I did have one strange encounter," Herleif mused.

"Hold on." Adrienne raised a hand that he likely couldn't see. "I don't want to hear any gruesome details of you hunting down some poor woodland creature."

She could practically hear Herleif's raised eyebrow in his

voice. "I don't hear you complaining about the venison you're eating."

"True." Adrienne grinned. "Go on, then."

"The creatures I actually saw were elves," Herleif said. "And I certainly didn't hunt them."

"Elves?" Adrienne repeated, surprised. "That's unusual, isn't it?"

"I thought so, but I wondered if I'd fallen out of touch with the area in my isolation," Herleif said. "So you haven't often seen elves in Toveham?"

"Almost never," Adrienne said. "I thought they'd basically abandoned the area altogether, on account of the magic being so scarce. Their main occupation is mining the magic from the ground, isn't it? Not much to interest them here."

She could just make out the dim shape of Herleif's head, nodding slowly. "That was my understanding as well. I wonder what brought that pair through this region."

"Besides," Adrienne added, pleased at how well they were making conversation, "I've always been told that elves despise giants even more than humans do. I can't imagine they'd be eager to make their homes this far north, so close to Battlement Wall and Kjemper beyond it."

Herleif remained silent and unmoving, the tone of the room suddenly frigid again. But Adrienne refused to be deterred by his humors. He wasn't alone in his reaction—many in Frossenland's north were touchy about giants. But surely if she kept pressing she'd find softness underneath, just like in his bear form.

"Your ancestors built the wall, didn't they? One of the greatest human feats in all history, my grandfather used to say. How long ago was it? You must know the history better than I do, since it was the monarch of the time who built it."

"I don't, actually," Herleif said, sounding a little begrudging.

"The records are very imprecise. No one seems to know exactly when or how they built it—just that it was a few hundred years ago, and they were very proud of the achievement."

"With good reason," Adrienne said with feeling. "My grandfather took me to see it, once, when he was still around. I was very small, but I remember it clearly. I would never believe it if I hadn't seen it. How they built it that tall and strong, all the while fending off the giants' attempts to stop construction, beats me."

"It is impressive," Herleif agreed gravely.

Adrienne chuckled. "Likely the records were vague because they were concerned other kingdoms might learn the secrets behind the construction, and seek to erect something as grand themselves."

"Very possible," acknowledged Herleif. "But if so, they damaged their own interests more than anyone else's. Thanks to the secrecy, the methods are lost to Frossenland as well."

"A lesson to learn from, I suppose," Adrienne said lightly. "Anything else to report from the day?" A thought occurred to her, and she gave him no chance to respond, instead barreling on. "I've just realized! You probably want news yourself, don't you? From the outside world."

Herleif seemed to be regarding her from underneath his hood, judging by his stillness.

"What makes you say that?" he asked. "Is there some major news from Sunniva?"

"Not that I know of," Adrienne told him. "But I wouldn't know of anything happening in the capital. No big news has filtered our way from within Frossenland, but there were some pretty sensational reports from Medulle recently!" She named the kingdom directly south of Frossenland, which stretched across the continent's whole southern coastline.

"You mean the tale about the mermaids?" Herleif's tone was disappointingly matter-of-fact, and Adrienne deflated.

"You already know," she said gloomily. "I was hoping to shock you."

Herleif gave a low, rumbling chuckle. "I only know the brief gossip I heard at the posting house a few days back. Honestly I thought it was nonsense, so if you have a credible report, you may still stun me."

"Well, I don't have any official details," Adrienne said, a little mollified. "But I believe it's all true. Apparently about six months ago, the Medullans discovered an entire empire of merfolk living in the waters south of the continent. Two of them had actually been living in Medulle disguised as humans! The sirens of legend are real, can you believe it?"

Herleif said nothing, leading Adrienne to suspect that he couldn't.

"The Medullans have all the excitement," she went on, her mouth quirking in a smile at the complaint she and her siblings had shared when the news came through. In her case, it was no longer apt. "What with sea legends coming to life, and an alliance with the mysterious island kingdom of Selvana, they—"

"Selvana?" Herleif cut her off, sounding startled. "The Medullans are allied with Selvana?"

Adrienne nodded eagerly, pleased to have found one piece of gossip he hadn't heard. "That's right. It all happened around the same time as the mermaids, I believe."

Herleif was silent for a moment, and she could feel his confusion. "But I thought Selvana was as isolated from the mainland as the Reviled Lands are. I thought no one had heard from them in hundreds of years, since the magic went wild and the ground became uninhabitable."

"That's right," Adrienne agreed. "But all that changed several months back. They reappeared—apparently they found a way to survive the magic, because the story is that the ground truly is just as deadly as rumor says. I remember hearing something about them living in the trees."

"Well." Herleif sounded troubled. "You managed to shock me."

Adrienne grinned. "You're the first person I've encountered who's more interested in the political alliance than in the appearance of real live mermaids. I suppose I shouldn't be surprised, given you're a prince. But why do you seem so glum about it?"

"I'm not thrilled that Medulle is securing diplomatic and political advantages while I'm...absent."

Absent? Adrienne's sense of humor was tickled by this polite way of phrasing his current condition.

"I can imagine it might be alarming," she said solemnly. "Is it more than you can bear?"

Herleif sounded surprised. "No, of course not. It's not as bad as all that. I just—"

"Well," she interrupted. "I'm sorry to have been the bearer of bad tidings, in any event."

"You...what?" Herleif seemed confused now, and Adrienne couldn't resist one more.

"If you ever find yourself returning to the capital, it will probably be difficult to get your bearings after so long in exile."

Even in the darkness she could feel Herleif's stare as he tried to make sense of her random chatter. Much as she tried to restrain it, a giggle slipped out.

"Are you...did you just do what I think you did?"

She was grinning openly, covered by the lack of light. "Too impudent?"

"No." She could hear the smile in his voice now, even if his tone was still a little confused. "Just impudent enough."

Her food was definitely finished now, and she was encouraged to have gotten Herleif talking. Sleep was beginning to call to her, and they'd had enough pleasantries for one evening. He hadn't even seemed offended by her cheeky references to his bear condition. It was time to be direct.

"Herleif," she said. "Can I ask you something?"

"You can ask," he said, his tone instantly wary.

Adrienne drew a breath. "Are you ever going to let me see your face? Or tell me why you're a bear, and why you're hiding here?"

The lighthearted mood that had gripped them a minute before was entirely gone now. The silence that followed her stark questions was so long and painful, Adrienne decided he wasn't going to answer.

"You basically said last night that you don't consider me a true wife," she said, trying not to sound petulant. "But you also said we're bound together, and it can't be helped. What's your plan for the future if you never intend to tell me the truth of what's happened to you? Of what's clearly *still* happening to you? Do you intend to cast me off when my presence becomes too inconvenient? Are you avoiding confiding secrets in me that you won't want me to have when I'm adrift out there?"

She waved a hand toward the window, pointless as the gesture was in the now total darkness.

"No." Herleif's reply was instant and unwavering. "However unusual the circumstances of our union, Adrienne, I take very seriously the vow I made and the responsibilities I undertook when I made it. I will never abandon you."

Adrienne ran a hand along the edge of the table, trying to understand all that was behind his impassioned words. It was clear that this new husband of hers took duty very much to heart. A good sign in a future monarch. On the whole she was pleased to have provoked some kind of response. And, if she was honest, she was pleased by his declaration of loyalty to her. In spite of the terrible beginning to their marriage and the restricted conditions of her new home, she didn't like the idea of him throwing her out. She was still trying to figure out how to respond when Herleif surprised her by speaking again.

"As to your earlier questions, they are not as easy to answer. I wouldn't wish to use the word never…it is a word too full of depth and danger. But you wouldn't be wise to expect me to do either of the things you asked imminently."

Adrienne sighed. "That's not really an answer," she informed him. "But I suppose it will have to do for now." She eyed his dark form. "I won't promise not to ask any more questions, but I'm not trying to make your life miserable, either. For what it's worth, there's no need for you to wander the halls until I'm sleeping before you can climb into your own bed. I won't try to look at your face when you're asleep, if that's what concerns you."

"Do you swear it?" Herleif asked.

Adrienne blinked. "If you really consider it necessary."

"I do."

"Very well," she said, a little irked. "I swear it."

Herleif seemed satisfied, but Adrienne couldn't help feeling put out. She stacked their dishes without comment, her movements chopped.

"Do you want me to help with—"

"No, I'll do it tomorrow," Adrienne cut Herleif off.

"I don't mind," said Herleif.

"Well, I do," said Adrienne tartly. "I prefer to wash dishes when I can see them."

Herleif made no reply, and Adrienne sighed. There was nothing to be gained from complaining about the situation.

"Come on," she said, turning toward the door. "The bed will be warmer with two."

She actually heard Herleif stumble behind her, and allowed

herself a small smirk. Even brooding princes could be thrown off balance, apparently.

She wasn't so sure of herself a short time later, when she eased into the bed beside Herleif. The mattress was so huge that there was no need for them to even be within arm's reach, but it was still completely unlike the night before. Even his breathing seemed to fill the space with unnecessary potency.

Adrienne lay awake for some time, listening to Herleif's breaths slow. If she disregarded the awkwardness of it all, it was actually incredibly comforting. It reminded her of the days before her sister's marriage, when she and Revna had shared a room. And yet, it was entirely different. She could chat casually with Revna instead of enduring the uncertain silence of her husband, it was true. But Revna's presence had never filled her with the confusing thrill that came from being so close to Herleif. Plus Revna hadn't been capable of defending her against literally any threat that might come her way.

"Good night," she whispered into the darkness, thinking that Herleif was asleep.

The shape beside her shifted ever so slightly on the mattress. "Good night," came her husband's deep rumble.

Adrienne sang to herself as she shouldered the rolled up bundle. She never would have guessed that such a thin rug could be so heavy. Of course, the room she'd taken it from was larger than her entire previous dwelling. She probably shouldn't have tried to tackle it on her own, but housework was so much more appealing during daylight hours.

She wrinkled her forehead, speculating on the likelihood of convincing Herleif to help her out in bear form. The thought made her chuckle. That would be quite a sight to see.

The laugh turned into a sigh as she heaved the rug over a sturdy branch on the edge of the clearing and began to beat it. In the month she'd been living at the castle, Herleif hadn't spent a single day with her. It wasn't as though she had nothing to fill her time. There was plenty to keep her occupied as she slowly made a decent section of the castle inhabitable again, and she didn't mind the work. The problem was the loneliness. In spite of the fact that Herleif remained a mystery in many ways, she found herself looking forward to evening with increasing eagerness each day. The time they spent together over a meal and conversation was the most comfortable part of every day, even though it all occurred in darkness.

And, if she was being brazenly honest, sleeping beside Herleif each night was almost as good. True to his word, he'd never tried to claim so much as a kiss from her, and the nightly ritual of getting into the same bed had ceased to be awkward. It was even becoming comforting. If the weather had been warmer, she might even have said cozy. Even the worsening weather was made better by his presence. They usually slept a few feet away from each other, but the warmth of the enormous figure beside her still permeated the bed, helping to keep the chill at bay.

Adrienne absently twisted the ring on her finger, her eyes unseeing as she stared at the thin gold band. Herleif had produced the ring—as well as one for himself—a couple of weeks after their unusual wedding. Adrienne still wasn't quite used to its presence. Although she'd certainly never been one of those little girls who dreamed of a wedding and a husband, she had thought occasionally about marriage in recent years. The reality, however, was nothing like any of her imaginings.

Pausing her task to glance up at the sky, Adrienne shivered. She pulled her borrowed shawl around her shoulders, reflecting on what was probably her biggest challenge. The days were definitely getting colder, and autumn had only just begun. It would get much worse as winter approached. She would have to find a way to get Herleif to budge on the fire issue. His bulk might keep him warm enough to survive, but her petite frame would wither away in winter's chill without any source of heat.

She wasn't entirely sorry about summer ending, however. The days would soon be getting shorter, and that would be a bonus. More time with Herleif in his human form would be a welcome change to her current loneliness.

She gave the rug one final beat, coughing in the cloud of dust that swirled out from it. The rain looked like it would hold off for a while yet, so she left the rug where it was, heading indoors to boil some water over the small fire she was allowed to maintain in the kitchen. She would welcome some tea to warm her up.

She supposed she could suggest that she sleep in the kitchen, away from Herleif's forbidden face. But she doubted he would approve that idea. He'd remained adamant that they share the huge canopied bed, in spite of showing no interest in any contact whatsoever.

Adrienne tried not to feel irked as she reflected on that fact. She'd been so relieved at his forbearance—she knew how perverse it was for her to now feel rejected. But she couldn't help it. Perhaps she'd let it go to her head when her father told her she was beautiful.

That memory banished any lingering resentment over Herleif's disinterest in her. She would do well to remember that being valued for her beauty was nothing to desire.

Adrienne realized as she traversed the corridors that she'd been clasping the bell in her pocket again. She kept doing it without meaning to. Slowly, she drew it out, careful not to let it ring. Herleif probably wouldn't thank her for bringing him lumbering in from his forest wanderings for no reason other than her clumsiness. She studied the small, slender bell. It was probably foolish, but carrying it around with her made her feel less alone. She'd given it a polish, and the silver surface now shone.

Silver. Everything in this castle was silver, she reflected. A glance to the side showed one of the numerous frameless pictures. She thought something decorative might have once stood on the plinth below it as well. Clearly whoever had carried off those items hadn't troubled to take the copious amounts of silver.

Adrienne found she couldn't settle over her cup of tea, rising quickly to tend to the little vegetable garden she was coaxing into life outside the kitchen. It wouldn't yield much before winter's frost set in, probably, but any fresh produce would be welcome. It was a limiting diet, eating only the food a bear could forage or hunt in the forest.

As always, while she worked, her mind turned back to Herleif. She barely noticed the hours passing, her hands busy with her work and her mind lost in contemplation of her mysterious husband. She'd spent such limited time with him in the month she'd known him, and he was surrounded by so much secrecy. And yet there were moments when she was overcome by the conviction that she actually knew him quite well. As well as she knew her own family.

But she always drove away this strange and rattling thought by reminding herself firmly that she didn't really know Herleif. How could she, when the most central question of their relationship remained unanswered?

Why had he married her?

What had he hoped to gain, and were his plans proceeding to his satisfaction? It didn't even trouble Adrienne all that much to know she must be a piece on the board for him, but it did make her uneasy to have no idea what purpose he intended to use her for. The irony of it all was that if he'd only tell her how her presence could help him, she'd probably be quite willing to further his cause. Contrary to what some men seemed to think, Herleif's undemanding approach to marriage had made his wife much more inclined to be loyal and generous, not less.

But none of that mattered while Herleif continued to maintain the charade that he wanted nothing from her. He must want *something*. He said it had been the impulse of the moment, but she'd seen him in that tavern. He'd watched for a long time before deciding to throw in his dice. He had some gain in mind, of that she had no doubt. She just wished she knew what it was.

Perhaps it related to his determination that they lie beside each other every night. It hadn't escaped her that it was the only thing he'd specifically required of her—other than the prohibition against looking at his face—and that he'd made a point of lying down beside her even the first night of their marriage, when they'd been trekking through the woods. It had been so bizarre, how could she forget it? She couldn't immediately think of how it would benefit him, but she'd be the first to admit she didn't have all the facts.

She wasn't so caught up in her thoughts that she failed to notice the sun setting. It was the most important part of her day, and she'd never yet missed it. Trying not to let her excitement show too much, she hurried back through the castle, eager to reach the steps. She didn't have long. She wasn't the only one who'd yet to miss a sunset—without fail, Herleif appeared through the tree line just as the sun was lowering. Was it possible that she wasn't the only one who longed for evening to come, who craved the companionship of a spouse they'd never planned to marry?

The thought made her heart thud erratically. It beat even more quickly when a familiar figure stepped through the trees, hood up but posture expectant, as though he trusted she'd be there, and didn't want to be late himself.

"Good evening!" she called happily, feeling her whole body relax at the end of another day's isolation.

"Good evening, Adrienne." Herleif's voice rumbled across the clearing, and Adrienne's smile grew. She always felt a pleasant little thrill when he said her name.

"Nothing but rabbit stew tonight, I'm afraid," she told him as he strode across the clearing toward her.

She didn't even try to peer under his hood now. She'd become accustomed to not seeing his face. She sometimes wondered what it looked like, but to her own surprise, the question didn't concern her much. It didn't seem especially relevant either to his personality or their relationship.

"A meal is made enjoyable or otherwise not by the fare, but by the company," Herleif told her, sounding as though he was smiling a little himself. "Or so my father used to tell me."

Adrienne scoffed. "Easy words for a king to speak, who probably never ate a mediocre meal in his life."

She turned away, knowing he would follow her to where their plates were laid out in the darkness, waiting for them. In spite of all the absurdities of life in the frigid, abandoned castle, she actually agreed with Herleif's departed father. And she fully expected to enjoy every bite of her meal.

CHAPTER TEN

Herleif

Herleif loped through the forest, his massive paws denting the damp earth in his haste. The sun was getting low in the sky, and he didn't want to be late returning to the castle. He could hardly remember the days before Adrienne came, when the transition from day to night—and consequently bear to man—made little difference to his life. He'd been equally isolated in both forms, and hadn't especially cared whether he spent his time in the castle or the woods. Sometimes he'd wandered the corridors as a bear, or slept as a man inside a hollowed out log. It had all been much the same.

Not now, though. Now he was becoming thoroughly domesticated.

The thought made him want to smile, but the expression didn't come naturally in his bear form. So he just kept padding forward, increasing his pace as the trees began to thin. Adrienne certainly had a knack for the domestic. In their nightly conversations he'd learned much of her previous life, and he knew that she'd always had to work very hard. He wouldn't have been surprised—and wouldn't have blamed her—if she'd taken her change in circumstances as an opportunity to indulge in idleness for once.

Instead, she was amazingly industrious. In the four months since their hasty marriage, she'd reclaimed much of the castle from its state of disuse. They only properly maintained a few rooms. It was all they needed, and trying to keep more of the castle free of dust would just create unnecessary work.

Much more important than the tidying and cooking and mending, however, was the company. In spite of knowing that she hadn't married him according to her own inclination, Herleif had made little attempt to shield his heart from the inevitable effect of sharing his life with someone after five years of solitude. From very early on he'd acknowledged—only privately, in his thoughts, of course—that Adrienne was an absolute delight to come home to. She'd made his lonely, frozen prison into a home, and the joy of it was almost like pain, since it came with the knowledge that he had no way to repay her for what she'd done for him.

Herleif's paw crunched over some frost, untouched in the undergrowth by the weak sunlight of the day that was drawing to a close. Winter was almost upon them. Soon snow would be falling. His body had run unnaturally hot since he was cursed to be a bear, but he knew Adrienne couldn't survive the winter without any source of heat.

He would love to be her source of heat.

The thought came unbidden, and he tried immediately to turn it aside. He might have accepted that Adrienne had softened him, but it was still too dangerous to think of her romantically. Much too fraught, given the barriers between them. It didn't help that she often crept across the bed in her sleep these days, unconsciously seeking his warmth and ending up nestled against him. He always shifted before she woke, so he didn't think she was even aware of her movement.

But he was aware. Having her so close was another type of joy that was equal parts pain.

The clearing came into view ahead, and Herleif put his tumultuous thoughts from his mind. His eyes pierced the gloom between the trunks much better than they would in human form. There she was, perched on the steps, the thickest blanket in the castle wrapped around her shoulders as she waited for him.

For him. She always waited for him, and it always made him feel like he was coming to life for the first time. She deserved so much more than this charade of a marriage. Sometimes when he was wandering the woods during the day, the guilt threatened to consume him. But it was hard to hold on to it when he returned to the castle and resumed his human form. How could he wallow in regret over forcing Adrienne into this life when she radiated cheerful energy every moment he was with her?

Judging by the low song he could hear with his excellent bear ears, she was literally radiating energy of some kind right now. He paused for a moment, enjoying the sweet sound of her song. She wasn't trained, that much was clear. There was often no sense of direction to her song, and she tended to make up words on the spot, hoping to manipulate the minuscule amount of power she could reach by simply telling it what to do. The results were sometimes highly entertaining, as Herleif didn't hesitate to inform her. The whole performance fell very far below what Herleif had witnessed from singers employed in royal business back in Sunniva. But he enjoyed it infinitely more, his whole being leaning toward the low, cheerful melody of his wife.

The ground shook abruptly as Herleif reached the edge of the tree line, and he paused. The quakes were a constant concern. Were they having them in the capital? He had no way to know. Iver had said, on that long-ago day, that the quakes had been happening for a long time. But he'd also said that they'd gotten much worse. That was over five years ago, and Herleif thought that if anything, they were even more frequent now. It was a worrying trajectory.

The tremor soon passed, however, just as the sun slipped properly out of sight. Herleif braced himself for the pain, welcoming it because it meant he could return to Adrienne. As soon as he was fully human, he hurried across the clearing, making sure his hood remained low.

As he neared Adrienne, he caught the words of her song. They were of heat and health, and he could indeed feel the warmer current of air that flowed around her. It wasn't much—either as a result of her lack of training or of the limited magic available to her—but it was an improvement on the frigid air of the evening.

"You're getting better at that," he commented when he stood near enough to feel the effects.

"Good evening to you too," Adrienne said with a smile. As her song broke off, so did the warm current. "And you're flattering me. I don't think there's any marked improvement in the heat I'm producing."

It was Herleif's turn to smile. "I don't think I'm given to flattery."

Adrienne laughed. "No, you don't seem the type. I suppose that means I'll have to take all compliments as sincere. Are you hungry?"

Herleif nodded. He'd gotten out of the habit of eating as a bear. He still spent some of each day hunting and foraging, but now he brought the food back to be shared.

"Good, because I've prepared an extra feast tonight," Adrienne said brightly. "Well, feast might be generous. But there's more food than usual."

"Why?" Herleif asked.

Adrienne flipped her pale hair over her shoulder in a businesslike gesture as she turned toward the doorway.

"I'm trying to get you into a good mood so that you'll be more likely to say yes."

"Say yes to what?" Herleif demanded. He should probably feel alarmed, but he just felt intrigued. It was hard to be suspicious around Adrienne, even knowing how much was at stake, and how much he had to lose. She just communicated trustworthiness with every move she made.

"You're rushing me," she complained. "I had it all planned out. It was going to be very subtle and convincing,"

"Adrienne." A hint of the bear's growl came out in the low rumble. Herleif reached out to grasp Adrienne's arm. She drew in a sharp breath at the contact, and Herleif dropped his hold quickly. "Don't keep me in suspense, I'll just imagine the worst."

"Nothing bad," she assured him, seeming to struggle a little to collect her thoughts. Was the touch of his hand on her arm really so unsettling? "I was just going to ask you if you'd stay with me."

"Stay with you?" Herleif repeated in bewilderment. "Of course I'm going to stay with you. Where did you think I was going?"

"No, I meant tomorrow," Adrienne explained. She took a breath, then added in a rush, "And maybe, possibly, the day after, and the one after that."

Slowly, Herleif's mind caught up. "You mean during the day?"

Adrienne nodded eagerly, the motion visible in the thin light that slanted through the window of the dining room, into which they'd just walked.

"But..." He frowned under his hood. "But I'll be a bear. All day."

"Yes, I'd grasped that, actually," Adrienne said, sounding half amused and half exasperated. "And maybe you don't get lonely as a bear, but as a human, I do. I'm alone all day, and I'd much prefer your company. Fur, fangs, and all."

Herleif didn't immediately reply because he didn't know what to say. Her request had completely thrown him. Surely she couldn't actually want to spend time with him in his animal state, could she?

But there was no reason she'd lie about it. If she'd asked for it, she must want it. In fact, given how rare it was for her to ask him for anything, she probably wanted it a great deal.

"I do get lonely," he said abruptly. "Even as a bear."

"Well then," said Adrienne, sounding surprised at the disclosure, but not displeased. "It seems that's settled."

She seated herself and drew a plate toward her. Herleif couldn't see what was on it, but it smelled good.

"I don't know if I'd say settled," said Herleif, seating himself as well. "I'm not sure it's safe. Those claws are sharp, you know, and I'm not sure if you've noticed my size in bear form. I could hurt you by accident."

To his surprise, Adrienne let out a peal of laughter.

"Herleif, have you seen yourself right now?" she asked. "Even in your human form, you're absurdly enormous. I knew the moment I laid eyes on you in that tavern that you could easily hurt me, by accident or by choice." He could feel her steady regard as she considered him. "And yet, with all the opportunity in the world, you've never hurt me but once."

"What?" Herleif sat up straighter, his food forgotten as alarm rippled over him. "When did I hurt you? Did I kick out in my sleep? Why didn't you tell me?"

"No, I didn't mean—" Adrienne cut herself off hastily, sounding flustered and clearly regretting her words. "I shouldn't have—never mind, I was being dramatic. You've never hurt me, Herleif, not physically."

Herleif remained silent. The discovery that she meant emotional pain didn't make him feel even slightly better. But she clearly didn't wish to elaborate, so he didn't press her.

"If you truly wish me to stay with you tomorrow, I'm willing to try it," he said gruffly.

"Thank you." Adrienne's good humor was apparently restored, given she tucked into her food with relish. "I'm hoping you can be especially helpful with shifting some of the heavier crates in the storeroom. I think there are some jams and preserves down there that might actually still be good! I'm not at all sure that I have sufficient stores for the winter."

"I don't know if I'll fit in the storeroom during the day," said Herleif dryly. "Do you want me to try now?"

He could just make out Adrienne shaking her head. "No, evening is too precious for housework. I'd rather just talk."

Herleif said nothing, but warmth seeped through him, the same warmth he felt when he returned from the woods each evening and saw Adrienne's petite form perched on the castle steps.

The meal passed too quickly, Adrienne doing most of the talking as she chatted cheerfully about her day. Herleif was more than happy to listen to her talk, but after a while he deftly steered the conversation in the direction he wanted to explore. He ate contentedly as Adrienne spoke fondly of her family and the home she'd left behind.

"You must miss them," Herleif commented.

He could feel her surprise at the question. "I do," she acknowledged. "And I worry about them. Are you confident my letter would have reached them?"

"Fairly confident," Herleif said. At Adrienne's request, he'd dropped a short note for her mother at the posting house a couple of weeks after their marriage, assuring her family that she was well and safe.

Herleif had been relieved on that occasion that Adrienne hadn't asked to come with him into the town. Most likely she'd wanted to avoid the possibility of seeing her father, and he certainly didn't blame her for that.

In any event, it had been for the best. He wasn't sure what would come of it if she accompanied him. As far as he knew, Adrienne had never even attempted to leave the castle surrounds on her own. Although Herleif had—of course— refrained from telling her as much, Adrienne seemed to have grasped that she was unable to leave the area. Whether she'd pieced together that it was only possible for anyone to enter or leave in Herleif's company, he didn't know. Unlikely, given Adrienne still knew nothing of the giant queen and her curse, so surely couldn't have realized how specific and intentional the magic's restrictions were.

I will break your spirit like I broke your father's weak human body. You think you're strong enough to resist me? You will yield before a year is out. I know how needy humans are. The loneliness will drive you mad.

The words danced in his memory, painful and enraging. Before Adrienne's arrival, Herleif had begun to wonder if the giant queen had been right. But since she'd come, he'd barely noticed his isolation from other humans. It was her isolation he regretted. For himself, he had no more interest in going into town. He'd done so a few times since delivering Adrienne's note, however. Each time he'd left after Adrienne was asleep and returned well before she woke. The purpose of those trips had been to spend some of his winnings on a few supplies to make life easier for his uncomplaining young wife. But he was reluctant to spend much of the gold, for reasons of his own.

"I hope they're well." Adrienne's soft words brought his attention back to his companion, seated on the far side of the dark table. Her wistful tone suggested she'd been as lost in reflection as he had. "It seems unlikely if my father is still around, but he's probably gone. He usually only stays a few weeks at most, and it's been four months now."

Herleif said nothing. From Adrienne's accounts, he had his own suspicions regarding her father's activities. But there was no need to worry her by reminding her that since he now held the majority of her father's debts, there weren't many angry creditors in Toveham to drive Svend away from the convenience of living at her mother's and brothers' expense.

"If I'm to spend tomorrow hauling crates for you, I think I'd better go to bed early," Herleif commented.

"Yes." Adrienne's voice was brisk, as if she was determined to banish her anxious thoughts. "I'm tired as well. I'd welcome an early night."

She continued to chat pleasantly as they made their way to the bedroom they shared. Herleif could hardly believe how natural and comfortable it was to be in each other's space. It almost felt like a real marriage, like the kind of easy companionship his parents once shared.

At least until they slid into opposite sides of the enormous bed, no part of them touching, and Herleif still wearing his hooded cloak. What husband didn't allow his wife to even see his face? Theirs was not a real marriage.

Herleif had become adept at recognizing the moment when Adrienne slipped into slumber, and he was glad that on this occasion he didn't have long to wait. Their conversation had prompted him regarding a task he'd long meant to do. And if he was to spend the following day in Adrienne's company, leaving her side while she slept wasn't such a loss.

He rose quietly, trying not to disturb her as he pulled on his boots and slipped from the room. He cast a concerned glance back at Adrienne, unable to make out any details in the darkness. She was covered by a dozen blankets, but it wasn't the same as having a fire. The air was already frigid, and winter had barely begun. Once the snow fell, he would need to find a better solution.

Herleif padded into the next room, retrieving the leather bag with his winnings from that night at the tavern. Not much of the gold had been spent, and all the notes of credit remained.

The journey through the woods and then the abandoned city was twice as quick as it had been when he'd traveled with Adrienne. Herleif alternated between a run and a jog, only slowing to walk occasionally for a rest. Even so, he knew it would be late by the time he reached Toveham. He would just have to count on his size and the presence his royal upbringing had undeniably left him with in order to convince the magistrate to play his part.

Sure enough, while Herleif's persistent banging on the right door brought out an irate magistrate, when the man got a good look at him, he was as willing as the shopkeeper had been to assist at the unconventional hour. At least it wasn't as late as it had been on that other occasion. The magistrate clearly hadn't yet been in bed.

He muttered to himself as they made their way through the town. "It's a bad business. Estrid and her children are good people. Seems a shame for them to be punished."

"I see no reason why they need to be," said Herleif dispassionately. "The name on these notes is Svend, not Estrid."

The magistrate said no more, shooting Herleif a sideways look that suggested he had no idea how to read the enormous stranger. Herleif kept his peace. All would become clear soon enough.

CHAPTER ELEVEN

Herleif

The walk to the rambling dwelling on the eastern outskirts of the town was achieved quickly. The moon was bright, and Herleif pulled his hood even lower over his face as their destination came into sight ahead. It wasn't a large building, but it looked well cared for, as much as he could tell in the moonlight. The yard was of a decent size as well, and Herleif could hear the sleepy clucking of a chicken. It was easy to imagine Adrienne here, singing softly to herself as she went about her chores, uncomplaining but hoping for a better future.

A future stolen from her first by her father, then by her husband.

Herleif pushed these bitter thoughts aside, focusing on the business of the moment. The magistrate knocked smartly on the door, and a moment later it opened to reveal a pale-haired woman with a wary expression and a striking similarity of features to Adrienne. She was much taller than her daughter, though, and years of hard work had given her a tougher demeanor than Adrienne still carried at eighteen.

"Magistrate," she said tightly. "You weren't expected. Is anything amiss?"

The magistrate cleared his throat. "I'm afraid it is, Estrid. I take no pleasure from it, but my duty is clear." He gestured back at Herleif. "This man has sought my assistance in the enforcement of the debts he holds."

Estrid's gaze darted to Herleif, skulking back in the shadows. He saw her eyes widen as she realized who she was. Her hand tightened on the door, and she started to speak. Before any word was out, however, she stopped herself, taking a moment before continuing with what Herleif was sure wasn't her original question.

"You've come to collect, have you? I wondered why we'd not heard from you in so long."

"Yes," Herleif responded, still well back from the doorway and the light that spilled from it. "I've come to collect."

"Like I said, Estrid," the magistrate interjected. "Unpleasant duty."

"No need to act like someone's died," said the older woman tartly. "We've been in full expectation of this event, and we have our four months of interest saved and ready."

"What?"

The angry voice issued from inside the building, and Herleif's hand clenched into a fist. So Svend was there, was he? Hiding behind his wife, letting her bear the brunt of his obligations. It was no surprise. Svend's diminutive form appeared in the doorway, his face scrunched in a scowl.

"What do you mean we have the money saved, Estrid? I've seen no hint of excess gold."

"Did you think I would tell you where to find it after what you did with the last gold you found?" she asked, her voice quivering with emotion. "Fifteen years we'd been saving that, Svend.

Fifteen years! Not content to gamble away your daughter's future, you gambled Adrienne herself, as if she was—"

She cut herself off, apparently remembering their company. With a deep breath, she turned to the two men in the doorway. The magistrate was shifting awkwardly, but Herleif remained silent and unmoving.

"If you'd given me the gold, I could have turned it into more," Svend said, sounding sulky. "This is different from last time. I came across a new opportunity which—"

"As I said," Estrid cut him off, her eyes on Herleif. "We have the four months of interest for all the debts you hold."

Recognizing his cue, the magistrate cleared his throat uncomfortably. "Mr Bjørn has informed me he insists on full payment of the debts. He's no longer willing to accept interest as a temporary measure." His tone was apologetic. "I've reviewed the papers, Estrid, and he's within his rights. All of these debts were due a long time ago."

The sound of a slamming door came from inside the dwelling, and a moment later two young men appeared behind their mother, arms full of wood.

"What's going on?" one asked sharply, dropping his load and all but pushing his father aside to join his mother in the doorway. "Mother?"

Estrid cleared her throat. "Felman, Kettil, this is the man who holds your father's debts now. He's come to collect what he's owed."

"That's the man?" one of the young men muttered to the other, alarm clear in his voice. "Look at the size of him—he'll snap Adrienne like a twig."

"Where's Adrienne?" demanded his brother. He took a half-step toward Herleif, anger clear on his face. "What have you done with her?"

"She is well," said Herleif calmly. He felt a pang of guilt for the fear Adrienne's family had obviously been suffering on her account. "She's at our home, asleep."

The man started to protest, but his mother cut him off sharply. "Not now, Felman."

"No, the boy makes a good point," Svend said quickly. "This man has already taken enough from us. Not only Adrienne, but all that gold! He has some nerve to come back here begging for more."

"Have you ever seen a man beg, Svend?" Herleif asked. Even he could hear the danger in his low voice as he shifted ever so slightly forward. "Because I have. And this is not what it looks like."

Svend swallowed visibly. Herleif waited for him to reply, but it quickly became clear that the other man had nothing to say.

"I have no interest in what you think of my nerve," Herleif said. "I'm here to collect the debts that are due, as the magistrate has told you."

"But..." Estrid's face was pale in the moonlight. "But we don't have that much gold."

"That's not my fault," said Herleif evenly.

"I don't know what to tell you." Estrid sounded dazed. "Even if we sold the house, I don't think it would be enough."

Herleif cast a glance over the dwelling, intentionally coloring his tone with disdain. "It wouldn't."

"Well, what do you want us to do?" Estrid demanded, a strain of strong emotion showing through beneath her calm tone. "You'd get much more from us in the long run if you continued to take interest."

"I don't want interest," said Herleif. He turned his hooded face to the magistrate. "What does the law say?"

"Well..." The magistrate cast an uncomfortable glance at the group in the doorway. "According to the law, if the terms cannot be met, the party who has defaulted is subject to detention until such a time as—"

"Debtor's prison?" Svend's voice swelled with outrage. "You can't intend to throw my family into debtor's prison. I won't stand for it."

Herleif's lip curled with disdain. "I don't intend anything of the kind," he said. He looked at the magistrate, whose expression was openly disapproving as he watched Svend.

"There is one name on these papers, Svend, and that person alone is subject to detention."

"Me?" The color drained from Svend's face, and Herleif could see that the contemptible man genuinely hadn't believed it possible for his actions to catch up to him to this extent. "You can't be serious," Svend protested. He glanced at his wife. "Estrid, surely you won't allow this!"

"What do you expect me to do about it, Svend?" she asked coldly, over the top of audible growls from her sons. "They're not our debts, but yours. And you've heard what the man said. Even our home—which I don't doubt will be taken and sold to partially recover the debt—isn't enough. I have nothing of sufficient value to rescue you from this, even if I were inclined to."

"Even if you were—?" Svend's fury was palpable. He struggled for a moment for what to say, then drew himself up in a flimsy attempt at dignity. "This is nonsense. I don't have to listen to these outrageous insults. You can't dictate to a man in his own home. I insist that you leave."

"I'm not leaving without satisfaction," Herleif said, the calm rumble of his voice a sharp contrast to Svend's bluster.

"Then I'll leave," Svend said, drawing a cloak from beside the door. "I expect you to be gone before I return." With a flourish, he pushed past the magistrate, giving Herleif a wide berth as he strode down the road.

"And there he goes," one of the boys muttered. "Doing what he does best, and running from his problems."

"Leaving us to pay for them," the other responded bitterly.

"Svend," called the magistrate. "You can't just walk away from this. The law is the law!" He turned grimly to Herleif. "I've no doubt where he's gone. I'll wake the sheriff to accompany me to the tavern and see he's taken into custody." He hesitated. "Are you sure you wish to take this drastic course?"

"Very sure," said Herleif.

The magistrate lowered his voice. "Estrid is right that you'll gain more financially if you allow the family to pay interest on the principal."

"I don't want a long term relationship with my debtor," Herleif said, his tone flat. "I want justice for his crimes."

The magistrate clucked his tongue, but made no more argument. "I suppose you'll want to accompany me while I seek support from the sheriff?"

He eyed Herleif, probably thinking the stranger could take Svend into custody by himself if he so chose. It was tempting, but it would be too hard to keep his face reliably concealed.

"No, I trust you to carry out your duty," said Herleif. He turned his face to the woman still framed in the doorway. "I wish to speak with the family."

The magistrate glanced anxiously at Estrid. "Now, that's not how we usually conduct these types of—"

"It's all right," said Estrid. "We wish to speak with him as well."

The magistrate still looked uncertain, but after a moment he turned away with a shrug. Herleif and the others all watched him out of sight before anyone spoke.

"I suppose you'd better come in," said Estrid.

Herleif shook his head. "No. We can speak here." A crowded tavern was one thing. Someone's family table in a well-lit room was another altogether. He studied the three tense faces before him, all of them apparently waiting for him to speak. "If you're concerned about your house, you—"

"I'm not thinking of my house," said Estrid tightly. "I'm thinking of my daughter."

"Adrienne is well and safe," Herleif said, warming to the woman. He could only be grateful that Adrienne's parents weren't *both* selfish and grasping.

"So you claim," one of the brothers said, his words laced with suspicion. "But how do we know you're telling the truth?"

The other brother nodded, his fists clenched at his side. "What are we supposed to think? Months with nothing but a brief note to say she's alive. When Revna was married, she went to live at a house a stone's throw away, where we can see her every day if we wish. Do you think we're all right with our sister being sold to pay our father's debts and whisked off where we can't find her or help her?"

"I guessed from what she's told me about you that you wouldn't be all right with it," Herleif said, speaking calmly in the face of the other man's rising passion. "It's clear that she loves you all dearly, and holds you in high regard. Our absence is due to circumstances we cannot control, not to the inclination of either one of us."

"What does that mean?" Estrid asked sharply. "What circumstances?"

Herleif studied her, knowing he had the advantage, since he could read her face and she couldn't even see his.

"I need to return to her," he said briskly. "It's a walk of some distance. But first we need to settle our affairs."

"I don't care what the law says, I'm not letting you take Mother's house," said one of the brothers fiercely.

Herleif smiled approvingly within the secrecy of his hood. "I'm not taking anyone's house." He held out the bag he'd brought, slipping the papers into it then tossing it at Estrid's feet. "I had no need or desire to win any of this. It's yours. I'm sure I don't need to tell you to hide it well until you're confident that Svend has been apprehended. I'm giving it to you in faith that you're strong enough not to use it to extricate him from his situation. If I were you, I would burn the notes of credit, and use some of the gold to pay whatever more honorable debts Svend had with tradesmen and the like, to free yourselves entirely. But that's in your hands. At any rate, you owe me nothing. The truth is very much the reverse."

Both the boys were staring open-mouthed at him by the end of this speech, but Adrienne's mother looked very thoughtful as she leaned down to pick up the bag.

"That's a great deal of generosity for no reason I can see," she said slowly. "Why would you do that?"

"Is it so strange for me to wish to provide for my wife's family?" Herleif asked. He nodded at the bag, although they likely couldn't see him do so. "Besides which, that's blood money, as far as I'm concerned. Or it would be if I kept it. Given what's passed, I think you can consider yourselves entitled to it."

He hesitated. He'd come here to make something right, not to connect with Adrienne's family in an emotional sense. But he found himself surprised by how much he wanted both to reassure them and to have them look on him with approval. Foolish desires, when he couldn't reveal himself in any way. But he should still try to set their minds at ease.

"I wish you to know," he said, his voice coming out more gruff than he would like, "that I do not support the practice of staking a daughter to pay gambling debts. Whatever you may think of how our marriage commenced, I give you my word that to the full extent that it is in my power, I will provide for Adrienne and see that she comes to no harm."

Even Adrienne's mother seemed stunned into silence by this

speech. It was very clear that whatever they'd been imagining since Adrienne's marriage, he'd defied their expectations. Hopefully they would believe him, and it would soften the pain of the separation from Adrienne that must inevitably continue.

Herleif didn't wait for a response. Drawing further back into the shadows, he turned and began walking up the lane.

"Wait!" It was one of the brothers calling out. "When can we see Adrienne? Where can we find her?"

A pang went through Herleif at the desperation in the man's voice, but he knew he couldn't answer. Allowing Adrienne's family to visit the castle was out of the question. Even bringing her to the cottage would be fraught with danger for them both, little as she knew it. He didn't acknowledge the question, not breaking stride as he made his way out of range of the dwelling.

He resisted the temptation to divert through the town and make sure Svend had been apprehended. He would have to trust those in authority within Toveham to fulfill their functions. Both the shopkeeper and the magistrate had showed concern for Adrienne's family, which was encouraging. Not everyone was as despicable as Svend.

At the thought of Adrienne's father, Herleif felt his hand curl into a fist. He'd almost forgotten just how vile the man's treatment of his daughter had been, but seeing Svend again had brought it all back. Herleif had been offended by it at the time, but now that Adrienne was his wife, and his responsibility to protect, his reaction was so much more potent.

Rage—there was no other word for the emotion that filled him. Adrienne was so young, so vulnerable, and so kindhearted. She deserved to be treated with respect, and to be cared for as the treasure she was. It wasn't just that Svend had neglected his responsibility to her, either. It was so much worse than that. He'd actually exploited those he was supposed to protect and provide for, using them for his own gain without thought for the devastation he left behind. Herleif could look on him with nothing but disdain.

It was certainly not the type of husband he strove to be, or the type of father he wished to become when he and Adrienne—

Herleif actually faltered in his steps, pulled up short by his own thoughts. Children with Adrienne? When had he started to picture a future with her, with a true home, and a family? It was too tantalizing and dangerous to imagine returning to a normal life—he'd kept sane for five years by not dwelling on that impossibility. Let alone daydreaming about a normal life with Adrienne.

And yet...they'd made it four months, hadn't they? Was it so impossible to think they might be able to see out the year without disaster? If they did, well...he would be free. And Adrienne would be by his side, because whether or not either of them had intended it, she'd bound herself to him for life. Herleif gave his head a little shake. It was too dangerous to paint such pictures. He just needed to focus on one day at a time, on what was right in front of him.

His sleeping wife, for example, who would be not just in front of him but beside him once he got home. She was probably very cold without him there. He picked up his pace, his thoughts on her request regarding the morning. Did she really want him to stay with her, even in bear form? He had to admit to some nerves about how she'd react to him, but he realized that was unjust to her. Except for that first time—one of his most painful memories—she'd showed no sign of fear when seeing him as a bear.

A whole new vista opened before Herleif. He'd honestly never considered spending his fur-bound hours with Adrienne. He knew she enjoyed his company in the evenings—she made no secret of the fact. But he'd assumed she would prefer solitude to being followed around by a gigantic bear.

But if he was wrong, well...he could only wish he'd been bold enough to live this way from the start. Almost able to feel another layer of loneliness peeling away, Herleif broke into a jog. Even before the curse, he couldn't remember a time when he'd been so eager to return to his home and family.

CHAPTER TWELVE

Adrienne

Adrienne woke abruptly, her mind taking a moment to grasp what was happening. This quake was surely much worse than usual.

Her confused eyes passed over the now-familiar room, and she let out a shriek as she realized the true source of the violent shaking.

"Herleif!" she squealed. "You can't transform in here. You'll break every piece of furniture in the room!"

Her husband jerked suddenly awake, his back remaining to her as he rolled from the bed straight into a crouch on the floor.

"I'm sorry!" he gasped. "I've never slept this close to dawn before. I must have—"

"Don't try to talk!" Adrienne scolded, cutting him off as his body began to ripple. "Just get your bulk out of the *one* room in the castle where all our breakable belongings are gathered!"

Herleif gave what might have been a laugh, although it ended as a grunt of pain. He struggled to his feet, pulling his hood low as he lunged unevenly toward the door. He'd barely disappeared from Adrienne's sight when she heard a shatter.

She hastened out of bed. As always she'd slept fully clothed, but she paused to slip on her boots before running across the rug. When she reached the doorway, she let out a snort of laughter at the sight of an enormous white bear crammed awkwardly into the corridor, his paws crunching on the broken shards of a vase as he tried to navigate around an upended plinth.

Herleif turned reproachful eyes on her, and she stifled her laughter with her hands.

"Sorry," she grinned. "I couldn't help it. You have no idea how funny it is to see a giant bear look sheepish." She dropped her hands, her expression sobering a little. "I am sorry it hurts so much to transform, though."

Herleif gave a dismissive huff, his furry flank upsetting a tapestry as he lumbered down the corridor toward the broader entranceway. Still grinning, Adrienne followed him. It had been a fortnight since Herleif had agreed to her request to stay with her during the day. He'd hung around the castle for most of every day since then, and she still hadn't gotten over the humor of watching a huge bear trying to be domestic. Why hadn't they done this months ago? It was so much better than only getting snatches of company in the evening.

She didn't mind Herleif as a bear, actually. He was comfortingly furry, and gave off a lot of heat. He'd even been known to let her snuggle against him on cold afternoons, while she read books from the castle's long neglected library. Neither of them would be comfortable enough to initiate that kind of contact when he was in his human form. But somehow, when he was a bear, it felt less fraught. And she very much liked being able to look him in the eyes rather than having him always hide himself —even if those eyes stood twice as high as hers.

Plus, as she liked to inform him, she could dominate the conversation when he was a bear, without fear of any interruption. She thought she could see a twinkle of humor in his bear-eyes when she said that. He wasn't exactly prone to chatter even as a human.

When they reached the entranceway, Adrienne edged around Herleif's massive form, taking the lead.

"Breakfast time," she said brightly. "And I think I'll boil water for some tea."

Herleif followed her to the kitchen. It was fortunate that the room had double doors, since even that was a squeeze. Adrienne had cleared the room as much as possible, pushing the large table that used to dominate it to the far wall with the help of Herleif in his bear form. As winter set in, it had become their base during the day. They even ate in there, with the exception of the evening meal, which Herleif insisted had to take place in the dark—and freezing—dining room. The light of the fire was no issue when he was in his bear form, however. Adrienne had barely entered the room when Herleif ambled straight past her, sitting down on his haunches in front of the embers of the previous day's fire.

"All right, all right, give me a minute," Adrienne told him indulgently. "I'll need to get more wood from outside."

Herleif pushed himself back up, his head brushing the low-hanging chandelier as he moved toward the outside door. He was always determined to help carry things, and even though it would often be easier to do it herself, Adrienne welcomed the assistance. She could tell it made him feel better about her situation.

Once the fire was lit and breakfast underway—they were both eating fish once again—Adrienne turned to her husband.

"Is that really the first time you've been asleep when the transformation started?" she asked him.

Herleif nodded his enormous head in a slow and deliberate movement.

Adrienne turned back to stoke the fire, a smile playing at her lips. Herleif might not know it, but she felt he'd just given her the greatest compliment on her influence as a wife. It seemed he was starting to relax, even in spite of his devastating curse. Clearly he felt safe in her presence, at the very least.

"I've been wanting to talk to you," she told him, swinging back around and adopting a serious tone. "It's important."

Herleif raised his head from where it had been resting on the warmer stones of the section of floor near the fire. Adrienne thought he looked apprehensive, but she was probably just projecting her own thoughts onto him. He had his bear face on, after all.

"Winter's here," she told him. "And it's only going to get colder. I can't manage without a fire to keep me warm. At night especially."

Herleif let out a low grumble, but the sound wasn't angry or menacing. He must know the truth of her words.

"I've been thinking about a solution," said Adrienne. "Actually, I've done more than just think about it. I've been working on it." She reached into a drawer, pulling out her handiwork with a flourish. "I've made you this."

Herleif stared at the misshapen garment with an intensity a real bear likely wouldn't manage.

"I know it's not the prettiest item," Adrienne said defensively. "And I doubt it will be the most comfortable either. I made it from a potato sack I found in the cellar. But it's thick, so at least it will keep your face warm."

Herleif's grunt somehow managed to sound startled.

"Yes, it's for your face," said Adrienne firmly. "If you wear it over your head, I won't be able to see your face. Then we can have fires through winter. I've sewn in holes for your eyes and your mouth, see?"

Not even her most optimistic interpretation of his bear expressions could claim any enthusiasm in Herleif's reaction.

"I know it's not ideal," Adrienne said with a sigh. "But unless you can suggest a better option, I really think we should at least try it."

Herleif let out a little huff, but to Adrienne's relief, he nodded.

"Excellent," said Adrienne briskly. "That's settled. Now the other matter."

Herleif cocked his head to one side in an eloquent gesture.

"I have a question for you," said Adrienne. "I know you either can't or won't tell me all the details about," she waved a vague hand, "everything. But I would like to know one thing. Will things continue as they are forever?"

Herleif was still for a long moment, during which Adrienne was sure he was trying to decide whether to answer.

"Just a nod or a shake of the head would be enough," she said hopefully.

After another moment, he shook his head once to each side. Adrienne left out a relieved breath.

"That's excellent news," she said, trying to speak unemotionally. "But for some time yet?"

Reluctantly, she thought, Herleif nodded.

"All right." Adrienne pondered for a moment. "In that case, we need to improve our system. We're not going to have enough food for winter just foraging like this. I think we should buy some serious supplies, and in the spring we should get some chickens as an investment for the future." She smoothed her skirts awkwardly as she looked at Herleif. "Do you...do you have any gold we can use to buy supplies?"

Herleif shook his head.

"We'll have to use some of the silver, then," Adrienne said. "There's plenty in this castle that's worth something. Would you be terribly sorry to part with it?"

Herleif gave a shrug of one large, furry shoulder.

Adrienne squinted out the window as she tried to think through the practicalities. "I don't think it would be a good idea to try to barter silver from the castle in Toveham. Not if you don't want anyone to know who you are, or where you're living. They have weekly markets in Kilv. We could go there. Do you know the town?"

Herleif shook his head.

"It's west of here," Adrienne informed him. "But it'll take us a couple of days, which means you'll have to be out there in your bear form. The road won't be busy at this time of year. I went to the markets a few times with my mother, and there are woods lining most of the way. With your superior hearing, you should have enough warning to duck out of sight if anyone's coming."

Herleif didn't respond. She had no doubt he had opinions, but he couldn't easily express them in his current form. There was a reason she'd broached the topic over breakfast rather than dinner.

"I found an old cart in the stables," she went on. "It would be perfect for bringing our supplies home." She gave him an innocent smile. "Like a carthorse."

Who knew bears could look so long-suffering? Adrienne's grin grew.

"I think it could be fun," she informed him. "We could travel through the woods anywhere sparse enough for the cart, and camp out overnight. To tell the truth, I'm pretty eager for a break from this castle."

Herleif's eyes seemed to soften, and his form relaxed a little. It seemed he had sympathy for her position, and it came as no surprise to Adrienne. Whatever his motivations for tying them together, whatever plans he had regarding her, he seemed to care about her comfort in the meantime. She even suspected sometimes that he felt guilty about whatever he was going to use her for. From time to time she caught his bear eyes watching her with a look of pain.

For a moment she was distracted, wondering as she had many times before what his reason was for their marriage. She could still picture his hooded form hovering in that tavern, watching each roll of the dice with great care. What had he gained, or would he gain in the future? He'd called their marriage a moment of weakness, but it hadn't been an uncalculated one. He'd also told her that he would never harm her or abandon her, which seemed inconsistent with the possibility of some future gain at her expense. But he wasn't gaining much from her current presence, that was certain. In fact, he had twice the work he'd had before, keeping her fed. He seemed to appreciate the companionship, but she couldn't believe that was the reason he'd married her. Not when it had taken him so long to unbend enough to really interact with her.

The crackle of their food over the fire drew her attention back to the present. She cast a glance over her shoulder at Herleif as she hurried to tend to the fish. "Are we agreed, then?" she asked. "Will we go to the market?"

His unsettlingly human eyes were full of unspoken thoughts as he held her gaze. But after a moment, he nodded his head again, and Adrienne was satisfied. The market was only days away. If they left in the morning, they'd make it. She would spend the rest of the day preparing.

Luck was not on her side, however. When she woke the following morning, her mind was full of the practical tasks necessary before departure, and it took her a moment to sense the difference in the air. Alarmed, she sprang out of bed, stumbling to the window to pull back the curtain.

She let out a groan at the sight of the familiar clearing coated in white. The first heavy snowfall of the winter. And the snow was still falling quickly enough to make visibility difficult.

There was no way they could set out in this. A glance back at the bed showed her that Herleif was gone, as she would expect given how light it was. He must have risen and changed form some time ago. They wouldn't even be able to properly discuss new plans for hours.

"I'm sorry," Herleif told her that night, dutifully wearing the potato sack over his face as they ate dinner by the kitchen fire for the first time. "I know you were excited to leave. But it will be some time before it clears enough to travel."

"It's all right," sighed Adrienne. "I am disappointed of course, but it can't be helped. I doubt the market will even be happening in this." She tried to keep her features straight as she glanced under Herleif's hood. "There are useful ways for me to spend my time here while we wait."

As it turned out, it was a month and a half before Herleif declared the weather clear enough to travel as far as Kilv. Adrienne had been at the castle for six months, and the worst of the winter had passed. Herleif had braved the initial snowfall on his own to go into Toveham and buy a smaller quantity of supplies, which had seen them through. Adrienne didn't ask how he'd paid for it, or why he'd slipped off when she was sleeping rather than inviting her to accompany him. She'd become so used to her husband's secrets, she sometimes had to remind herself that it wasn't normal to know so little of the person you were married to.

They'd been fortunate that no amount of snow stopped Herleif from hunting in his bear form—he didn't seem to feel the cold at all when he had his fur. Still, the winter had been far from luxurious.

Once assured Herleif was willing to accept her solution,

Adrienne had made him a better face covering out of a thick woolen tunic she'd found in a drawer, and he'd dutifully worn it through the hours of darkness. He'd even allowed them to have a fire in their room.

She could see it made him nervous, though. He didn't sleep as deeply, and he checked the covering every time he stirred, as though worried she'd pulled it off while he was dozing.

It was disheartening, because it suggested he still didn't fully trust her. And maybe he was right. If she was honest with herself, there were times she was tempted. More than once she propped herself up on an elbow while he slept uneasily, studying the eyelids that were all she could see of his face. Those and the lips, but even she knew it was too dangerous to stare at those. Her marriage was in no way what she would have expected, but it wasn't just because of Herleif's strange situation. Based on what she'd witnessed in her parents' marriage, she'd never expected to feel such fondness for a husband she hadn't even gotten to choose. It was more than fondness—it was a deep and confusing ache, occupying the space somewhere between acute pain and deep joy, and it was strongest when she watched him sleep. It was unsettling, and Adrienne tried not to dwell on it.

When the snow had melted enough to allow travel, Adrienne once again raised the idea of the market. Herleif agreed, but he also took the opportunity to inform her that once they returned, they would go back to having no fires. Adrienne wasn't surprised and didn't argue. In some ways she would prefer it, if it meant Herleif would be more relaxed.

Given the staggering amount Herleif could carry even in human form, they decided the cart was unnecessary. Adrienne still had hopes of raising chickens, but she figured they could transport a couple home without the cart, and consider getting more later.

They set out at first light, as soon as Herleif had transformed. The first few hours they walked in silence, Herleif's tension palpable once they left the safety of the castle woods. But when they successfully crossed the main road without being seen, delving into the shelter of the forest beyond, he seemed to relax. The rest of the day passed smoothly, Adrienne chatting away to her silent companion as they traversed the woods—her picking her way, Herleif tramping over the top of anything in his path. Their pace was necessarily set by Adrienne, and they didn't make it as far as she'd hoped before they stopped to camp for the night.

"We'll have to make better time tomorrow if we want to reach the market the following day," Herleif told her as they ate a simple dinner after darkness had fallen, his voice coming out muffled through the face covering he'd brought with him.

"Well, we can't all be enormous and four-legged," Adrienne said. She was weary after the day of walking, and the words were a bit waspish.

"You could ride on my back," Herleif suggested. "I'm sure it would be much faster."

"On your back?" Adrienne cast a doubtful glance at him. "It's a long way off the ground."

Herleif seemed amused. "I won't let you fall," he assured her.

So the next day, as soon as Adrienne's sore feet began to slow her down, Herleif drew up alongside a large, mossy boulder. Feeling self-conscious, Adrienne scrambled onto his back, gripping his fur more tightly than could be pleasant for him. He made no sound of complaint, however, and they certainly traveled much more quickly. Three times they had to cross a section of ground not covered by trees, and on one of those occasions they were delayed for some time as they waited for an opportunity with no passersby. But even so, they were most of the way to Kilv by the time they stopped to make camp.

The second night passed just like the first. They had a fire, and no creatures bothered them. Even in human form, Herleif's presence seemed to have that effect. Although the snow had mostly melted, it remained bitterly cold. As the fire died down, Adrienne found herself drawing closer and closer to Herleif for warmth. When she woke shortly before dawn, she was curled right up into him, her back to his vast chest. She could tell by his breathing that he was already awake, but there was no sign of tension or discomfort in the muscles of the arm that was around her, holding her in place. For a moment she lay still, allowing herself to bask in their nearness. Then she started to sit up, and he immediately lifted his arm away.

She didn't comment on their embrace, and neither did he. Within minutes, the sun had begun to rise, and her companion was once again a large bear. It was a convenient way to escape any potentially awkward conversations, honestly.

They reached Kilv only a few hours after sunrise, and the market was bustling. Helpfully for their purposes, the market was held in a large square of cleared land outside the town, with the forest growing right up close. Herleif was able to linger in the trees only about ten minutes' walk from the market in relative safety from being spotted.

Adrienne felt nervous without his presence, but she tried to look confident as she entered the chaos of the market. It wouldn't help her bartering if she let herself look as lost and alone as she felt.

She hoisted her heavy satchel higher up her shoulder, scanning the stalls. Her first priority was certain food supplies, but she seemed to be in a part of the market where the stalls primarily sold clothing. Glancing curiously at the beautiful bolts of fabric, she pushed her way through the throng. She felt more anxious the further she went from the forest and Herleif's reassuring presence, but at the same time, the market was a fascinating place. A stab of regret went through her as she pictured wandering through it with him at her side, in human form of course. Things had never been that easy for them. But he'd told her it wouldn't be forever. She just had to hold on to that hope.

Adrienne's first few transactions went smoothly, the merchants very ready to accept the small silver items she paid with. She and Herleif had debated their value during the journey, but the truth was neither of them really knew. Adrienne had no experience with valuable royal silver, and Herleif had no experience with bartering in a market. He might have grown up surrounded by extravagance, but that didn't mean he knew what a silver candlestick was worth in terms of root vegetables. She suspected she'd overpaid for a number of items, but it couldn't be helped.

Once she'd used up the few small objects, things became trickier. As she'd feared, her attempt to barter more costly furnishings from the castle attracted significant attention. Two merchants turned her away, and the third considered her with an expression she didn't like at all. She had no doubt they all thought she'd stolen the silver. Herleif had expressed that concern around the campfire the night before, but Adrienne had told him that even if they did think she was a thief, they wouldn't be likely to raise a fuss if they were in a position to benefit from it. They'd cheat her in turn, no doubt, but at least she'd be able to get the supplies they needed.

She had thought Herleif's silence in response to this comment was a little troubled, but the third merchant's behavior seemed to support Adrienne's guess. The man cast an eye over Adrienne's satchel. It was bulging now, mainly with her purchases, although there were still some valuable keepsakes in there.

"What else you got to offer?" the merchant asked, his gaze greedy.

Adrienne kept her voice cold. "I think this is more than enough to cover what I'm asking." She brandished the silver urn which Herleif had assured her wasn't an important family heirloom or anything of that nature. It was a struggle to hold it along with the box in which four chicks were nestled.

"I'll be the judge of that, lass," the merchant said in a self-satisfied way. "If you want to buy my wares, you'll have to pay the price I ask."

Adrienne scowled. This was the reason her family had never sent her to barter when traveling markets came through Toveham. It wasn't an issue of her capability—her diminutive stature always made people think she was younger than she was, and apparently that meant easily manipulated in the minds of many.

She cleared her throat, ready to argue, when a new voice joined the conversation.

"Where did you get that, girl?"

Adrienne spun around at the stern question, alarm rushing over her as she recognized the uniform of a marshal. There were a pair of them, actually, and they were looking at her with suspicion. The speaker seemed surprised when she turned fully and he got a good look at her. He'd probably thought she was a child. But her adulthood would probably make things worse—she'd be less likely to be shown lenience.

"It comes from my family home," she told him evenly. She didn't like to lie, but a moment's reflection made her realize the words were technically true. Their marriage made Herleif family, and it had come from their home. "We treasured it once, but times are hard," she said, letting some of her bitterness about her own family's struggles seep into her tone. "We must do what it takes to survive, and we can't eat silver."

The marshal narrowed his eyes, clearly not convinced. "Let me see it."

Adrienne pulled it back, her skin crawling as she realized how much interest their confrontation was gaining. Many market-goers had stopped to watch.

"I don't believe I'm obligated to let you take my possessions from me," she said, trying to sound confident.

The marshal snorted. "If it were really yours, that would be true. Give it here." He reached out.

Adrienne tried to pull it back, but he was too quick and too strong. After the merest moment of scuffle, he wrested it from her hand. To Adrienne's dismay, he flipped it upside down, frowning as he took in the engraving on the bottom.

"That's the royal crest," he said grimly. His eyes traveled up to Adrienne's face. "From your family home, is it? Are you some kind of lost princess?"

"No," said Adrienne tightly. "It may have belonged to the royal family once, but it belongs to my family now. I come from Toveham—the royals probably gave it as a gift to my grandparents when they used to frequent the area. Many in the village once worked for them at some time or another."

"From Toveham?" the marshal repeated. "Enough said, lass. Do you think I know nothing of the geography of my own land? If you've been pilfering from the northern castle, you'll answer for it. The royals may not go there anymore, but everything in the building still belongs to our monarch."

"Of course I haven't," said Adrienne, increasingly desperate. "Clearly you *don't* know the area as well as you think. No one can get into that castle. No one's been near it in years."

"A plunderer's dream," the other marshal said dryly. He nodded to his fellow. "Come on, let's take her in. A night in the holding cell should bring out the truth."

"No!" Adrienne protested. "No, you don't understand. I didn't steal it, I swear! You can't lock me up!"

"Can't we now?" The marshal sounded amused. He and his fellow moved in unison, each grabbing one of her arms in a hold she knew she wouldn't be able to break. If only she'd been given the chance to study her craft! She might know how to break free by the use of magic. Not that there was much power to be found in the magic-parched earth.

"Please!" she cried again. "Let me go. You don't realize what you're doing."

The men ignored her words, yanking her away from the stall. The box fell from her hand, the chicks breaking into a frenzy of chirping.

"We'll be having a look through the rest of that satchel, too," said the marshal who still held the urn.

Adrienne gave a wordless protest as panic clouded her mind. What would Herleif think when she didn't return? What would happen to him if she was locked up overnight, and he was unable to insist that they sleep side by side? What would happen to *her* if she spent the night in a holding cell, along with who knew what other criminals? She knew the law wasn't kind to unprotected waifs of her class.

She opened her mouth to cry out to Herleif, but stopped herself. Who knew what kind of attention it would attract if she called out the name of the missing prince after producing silver with the royal crest? He wouldn't be able to hear her anyway.

A memory came back to her, of Herleif telling her of the enhanced hearing of bears, and the even greater superiority of his in his oversized bear form. She remembered exactly what they'd been speaking of—she'd gotten in the habit of keeping it always in her pocket during the day, and never stopped, even once Herleif started spending the days with her.

Adrienne went limp, stopping her struggles for a moment.

Thinking her docile, the marshals started moving through the market, even further from the forest where Herleif lurked. If she was going to act, the sooner the better.

Springing suddenly into motion, Adrienne yanked one arm down, plunging her hand into her pocket. The movement was so unexpected, the marshals didn't respond quickly enough to prevent her getting her fingers around the slender handle of the silver bell. She pulled it out, ringing it fiercely.

One of the marshals grabbed it, bringing the noise to an abrupt halt. But Adrienne could still hear it ringing in her ears, even as she barely dared to hope.

"What are you doing?" the man asked sharply. "Is that some kind of signal to your band? How many thieves are loose in the market right now?"

"Probably a fair few, but I'm not one of them," Adrienne grunted, once again struggling.

The two marshals continued to tug her through the crowd, tense and watchful now. But no amount of vigilance could have prepared them for the response to Adrienne's signal. Even she felt a thrill of instinctive fear several minutes later, when screams ripped through the bustling market, giving them mere moments' warning before a gargantuan white bear came crashing through the stalls.

CHAPTER THIRTEEN

Herleif

Herleif was only dimly aware of the utter pandemonium he was leaving in his wake as he plunged through the market. He felt more like a bear than a man in that moment, his usual human reason further from reach than he could ever remember it being in all the years of his transformations. When he'd heard the ringing of that little silver bell, he'd simply charged. The fear that consumed his mind left no room for rational consideration of the risks.

He'd been wary from the start about the idea of Adrienne venturing into the markets alone with a bag full of suspicious silver. But he'd had no other ideas to suggest. The markets didn't operate after nightfall, so he couldn't go with her.

He vaguely remembered that at the time he'd been convinced he couldn't venture into sight in his bear form. But that conviction was nowhere to be found the moment he caught Adrienne's signal for help.

People fled before Herleif, eyes wide and screams trailing behind them. His ears rang with the volume of it, and his mind was overwhelmed by all the potent senses assaulting him. But he pushed it all aside, desperate to find Adrienne. The ringing had stopped, so he wasn't entirely sure of his direction, but he kept moving between the stalls, sniffing the air as he went.

Even in his panic, he was enough in control to take care not to hurt anyone, even to minimize the inevitable damage to the stalls he brushed past with his monstrous flanks. But from the way the humans were reacting, anyone could be excused for thinking he was batting people with his claws and sinking his teeth into anyone who got too close.

His nose caught a familiar scent, and he paused, swinging his vast head around. Adrienne. He changed course, charging off again, to the great distress of a group sheltering under a wagon now in his path. He ignored their hysterical screams, lumbering forward as quickly as he could without causing carnage. It was nothing to the speed at which his paws had eaten away at the ground as he sprinted through the woods. But thankfully it was enough. In another moment Adrienne came into sight, her arms gripped firmly by two marshals whose expressions would have been humorous to Herleif if they weren't in the process of arresting his wife.

Herleif let out a rumbling growl that had the desired effect of making both men drop Adrienne's arms at once. She stumbled forward immediately, relief evident on her face.

"Your hearing really is excellent," she said, sounding dazed.

Herleif gave another growl, this one full of warning rather than anger. He jerked his head meaningfully, and Adrienne seemed to come out of her stupor. With a quick nod, she hurried toward him, using a nearby barrel to scramble onto his back. Her heavy satchel banged against his side, and her hands shook a little as she gripped his fur.

Herleif barely waited for her to be settled before he took off again, retracing the trail he'd already left. No one challenged them, or attempted to stop them. Everyone was still diving out of the way, eager not to be in the bear's path. He heard Adrienne draw in a breath at the sight of the damage he'd left in his wake, but she made no comment until they were halfway back through the market.

"Stop!" she called, and Herleif careened to a sudden halt.

Adrienne slipped from his back, hurrying toward a box that lay abandoned under a half-collapsed stall. She picked it up, her evident anxiety dissipating as she peered inside it.

"They're all right," she told him reassuringly, just as if he'd expressed concern about whatever unnecessary detail had made her stop their flight. "The chickens," she added, cradling the box as tenderly as a mother might hold her child.

Herleif tilted his head, trying to make his expression as exasperated as possible. He could tell from the ghost of a grin on Adrienne's lips that she'd understood his silent message, but she didn't acknowledge it aloud. With more difficulty this time, she climbed up onto his back again, and they set off.

Herleif didn't stop when they cleared the market, maintaining a rapid pace until they were well into the woods. When his hearing and smell both told him they were safe, he slowed to a walk, his pulse still pounding. Gradually, the rush of bear instinct began to wear away.

"Thank you for coming to my rescue," Adrienne said. A note of anxiety entered her voice. "We made quite a mess back there, didn't we? I hope I didn't overreact by ringing that bell. They said they were going to lock me up overnight. I didn't know what would happen to you if I wasn't with you at night. It seems..." she hesitated, "important to you to have me close when you're sleeping."

Herleif slowed still further, thrown by her words. It wasn't a surprise that she was observant enough to put the pieces together to that extent, but he still hadn't expected her to say it aloud. He was also rattled to realize that she was right—it would have been disastrous if he'd been unable to recover her before the night was over. And yet, he hadn't even thought of that. His reaction had all been for Adrienne, his fear all about her safety.

Some kind of awareness intruded on his mind, insistent and unyielding. All the things he'd spent six months shying away from, or hiding under the guise of unemotional husbandly duty refused to be ignored any longer. He had to acknowledge to himself how much he'd come to care about Adrienne. It was much more than duty to the vow he'd made, or guilt over how he'd trapped her. It was deeply personal, to the point of discomfort. He'd known the moment he heard her ring the bell—it would kill him if anything happened to her. It was a confronting realization, one that had never been part of his plans.

"A lot of people saw you," Adrienne said tentatively. "I'm sorry I put you in that position."

Herleif shook his head violently. He wished he had his words, so he could have told her that he begrudged none of it, in spite of the risk. She'd been in danger, and he would have done much more than wreck a market and expose himself to witnesses in order to save her.

Then again, even if he did have words, he probably wouldn't have said that.

There was no more conversation between them, and Herleif didn't pause to let Adrienne dismount. Speed was crucial now, and they would move much more quickly at his pace. He wouldn't tire anytime soon in his current form. By the time they stopped for the night, they were almost halfway back to the castle. Even so, Herleif allowed them only a few hours of sleep, continuing to walk in his human form, and starting the next day before he transformed. The absurd and uncomfortable covering Adrienne had made for his face came in handy, at least.

He knew that the story of their exploits at the market would spread quickly, and a team of hunters would likely be dispatched to try to deal with the savage bear running rampant throughout the region. Herleif wanted to be well within the safety of the castle's boundary before any such hunters caught up to them.

It was a strange thing, to be thinking of the boundary as a bubble of safety rather than a prison. And yet, it had been a long time since it felt like a prison to him. Even his initial feelings of guilt after Adrienne first arrived, when he chastised himself for trapping her as well, had begun to fade. He'd made discreet inquiries in town when he went for basic supplies, and he knew that his worthless father-in-law had indeed been taken to a debtor's prison. But even so, he rarely thought about whether Adrienne would prefer to be at home with her family.

She just seemed so happy most of the time. Particularly—if he dared think it—when she was with him.

Or perhaps he was just telling himself that to avoid thinking about the reality—that it didn't matter what either he or she wanted, because she couldn't leave him and return to her family without catastrophic consequences not just for him, but for the whole kingdom. The mess might be of his making, but he couldn't just excuse her from dealing with the consequences. Not without making a bigger mess again.

These thoughts plagued Herleif's mind all the way back to the castle. Their journey took another full day, but by the time he changed form at sunset, they were within reach, and decided to push on rather than spend another night camping.

"I'll be glad to be back in our own bed again," Adrienne said cheerfully, as they picked their way through the familiar woods.

Herleif felt something deep inside him warm at the casual words, and for the first time in a long time, he didn't try to push it down. Wise or unwise, he'd let her into his heart, and he saw no point in denying it to himself.

Adrienne chattered on, her initial unease after the market fiasco long since faded. Herleif was in human form now, and he was carrying not only the heavy satchel of supplies, but the box of chicks. He cast them a resigned glance. What they'd discussed was buying mature chickens, who could produce eggs immediately. But he didn't have the heart to point this out to Adrienne when she'd been so enthusiastic about how much fun it would be to raise them. She clearly had a nurturing disposition. She would make a wonderful mother one day, if...

But some thoughts really shouldn't be indulged, no matter how Herleif's heart might be softening. The future was still much too uncertain.

He responded as required, but was generally happy to listen to Adrienne talk. A memory struck him, of the first time they'd walked through these woods together, the night they were married. Adrienne had been making a great effort to communicate, and put on a good front. She'd even said she wasn't afraid, and in that moment, he believed it. But her demeanor now was so entirely opposite to how it had been then, that Herleif felt he was only just beginning to understand exactly how afraid she'd been.

Not just of him, either. She'd had reason to fear him, given he was a stranger. Especially since he'd offered no explanation either of his bizarre behavior or his decision to gamble for her hand in marriage. Then he'd turned into a bear, and well...that was a whole different matter.

But her fear had been deeper than that. It was still deeper. It was such an intrinsic part of her, Herleif doubted she even noticed it. If she did, she wouldn't think of it as fear, most likely. But he saw it. It came out all the time, like in the way she'd assumed that any merchant would turn a blind eye to her supposed theft as long as they could gain from it.

He didn't blame Adrienne for this cynicism. Given his own

experiences, he had reason for bitterness as well, and he knew his heart often wasn't what it should be. But at least his parents had both been good people, consistent in their treatment of him and his sister. A familiar pang went through him at the thought of the father whom he'd loved fiercely. He doubted the memory of his death, sudden, pointless, and vile as it was, would ever lose its sting. And thoughts of his mother brought no relief. What she must be suffering from her losses, how heavy must her crown sit on her head as she held the reins of government for a daughter who was still seven years from claiming a burden she'd never been intended to carry.

In spite of all the pain he felt, Herleif recognized the difference. His wounds came from external sources. Adrienne's came from within her own family. It was no wonder her view of the world seemed confusingly contradictory at times. Her mother had raised her with love, and Herleif had seen enough in his one meeting with Estrid to know that she was hardworking and responsible. Adrienne's father, on the other hand, had been worse than a burden. He'd taught Adrienne to expect that affection was a mask for wanting something, and a husband only shows his face when he wants to manipulate the family for his gain.

And somehow, out of that convoluted mess of a household, Adrienne had emerged. Beautiful, kind, tender-hearted, determined, indomitable Adrienne. A woman born to have magic course through her being, who instead was stuck tending chickens and preparing cold meals in the darkness, but who somehow managed to be cheerful and industrious through it all.

Even discounting his cursed form, Herleif didn't deserve such a prize.

"There it is!" Adrienne's glad cry caught his attention, and he followed her pointing finger to see stone walls between the trunks ahead, glinting in the moonlight. "Home at last," Adrienne added.

Herleif's heart swelled once again as he followed her across the clearing. He was beginning to get the feeling that whatever came next, home would be wherever Adrienne was, for the rest of his life.

CHAPTER FOURTEEN

Herleif

"Herleif, is there any way you can carry this wood for me?" Adrienne's voice drew Herleif's attention, and he lumbered toward her, obliterating the undergrowth with his massive paws.

They'd been back from the markets for two weeks, and although their supplies were still going strong, Adrienne had been determined to hunt through the woods for berries to supplement their dinner that night. If he'd been able to speak, Herleif would have informed her that it was still too early for berries, but as it was, he wasn't opposed to a wander through the woods together in the relative warmth of late afternoon. Spring was on them now, and the days were steadily growing more pleasant.

He reached Adrienne in time to see her stagger, dropping her armful of wood. The load was almost as big as her petite form. Herleif gave her a look, and she sighed.

"I know it's too much for me to carry, but I couldn't find any branches this large nearer the castle. When I saw these, I thought they'd be perfect for the bigger coop we're building."

Herleif gave a long-suffering huff. Those chickens. It wasn't that he resented building the coop—Adrienne's use of the word *we* was generous, to say the least—but the way the chicks fawned over Adrienne, following her around, and even swarming Herleif when he dared to enter the kitchen in bear form, was a little much. One of these days he would step on one by accident, and break his poor wife's heart.

Stupid poultry.

"You can't really carry it though, can you?" Adrienne asked, looking him over.

Herleif didn't attempt to reply, knowing she could figure it out herself. If they'd had the sling they'd rigged up for the market trip, he could probably have managed. The weight certainly wasn't an issue for him. But since they'd only been planning to pick berries—nonexistent berries—all they had was Adrienne's basket. It was much more than he could carry in his mouth, and he couldn't exactly walk home on his hind legs while carrying the bundle with his claws.

"Never mind," said Adrienne, resigned. She dropped the last few branches and picked up her basket. "We'll have to come back tomorrow better prepared." She glanced up at the canopy of trees above. "It will be dark soon. We should get home, and get some food going. It will be much slower if we have to walk back after dark."

She sent a calculating glance at Herleif, who would have smiled if his face would allow it. Adrienne had changed her tune considerably since the first time, when she'd been nervous about climbing onto his back. She now seemed to consider it her right to hitch a ride anytime they were going anywhere outside and Herleif was in bear form. He liked to complain to her in the evenings that he felt like a steed rather than a person, but in truth he didn't mind at all. He tried to keep a careful distance when he was in human form—not trusting his heart to listen to his better sense if he let himself be too close to her—

but as a bear it was entirely different. They'd found an easy companionship that could include physical touch without being fraught. Honestly, if they made it through all this, he thought he might miss that.

In spite of Adrienne's words, she wandered a little further through the woods, apparently not quite having given up hope of the elusive berries.

A sound caught Herleif's sensitive ears as he stepped after her, and he paused, glancing around. They were well outside the protective boundary now, and he felt a sudden unease. It was time to return home for certain.

Herleif lowered his enormous head, nudging Adrienne's back. When she looked around inquiringly, he jerked his head toward the castle, then gave it a little shake to restore his balance. Even after five years, he was sometimes caught off guard by the sheer weight of his bear body.

"Yes, all right, I'm coming," Adrienne said, her tone suggesting she felt none of the tension that had overtaken Herleif.

She'd just turned toward him, some other casual question on her lips, when an unfamiliar scent reached Herleif's nose. He stiffened, inhaling deeply and turning his head to better listen. With one large paw, he batted Adrienne to the side, trying to silently communicate that she should get behind him.

Whether she understood or not, he couldn't tell, but she fell silent at his contact. Herleif scanned the trees tensely, his ears pricking as he heard the sound of a creature approaching. It could be a deer, of course...but he didn't think so.

With a huff, he turned back to Adrienne, urging her onward with another firm push of his head. She stumbled a little in her haste, her face pale as she hurried through the undergrowth. It was the first time they'd encountered danger in their woods, and she'd clearly picked up on his difference in demeanor. If they could just get back inside the invisible boundary, whoever it was wouldn't be able to follow. But out here, they were vulnerable.

The thought had barely passed through Herleif's mind when something whizzed past his ear, missing Adrienne by inches and burying itself into the trunk of a nearby tree. Herleif stared at the arrow for one paralyzed moment before spinning with a roar to face the one who'd fired it.

He'd expected to see a whole group—a hunting party sent in response to the market incident, perhaps—but instead it was one young man. Herleif didn't know him, but the rage and determination on his face suggested a much more personal vendetta than would be caused by a ruined stall. Had he accidentally killed someone back in Kilv without even realizing it?

The man was pulling out a new arrow as he ran, and Herleif heard Adrienne gasp in horror.

"Come on, Herleif," she said frantically. "We need to get out of here!"

Her voice recalled Herleif to the fact that she'd nearly been hit, although the focus of the hunter made it clear she wasn't the target. Turning his back on the stranger, Herleif lunged at Adrienne, closing his teeth around the back of her gown before she had time to figure out what he was doing. He hoisted her into the air, running as quickly as he could without endangering her as she dangled by her clothes from his jaws.

A wordless cry of outrage came from the man behind him, and Herleif immediately caught the sounds of pursuit. He knew that at his reduced speed, he would struggle to get fully clear of the range of a good archer. But he didn't have to outrun the man indefinitely—only until they reached the boundary.

He heard Adrienne's voice, sounding winded as she attempted to sing. What she was trying to do, he couldn't tell, but she broke off quickly in frustration. There just wasn't enough magic in Frossenland's ground. Not anymore.

Another arrow flew past them, and Herleif crashed more quickly through the brush. The man was a fast runner, he'd give him that. If they'd had time for Adrienne to get onto his back, Herleif could have outpaced him with ease. But then Adrienne would have been in more danger. At least in her current position, Herleif's bulk shielded her from the arrows.

"You won't evade me!"

The furious roar from behind him made Herleif falter. He hadn't expected the human to speak to him.

"Five years I've waited! I won't let you kill that poor girl like you killed my father, you foul creature!"

Herleif's breath caught in his throat, and he stumbled over a fallen log, nearly dropping Adrienne. Five years? This was no reaction to the pandemonium at the market. This was about the day his father had died. He'd known before Adrienne told him that popular opinion believed him—the bear version—to be King Eerikki's killer. It was a natural conclusion, given no living witnesses but him had seen Grograna the giant queen. But there was another man who'd died that day. Another father.

Iver.

Could the young man behind him, the one with such hatred in his eyes, be Iver's son? Hagen was his name, if Herleif recalled correctly. Herleif had only ever seen him in passing, but the age was about right. The hunter looked to be seventeen or eighteen, which would fit with the five-year gap. The child had been on the cusp of an apprenticeship at the time. Herleif remembered Iver telling him that the boy's mother wished them to move to Sunniva for Hagen to study songcraft instead, because he'd inherited his father's gift.

As if in confirmation of his guess, the young man behind Herleif began to sing. A glance back showed that he'd stowed his bow to better sprint, and was turning to a different method of attack.

Herleif knew Iver's family had left the area, and had assumed they'd settled in the capital. Hagen's singing supported that idea—in strong contrast to Adrienne's attempts, it was targeted and confident, both in tone and in meaning. Herleif couldn't feel power, but he felt Adrienne stiffen, and was sure that she could sense the magic Hagen was pulling from the ground.

Something invisible seemed to grab at Herleif's back, slowing him down. It was like the hands of a giant itself were restraining him, trying to stop him from running. But as he struggled, the sensation slipped away. Hagen's angry cry suggested he'd gained considerable ground during Herleif's struggle, but Herleif didn't pause to check. No wonder Hagen was frustrated. He was surely used to the more fertile ground of the southern part of the kingdom, where magic was relatively plentiful. His skills would be less effective here.

Herleif might not be able to sense magic, but he was intimately familiar with his domain, and he recognized the boundary of his prison approaching. Just as he put on a final burst of speed, he felt it. The blazing heat of something piercing his flank. He fell heavily, Adrienne flying from his jaws with a cry.

"Herleif!" she screamed, the terror in her eyes all for him. She threw herself forward, her hands coming away from his white fur stained with red.

Although he knew it was his own blood, panic clouded Herleif's mind at the sight of Adrienne covered in it. Hagen was almost on them, and the boundary was so close. If she made it inside, she would be safe. She wouldn't be able to come back out even if she wanted to, not without Herleif's company.

But it was clear she had no intention of leaving him and running to safety. Herleif struggled to his feet, the searing pain in his flank a dull ache compared to his terror for his wife. He charged at her, lowering his head as he pushed her ahead of him, his only thought forcing her over the boundary line.

"No!" she cried, obviously grasping his intention, just as another arrow pierced Herleif's back, bringing him crashing down once again.

Hagen's voice cut across the agony, frantic and alarmed.

"Where is she? What did you do with that girl?"

Herleif raised his head painfully, looking between his wife and the furious young man. He could still see and hear Adrienne, who was trying fruitlessly to get to him, but obviously Hagen couldn't. She must have seemed to simply disappear when she crossed the invisible line.

"I'll finish you once and for all, and then I'll find her," said Hagen, lowering his bow and pulling out a sword. "You'll take no more victims from their families."

Herleif had no fight in him. He felt broken, and his physical wounds were the least of it. The grief and impotent rage in Hagen's eyes were all too familiar, like Herleif was looking in a bitterly painful mirror. He didn't blame the young man in the least. Hagen had no way of knowing that they had both lost their fathers to the same monster that day.

And didn't Herleif deserve the death the other man was determined to mete out upon him? He'd never intended Iver to die, but the groundskeeper had died on Herleif's account nonetheless. If not for Herleif and his father making their foolish unannounced trip to Tove, if not for first King Eerikki's crown, then Herleif's size, catching Queen Grograna's eye, Iver would still be alive. He could even have fled when he found Herleif in the giant's clutches, the king dead at their feet. But Iver had stayed, to try to save Herleif, and it had cost the groundskeeper his life.

If different decisions had been made that day, right now Iver would probably be receiving a visit from his beloved son, returning from training at the Singers' Academy in Sunniva, ready to make his family proud.

"HERLEIF!" Adrienne's scream pierced the air, but Hagen gave no sign of hearing it. "Herleif, don't you dare die!"

That brought life back into Herleif's limbs, a new kind of shame coming with it. How quickly he'd forgotten that his life belonged to more than just himself now. He'd taken a vow, and what would become of his wife if he died here? Would she even be able to leave the boundary? Would the magic dissipate once he died, or would she truly be stuck? Herleif didn't know, and he didn't care to test it.

He struggled up, his massive paws scrabbling to get purchase through the pain shooting through him. Hagen was advancing, his bow forgotten and his sword in his hand.

"Come on, then!" His voice shook as he shouted his challenge to the bear. "Aren't you going to try to kill me like you killed them?"

A familiar pain washed over Herleif, one that had nothing to do with either emotions or his injuries. The sun must have set behind the trees. The transformation was about to occur, and he couldn't let that happen in front of Hagen, not when he was in such a vulnerable state. Adrienne had been unbelievably accommodating in not trying to sneak a look under his hood, but there was no chance Hagen would grant the same consideration.

It went against all his instincts both to flee a fight and to turn his back on his enraged attacker, but he knew he had only moments. With a sudden lurch, he swung around, throwing himself toward Adrienne with all his strength. He felt the moment he passed over the boundary, his body curling inward in an instinctive gesture of concealment as he transformed back into a man.

"Herleif!"

Adrienne's shriek came from right next to him, and a moment later he felt her hands on his shoulders, trying to roll him over. He hastily pulled his hood up to cover his head. It was a shame he'd abandoned the face covering as the weather grew warmer, trusting instead in the darkness he found more secure. Otherwise he would have had the covering in his pocket. Even in the gathering darkness, it wouldn't be an easy task to keep his face concealed when he was so injured.

"Herleif, you're hurt." Adrienne sounded panicked, and Herleif tried to make his own voice calm as he struggled to a sitting position, head bowed low for safety.

"I'll be all right," he panted. "Just need...a minute."

"You need considerably more than a minute," Adrienne protested. "You have two arrows sticking out of—"

Her voice broke off, and Herleif opened his eyes. In the gloom, he could just make out her shape, her head moving as her gaze passed over his form.

"Actually, the arrows seem to have fallen out when you transformed," she said, her voice still anxious. She picked one up from the ground, then cast it aside in order to lay a hand on Herleif's side. "Sorry," she gasped, when he flinched.

Herleif shook his head, taking stock of his body. "No, I'm sorry. It was an instinctive response. The pain is actually very manageable. I think the transformation was timely—the arrows had pierced deep into my bear body, but most of that bulk is gone now."

Adrienne ran a hand over the top of her head and through her hair, which was glinting silver in the moonlight beginning to creep through the trees.

"I still don't like it," she said. "I have a feeling your idea of *manageable* pain is another person's idea of agony."

Herleif said nothing, warmed by her concern. She was right that the wounds were still considerable—pain assaulted his senses, but it wasn't the rampant pain of irreparable damage. It was more like a strung-out version of the transformation pain. He had no doubt it would pass. He would heal.

"That man was a singer," Adrienne said tightly. "Did you hear?"

Slowly, Herleif nodded.

To his surprise, his wife let out a groan. "If only I was trained in songcraft. I'm sure there are ways to heal your injuries using magic, if I only knew them."

"Truly, Adrienne, I'll be all right," Herleif tried to assure her. But given he shifted position at that moment and the movement elicited an involuntary grunt of pain, Adrienne didn't seem convinced.

"I'll be the judge of that," she said tartly. She cast a look back toward the darkening woods. "Am I right that we're safe from him now? He can't get in here, can he?"

Herleif made no answer, unsure what was safe to say.

Adrienne's soft sigh was more impatient than annoyed. "Of course you won't tell me," she muttered. "It's only your life on the line."

Herleif smiled wryly under cover of his hood. His life was exactly what was on the line, if only she knew it.

"Let's have a look," said Adrienne, scooting around to better examine his back. "I can't see much," she said. "But it does seem as though the bleeding is slowing. I think you're right—the wounds are superficial in your human form. That's very lucky."

"I'm just hounded by good luck," Herleif commented.

"Very funny, bear-man," Adrienne said, unimpressed.

Herleif smiled again. She seemed to get snarkier when she was concerned.

"I wasn't joking," he said solemnly. "I was referring to my luck in games of chance. I've been known to win fabulous prizes."

Adrienne made a scoffing noise, but when she came back into sight and Herleif caught a look at her face in the dim light, he thought she looked a little pleased.

"Superficial or not, these wounds still need to be dressed," she informed him. "But I can't do that out here. How do I get you back to the castle?"

"I'll walk, of course," said Herleif. He pushed himself to his feet, moving a little too quickly in his determination to prove he was fine.

"Whoa!" Adrienne cried, when he began to sway.

She ducked under his arm, drawing it around her shoulder. She was so petite, Herleif had to actually lean down to rest on her. He knew she wouldn't be able to hold much of his weight. But she did help balance him.

Abandoning the basket, they began to walk slowly through the woods, Herleif's senses almost as captured by the girl pressed against him as by the pain that lanced through his body with every step. It was rare for Adrienne to be so close when he was in his human form. He could feel her trembling, although whether that was from their nearness or just from the pressure of carrying the weight of his massive arm, he couldn't tell.

Adrienne had taken it on herself to guide them home, and taking advantage of the opportunity, Herleif studied her face. He could look at her anytime during the day of course, but it was different through his human eyes. Her pale hair was disheveled across her forehead, and her brows were pinched together in concern, but no such details could obscure the reality. When he'd first seen her, he'd thought her pretty. Now he thought her stunningly beautiful, more than any other woman he'd ever laid eyes on. It was a delicate type of beauty, almost ethereal. In fact, her features were delicate enough to make her look elfin, although she wasn't quite as small as all that. At any rate, the moonlight suited her somewhat wistful aspect well, increasing her allure.

Adrienne must have felt his scrutiny, because she leaned her head back as if to look at him.

"Don't look up," he said, the words coming out sharper than he meant them to. He started to pull away from her support, but Adrienne tightened her grip, her head no longer leaning back.

"No, let me help you," she said quickly. "I wasn't thinking, I'm sorry. I won't try to look."

She lowered her head pointedly, staring at the ground just before her feet as she picked her way through the forest. Regret knifed through Herleif as he took in the defeated posture. But what choice did he have?

Twice on the journey Herleif had to stop and rest, and by the time they reached the clearing, both of them were exhausted. Herleif's wounds had begun to bleed again from the exertion, although the pain had settled to a powerful but consistent ache.

To Adrienne's evident frustration, Herleif refused to go into the kitchen, knowing the remains of the day's fire would still be there. After a moment's thought, Adrienne led him to the dining hall instead, settling him in a chair before hurrying to fetch water and clean linen.

"This won't be easy to do in the dark," she informed him when she returned. "I'll probably make a mess of it."

"I'm sure you'll do better than I would alone," Herleif said, his tone uncompromising.

He heard Adrienne's sigh as she clearly grasped the message. No light.

"So whose son was that man?" she asked bluntly, as she poured water into a bowl. "The groundskeeper's, or the guard's?"

Herleif paused before answering, surprised by how much detail she knew of the incident that had ruined his life.

"The groundskeeper's," he said gruffly. "His name was Iver." His voice dropped. "He was a good man. A friend as well as an employee."

The sounds of Adrienne's preparations paused. "I'm sorry."

Herleif let out a breath. "So am I. His son's name was Hagen, I believe."

"Well, he was quite valiant, trying to rescue me from the bear," Adrienne said in a half-hearted attempt at cheerfulness. "But I think I'll stay inside our area for a while, all the same."

Herleif was unable to think of a response.

"He was looking for you specifically, wasn't he?" Adrienne mused, undeterred by his silence. "The bear you, I mean. How did he know where to find you? There have been rumors of the huge white bear for years, so why now?"

"He heard something more concrete than rumors," said Herleif grimly.

Adrienne drew in a sharp breath. "The markets?" she asked. "You think word has spread? As far as the capital?"

"I don't think there can be any doubt word has spread," Herleif said. "And it could easily have reached the capital."

He tugged on his hood in an unconscious gesture as he pondered the fear he couldn't risk saying aloud. If the tale of the rampant white bear on the loose had reached Hagen, had it reached the giants as well? Had Grograna heard that the bear had been traveling with a young, beautiful—and worst of all, petite—human woman? Herleif didn't know what the giant queen would do if that information reached her, but he was confident it would be something he didn't like.

Herleif was ripped from his thoughts when warm hands suddenly brushed the bare skin of his sides. Adrienne was sliding his tunic up.

"What are you doing?" he asked, his voice embarrassingly breathless as his hands closed over hers, restraining them.

"I need to treat the wounds," Adrienne told him. She spoke as though his question were foolish, but the tone was a little forced. She felt how charged the moment was as well as he did.

Herleif hesitated, his hands still over hers.

"Herleif." Adrienne's voice was soft now. "I really don't know how I can treat your injuries unless I can get to them."

Herleif swallowed, giving a slow nod as he released her hands. She was right, of course. This wasn't a romantic moment. It was medical attention. However much he might enjoy the sensation of her hands on his skin, it couldn't violate the terms of Grograna's curse.

Surely.

The possibility that he was wrong certainly added tension as Adrienne removed his blood-soaked tunic. But if Herleif was honest, the danger was only secondary in his mind as her gentle fingers searched his back and side, examining the injuries in place of her eyes.

"This one is very superficial," she told him, her breath against his skin telling him she was leaning close to the arrow wound on his back. "It barely needs dressing."

"Yes, that one is the least painful," Herleif confirmed.

After giving the area a gentle but thorough clean, Adrienne moved her focus to his side, searching by touch for the first wound Hagen had inflicted. Herleif's indrawn breath when she found it made her murmur an apology, but a moment later her hand was back, sponging the wound with a wad of linen.

"I don't think it's deep," she said, her words soft and close in the darkness. "But it should definitely have a bandage."

The warmth of her touch disappeared, and a ripping sound cut through the air. With unexpected deftness, Adrienne secured a clean wad of linen to the gouge left by the arrow.

"You seem to know what you're doing," Herleif commented.

"I have two brothers," she reminded him, and he could hear

the smile in her voice. "I've helped tend my fair share of injuries."

As she spoke, she began to wrap the linen strip all the way around Herleif's torso. The fact that he was seated evened their heights considerably, but for her to reach all the way around his broad torso still required her to lean right into him. Every point of contact was a blossom of flame, the skin of her face and arms searing his, now that his tunic was no longer between them.

Could she hear the way his heart was pounding, with her cheek pressed to his chest like that? Surely she must. Suddenly Herleif was desperate to hear her thoughts, to know the effect this closeness had on her.

"Adrienne," he murmured.

Perhaps misunderstanding his meaning, she pulled back, her face giving off heat he could feel even if not see.

"That should hold," she said, her voice not entirely steady. She ran a hand over the fabric across his chest, her fingers pausing halfway across. "What's this?" she asked. "Did he get you in the chest as well?"

Herleif shook his head. "That's an old injury."

Adrienne's head tilted to the side, her expression unclear in the gloom. "The guard who went back for the bodies said he got the bear with his spear," she murmured. "He thought he'd killed the creature." She let out a slow breath. "Oh, Herleif. And that time you had no one to tend your wound, or care for you as you recovered. It breaks my heart to think how unbearably you must have suffered in those first days. How much you're still suffering."

The grief in her voice made Herleif catch his breath. What had he ever done to justify her caring so much for what he felt? How did she manage to make him feel more important in his isolated, cursed existence than he'd felt as the kingdom's celebrated crown prince?

"I'm not suffering now," he said.

He swallowed, still thrown off balance by her nearness as she hovered in place, her other hand coming up to join the first as she explored the old scar on his chest. Part of him wanted to draw back from the vulnerability required to speak his thoughts, but he pushed on, forcing his discomfort aside. He owed her what little honesty he could give.

"Not since you came."

CHAPTER FIFTEEN

Adrienne

Adrienne looked up sharply, causing Herleif to lower his head so that his hood draped low.

"Do you mean that?" she asked. Her fingers tensed where her hands still rested on the bandage across his chest.

"Why would you doubt it?" Herleif's voice was a deep rumble that seemed to reverberate inside Adrienne's core. "I know I'm not open about many things, but I've never lied to you, Adrienne."

It was Adrienne's turn to lower her head, and she gave no answer.

"If you doubt me, I don't blame you," Herleif said heavily. "I know it must seem like I don't trust you, but it's not the case." For a moment the silence drew out, then he lifted his hands, laying them over hers on his chest. "Adrienne," he breathed. "I never meant to hurt you with any of this. I know I have, you've told me as much, but I—"

"I remember," Adrienne cut him off. "I was referring to our first evening at the castle, when you called our marriage a moment of weakness." She shook her head, a strand of her pale hair flashing before her vision. "It was foolish of me to be hurt by that. I had no reason to expect warmth from you then, or even to want it. We were strangers."

"I was selfish to say it," Herleif said, his voice tinged with disgust. "I was thinking of my own troubles—none of which are of your making—and not of what you must feel."

"It's all right," Adrienne said, her voice a whisper, and her hands clenching a little under his. "We were both taken by surprise that night." She swallowed, then spread her fingers under Herleif's hands. The skin of his chest was warmer than it should be in the evening's chill, and she felt a muscle jump under her touch. "I do wish..."

She trailed off, losing courage.

"What?" Herleif prompted.

She could tell from the sound of his voice that his head was angling up toward hers, and it took all of her self-control not to sneak a look at his face. The curtains were drawn, and there was very little visibility in the dark room. But maybe she could catch just a glimpse.

No, she told herself. *Whether he's telling the truth about trusting me or not, I don't want to give him any reason not to.*

"Adrienne," Herleif tried again, his voice almost desperate. "Tell me. What do you want? There's nothing I would deny you if it was in my power."

Adrienne kept her head lowered, afraid of giving in to temptation. "I wish I could see your face," she whispered. She felt him stiffen, and she rushed on. "It's not that it matters to me what you look like. I just...hate the secrets. And even more than that, I hate the distance."

Herleif was still for a painful moment, then abruptly he shifted. Adrienne kept her face dutifully averted as he rose to his feet. She thought he would leave the room, and she let out a tiny gasp as he instead stepped toward her, his hands coming to rest gently on her shoulders, which they completely encased. Adrienne no longer had to be careful not to see Herleif's face. She found herself looking straight ahead at his broad, uncovered chest, her breath coming a little too quickly.

The next thing she knew, Herleif moved again, and his forehead was resting on the top of her head. He must be bending uncomfortably low to reach her, but he gave no sign of wanting to cut the moment short. Adrienne's heart picked up speed, and again she had to fight the urge to lift her face to his. He'd always kept such a careful distance between them, rarely even touching her in his human form, certainly never bringing his face this close to hers. But his movement had definitely crossed an invisible barrier between them. She could actually feel his breath stirring her hair. In that moment, it felt like it would be the most natural thing in the world to step right into him, let his arms close around her, and raise her eyes to meet his. Perhaps he would pull her into his arms, lifting her up against him to close the height difference, then lower his head, and—

Adrienne cut her thoughts off, not wanting to ruin the most intimate moment she'd shared with her husband by pining for what she couldn't have. Because in spite of his current posture, she had no expectation that Herleif would abandon his rigid rules just because she'd said she wanted him to. The restrictions had never been there for her convenience.

"Adrienne..." Herleif's voice was a deep thrum in her chest, his anguished tone sending a strange thrill through Adrienne's body as his voice cracked in a way she'd never heard before. "Adrienne, I wish..."

He trailed off again, and she had the distinct impression that he was desperate to speak but prevented. Not by magic—she felt nothing like that on him, not when he was in his human form. It was by his iron will, and she'd begun to despair of ever understanding the reason behind it.

She shifted her hands from under his, not pulling them away, but sliding them further up his chest.

"I know I'm not allowed to see your face with my eyes," she whispered. "But there are other ways." One of her hands moved hopefully up his neck, and she could feel his pulse pounding under her fingertips.

"I...I don't know. It's so easy to make a mistake."

With her hand still in position, she could feel Herleif's nervous swallow. She'd never heard him so uncertain.

A mistake like marrying me?

Adrienne didn't speak the thought aloud. She didn't even know where it came from. She didn't want to think it had been a mistake for Herleif to marry her. But the only other option was that he'd made an intentional decision with a worthwhile reward. At the start of their marriage she'd accepted that reality, and it hadn't troubled her too much. But she hadn't reckoned on growing so close to him, so desperate for his presence and approval. Now, with Herleif's face pressed into her hair, and his skin warm under her fingers in the darkness, she could hardly bear the knowledge that he planned to use her to gain some unknown benefit in the future.

No, she told herself sharply. She wasn't going to think that way. Not now, when he was letting her closer than she'd ever been. Not when he sounded like he was wavering as to her request to come closer still.

"How about this?" Adrienne lowered her hands and stepped slightly back.

Reluctantly, she thought, Herleif released her shoulders and moved back as well. But Adrienne was far from finished with their moment. Reaching down to the nearby table, she picked up an unused length of clean linen. She wrapped it around her eyes, covering them completely and tying it firmly at the back.

"I swear I can't see a thing. You can check the knot yourself."

Herleif didn't answer, which meant he wasn't refusing outright.

Feeling bold, Adrienne felt her way back to his chest. If he wanted her not to touch him, he'd have to say it. With her eyes covered, she dared to raise her face, stepping even closer than she'd been before. Her hand traveled up his neck again, and although his breathing quickened even more, he didn't protest.

She reached the edge of his jaw, and traced her fingers along its line, down to his chin. It was scratchy, as one would expect at the end of the day on a usually clean-shaven man.

"You don't have a beard," she commented.

"You sound surprised." Her fingers were still cupping Herleif's chin, and his breath was a warm breeze as he spoke.

"I pictured you with a beard," she informed him.

She trailed her fingers back up his jawline, spreading them over his cheek and running her thumb along his nose. His skin was rougher than hers, and his nose was straight and strong. She ran her thumb up it, feeling along his brow. Herleif seemed to be holding his breath, his whole body taut with tension, but not the fearful kind. She got the sense he was as lost in the moment as she was.

The back of her hand brushed Herleif's hood, and, seized by a sudden recklessness, Adrienne threw it back. She lifted her other hand as well, running both through Herleif's hair. Like she'd seen through the window months ago, it came down to about his ears, thick and—if her assessment was correct—a little on the wavy side. She remembered on that occasion that she'd had a desire to do just what she was doing now. How little she'd guessed, even then, what Herleif would come to mean to her, and how desperately she'd long to be close to him.

"You're very handsome," she breathed. "But I suppose you know that."

Herleif let out a throaty, unsteady laugh. "I'm not sure how *you* could know that given you can't see me."

Adrienne smiled. "I can see well enough, even without my sight."

Again she felt Herleif swallow. "That makes no sense," he informed her.

"It makes perfect sense to me," Adrienne murmured. Her hand settled back on his cheek, and, drawn by an irresistible impulse, her thumb traveled to his lips. She traced their shape with a boldness she never would have possessed without the comforting cover of darkness. His lips parted slightly under her touch as he drew in a sharp breath.

Adrienne's hand stilled, her mind full of all the things she'd seen about Herleif's character, even without ever looking at his face. She could never have predicted any part of her unplanned marriage, not least the kindness of her strange, distant husband.

Not least the intensity of her own desire to close that distance.

That desire swept over her in a terrifying, exhilarating rush, and before she'd consciously decided to do it, Adrienne found her hands on either side of Herleif's face as she pushed herself blindly up on her toes, her lips seeking his.

In her folly, she hoped he would lean down to help her close the distance, but instead he jerked back, the moment instantly shattered.

"Adrienne!" he gasped, horrified. "What are you doing?"

"I...I...I thought..." Adrienne stammered, scrambling to adjust to the abrupt change in tone.

"Don't you remember what I told you?" Herleif demanded. "The first night you were here, I told you I won't force so much as a kiss on you."

"Yes, I remember," said Adrienne helplessly. She felt absurd with the blindfold still on, but she didn't dare take it off with

Herleif in this humor. "But don't you understand, Herleif? There's no question of forcing now."

Well, that wasn't strictly true, she realized. She'd almost forced a kiss on him just now. But that hadn't been her intent. In the moment, she'd genuinely thought he would welcome it. Clearly she'd been mistaken.

Embarrassment rushed over her, and she took another step back.

"Adrienne…" Herleif's voice sounded strangled, and she was almost glad she couldn't see whatever expression was on his face. "I stick to what I said. I won't kiss you."

"Obviously," said Adrienne quietly, wishing desperately to be alone with her humiliation. "I'm sorry I made you uncomfortable."

"You have nothing to be sorry for," Herleif said miserably.

"Don't I?" Adrienne struggled for a moment to keep her emotions at bay. "How have I failed so miserably as a wife that you won't even let me kiss you? What kind of a marriage is that?"

"You haven't failed at anything," said Herleif fiercely. "You're perfect, Adrienne, you're—"

"Don't." She raised a hand to stop him.

He fell silent, presumably seeing the gesture. After all, he wasn't blindfolded. He was allowed to see her face anytime he chose. She stepped further back.

"I don't think your injuries pose any ongoing danger," she said, her voice a little choked. "But I'll check them again tomorrow evening to be sure the transformations don't worsen them."

Abandoning all the materials she'd used to dress his wounds, she pulled the blindfold from her eyes and turned for the door.

"Adrienne," Herleif tried again. She paused, but apparently

he had nothing to add. She'd caught the movement that suggested he'd already pulled his hood back up.

No exceptions. No mistakes.

"Good night, Herleif," she said, hurrying from the room.

Her face burned with disappointment and humiliation as she made her way along the familiar route to their bedroom. She'd been a fool to think Herleif would let her that close. Even though she knew there was more to the situation—there had to be—and that Herleif may not have control over it all, she couldn't bear the sting of his rejection.

If she'd been told, back in that tavern, that the man who won her as his wife would wish to keep distance from her, and never want so much as a kiss, she would likely have been delighted. But that was before she'd known Herleif. Before she'd been foolish enough to let him into her heart. She hadn't planned to, or meant for it to happen. But that was because her plans hadn't accounted for the person he was. He was patient, kind, steady, strong...he was so easy to be around, whether human or bear, that she usually found his company as comfortable as her own.

He'd become her closest friend, but it was more than that. The desire for more had been growing steadily in her for months now, and to let it out into the open like she just had could only make it worse.

For the first time in a long time, Adrienne fell asleep alone in the big bed. She knew Herleif wasn't actually sleeping elsewhere, just waiting until she was asleep before coming in, so as not to disturb her or force his company on her. He would sleep beside her—he always did.

This time, the thought brought her no comfort.

Adrienne woke to the pale light of dawn. The bed was empty, but when she stretched out a hand, the warmth of the sheets told her that Herleif had been there. He must be a bear by now, though, since she could see light creeping around the edges of the curtain.

For several minutes, Adrienne lay awake, staring at the canopy. Try as she might to resist it, her thoughts were pulled inevitably back to the evening before. She remembered the shape of Herleif's face under her fingers and the warmth of his breath as their faces were closer together than they'd ever been. Or ever would be again, probably.

Adrienne pulled herself out of bed, eager to distract her mind. Something told her Herleif wouldn't be meandering around the castle in his bear form with her today. After consuming a simple breakfast, she threw herself into the sort of cleaning and organizing tasks that had occupied her time when she first came to the castle. Once Herleif had joined her, they'd often preferred to be idle together after the necessary chores were done. But solitary idleness was the last thing Adrienne wanted.

It was midmorning when Adrienne decided to venture to the other side of the castle in search of any undiscovered garments. One of her gowns needed mending, and she was hopeful of finding another with fabric similar enough in color. She searched a few sleeping chambers without success before a storage room caught her attention.

She was walking down the corridor past it when she felt a strange pulse. She paused, wondering if she'd imagined it. But no, there it was again. It felt like magic, but it was hard to be sure. She had so little experience with her own craft. Cautiously, she began to sing, trying to pull power from the ground. Little wisps danced up toward her, passing into her and wafting out with no defined purpose. It was definitely the same sort of sensation. But what Adrienne had first felt came from the room, not the ground below her feet. A talisman, perhaps? It must be a powerful one to emit such an easily detectable level of magic even when not in use.

Intrigued, Adrienne pushed her way through the door. It was a small storage room, but even so the shelves were only half full. And judging by the layer of dust, no one had been in there in years. She'd certainly never entered it before. Her eyes passed over the various items, trying to identify the source of the magic. She could still feel it, and she followed the trail back to a small chest placed at about the height of her shoulders.

It wasn't locked. When she lifted the lid, a cloud of dust flew out, making her sneeze. There were a number of items in there, but she couldn't get a good look at any of them. There weren't any windows in the storeroom, and only minimal light found its way in from the small windows on the far side of the corridor off which the room came.

Adrienne tested the chest and found that it wasn't heavy. Reflecting that there was no hurry whatsoever, she decided to take it downstairs and look through the items at her leisure in the sunshine. It was a pleasant spring day, and she could do with the fresh air after all this dust. If she was hoping to catch a glimpse of her fur-clad husband who was almost certainly outside the castle rather than within it, she didn't acknowledge it to herself.

On her way out of the room she grabbed a blanket from another shelf and threw it over her shoulder. Though the chest was small enough to comfortably lift in her arms, it seemed to grow heavier as she trekked down the corridors. By the time she emerged into the clearing, she was very glad to set it down. She threw the blanket over the still-damp grass and settled on it with the chest.

The first few items she drew out were of no particular interest. It looked like a collection of broken odds and ends that someone had intended to fix and never gotten around to. But nestled underneath was a length of fabric, wrapped around something flat and circular.

This was the source of the magic, Adrienne was sure of it. She lifted the bundle carefully from the chest, setting it down on the blanket. Magic pulsed out from the hidden item, and an instinctive song stirred in Adrienne, wanting to take hold of the rare source of power. She refrained from singing, not sure either of the origin of the magic or of her ability to channel it to something productive.

She did, however, lift the wrappings carefully from the object, her breath catching at the sight of a thin, golden circlet. It was the first gold she'd seen at the castle, excepting her own and Herleif's wedding bands. She was just reaching for the circlet when a growling roar sounded from across the clearing. Adrienne's head shot up to see the terrifying sight of a huge white bear charging toward her at full speed. She'd never seen Herleif move like that, and for a fleeting moment, she wondered if he'd lost his human reason somehow, and truly become the bear.

Adrienne fell back, scrambling away from the blanket in genuine fear. Herleif didn't chase her, however. He skidded to a stop on the grass, his teeth clutching the edge of the blanket and yanking violently. Everything from the chest—the talisman included—flew through the air, landing in a jumbled heap out of Adrienne's reach. With another yank of his head, Herleif sent the blanket flying clumsily after it, so it landed on top of the pile, covering most of the items.

Adrienne got the message. Without a word, she pushed herself to her feet, half-running as she retreated to the safety of the castle. A glance back showed Herleif hovering, watching her out of eyes that were much too human and much too anguished.

She could see that he wasn't a senseless animal. He clearly retained his right mind, and no doubt he had a reason for his actions. But the fact remained that she'd been frightened of the bear for the first time since witnessing the initial transformation. She needed some distance between herself and Herleif's current form.

The rest of the day passed miserably and anxiously for Adrienne, huddled in front of the fire in the kitchen. Between the man's rejection of her kiss the night before and the bear's angry charge that morning, her emotions were in such a snarl she hardly knew what she thought or what she wanted. She was tempted to avoid Herleif in the evening as well, but she told herself that was cowardly. So instead she went about her usual preparations. She didn't wait for Herleif on the castle steps, but when he appeared in the dining hall just after sunset, she was waiting with a hot meal.

Even in the usual darkness, it was immediately obvious that Herleif was as uncertain and uncomfortable as she was. For once, Adrienne didn't try to fill the space with chatter, leaving it to Herleif to initiate conversation if he chose.

She expected him to remain silent, so was surprised and a little mollified when he spoke.

"I'm sorry about this morning, Adrienne. I didn't mean to scare you." Adrienne said nothing, and he added, "As I've told you before, I would never hurt you. I panicked, and I regret it. If I'd had the luxury of words, I would have been able to communicate more clearly rather than being so aggressive."

"You communicated very effectively," Adrienne assured him in a clipped tone. When he remained silent, she sighed. "I know you wouldn't hurt me, really. But in the moment…"

She trailed off, and Herleif's hooded head dipped in a nod. "I understand. I'm sorry," he repeated.

"That circlet," Adrienne pressed, figuring since they were

speaking after all, she may as well try for some answers. "Is that your crown?"

"One of them," Herleif acknowledged.

Adrienne raised an eyebrow. How many crowns did a prince need? In moments like this she was thrown by the reminder of how very different Herleif's life had once been both from their current life together and every aspect of her own life before they met. And perhaps he would someday return to that life. Impossible to know how and when, and impossible to know what would happen to her in that eventuality. She usually tried not to think about it.

She didn't say any of those thoughts aloud, returning instead to the matter of the circlet.

"It's a talisman, though." She didn't phrase it as a question. "Why is it a talisman?"

Predictably, Herleif gave no answer, and she could tell it wasn't just because he was thinking about it. He would say no more on the topic.

"I'm tired," said Adrienne, standing. She'd barely touched her dinner, but her appetite had fled. "Good night."

Herleif said nothing as she left the room. His silence was almost more painful than angry words. Adrienne knew with gloomy certainty as she settled into bed a short time later that he would make no appearance until after sleep had claimed her.

CHAPTER SIXTEEN

Herleif

Herleif smiled down into Adrienne's upturned face. Gentle sunlight played on her features, bringing out the yellow in her pale hair, and lending color to her cheeks. Her eyes were sparkling back at him, holding the same hint of laughter that had those full, pink lips curling up into a smile.

A light breeze sent her hair flying in wisps across her cheeks, and he reached out to pull a strand away from her lips. She closed her eyes at his touch, leaning forward slightly. There was no fear, no hesitation in her demeanor. With her eyes still closed, she slid her hands up his chest, bringing them to rest on either side of his face. When she leaned up onto her toes, Herleif leaned down. In the most natural movement in the world, their lips met. Heat exploded inside Herleif, along with a joy so intense it was fierce. The whole world seemed to shake as they drew each other close.

Suddenly, Herleif realized that the ground truly was shaking. The breeze of a moment before had also risen, and wind now howled around them. A deafening crack made him draw back from the kiss, and he realized with horror that he was standing not on solid ground, but on ice. Ice which was now splintering beneath his feet.

"Herleif?" Adrienne gasped, confusion crossing her lovely features as she took in his expression.

Herleif glanced around, bewildered by the unfamiliar mountains of ice that rose up behind his wife. Where were they? Without warning, another crack resounded through the air, and a fissure opened up right underneath Adrienne.

"Herleif!" she screamed. "HERLEIF!"

He tried to reach for her, but she was already falling, falling, into the endless darkness of the chasm.

Herleif woke with a start, his breath coming in frantic, frenzied gasps. It took a moment to recognize the canopy of his own bed in the darkness, and to realize that he wasn't stranded in a frozen wasteland, powerless as he watched his wife fall to her death. The dream had felt horribly real, a sensation that wasn't helped by the very real tremor currently making the castle creak. It was a particularly bad one, and it was no wonder his sleeping mind had incorporated it into his dream.

Gradually, the shaking died away, and his heart slowed, although the sense of unease lingered. Even though it had been two months since Adrienne had tried to kiss him, he still dreamed about it nearly every night. But the dream tremors and the cracking ice were new. Did they mean something? Or was it nothing more than an absurd dream, brought on by the tremor happening in the waking world?

Herleif could tell from the hint of gray around the curtains that dawn wasn't too far off. It was time for him to be leaving, so as not to burden Adrienne with his presence when she woke.

And yet, he couldn't bring himself to slip away like he normally did. The dream was too near, both the terror of its ending and the longing of what had come before. His eyes found Adrienne's form in the slowly lightening darkness. She was sleeping peacefully, her back to him as she occupied the far side of the enormous bed. Herleif sat up, disturbing the covers as little as possible as he studied her face. He couldn't make much out, and not just because it was still so dark. Her hair was plastered over her cheeks, not unlike in the dream. Holding his breath, he reached across the distance separating them, gently brushing the strands away. Adrienne stirred, mumbling a little in her sleep as she shifted position, but she didn't wake.

Herleif's eyes had adjusted enough that he could see her features. She was achingly beautiful, and repeated exposure didn't dull the impression. If anything, she was more beautiful every passing day.

And further out of reach.

Herleif's heart ached as he remembered the fear in her eyes when he'd charged across the clearing. He'd never meant to frighten her. Too late he'd remembered how terrifying his form was. He'd become so accustomed to her apparent comfort around him. But worse than that memory was the distance she'd maintained between them ever since. Although he couldn't blame that entirely on the incident on the lawn. It might have more to do with her attempt to kiss him.

Herleif let out a soft groan. That had been torture, being forced to refuse Adrienne exactly what he wanted to give her. He'd hardly dared hope she felt any sliver of what he did, and then suddenly she'd been all but in his arms.

And he'd pushed her away.

Then the incident with his circlet the next day. Two close calls in as many days. He'd become careless. He'd been so focused on removing every candlestick, every lantern, every possible source of light that might reveal his face, he'd never even thought about the circlet. He should never have left it where Adrienne could find it. He'd returned to the clearing after their short and miserable dinner that evening, using his human dexterity to pack it safely away and stash it in a new hiding place.

How he hated that circlet. The only gold Grograna had left him when she cleared the palace of every other scrap. And she wouldn't have left even that if there hadn't been a price. Herleif closed his eyes, blocking out the pleasant vision of Adrienne's features—more relaxed in sleep than they were around him these days—and letting the image of Grograna's enraged face fill his mind instead. He heard again the words she'd spoken before she transformed him.

You think you can find a better bride than my daughter among the humans? I will make you so hideous no one will ever want to so much as look at you again let alone marry you. Then we'll see who will yield.

Little had he guessed when he heard those words just how dramatic a transformation the giant queen's magic was capable of inflicting on him. And yet, against both his own and Grograna's expectations, his bear form hadn't prevented him from acquiring a wife. And not just any wife—the most amazing woman he'd ever met. And the giant queen had been so scornful of the idea that Herleif could find a human bride better than her ghastly giant daughter. The wonder of it was that even when he was a bear, Adrienne didn't find him hideous, as Grograna had predicted all humans would. At least, Adrienne hadn't found him that way until he rushed at her like a senseless fool.

Of course, Grograna had intended for him to be a bear all the time, and in that state, he wouldn't have been able to marry Adrienne. It was Iver's intervention that had introduced that chink in the armor of Grograna's transforming curse. Herleif remembered learning, in the basic study of magic that formed part of his training as prince, that sunrise and sunset were often meaningful in magic. He doubted Iver had intended to specify that he was a bear by day and a man by night. He'd probably tried to undo the transformation entirely, but there simply wasn't enough magic available in the northern wastes for that, even for a singer as skilled as Iver had been.

And Grograna had killed Iver for it—thrown him across the room like a child's doll. Herleif remembered with painful clarity his own panic as he'd stumbled four-legged toward the downed groundskeeper, struggling to master his new form.

Iver had been clinging to life, but he'd sustained a head injury that Herleif had seen at a glance would claim him.

I have…no more…magic, Iver had whispered brokenly, the light already fading from his eyes. *But the magic she used to curse you is…also spent. She can't make it permanent. You just have to… outlast…her.* Iver's eyes had flickered closed then, and a whine of terror had escaped Herleif's strange new lips. But the groundskeeper made one final effort. *There's power in your blood, Your Highness…Your Majesty.* The use of the new title had terrified Herleif more than all the rest. *Even with you in this form, I feel the power…hold on to your determination…it will counteract the power of her magic.*

Those were the last words Iver had ever spoken, and the memory of the groundskeeper's sacrifice had kept Herleif going any time he was tempted to yield and be free of the nightmare. He couldn't let Grograna win. He couldn't let her foist her daughter onto Frossenland as its queen.

You will yield before a year is out, Grograna had scoffed. *The loneliness will drive you mad.* Herleif hadn't even thought to ask how he could yield, too full of shock and rage at the deaths he'd just witnessed. It was only after she'd so maliciously outlined the details of his curse, then used another talisman to draw all the gold in the castle to her, that she'd found his circlet and let out a laugh.

How appropriate, she'd told him. *You will give me this crown, when you give my daughter your kingdom.* Before his dazed but defiant eyes, she'd produced another talisman and poured magic into the circlet. *When you're ready to yield,* she told him smugly, *you must only touch it. The rest will be taken care of.*

Bear that he was, he'd been unable to speak in reply, but he'd sworn to himself in that moment that he would never yield, no matter what his defiance cost him. He had to admit to himself, however, that in spite of that determination, he'd never tried to destroy the circlet, or lose track of it. He'd taken the first opportunity to place it somewhere out of sight and—as he'd thought—secure, but he'd always known where it was. He'd always left himself a way out. Perhaps that was weakness. Even now, the location of the circlet burned in his mind, locked safely in a desk in the adjoining suite.

But he'd never use it, he assured himself fiercely. Even at the time he'd been repulsed by the idea of marrying Grograna's daughter, but now that he had a wife, it was doubly unthinkable to imagine exchanging her for a giant. For anyone, if truth be told.

The question of what would have happened if Adrienne had touched the circlet had plagued him for the last two months. Would she have triggered his own unwilling capitulation? Or would whatever horrors Grograna had planned for him upon touching the circlet have fallen instead to her? Unthinkable.

They'd been so close to disaster, and Herleif couldn't even explain it to Adrienne. Not that she'd been in any doubt as to his views on her touching that circlet. And she was smart enough to know that his outburst must have been brought on by some crisis. But it was infuriating to never be able to communicate freely regarding his strange behavior.

Herleif buried his face in his hands. In his absorption, he forgot to make his movements gentle, and Adrienne stirred once again. This time she emerged from sleep with a sigh, shifting from side to side as she came to full awareness.

"Herleif?" Her voice was groggy and confused, and no wonder. It was the first time in two months that Herleif had still been there when she woke.

He checked that his hood was low enough, then spoke.

"Yes, it's me. It's almost dawn."

Adrienne sat up, making no move toward him. Gone was the bright smile that used to greet him in the mornings. It broke Herleif's heart how much she'd withdrawn from him since he rejected her attempt to kiss him.

"Oh." Adrienne didn't seem to know what to say. "I didn't expect to see you."

Herleif didn't respond to this comment, his eyes searching her face. She looked tired, the peace of her sleeping state gone. Now that she was awake, all her troubles had returned. Troubles of his making.

"Are you all right, Adrienne?" he asked, the words soft and sincere.

To his dismay, he saw moisture building at the corners of her eyes. He'd never seen her cry before, and it made something deep inside him hurt unbearably.

"No," Adrienne whispered. "I'm not."

Herleif's heart twisted again. He'd expected her to politely and untruthfully deny any distress, and the simple admission was more powerful than any showy display of grief could ever be.

"I'm lonely," Adrienne continued. "I miss...company."

Herleif had the impression she'd changed her sentence partway through, but he didn't pry.

"What can I do?"

Adrienne looked at his hooded form, her expression

suggesting surprise. "Well, I'd like to see my family. It's been over eight months, and I miss them. And worry about them."

Alarm swirled through Herleif, but he tried to think of Adrienne rather than himself. There was danger in this course, undoubtedly. But she'd already paid more than enough for his curse. Really, it was amazing she'd lasted this long before asking him outright to let her leave and see her family.

Adrienne's demeanor changed as Herleif thought it over. She clearly sensed he was considering it, and her next words were hopeful.

"I can't imagine my father would still be there after all this time."

Herleif knew for a fact that Svend wasn't in Toveham anymore, but he didn't say so. He was still trying to think through the implications of Adrienne's request. Perhaps fortunately, at that moment he felt the first familiar prickles.

"The sun is about to rise," he said gruffly. "We can discuss it more this evening."

He rose from the bed, hurrying into the corridor and toward the entranceway as the pain gripped him. By the time he emerged through the castle's front doors, he was already on all fours and covered with fur.

He spent more time wandering than hunting that day, staying within the boundary of the curse. Hagen had hung around for days after his failed attack, trying to find a way into the castle's surrounds. But he'd long since given up and left. Even so, Herleif thought it safer not to venture out unnecessarily.

All day Herleif argued with himself as he patrolled his territory, weighing the risks of letting Adrienne visit her family against her right to such a basic courtesy. It was less than four more months...Grograna had said that if he married, he would only have to last a year. If he'd thought it achievable, he would have considered marriage as a strategy years ago. But he'd never believed anyone could be so accommodating as Adrienne had been. She made it positively easy. His mind flashed once again to how it had felt when she'd stepped into him, her hands on his face and her lips moving toward his.

In some ways she made it easy. In others, it was unbearably difficult. But still, they'd made it more than eight months. It would certainly have been simpler if she'd held out that extra time without asking to see her family. But she hadn't, and four months wasn't nothing. If he said no, she would suffer in that time. The cost to her was too high.

When Herleif returned to the castle in his human form, Adrienne was waiting for him on the steps, like she used to do when she first came to live with him. Her demeanor convinced him that she'd thought of little but her request all day, but she didn't immediately bring it up. She led him to the dining table, initiating conversation about her day for the first time in weeks.

"Did I tell you that I raided the library last week?" she asked, as she served up the rabbit stew.

"No," Herleif informed her.

She nodded. "Well, I did. I found some books on magic, actually."

"You've been reading up about songcraft?" Herleif asked, his attention caught. "That's a good idea."

"I thought so," Adrienne agreed. "It's definitely interesting reading. I just wish there was more magic available for me to practice as well as learn the theory."

"What have you learned?" Herleif asked.

"Well, my main interest was in healing," Adrienne said. "I didn't ever again want to be in a position like we were after that man Hagen's attack, where you might be more seriously wounded, and my power would be useless to help you."

Herleif didn't know what to say. It was both touching and

painful to think that even while distant and wary toward him, she'd been researching ways to keep him safe.

"Do you have any minor injuries?" Adrienne asked. "I mean *very* minor."

Herleif searched his hand, finding a small cut from a bramble. "Like this?" He extended it toward her across the table.

Adrienne leaned forward to peer at it, a little too careful not to touch it. "Yes, that's a good example," she said. She cleared her throat, then closed her eyes, beginning to sing in a soft, wistful voice that captured Herleif immediately.

"Bind the pain, the fever still. Heal the hurt, make well the ill."

She opened her eyes, her expression hopeful. "Any difference?"

Herleif turned his hand over a couple of times, looking at the cut. "I think it stings a little less," he offered.

Adrienne leaned back in her chair with a sigh. "You're being generous," she said dryly. "I'm not surprised. I could hardly pull any magic in just now. And that song is a very general catch all. From what I read, it tends to be more powerful when it's more specific."

"Well, it's time well spent to learn about it, anyway," said Herleif.

Adrienne nodded. "I came across another topic that might be interesting. It's about putting power into objects."

Herleif frowned. "Making talismans? I thought only elves did that, with magic they'd mined from the ground. I thought singers didn't store magic, but channeled it through their bodies for immediate use."

"Yes, that's what I understood, too," said Adrienne. "And I think that's correct. This wasn't about making talismans. That's when you store magic to be accessed and molded at a future time, and like you said, only elves do that. What I read today was about giving an item a certain property. Tying your magic to it so that you can manipulate the object later, without needing any new magic to do it."

"Sounds like a fine distinction to me," said Herleif doubtfully.

Adrienne laughed. How he'd missed that sound. "Yes, I don't fully understand the difference, either," she said. "It would be much easier with an instructor rather than just muddling through a book. But I gave it a try according to the instructions, and I think I now have some kind of minimal control over the salt cellar."

Herleif laughed as well, recognizing from her tone that she was trying to make a joke. He was glad she'd found some way to learn about her craft, though. He longed to give her all the opportunities her family had worked so hard to offer, and much more. If they emerged from all this unscathed, he would see to it that she had the chance to study under the best masters the academy had to offer.

"Have you thought any more about my request?" Adrienne asked.

Herleif took a moment to answer, startled by the abrupt change in topic. "Yes," he said slowly. "I thought of little else all day."

"And?" Adrienne pressed, unable to hide her eagerness.

Herleif looked at her face, barely visible in the darkness, but still communicating her hope. How could he deny her something so reasonable, so utterly deserved?

"We can go tomorrow," Herleif said abruptly.

Adrienne's gasp was audible. "Really?"

Herleif nodded under his hood. "I'll travel with you to the edge of the woods, but no further, for obvious reasons."

"I can find my way," Adrienne said quickly.

"There are conditions," Herleif warned her. "I'm sorry it must be so, but I cannot compromise on them."

"What conditions?" Adrienne asked.

"You must return in the evening," said Herleif. "You're not to stay there overnight."

Adrienne nodded. "I'll return before that," she assured him. "I have no desire to travel alone through the darkness."

"Thank you," said Herleif, relieved by her easy agreement. Not only would he be lost if she didn't come back to him overnight, but he also didn't relish the thought of her traversing the woods or the abandoned city after nightfall. He wished desperately that he could accompany her, meet her family under better circumstances than their last interaction. But he obviously couldn't do so during the day, and it was far too dangerous to enter the light and warmth of their home at night.

He hesitated, trying to picture the scene Adrienne would share with her family. He was reluctant to put any stipulations on that time, but so much could be lost if they weren't careful enough.

"What will you tell them?"

Adrienne considered it for a moment. "I don't know. I don't think I should tell them your real identity, or the fact that you turn into a bear during the day, do you?"

"I do not," said Herleif, once again profoundly relieved.

Adrienne nodded wisely. "Much simpler not to. Since I can't explain any of it."

The stiffness of her tone on the last sentence sent a barb through Herleif's heart, but he knew it was deserved. "Will you really be comfortable lying to your family, though?" he pressed.

"I won't lie to them," Adrienne said, sounding a little irked. "I'll speak the truth, just not all of it. Leaving things out is not the same as lying."

Picturing Adrienne's mother from their one meeting, Herleif wasn't convinced. Estrid had seemed both perceptive and determined. He doubted she would meekly accept her daughter's detail-sparse account of her new life.

"Even your mother?" he asked. "Will you really leave so much out when she asks you how you are?"

"I'll have to," said Adrienne, her voice once again tight. "I can't tell her what I don't know."

"And..." Herleif hesitated. "And you're sure you want to go now? You don't want to wait...a little longer?" He dared say no more, for fear of revealing too much.

"I'm sure," said Adrienne, sounding bewildered. "Why would I want to wait?"

"No reason I can think of," said Herleif, his voice heavy with resignation. Nerves rushed over him, but he told himself not to be selfish. Adrienne deserved this, and much more. "Tomorrow, then."

CHAPTER SEVENTEEN

Adrienne

Adrienne woke before sunrise, tingling with excitement. Today she would see her family. She should have asked months ago—she'd honestly never dreamed Herleif would just agree.

But months ago she hadn't been pining for her family, she reminded herself. Months ago she'd been bizarrely happy in her life at the castle, in spite of its restrictions. Months ago, all her focus had been on the man who occupied her every waking thought, and quite a few of her sleeping ones, if she was honest.

Now, the affection for Herleif that had grown within her made the new distance between them all the more unbearable. She needed a change, a chance to clear her head, or she'd go mad with the solitude, and the constant reliving of Herleif's rejection. Part of her was sorry Herleif couldn't stay with her on the visit to her family, but another part was glad. The distance might do them both good.

Although dawn hadn't yet broken, Adrienne was unsurprised to note that Herleif had already left the room. He was probably waiting for her outside—they'd planned to leave as soon as it was light. Adrienne dressed quickly, donning the same gown she'd traveled to the castle in, and the cloak Herleif had bought her immediately after their wedding. It wouldn't do to show up to her family's cottage in the finery of royalty, however worn and faded the gowns might be.

As predicted, Herleif was waiting downstairs, and after a quick breakfast, Adrienne joined him in the clearing. They walked in silence across the grass and into the trees, the mood of the bear impossible to read. Herleif didn't indicate for Adrienne to ride on his back, and she didn't ask. Their progress through the woods was therefore slow, and the sun had fully risen by the time they reached the tree line.

Adrienne's gaze passed over the abandoned city that stood between her and the village where she'd grown up. Strange that she no longer thought of Toveham as home. She turned to Herleif.

"Goodbye, then," she told him, feeling foolishly emotional. It wasn't as though it was a permanent parting, or even a long one. So why was a lump rising in her throat at the idea of leaving him?

Herleif dipped his head in acknowledgment of her words. His bright, intelligent eyes seemed to bore into her soul, giving the impression that there were things he wished to say, if only he had his voice.

"I remember the restrictions," Adrienne assured him, taking a guess at his thoughts. "I'll be back before dark. And I won't tell them about," she waved a hand at his bear form, "this. I promise."

Herleif's eyes looked no less troubled, and it was impossible to tell if that was what he'd wished to say. Was it her imagination that she read in his gaze the same sense of impending separation that she felt? Why was she suddenly seized by the sense that their time was limited, that some kind of countdown had begun, and she was the only one who didn't know it?

She said none of this aloud, and of course Herleif couldn't speak. After a moment, he nodded again.

Still Adrienne hesitated, then she reached out and laid a hand against his furry flank. "I'll see you soon," she promised.

Herleif turned his huge head suddenly, nuzzling his snout against the hand. That brought a smile to Adrienne's face. She'd missed the cuddliness of the bear almost as much as the conversation of the man these last couple of months. When Herleif withdrew his head, she turned away, drawing her cloak around her. Spring was moving toward summer, and it was nothing like as frigid as it had been a few months before. But it was still brisk, as northern Frossenland always was.

As she entered Tove's empty streets, she glanced back. Herleif still hovered, just inside the tree line. He looked so forlorn, kept captive by the need to hide his terrifying form, that it pricked at her heart. Did he wish he could come with her? Or would he have no interest in spending a day with her family?

She moved quickly through the streets of the former capital, spooked by the forlorn aspect of all the abandoned buildings. She knew rumor said thieves sometimes made camp among the ruins, but she wasn't really worried. Herleif was nearby, and as always, she carried her silver bell with her. The incident at the markets had proved both that he could hear her across a great distance, and that he was willing to expose his bear form if she was in danger.

Happily, it wasn't necessary. Adrienne crossed the city without incident and made her way into the outskirts of Tove-ham. She was tempted to go through the town, and see if it had changed much. But on reflection, she decided it would be wiser not to draw attention to herself. So she skirted around the town's southern edge, making for her family's home just east of the village. It was surreal to pass through such familiar surroundings after so long. She'd been with Herleif for over eight months, but honestly it felt like longer. Her new life was so removed from her old, she could hardly connect with the person she'd once been.

In spite of all that, her heart lifted when she saw a familiar building up ahead. The clucking of chickens, and the smell of tilled earth from nearby fields where crops were still being planted, washed powerfully over her, taking her immediately back to a different time. Her eyes drank in the cottage eagerly. Everything looked the same, and yet different. It was all still there, but it was...better. The rundown fence had been mended, there seemed to be twice as many chickens, and smoke curled from the chimney, even though it was nearly summer.

Intrigued, Adrienne increased her pace. She'd almost reached the edge of the yard when a well-known figure emerged around the side of the building, a stack of cut logs on his shoulder.

"Adrienne!" Kettil dropped his load, sprinting toward her. "Adrienne's here!" he cried over his shoulder.

By the time he reached her, the door had flown open, both Felman and Adrienne's mother appearing. The four of them converged outside the front door, Adrienne laughing and crying at the same time as three pairs of arms engulfed her.

"Adrienne, you've escaped!" Felman cried delightedly. "You're free!"

Adrienne clucked with her tongue. "Nonsense, Felman, it's nothing like that. I've come for a visit, that's all. No escape necessary."

Her brother scowled, and Adrienne couldn't help laughing at him.

"You don't look pleased, Felman. Would you prefer me to have been a mistreated prisoner?"

Felman gave her an unimpressed look, but it was her mother whose shrewd gaze drew Adrienne's attention. Herleif had been very perceptive when he'd guessed that the older woman would be the one to dig for more answers.

"We can talk more comfortably inside," Estrid said briskly. "Kettil, run over to Revna's, and tell her that Adrienne's here." She gave Adrienne a sharp look. "You have time to come in, don't you?"

Adrienne nodded happily. "I have all day, if you can spare it."

"We can spare it," her mother assured her. With one arm around Adrienne's shoulders, she led her inside. Within minutes, Revna had arrived, her three children in tow. Unhesitatingly, she turned them out of doors to play in the yard as soon as they'd all hugged their aunt and exclaimed over her unexpected return.

"What do you mean, you didn't have to escape?" Felman demanded, once the adults were alone. "I thought your husband was refusing to let you come here."

"Not at all," said Adrienne, a little thrown by her own defensiveness. It felt strange to take a different position from her brother in a matter involving family. "I told him yesterday that I'd like to visit you all, and he suggested today. He accompanied me part of the way, but he had other...commitments that prevented him from joining us."

Commitments like roaming the woods as an oversized bear. And hopefully catching something good for that night's dinner, of course.

"Why did he change his mind, though?" Kettil pressed, frowning. "When he hasn't let you visit all this time?"

"Well..." Adrienne bit her lip, chastising herself for not having foreseen this very natural question. "Well, actually, I didn't ask to visit until now."

"Why not?" Revna demanded, sounding affronted.

Adrienne sighed. "It's not easy to explain," she said. "I know that's an unsatisfying answer, but it's all I have."

"Unsatisfying is an understatement," Felman said. "I can't think of any reason why you wouldn't want to come back to us for eight whole months!"

"Can't you?" Revna sounded a little amused, and Adrienne had the uncomfortable feeling that her sister had noticed the way her cheeks were heating.

"No." Felman stared at his older sister, then swung back to Adrienne. "Unless...does he have you under an enchantment?"

Adrienne laughed. "No, of course not. He's used no magic on me." She glanced around. "The place is looking wonderful. Did I see extra chickens out there? And you've mended the fence!"

"Yes, we're doing better than we have in a long time," her mother told her, something behind the words that Adrienne couldn't quite place.

A sudden thought struck her. Was it possible that the change in their circumstances arose purely from no longer putting aside money for her future schooling? Not to mention one mouth fewer to feed. Guilt pricked her at the idea. She'd cost her family so much for so long, and all for absolutely no gain.

"Well, I'm glad for that, anyway," she said.

She tried to speak cheerfully, but it felt unnatural. Everything was changed, herself more than the rest. She'd been so excited to see her family again, and of course it was good to be with them, but it wasn't the same. She'd barely been there ten minutes, and already she found her thoughts straying to the castle, wondering what Herleif was up to right now.

Then she remembered the distance between them. If she was home, she'd probably be alone right now, not curled up against her personal giant cushion to read or mend. She looked over at Revna, intending to ask after her husband, but found her sister's eyes scanning her in a measuring way.

"What?" Adrienne asked self-consciously. "What are you staring at, Revna?"

"You," her sister said unashamedly. "It's been eight months, hasn't it? I thought maybe you'd come to tell us some news, but you don't *look* like you're carrying."

"Carrying?" Adrienne repeated, momentarily confused. Her sister gave her an incredulous look, and her meaning suddenly became clear. "Oh," said Adrienne. If she'd been blushing before, it was nothing to how fiery her cheeks were now. "No, of course I'm not."

"No baby yet?" Revna asked, frowning. "Well, I suppose it's not so unusual. Hopefully it won't be too long."

"Actually..." Adrienne swallowed, not at all sure how to explain, or whether she wished to.

"I don't want to hear about this," Felman cut in, sounding horrified.

"Agreed," said Kettil, his expression faintly disgusted. "You're our sister."

Revna looked between them in bewilderment. "I'm your sister, and I don't remember you having any issue when I was pregnant. It's all perfectly natural."

"That's different," Kettil assured her. "You're older. Adrienne's our baby sister. We don't want to think about her being pregnant."

"I'm not pregnant," Adrienne said, the words coming out more brittle than she intended. "Can we drop this?"

"Hm." Revna had never been known for her tact, and Adrienne wasn't surprised that she ignored her little sister's request. "Sore spot, is it? Definitely more to this."

"All right." Felman stood up, shuddering a little. "The woodpile still needs restocking."

"Yes, I'll help," Kettil agreed, hurrying after his brother.

Revna rolled her eyes as she watched them go. "Given

they're being such babies themselves, you'd think they'd be more comfortable talking about the topic."

Adrienne fidgeted with her skirt, fighting a cowardly wish that she could flee the conversation like her brothers had.

"Is everything all right, Adrienne?" Her mother's voice was softer than Revna's had been, but her expression was just as shrewd.

"Yes, truly it is," Adrienne told her.

"Then why did you go as red as a beet when I asked you if you were carrying yet?" Revna asked skeptically.

Adrienne kept her eyes on her hands as they smoothed her dress across her knees.

"It's just...our marriage is a little...unusual."

"What does that mean?" Revna demanded.

Adrienne sighed. She knew her sister. There was no point dancing around it. "It means that my husband hasn't so much as kissed me yet." She seriously hoped the *yet* wasn't just optimism on her part.

"What?" The startled reply came from her mother. She exchanged a look with her oldest daughter. "Isn't he...isn't he fond of you?"

Adrienne shrugged. "I think he is." She forced herself to look up into her mother's eyes. "It's...difficult to explain."

Her mother looked troubled, but she said nothing. Something about her obvious confusion surprised Adrienne. It was as though her mother knew something Adrienne didn't, and Adrienne's information didn't fit with it.

"But he treats you well?" Revna pressed. "Other than whatever strangeness is behind that?"

Adrienne nodded vigorously. "He treats me very well. I've been happy with him, honestly."

Until recently, she added silently. She didn't even consider saying it aloud. Now that she was with her family, she was gripped by an overwhelming desire to make them understand how kind and trustworthy Herleif really was. And that realization made her feel foolish for the excessive distance she'd placed between them in recent months. She'd been hurt by his rejection, and she'd been punishing him for it. That was the plain and simple truth. But it made no sense for her to punish him when she was certain he wasn't free to act as he might wish to.

"Well, I'm glad to hear it," her mother said. "It's what I thought, but it's a load off my mind to have it confirmed."

Adrienne stared at her. "It's what you thought? Really?"

"Why are you surprised?" Revna asked.

"Well..." Adrienne shrugged. "If I'm honest, I pictured you all frantic with worry over my wellbeing. I'm glad you haven't been suffering unnecessarily, of course. But I'm surprised you assumed that a man who won me in a sordid game of chance would treat me well. He's certainly nothing like I expected him to be based on those circumstances."

"We were desperately worried at first," her mother assured her. "I wouldn't want to give you the impression that we didn't care—we were all sick with worry. But then Bjørn came to visit us, and—"

"What?" Adrienne sat up straighter, her mouth falling open. "He visited you? When?"

"Months ago," her mother said. "Four, maybe. You didn't know?"

Adrienne shook her head. "I wonder why he didn't tell me," she mused, troubled.

The door to the yard swung open, and Adrienne tensed, her eyes flying to the figure in the doorway. When she saw it was Felman, she relaxed. Kettil filed in behind him as well.

"Please tell me you've moved on from the last topic," Felman said darkly.

Revna rolled her eyes at him, but her next words were directed at Adrienne. "Are you sure you're all right? You just jumped when that door opened. You seem on edge."

"I was worried it might be Father," said Adrienne. She cast a glance around the cottage. "He's not still here, is he? I assumed he would have left months ago, but it occurred to me that he might have gone and returned by now. It wouldn't be the first time his visit was horribly timed, would it?"

No one immediately answered, and when Adrienne looked back around, she realized that all four members of her family were staring at her.

"What?"

"You don't know?" Kettil asked. He exchanged a look with his mother.

"Know what?" Adrienne looked uneasily from one face to the next. "What are you talking about?" Her eyes widened. "Don't tell me he's died?"

"Not that we know of," Felman said. "But he's definitely not coming back for a visit anytime soon. That mountain of a husband of yours had him thrown in debtor's prison."

CHAPTER EIGHTEEN

Adrienne

"Herl—*he* did what?" Adrienne shot to her feet, only just catching her slip in time. If Herleif had introduced himself to her family as Bjørn, she would honor that. Thankfully no one seemed to notice it, everyone's attention still on the topic of her father. "Please, someone, explain," she said desperately.

"I'm astonished you don't know," Kettil said. "A few months back he showed up here, late at night, with the magistrate in tow. He produced all Father's notes of credit and made a big show of demanding full payment of the debts. Mamma tried to reason with him, told him we didn't have enough, explained that we had the months of interest saved, and he'd get more from us in the long run if he kept the debts alive. But he was adamant. Said he wanted justice, and wouldn't accept credit any longer. He appealed to the magistrate, who said that if Father couldn't pay, the law demanded he be detained in debtor's prison. Father blustered and protested—you can imagine it. He tried to run off to the tavern, but they rounded him up quickly enough. He's been detained ever since."

Adrienne said nothing, too stunned by this information to find a response.

"There's more," her mother added. "Once the magistrate had left, your husband gave us the notes of credit. He recommended we burn them, which we did immediately. He also gave us a bag of gold—greater in value than what your father took the night we last saw you. He said that in his hands it would be blood money, and he had no need or desire to win it."

"Which makes no sense to me now," said Revna thoughtfully. "When the boys told me what he'd said, I assumed he'd entered the game because he was so struck by your beauty. I thought maybe he'd fallen in love with you on the spot, and was determined to have you for his wife. But if he doesn't even want you…"

Adrienne winced. She hoped that wasn't true. She would like to think that Herleif wanted to be with her, and was prevented by something outside of his control. But it was difficult to be sure with him.

"No, I can't make sense of it," Revna declared. "I don't understand why he threw in his dice."

Adrienne said nothing. It was the same question that had plagued her for eight months, and she had no answer.

"What does he look like?" Felman asked curiously. "When he came here, he skulked in the shadows the whole time with his hood pulled low, and refused to come in—we never actually saw his face."

Adrienne had to hold in a snort. No doubt. It was reassuring to know that Herleif's strange restriction wasn't specific to her.

"What do you care what he looks like?" she said evasively. She shook her head slowly. "I didn't know any of this. I don't know what to say." Her eyes found her mother's. "What did you do with the gold?"

"Paid off the rest of your father's debts," her mother

answered. "And there was still a decent bit left over, since most of his creditors were part of that game, and lost their credit to this Bjørn. We've been able to make some improvements, and still keep a bit aside for emergencies."

"What are you going to do about Father?" Adrienne asked.

Her mother leaned back in her chair with a sigh. "I don't know," she admitted. "I don't have enough funds to bail him out. Although now that we've burned the notes, I suppose the amount is immaterial. Only your husband could challenge him being released, and he's not likely to do so without the papers." Her brow was unusually stern. "I suppose I could plead his case, but I'm not inclined to do so. Once, perhaps. But not after what he did to you." She held Adrienne's gaze, and the grief and regret in her eyes made Adrienne's heart squeeze. "Adrienne, child..."

"Don't apologize, Mamma," Adrienne said quickly. "You're not at fault in any of this."

"I let you go with him that night," her mother said, her voice strained. "I even encouraged you to go, thinking it wiser than making a scene. I swear to you, I never thought he could do anything so irrevocable in one evening."

Adrienne shook her head, her throat tight and a strange smile tugging at her lips. "It was horrible at the time, I acknowledge, but it hasn't turned out so bad in the end. I...I don't know how else to explain it, except to say that I don't regret my marriage. I wouldn't change it if I could."

"You've fallen in love with him." Revna's words were so stark and matter-of-fact, they fell on Adrienne with the force of a boulder. "It's not surprising, if he's been kind to you."

Adrienne opened her mouth, but no words came out. She closed it again, swallowing. Was her sister right?

Of course she was.

Adrienne had been in love with Herleif for months. She'd

known it well before she tried to kiss him, and the intensity of her devastation over that incident was more than enough to confirm it. Something deep within her was uncomfortable with the realization, given the fact that she still didn't know his reason for marrying her, still didn't know if he could fully be trusted, or if the purpose he had for her would prove to be sinister. But even more immediate a concern was the question of how he felt about her. Like the other mystery, that remained unanswerable.

"I'm still not sure about all this," Felman said, his brow heavy and his tone disapproving. "Whatever he's duped you into thinking, that man stole you from your family."

"He bought us all out of debt, Felman," said Revna, sounding exasperated. Clearly they'd had this argument before.

"Blood money. He said it himself," Felman retorted. "He felt guilty for what he'd done, and he tried to pay us for her. That just makes it worse, in my opinion. She's not a slave to be bought and sold."

"Give it a rest, Felman," said Adrienne sharply. "You're wrong about him. He wouldn't treat my life like that, like something to be traded."

She believed the words, mostly. She wished there wasn't a small part of her wondering if she had been duped, wondering yet again about the true reason behind Herleif's decision to vie for her hand. But deeply as that fear was rooted, the affection she had for Herleif dominated it, and compelled her to defend him against her brother.

"We only have you for a day," her mother cut in. "We're not going to waste it arguing. Come, Adrienne, you can help me get started on lunch. I want to hear more about your life."

"I'd rather hear what you've all been up to," Adrienne said, as she hopped up and moved into the kitchen area to help her mother.

It was such a familiar task, and yet it felt as surreal as all the rest. She was used to a different kitchen now, with different ingredients to work with, and an entirely different companion. A smile curved her lips as she thought of Herleif, in his bear form, sniffing interestedly at the soup she had over the fire, and getting scolded for it. It was endearing, the way he often dropped his reserve when in bear form. She didn't think he even realized he was doing it.

Her nieces and nephew re-entered the cottage soon after, and they at least were very willing to chatter excitedly about their own lives rather than press Adrienne for details of hers. The day passed much too quickly, full of cheerful conversation and tales of domestic adventures. The difference in tone was marked compared to the last time Adrienne had been in the dwelling. Her father was absent now. Not just in person, but truly absent. The burdens he'd placed on the family were gone, as was the threat that at any moment he might reappear and wreak havoc on their lives once again.

Herleif was responsible for this relief. And Adrienne hadn't even known.

When the afternoon was wearing on, and the light beginning to adopt a yellow hue, Adrienne rose reluctantly. "I need to go," she said. "I promised I'd be back before dark. Neither of us thought it a good idea for me to be walking home alone after nightfall."

"Very sensible," her mother said approvingly. She stood also. "I'll walk you to the end of the lane."

Adrienne smiled, trying to ignore the strange sense of unease brought on by her mother's manner. Something was a little off, but she couldn't tell what. The others all embraced Adrienne, adjuring her to visit them again soon, but only her mother accompanied her out into the afternoon sunshine.

The two women walked up the laneway arm in arm, the moment tasting very bittersweet. It wasn't the fact that she was leaving that played with Adrienne's emotions. It was the realization that had struck her in the familiar, beloved cottage—that she could never truly return. She could visit, but the life she'd known there was gone, over, out of her reach. She found she wasn't sorry for it, but it was still a strange and confronting revelation.

"He really is kind to you?" her mother asked, once they were clear of the house.

Adrienne nodded. "I swear it."

Her mother seemed satisfied, but Adrienne couldn't help frowning.

"I just can't believe he did all that, with the credit and the coins, and I had no idea."

"Can't you?" her mother asked. "I assumed you knew, but when you said you didn't, I realized it wasn't so surprising."

"What do you mean?" Adrienne demanded.

Her mother shrugged. "A good man doesn't show kindness to be admired by others. He had no need to tell anyone in order for it to be worth doing."

"Not even to tell those nearest to him?" Adrienne demanded. Her voice caught a little. "I'm his wife!"

Her mother reached out, smiling as she smoothed a wisp of Adrienne's hair behind her ear. "Especially those nearest to him. A man like your husband doesn't act with kindness for show. He does it because his heart *is* kind. If he boasts about what he's done, it was done out of vanity, not kindness. A good man does more and says less about it."

Adrienne frowned as she thought this over. It was impossible not to draw a comparison between her own husband, and the husband of the woman next to her. How many times had her father boasted about integrity he hadn't actually shown, like his claims that he regularly sent money home to his family because he'd done it once or twice?

My father is selfish, she thought, remembering how forcefully the acknowledgment had struck her the day her father returned for his most recent, most disastrous visit. *And Herleif is the opposite. He has genuine, unselfish generosity. It shows in everything he does.*

Behind the thought was another realization, something Adrienne couldn't fully grasp onto, but sensed to be crucially important nevertheless. It lurked just out of reach, waiting for her to explore it. But she could ponder her own marriage later. Who knew when she would next get a chance to ask her mother some of the questions that had been burning in her mind since she became a wife herself?

"Why did you marry Father?" She blurted it out, no time for tact. They'd reached the end of the lane, and soon she would have to hurry home. "Did someone force you? Or were you in a corner, like I was?"

Her mother shook her head, the smile on her lips sad. "No, I chose him of my own free will. I was young, and I acted in haste." She squeezed Adrienne's arm. "Not that I mean to say I regret my family."

Adrienne shook her head. "I understand," she assured her mother. "You don't need to guard my feelings. I know you love me, and the others. You can speak honestly."

Her mother nodded gratefully. "You have to understand, Adrienne, that your father wasn't always the way he is now." Her smile turned a little wistful. "Well, he was always a bit unpredictable, and if I'm honest with myself, a bit unreliable. But back then it was exciting rather than frustrating. He was so charming, you see. And many girls admired him—I was delighted he chose me. I knew I was capable of running a home, and I thought I could fill in the gaps where he wasn't reliable."

She sighed again, and the sadness in her eyes made something inside Adrienne ache.

"Then he discovered games of chance. Not that he didn't know what they were, of course. But his father had rigidly prevented him from engaging in them when he lived under his roof. I quickly came to understand why. There's a weakness in his family. His father was conscientious about it, but his grandfather ruined his family with it." She shook her head. "I suppose that's what made his father so determined not to fall prey to the same affliction."

"Watching our father has certainly given all of us a distaste for any such pastime," Adrienne said. "But what do you mean, affliction? You make it sound like it's a disease he can't help."

"He can help it," her mother said quickly. "I don't mean to make excuses for him. He makes his own choices, and he has at last been brought to face the consequences of them." She gave Adrienne a searching look. "Thanks to your husband. But your father is more susceptible than some men, there's no doubt. And once he began to indulge his love for the dice, it was ruinous. Things were never really good again."

"Except for when he was gone," Adrienne said. Unlike her mother, she had no fond memories of a better time with her father, and accordingly she had less sympathy than she sensed lurking behind her mother's words.

"Adrienne." She could tell at once from her mother's tone that the topic was changing. "There's more you're not telling me, isn't there? A great deal more."

Adrienne bit her lip, silent.

"There's some kind of magic at work in your marriage, isn't there?" her mother pressed. "Your husband is affected somehow."

She didn't phrase the last part as a question, and Adrienne's unease returned. It was strange how accurately Herleif had predicted that her mother would be the one difficult to mislead or withhold information from. Perhaps not that strange, actually, now she knew that he'd met her mother.

"Just answer me one question," her mother asked. "You'll likely think me mad, but humor me. Have you ever seen your husband's face?"

Adrienne drew in a sharp breath, her heart racing. How did her mother know so much?

"Don't tell me it's true," her mother breathed, her eyes widening at Adrienne's prolonged silence. She gave her head a slow shake. "I won't press you to tell me more. I can see you're reluctant. But if you actually haven't seen his face, there's something I need to tell you."

"What?" Adrienne demanded, alarmed at her mother's expression. She glanced up at the sun. She really needed to get going, but she couldn't leave without an answer now.

"I was approached a short time ago," her mother said, speaking in a rush as if she knew time was limited. "By an elf."

"An elf?" Adrienne repeated. Whatever she'd expected, it wasn't that. "Here?"

Her mother nodded. "I was as stunned as you are. I thought they'd basically forsaken the north. It was a very strange visit. The elf gave me this cryptic message about your husband." She searched Adrienne's eyes carefully as she went on. "He claimed that your husband is not Bjørn, but Crown Prince Herleif, rightful ruler of our kingdom."

Adrienne couldn't help the gasp that escaped her. She tried quickly to school her features, realizing too late that doing so just made her earlier deception more obvious.

"So you did know," her mother murmured, clearly reading Adrienne's reaction with ease. "I'm glad of that." Her expression became troubled. "But if that information is true—as unbelievable as it seems—then the rest of the message is likely true as well. And I'd much rather believe it wasn't."

"What do you mean?" Adrienne demanded. "What was the message?"

"That he's under a curse," her mother said. "That his father was actually killed by a giant, not a bear, and that the giant tried to curse the kingdom."

Adrienne's mouth fell open, her mind spinning at this new thought. A giant? She'd never considered that option, and why would she? Giants didn't have magic.

"I was skeptical as well," her mother said, once again comprehending Adrienne's silent response. "But the elf claimed that the giant had gotten her hands on some powerful talismans. Apparently she tried to throw a curse on Frossenland, and the prince got in the way of it, taking it onto himself instead, and protecting the kingdom."

Adrienne could feel the color drain from her face. She had no difficulty whatsoever picturing Herleif doing exactly that.

"What's the nature of the curse?" she whispered, her voice thin in her own ears.

"That no one is allowed to see his face for six years," her mother said. "Not a living soul."

"Six years?" Adrienne repeated, her mind churning as she tried to work out the timeline. At the time of their marriage, five years had passed since Herleif's supposed death. That meant that he had only months left before six years was up. "What happens at the end of six years, if no one sees his face?"

"He dies," said her mother simply.

"What?" Adrienne gripped her mother's arm, horror rising in her.

"That's what the elf told me," her mother said in somber tones. "He'll absorb the curse fully, and it will kill him, but the kingdom will be free. If someone sees his face, on the other hand, the curse will be unleashed on Frossenland."

Adrienne's breaths were coming in short gasps. It was all too horrible to believe. Could it be true? She had a terrifying feeling that it was. Unlike her mother, she had very specific reasons to think her husband was under a curse. The intercepted magic must have taken the shape of forcing him into a bear's body during daylight hours. It was what she would expect from magic wielded as clumsily as an untrained giant would likely manage. And it would be exactly like Herleif to take the cost on himself in order to save his kingdom.

But he'd sworn to her that he took his marriage vows seriously, that he wouldn't abandon her. There was an obvious answer for that. He clearly didn't consider his death to count as abandonment. *Until death parts us*, wasn't that what they'd said?

Well, she considered it abandonment, she thought fiercely. If he let himself die and thereby left her alone, knowing it was coming and doing nothing to stop it, she didn't know how she would forgive him.

She couldn't let it happen.

"What will happen if the curse is unleashed on Frossenland?" she asked her mother urgently.

"The elf wasn't sure," her mother said. "But he claimed that the curse would lose potency with every passing month the prince resisted it. If it had been unleashed immediately upon being cast, it would have been devastating, but if it was unleashed near the end of the six years, it would likely be all but spent. The damage might well be minimal."

Adrienne frowned. It was too uncertain. *Likely...might well be...*Herleif wouldn't like that. He would want a guarantee that the curse wouldn't harm anyone if he freed himself with it. But would he really sacrifice his own life on merely the *possibility* that letting himself live might harm others?

The answer came to her instantly. Yes, he would. Herleif would.

"So you've really never seen his face?" her mother asked, her voice grim.

"There are no sources of light in our home," Adrienne whispered. "He won't let me have so much as a candle."

Her mother looked deeply troubled, and Adrienne didn't blame her. She'd no doubt hoped the elf's account was nonsense, with no basis in fact. And not just for her daughter's sake. The whole kingdom could be affected.

"I can't let him die, Mamma," Adrienne said. "Not without at least trying to save him." She remembered the moment when Herleif had collapsed, his bear form pierced by two arrows. She'd seen in his eyes that he'd given up, and it terrified her. "I'm scared that he won't save himself."

"Wait here." Her mother was already hurrying back toward the house, and in a few minutes, she returned with something clutched in her hand. "Here." She held out a simple tallow candle to Adrienne. "I don't know if you want to use it—I don't know if you should. But now you have the choice."

Adrienne reached out slowly, taking the candle. She hated the feeling that she was betraying Herleif's trust, but also knew she might regret it if she didn't take the opportunity. Having the candle didn't mean she had to use it. And the trouble with blindly following Herleif's restrictions was that she couldn't be confident he would take his own interests into account. And she certainly couldn't trust him to be up front about his situation and his intentions. Experience had shown that. Now she thought about it, she probably had her answer as to why he'd never told her the details of his curse. He didn't want to give her the chance to protest, or to try to stop him. But she didn't want to be part of him sacrificing himself unnecessarily, no matter how willingly he did it.

"It's too much for you to carry," her mother said, anxiety creasing her forehead.

Adrienne shook her head firmly. "He's my husband. If it's not my burden to carry, then whose?" She hugged her mother. "I don' t know what I'm going to do, Mamma, but I'll figure it out."

The afternoon was melting into evening, and Adrienne knew it was time to be gone. With a final word of farewell to her mother, she stowed the candle in the pocket of her cloak and hurried toward the woods.

Herleif was waiting.

CHAPTER NINETEEN

Adrienne

When Adrienne crossed the last stretch of the abandoned city, the sun was nearly at the horizon. Her eyes scanned the trees tensely, looking for a patch of white fur hidden behind the trunks. Sure enough, as she drew close, something large shifted in the shadows.

Adrienne's heart picked up speed, a rush of emotions overcoming her as she recognized her husband. She'd discovered a great deal about him during their day of separation, and part of her wished she could go back to the simpler time when she'd known none of it.

"Herleif," she said, as soon as she entered the woods. She reached out to lay a hand on his furry neck. "You haven't been standing here all day, have you?"

Herleif didn't answer, his body beginning to quiver under her touch. At first Adrienne thought he was responding to her words, but the shaking rapidly intensified, and a glance at the sky told her the real explanation. The sun must be setting beyond the trees.

She pulled her hand back as Herleif turned away, curving in on himself in his usual posture of protection. She'd long understood that the purpose related not to the transformation, but to the need to hide his face.

Because heaven forbid anyone see his face and thereby save his life.

Fear raced through Adrienne at the unbidden thought. The candle in her pocket suddenly felt heavy, and the guilt of her secret made her cheeks burn. But as Herleif drew himself up, his now-human back to her while he adjusted his hood, Adrienne felt a flash of defiance. Why should she feel guilty for keeping the candle secret from him? Their entire marriage was nothing but a long series of secrets, at least on his side. And if she used it, it would only be from a desire to save his life.

"Adrienne." Herleif turned, hanging back a little as the light continued to fade. "You're back. Is everything well?"

Adrienne nodded. "I said I'd be back before dark, didn't I?" She searched the darkness under his hood. "Are you well?"

"Of course," said Herleif dismissively. "I've done nothing of note today. I want to hear about your visit to your family. How was it?"

"It was illuminating," Adrienne said. She moved forward into the trees, Herleif keeping pace a step behind her, where she couldn't look at him without swiveling. "Herleif, why didn't you tell me you'd visited them?"

Herleif expressed no surprise at her words. He must have realized her family would tell her of their interaction.

"Perhaps I should have," he acknowledged. "I wasn't sure if you would welcome the information that I'd gone to your family's home uninvited. It was months ago, and we didn't know each other as well then. It was just before we started spending the days together."

"You didn't just go to their home though, did you?" Adrienne accused. "You used my father's debts to free them of him and gave them all that other money you won."

Herleif took a moment to answer, and when he spoke, his tone was cautious. "You disapprove?"

"Of course I don't disapprove!" Adrienne came to a stop, and Herleif mirrored her. His hood was so large that it hung halfway down his face, the rest fully hidden in the darkness, but they faced each other nonetheless. "Herleif, how could I be anything but grateful for what you've done for them? But I wish I'd known."

"Why?" Herleif asked. "Would it have changed anything for you to know?"

Adrienne raised her hands helplessly. "I don't know. I just feel...unmoored." Herleif seemed puzzled, and she didn't blame him. "I just don't understand why you did it," she said at last. "No one would have expected it of you—no one *did* expect it of you."

Herleif took a long moment to answer. Adrienne had the impression he was confused. "I did it because...well, do I need to explain? From what you've told me, your father stole that money from your family. That and more. And I won it in a sordid game of chance, which I entered with great reluctance and with no desire to acquire Svend's gold. Not to mention I'm a prince with a castle full of wealth. What possible other course makes sense but for me to return it to those to whom it actually belonged?"

"With great reluctance?" Adrienne repeated, her mind traveling back to the evening in question. "But you were so intentional. You were about to leave, and then my father announced that I would be his final stake, and you changed your mind. You hovered for hours, and I know you were clear-headed, because I didn't see you drink a thing. You only threw your dice in when it was close to the end, when..."

She trailed off, comprehension slowly trickling in. *When my hand had been staked*, she'd been going to say. She'd always understood from that sequence of events that Herleif's true purpose in joining the game had been to win a bride, not gold. She'd just never been able to comprehend why he wanted a wife in name only, sure there was crucial information she was missing, regarding his ultimate purpose for her.

But it had been months since she'd really contemplated the evening in question, and as she did so, knowing Herleif as she now did, the thought that had lurked just out of reach when her mother spoke of Herleif's quiet generosity suddenly burst into focus.

"You did it for me," she said, the words not much above a whisper. "Purely for my own sake, for no other reason than to save me from my father, and those other men."

Herleif was silent, seeming almost wary.

"I wish you'd told me that," Adrienne said, taking his lack of a denial as confirmation.

For some reason, her throat was suddenly clogged with unshed tears as she found herself rapidly reviewing all their interactions. Embarrassment washed over her afresh at the memory of how she'd tried to kiss him. Her own conduct on that occasion was doubly painful now she knew he hadn't married her because he wanted to, or because he was moved by her beauty or any such nonsense. He'd never actually wanted her as a wife at all.

But then, they'd been so happy with one another's company before that incident. She was sure she hadn't imagined his enjoyment of their time together. And although he'd rebuffed her, he hadn't exactly seemed repulsed. Anguished was more the word that sprung to mind.

The silence stretched out between them, eventually broken by Herleif.

"Adrienne? This reason for our marriage is a surprise to you? Did you assume otherwise?"

"Of course I did," Adrienne said, her words coming out more

passionately than she intended. "It never even occurred to me that you did it just to protect me. We were total strangers!" She passed a shaky hand over her eyes. "I should have realized, I suppose, now I know you. But..."

She shook her head helplessly. How could she explain the assumptions that had shaped her thinking to someone as honorable as Herleif? She was only just beginning to understand them herself.

"My father only ever showed up when he wanted something," she said, her voice strained and quiet now. "I assumed you had something to gain from our marriage. It's no secret that there are many things hidden between us. I assumed you had some purpose for me, or for our union, that you wouldn't or couldn't tell me about. I assumed when the time came you would...make use of me."

"What?" Herleif's horror was clear, even though she couldn't read his expression. "Adrienne, I would never *use* you. I'm sorry you were left with that impression. I—"

"It isn't your fault," said Adrienne, cutting him off with a sharp shake of her head. "The true answer is far more obvious, I was just too prejudiced to see it, or to have that much faith in your generous heart."

All the hours she'd spent worrying about what Herleif might have planned for her! All the times her unformed suspicions about the likely answer had prevented her from fully trusting him! Now that his true motivations were before her, his worth blazed across her consciousness so brightly it was almost painful. He was the best man she'd ever met, and she'd somehow ended up married to him. And, if her mother's mysterious informant was telling the truth, she might be about to lose him forever.

"Adrienne, you give me too much credit." Herleif sounded pained, even by the moderate praise she'd spoken aloud. "It would make more sense to me if you were angry with me. What difference do my motivations make to the reality I forced you into? You were given no true choice in the matter—I had a choice, and I trapped you into this marriage, fully aware that you knew nothing of..." he gestured at himself and the hidden castle, "all this. I'm truly sorry, Adrienne. I've wanted to say it so often, but I didn't know how to say it without..." He shifted back from her, letting out an audible breath. "It will be easier soon," he said, something in his voice she couldn't read. "I promise."

"You trapped me?" Adrienne repeated. "Is that what you call our life together?"

Unreasoning anger was growing inside her as his words stirred up all her fear again. What would be easier? Was he referring to his own death?

"Do you think I'd rather be married to that other man?" she demanded. "No doubt treated worse than one of his dogs?"

A shudder went over Herleif, and to Adrienne's surprise, he stepped forward, gripping her arms in his strong hands. She looked down out of habit, not yet willing to abandon the respect she'd so far shown to his wishes regarding her seeing his face.

"I would never let that happen," he said, his voice low and intense. "I would die before I saw you married to that vile man."

Adrienne's heart fluttered traitorously at the passion in his voice, but the sane part of her mind told her this reassurance was the opposite of comforting. Why did his thoughts fly straight to sacrificing his life to save others? Was it because he'd been living that reality for almost six years already?

She raised both hands to her face, pressing her palms against her eyes as she tried to gather her thoughts.

"So you stood to gain nothing from marrying me," she said, her voice coming out muffled. "But you did it anyway. Even though it cost you something."

Her mind flew to all the awkwardness they'd endured

regarding Herleif's unwillingness to share any romantic touch. There was definitely something at work there. She lowered her hands to peer up at him, and he quickly released her and stepped back, his hood as concealing as ever.

"Didn't it?" she pressed. "It cost you more than I've understood, I'll wager."

Herleif didn't acknowledge it, but again his silence felt like confirmation. Adrienne's mouth was suddenly dry with fear as her mother's words rang in her ears. It was entirely in character for Herleif to sacrifice his own interests for those of others.

"Herleif," she said, gathering her courage. "Will you just tell me why I can't see your face?"

There was no hesitation in Herleif's reply. "No. I won't."

Disappointed but not surprised, Adrienne tried again. "Or why you won't kiss me?"

This time it took Herleif a moment, and he audibly swallowed before speaking. But his answer was just as unequivocal. "No."

Adrienne frowned. Was it possible that particular mystery was just a case of his own restraint? Had he decided that since his death was impending and they had no future, it would be irresponsible to kiss her and start something he couldn't finish? Her sister's blunt questions came to mind, and her cheeks heated. Maybe his concern related to fathering an heir. Maybe he wanted her to be fully free once he was gone.

The horror of that idea loosened her tongue.

"You were right," she blurted out.

Herleif's voice was wary. "About what?"

"My mother was the hardest to distract from all the unanswered questions." She swallowed. "She asked me directly if I'd ever seen your face."

Herleif stiffened visibly. "What did you say?"

"I didn't admit it in as many words, but she knew," Adrienne told him. "She already knew before she asked me, because someone else had told her."

She could feel Herleif's astonished stare, even from under the hood. "What do you mean? Who told her?"

"An elf," Adrienne said, the words tumbling out. "An elf came to see her and told her something...something absurd. Something that couldn't be true, surely."

Herleif remained silent, and after a moment Adrienne pushed on.

"The elf knew who you really are. And he said that you're under a curse. A curse placed by a giant."

Herleif's sharp intake of breath made Adrienne pause.

"Is it true?" she demanded.

Her husband said nothing.

"Herleif, why don't you tell me the truth?" she begged. "Please, I can help you."

"You're already helping me," he said gruffly. "You've already done more for me than I could ever have been justified to expect. Let us say no more about it."

"That's not good enough!" Adrienne cried, panic rising. "I need answers, Herleif! The elf told my mother that the giant's target wasn't really you, but the kingdom. Surely you needn't suffer so much just in the hope that—"

"It is the duty of a prince to do whatever must be done to protect his kingdom," said Herleif, his voice as stiff as it had been back when they were little better than strangers. "I do not wish to discuss it, Adrienne."

Adrienne's breaths were coming in short gasps now. Everything he said was convincing her that what the elf had told her mother was true. But she couldn't let him die.

"Please, Herleif," she begged. "Please just tell me the truth. Tell me exactly what happened that day, and exactly what the curse involves."

"Don't ask it of me, Adrienne." Herleif's words came out rough, almost angry as he stepped away from her. "Can't you just leave it be?"

"No!" Adrienne cried. "I can't. I've left it be for eight months, Herleif, and it's too much to expect me to ask no questions when the stakes are so high."

"I know I've expected too much from you," Herleif acknowledged. "But I told you at the start that I wasn't offering you the full confidence a true wife should expect."

Adrienne remembered when Herleif had told her that, but the words hadn't stung then like they did now. She didn't want to hear that he didn't consider her a true wife, not now she'd lost her heart to him.

"Our marriage might be nothing but a sham to you," she whispered. "But you're the only husband I've ever had, and I want to be a real partner in whatever you're facing."

"I didn't say that," Herleif said, sounding anguished.

"Why are you so determined to make a sacrifice of yourself?" Adrienne demanded. "Especially when it might be needless!"

"Needless?" Herleif sounded irritated now. "Do you think I do anything without careful thought, Adrienne? I am not a fool —I have only ever sacrificed what I must for the sake of my duty and those I love." He ran a massive hand down his hidden face. "Adrienne, please, let us say no more of this."

Adrienne hesitated, unsatisfied. He might consider it necessary to sacrifice his life, but she wasn't convinced. From what her mother said, it sounded like there may well be another way. Like the force left in the curse might be within the level Frossenland could handle, especially considering how much more plentiful both singers and magic were in the southern part of the kingdom.

She was tempted to blurt out everything her mother had

told her, and demand to know if the details of the curse were as the elf had claimed. But she was afraid to show Herleif how much she knew. If he suspected she was considering looking at his face, he would surely take steps to make it impossible. If he found out about the candle, for example, she had no doubt he'd take it away. And she didn't want to relinquish the power of making the choice. Swallowing all her questions and fears, and trying to ignore the guilt burning inside her at her secret, she turned toward the castle.

"Very well."

To describe the mood of their little household that evening as tense would be generous. Herleif informed her that he'd caught food for the evening meal, but Adrienne's appetite had fled. She told him as much, and he made no protest when she retired to bed early. Sleep was a long way away, but she feigned it quickly, not wishing to keep Herleif from his own rest.

She lay awake for a long time after he slipped into the far side of the huge bed, wrestling with herself. She knew what he wished her to do—or rather not do—and in principle she had no desire to go against his wishes. It wasn't just that she wanted him to trust her...she wanted to actually *be* trustworthy.

But much as she would trust Herleif with her life, she wasn't sure she could trust him with his own. He would never act unselfishly, and she would never be able to convince him that it wasn't his duty to take the whole force of the curse on himself.

The candle her mother had given her was heavy in her pocket, assuming a significance out of alignment with the ordinary, everyday object. It was no longer just a candle. It represented a decision—one she felt ill-prepared to make, knowing how completely it could change everything. She'd sworn to Herleif that she wouldn't try to see his face when he was sleeping. Months had passed since then, and their relationship had changed so much, but he'd never released her from that promise. Did her word mean so little to her, that she was considering breaking it? But she couldn't just let him die in some misguided attempt to protect his kingdom!

But then again, what if she was wrong about the curse? What if it was still potent enough to wreak havoc on the kingdom? She didn't know the true nature of it, but the fear that others might lose their lives on account of her saving Herleif's stayed her hand as the hours of darkness slipped by. How could she find out for certain? It seemed likely that no one but Herleif could tell her the truth of the curse, and he'd made it very clear that he wasn't going to do so.

Adrienne sat up, disturbing the covers as little as possible as she inched toward her husband's sleeping form. As she got closer, the mattress sloped, responding to the sheer bulk of him. Looking at his size just increased Adrienne's frustration. He was so strong, so capable. Surely it was worth at least fighting. Surely if the weakened curse was released on Frossenland, the combined might of the crown and the kingdom's singers could fight it off.

How different it had been only one night before. Adrienne could hardly remember the distance she'd been putting between herself and her husband, or the reason for it. None of that mattered now, not with his life in potentially imminent danger.

Herleif's strange manner when they'd parted at the edge of the forest that morning suddenly sprang to Adrienne's mind. He'd nuzzled her hand so wistfully, and his eyes had seemed too sad for the single day's separation, especially since they hadn't been spending the days together for weeks, anyway. The thought had crossed her mind that he was acting like the goodbye was final. Or, perhaps, like it was a foreshadowing of another, more permanent goodbye.

That thought decided her. It was hard to tell the time, but

for all she knew, the sun might be about to rise. She might be about to lose her opportunity, and she was done hesitating. It was time to take a more active role in her own marriage.

Holding her breath, Adrienne drew the candle from her pocket. The light in the room was so dim, she could barely make out its shape in her hand. She had no flint, but after months of practice with the kitchen fire, she didn't need one. Keeping her voice soft so as not to wake Herleif, she began to sing. The weakness of the flame that winked into existence on the wick of the candle matched the tiny flicker of power that responded to Adrienne's song. But it was enough. The wick caught, and the flame became stable. Leaning right over Herleif, Adrienne slipped a hand under his hood, drawing it back with a pounding heart.

In the flickering light of the candle, Herleif's face was finally revealed.

Adrienne's breath caught in her throat as her eyes moved hungrily over his features. It was strange to see someone for the first time, and yet to already know that they were as dear to you as your own self, their every feature perfect in your eyes. There was the strong nose she'd felt in the darkness a couple of short months before, the uncompromising, somewhat square jaw.

He was incredibly handsome to her. Whether she would have thought so when they first met was impossible to tell. When she looked at him now, all she could see was Herleif, and that made his face incredibly precious. His was a rugged kind of charm, more suggestive of raw strength than sensitivity, but no less appealing as far as she was concerned.

Adrienne was so lost in the wonder of finally seeing the face she'd spent so much time imagining, she momentarily lost sight of the real purpose of her actions. She forgot to wonder whether she'd just saved his life, and what she might have unleashed in the process. All she could think about was Herleif.

He stirred, his forehead creasing as if in pain. Adrienne

smoothed it with her finger, her heart pounding as she waited for him to wake and see what she'd done. But he didn't. His eyes remained closed as his hand reached out blindly in the candle-light, a grunt escaping him. She took the hand in hers, and Herleif squeezed, momentarily stilling. Impulsively, Adrienne leaned down and pressed a kiss to his cheek.

Herleif went utterly still for a moment, then his head turned, and before Adrienne well knew what was happening, months of hopeless wishing finally became reality as her husband's lips found hers.

CHAPTER TWENTY

Herleif

Herleif could barely keep up with his dream this time, its change from joy to pain and back again so rapid. It felt different from his usual visions—how did he know he was dreaming while still in the dream, for example? He was sure that Adrienne had been holding his hand a moment before, but he'd lost all connection with the sensation in the unimaginable pain that had suddenly assailed him.

And now he was kissing her, as he had in so many dreams before, and the pain was completely gone.

No reason to fight it, he supposed. He would wake soon enough—he may as well enjoy her nearness while he could.

But as he leaned into her, the light began to change, something like fire dancing before his confused gaze.

Herleif's eyes flew open, and he let out a cry of horror as he realized that it was no phantom, but the real Adrienne pressed against him. It took less than a moment for him to take in the significance of the candle in her hand, and her position as she knelt on their bed. It was exactly the scene he'd feared for months after they first married.

"Adrienne!" he groaned. "What have you done?"

Adrienne's eyes were wide and fearful, and Herleif immediately regretted his words. None of this was truly her fault, as he knew better than anyone.

"I'm sorry," he said quickly. "I don't blame you. But we were so close, and—" His words broke off as he realized that her expression was only growing more terrified. Fear tore at his own heart. "Adrienne?"

She drew in a rattling breath, and he realized it was the first he'd heard her take since opening his eyes.

"Her-leif."

Her gasp was barely audible, and panic flared to life inside Herleif. His arms shot out automatically as Adrienne toppled sideways, reflex causing him to grab the lit candle from her hand and deposit it in a cup on the chest beside his bed. With his other hand, he caught Adrienne and laid her gently on the covers. Grograna hadn't exaggerated her power. The curse was taking Adrienne, just as she'd promised it would.

"NO!" Herleif cried, his own total lack of pain the most terrifying and agonizing feature of the whole situation. "No, I won't let this happen!"

But how to stop it? There was only one way, and he knew exactly what needed to be done. Without a moment's hesitation, he leaped down from the bed and tore across the room. Bursting into the adjoining study, he threw himself at a locked writing desk.

He vaguely remembered storing the key somewhere secure, but he didn't try to conjure up the location. He fell on the desk, ripping at the wood with his bare hands as images from the past streamed through his mind, as vivid as if it had been yesterday, instead of almost six years earlier.

· · ·

Herleif turned from Iver's dying whisper, a feral snarl escaping his bear's snout as he faced the murderous giant queen.

"Fool," growled the giant, her eyes on Iver's unmoving form. "He gave his life for nothing."

The irritation in her voice told Herleif that she wasn't as disdainful of Iver's magic as her dismissive words suggested. Iver had said not only that he'd softened the curse on Herleif, but also that Herleif's own determination could counteract it, and Herleif could see from Grograna's reaction that there must have been truth in those claims.

"I feel how he's attacked my curse," the giant said irately, "but his intervention is pathetically weak, like the magic in your parched land. He hasn't thrown it off. You may regain your human form temporarily, but the power of my curse will return again and again— you will never fully be free of the bear until you yield to my wishes."

NEVER. Herleif couldn't speak the word, but Grograna seemed to understand from his furious roar. She narrowed her eyes.

"Do you think you can defy me?" she growled. "If you won't yield, I'll simply kill you." She gestured to the lifeless body of Herleif's father. "You've seen how easy it would be."

Responding to some new instinct, Herleif braced himself in a defensive position, his hackles rising as a low snarl emerged from his unfamiliar throat. Let her try.

Grograna's eyes narrowed in anger—clearly she was annoyed that he wasn't cowering in fear before her threats, choosing to give in rather than face death. Did she truly think him such a coward?

"I feel your blasted determination resisting my magic," she muttered. "Curse the latent power in royal blood."

Herleif didn't know what she meant by that, but he had no time to consider it. Her temper—which seemed fragile—was giving way once again.

"That man spoke nonsense," she hissed. "He thinks you can outlast me?" She gave a laugh that was far from sane. "The transformation may be neither complete nor permanent, but there's plenty of power left in the magic I've coated you with. It will last twenty years at least. Can you hold on that long, little king?"

Again Herleif let out a low, wordless growl.

The giant's lips curled in a sneer. "Let me help make the choice easier for you." Ominously, she drew another object from the folds of her dress. "You claim you won't marry my daughter even if another human never even looks at your face again? Let's put that to the test."

She crushed the object in her hand, and another wave of hot pain washed over Herleif. She was unleashing more magic on him, and he was powerless to stop her. How did she have so much at her disposal?

"How often you will be human in form, I do not know," Grograna said maliciously. "But the magic will be with you every second that you are. Your own words will snare you—if anyone sees your human face, even for a moment, the magic will be unleashed on you. If you tell a soul a single detail of your curse, the magic will claim you." Her smile grew even more sinister. "Oh, I forgot to tell you what the magic will do, didn't I? It will kill you...slowly and painfully. The only way to halt its progress will be to yield." She cackled. "What do you think of that, little king? I will break your spirit like I broke your father's weak human body. You think you're strong enough to resist me? You will yield before a year is out. I know how needy humans are. The loneliness will drive you mad."

Herleif's growl was long and low. His posture communicated his defiance, and again it provoked the giant's ire.

"Why hold on to your determination?" she spat. "Do you want twenty years of loneliness and misery?" Her eyes narrowed. "You still think marrying my daughter would be worse? You're still so determined to marry a human girl? Go ahead. A wife who can't even see your face? To whom you can't tell a single detail of your curse? What kind of a marriage would that be?"

Her eyes narrowed as she looked Herleif's bear form over.

"I feel your determination burning fiery hot," she said through *clenched teeth. Her voice dropped to a mutter. "Your obsession with marrying a human could ruin everything. Fine, little king," she said, just as if Herleif understood the supposed power his determination carried, just as if he was arguing back instead of paralyzed in pain. "If you marry, the curse won't last as long, your resistance has won you that much."*

She rattled the broken shards of talisman in her hand, and the pain assaulting Herleif peaked. "But there's some life left in this other curse to counteract your defenses. I will make sure your marriage does nothing but increase your loneliness. The moment a wife binds herself to you, she'll fall under your curse. If you can lie beside her every single night without ever sharing so much as a kiss, you will both be free. But if you fail—if you tell her about your curse, if you let her see your face, if you give in to your need for her—as you will—the curse will fall on her. She will be the one to die if you don't yield."

Her lips curled into a feral smile. "So what will it be, little king? Do you think you can last twenty years alone? Or one year in the coldest marriage imaginable? I think you can't manage either. I know humans—they're weak and needy, dependent on each other to soothe their turbulent emotions. One way or another, you will yield, and I will see my daughter as queen of your little human kingdom."

Herleif's thoughts were pulled back to the present as the desk gave way with a splintering crunch. There was the circlet, still wrapped in linen. Hateful as the talisman had always been, the sight of it flooded him with relief. Grasping hold of the whole bundle, he catapulted himself back to Adrienne's side.

She was drawing slow, rasping breaths, her eyes staring unseeingly at the canopy above her head as whimpers of pain escaped her lips. Lips that a mere minute ago had been pressed to Herleif's, making him feel truly alive for the first time...and in the same moment, bringing his world to a violent end.

"Adrienne," Herleif cried, anguish rocking him at these signs of her suffering.

Grograna's words echoed horribly in his mind. *It will kill you...slowly and painfully.* And now that death had been unleashed on Adrienne. But Grograna's next words were just as clear. *The only way to halt its progress will be to yield.* It wasn't too late.

"Adrienne, I'm so sorry," he choked out, pulling her into his arms. Her petite form fit so comfortably, nestled fully against him as his arms encircled her. Indomitable as her spirit might be, physically she was so fragile. And never more so than this moment. "I never meant for you to suffer because of me," he said, a dry sob escaping him. "I wish I could explain, but I have to go—there's no time."

In spite of her evident pain, Adrienne struggled up, a noise of protest escaping her lips. Her normally pale face was so devoid of color she looked half-dead already. The sight was terrifying.

"There's no other way, Adrienne," Herleif said, lifting the linen from the circlet. "You were right about the curse—it was a giant. It was their queen, and she's determined that I marry her daughter."

"Herleif, no!" Adrienne's eyes were wide, her voice garbled and her limbs shaking. She reached out and seized the still-lit candle, the better to search Herleif's face as her eyes pleaded with him.

Herleif laid a hand against Adrienne's face. His palm encased her cheek completely. He knew he had to hurry, but he could hardly bear to say goodbye, knowing it was their last moment together.

"If I don't go, you'll die," he told her, his voice unsteady. "And I can't let that happen."

"Don't go," Adrienne begged in a painful whisper, her breath coming in ragged gasps as her hand rose feebly to rest over his. "There must be another way." Something flickered in her eyes. "I've been studying healing magic, remember? I'll sing."

A look of great determination came over her pale, pinched face, and she began to sing a wordless melody. Herleif could tell she was putting everything she had into it, but even if magic hadn't been so scarce, he could tell it would be no good. How could she sing when she could barely breathe?

"Adrienne," Herleif said, clutching her to him. The impassioned movement brought her fully against his chest, causing the candle in her hand to drip wax onto his tunic. "I just want you to know that whatever the giant queen makes me do, whatever she inflicts on Frossenland, *you* will always be my queen." He drew a shaking breath, but his voice came out steady. "I love you."

Tears poured down Adrienne's cheeks, hot and fast. "Herleif, no," she croaked out, her eyes raised to his, their expression wild. "You can't give in. You can't...go to...her. You promised you'd never...abandon me."

"I'm sorry, my love," Herleif whispered. In a sudden rush of realization, he remembered that nothing he did mattered, now the curse had already been activated. His arms tightened around Adrienne, crushing her against him as he pressed a fierce kiss to her trembling lips. The hand not holding the candle pressed against his chest, tremors rocking her as Grograna's curse ate away at her life.

Enough, Herleif told himself. She shouldn't suffer another moment's pain on his account.

Wrenching himself away, he ripped the linen fully clear and grasped hold of his golden circlet.

CHAPTER TWENTY-ONE

Adrienne

"No!" Adrienne cried, reaching for Herleif.

But it was too late. The moment his hand closed over the circlet, a violent wind swept into the bedroom. It shattered the windows and blew the door from its hinges. Adrienne was pushed flat against the bed, curling her body inward to try to protect her face from the gale battering against her.

The crippling pain of a moment before was instantly gone, but Adrienne felt no relief. Instead terror gripped her, as sharp as the icy chill pouring in through the windows. Her senses were saturated with the magic carried on the wind. It filled the room in its potency, but its path was targeted and specific.

Adrienne forced her eyes back open, watching in horror as the magic-laden wind surrounded Herleif and lifted him bodily from his feet.

"Herleif!" she screamed. Fighting the wind, she surged from the bed and stretched her arm out toward him. His eyes found hers, emotions too deep for words flitting across that unfamiliar and yet intimately beloved face.

Herleif's hand reached for hers in instinctive response, but they couldn't bridge the distance quickly enough. The wind swept between them, sending Adrienne tumbling back onto the bed as Herleif was blown straight through the jagged hole where the window had been.

The wind died immediately, and Adrienne flung herself from the bed and across the room. The sky was still dark, dawn not yet upon them. In the moonlight, Adrienne could see the dark blood on the edges of broken glass. The wind hadn't been gentle with Herleif as it threw him out of the opening.

"Herleif," Adrienne moaned, sinking to her knees and covering her face with her hands. She borrowed her husband's words to her a short time before. "What have I done?"

She'd broken her word, that's what she'd done. She'd trusted the second-hand gossip of a stranger instead of her own husband, and done precisely what she knew he didn't want her to do. Whatever happened next, to Herleif and to Frossenland, would be her fault. The fact that Herleif had immediately tried to take back his accusation didn't make her feel better. On the contrary, the reminder of his generous heart made her own unfaithful conduct all the worse.

His face swam before her vision as she knelt in a pool of her own misery. She'd so longed to see that face, and now the image of it fixed in her mind wore a look of horror and reproach. How much magic had been in that wind? It had swept him up like a rag doll, instead of the enormous human he was. She'd thought him so strong, so unbreakable, and yet he hadn't even tried to fight the wind. He must have known it would be pointless. She remembered thinking, when she first slept beside him, that he was strong enough to defend her against any threat. How foolish she'd been. In the end, the threat he couldn't defend either of them against was herself.

What had she done?

Whatever the giant queen makes me do, whatever she inflicts on Frossenland, you will always be my queen.

Herleif's words seared her memory, causing her breath to come in shallow, grating gasps. The words that had come next were almost too exquisitely painful to remember.

I love you.

He'd told her he loved her. He'd kissed her with a fierce passion that had taken her breath away, even in the midst of the agonizing pain she'd been suffering. And she hadn't even replied, hadn't even told him how completely he held her own heart.

No. She couldn't think about that now. She couldn't afford to dwell on the feel of his arms around her, or the throaty tenderness in his voice when he called her *my love*. It wasn't time for moping, it was time for action.

Adrienne rose to her feet, shivering in the ordinary gust that came through the broken window as she cast her gaze across the moonlit room. A glint of gold caught her eye from among the wreckage the magical wind had made, and she stumbled forward eagerly. The circlet! It must have been blown from the bed. Herleif had only needed to touch it to be swept up and away—could she follow him if she did the same?

But when Adrienne grasped hold of the intricate golden band, nothing happened. The metal was cold against her skin, unfeeling and unresponsive. Nothing like the man who'd once worn it, in an old life in which she'd played no part. She realized that it no longer held any trace of magic. Whatever enchantment had been in the talisman had been used up. It had served its purpose.

Her eyes traveled over the bed, rumpled and empty, to the doorway on its far side. This door led into an adjoining suite and, like the one leading to the corridor, it had been ripped from its hinges. Adrienne couldn't make much out in the darkness, but she was surprised that the damage seemed to have extended even into that other room. She needed light to see for sure.

"Where's that candle?" she muttered.

At once, awareness flared inside her, and in confusion, she followed the direction her mind was prompting and saw the candle lying amongst the covers, thankfully extinguished. How had she known exactly where it was? Without quite knowing why she did it, she held out her hand, mutely seeking the source of light. To her astonishment, the candle rose in the air, soaring neatly into her outstretched fingers.

Adrienne stared down at it. What was that? She'd never made something move without touching it before. And she hadn't even sung. She cast her mind back over those frenzied moments before Herleif had touched the circlet, and drew in a sharp breath as understanding hit. It was all a blur of pain and terror, but she remembered trying to use magic to heal herself of whatever was crushing her heart in her chest.

No wonder it hadn't worked, she thought bitterly. As both wife and singer she'd been utterly useless. In her confusion and panic, she'd mixed up the two types of magic she'd been so clumsily trying to study in the castle's library. Instead of a healing song, she'd released one that attempted to put power into an object, allowing the singer to manipulate the object later, even without magic. Apparently it had worked. Although she hadn't consciously intended to put the magic into the candle, she seemed to have done so, since she could now make it move without touching it and without using new magic.

A lot of good that did her.

Holding the candle before her eyes, Adrienne raised her voice in a feeble song. Barely a trickle of magic responded from the barren earth below, but it was enough. A tiny flame flickered into life on the wick, and Adrienne carried the light into the adjoining suite.

It was a study, into which she'd wandered many times. The only item of furniture that seemed to have been affected by the recent crisis was the writing desk. Adrienne held the candle close, frowning as she tried to make sense of the damage. It didn't look like the result of wind. It looked like it had been ripped apart by a wild animal. Dimly, she remembered Herleif leaving her side when the pain took her, and sprinting away with panicked urgency. Was this where he'd gone? The circlet must have been inside the desk.

Adrienne had half turned away when a piece of parchment caught her eye. It was now exposed to the air, which meant it must have been in the locked section of the desk. What document had been precious enough to Herleif to secure it away?

With trembling fingers, she raised the crumpled parchment into the candlelight. Tears pricked at her eyes as she recognized her name, in her own hand. This was their certificate of marriage, pulled from the drunken notary's pocket and shoved into Herleif's hand in that tavern. She could see the man's seal, the wax smeared untidily across the surface. And the notary's own entry was barely legible.

Hardly knowing whether her heart could take it, Adrienne let her gaze travel up the paper, to where Herleif had written his own name. Her eyes widened. She'd expected to see the name Herleif rather than Bjørn—she remembered her surprise during the hasty ceremony when he'd given a name different from the one her father had used. But what she hadn't anticipated was his full title.

She stared at the seven names, most of them unfamiliar. Herleif was the first one, and Bjørn was the fifth. He'd obviously used one of his names, if not his primary one. The name of the royal family's house appeared at the end, and the names themselves were followed by Herleif's official titles. In addition to *Crown Prince, uncrowned heir apparent*, he was the duke of two provinces. It was an overwhelming sight, but that wasn't what made Adrienne's breath catch.

She remembered the tawdry scene in the tavern. It was far from the wedding a future king should have. And she knew now that Herleif had acted not on his own inclination, but out of a selfless desire to shield her from harm. They'd been total strangers, and he'd had reason not to wish for exposure. He took a great risk, trusting that the notary wouldn't pore over the records once sober. It would have been so easy for him to give a fake name—no one could have called him out on the deception. But he'd still provided his full name and title on their certificate of marriage. Even knowing their union would bring him only cost and no benefit, he'd left himself no loopholes to try to wriggle out of his responsibility to her when he reclaimed his position.

Her husband was the most honorable man in Frossenland. In Providore.

And she'd betrayed his trust, unleashing magic on him that forced him to leave her, and doomed him to be tied to a giant princess whom he didn't want.

Defiance burned within Adrienne, sudden and fierce. No. *She* was Herleif's wife. He'd already pledged himself to her. And from what he'd said before the wind took him, she held his heart as well. She wasn't going to surrender him to the giants without a fight.

She folded the document carefully, stashing it in a pocket of her dress. She grabbed the circlet as well, and pulled on the cloak Herleif had bought her immediately after their wedding. Not pausing for anything else, she ran out into the gathering dawn.

Her eyes were drawn across the clearing as she ran. Even in

the dim light, she could see the trail of devastation left by the wind that had swept Herleif away. Fully grown pine trees, some taller than the castle, had been flattened, roots ripped from the earth, and stone debris littered the grass where chunks of the castle wall had been torn apart.

With a shudder, Adrienne turned away, blundering blindly through the forest. By the time she emerged into the abandoned city of Tove, the sun had fully risen. The journey seemed interminable, but she didn't stop to rest even once. It was only after she finally banged on her mother's door, and it swung open to reveal Felman's astonished form, that she collapsed in an exhausted heap.

"Adrienne!" Felman cried, catching her as she fell. "What's happened?" His face darkened. "He's mistreated you. I knew it. I knew we should have—"

"No!" Adrienne cried, energy returning to her at this injustice. "Herleif has never mistreated me. None of this is his fault!"

"Herleif?" Felman looked bewildered as he helped her over the threshold and into a chair. "Who in Frossenland is Herleif?"

"My husband," Adrienne said. "His name isn't really Bjørn, it's Herleif. He's the crown prince—the king, by rights. And he's been taken by the giants, and it's all my fault!"

"Whoa, whoa, whoa," Felman raised a hand to try to stem this flow, his eyes wide and confused.

"What's going on?" Adrienne's mother hurried in from the yard, her forehead creased with concern at the sight of her youngest daughter collapsed in a chair.

"We were wrong, Mamma," Adrienne said, tears pricking at her eyes. "Seeing his face didn't free him. It unleashed the curse on him. I don't understand exactly what happened, but I know I've made a terrible mistake."

Her mother sank into a chair herself, her hand flying to her mouth in horror. "I'm so sorry, Adrienne," she whispered.

Adrienne shook her head fiercely. "It's not your fault. This was my decision, and I'm the one who should have known to trust him."

"Adrienne?" Kettil joined the group, almost breaking the eggs he held in his haste to deposit them on the table. "You're back so soon! What happened?"

"It's too much to explain it all," Adrienne said helplessly. "Mamma knows some of it already. Herleif is the prince, and he's the bear. I don't know how it all happened, but a giant cursed him. The huge white bear didn't kill the king and those other men—the giant did. And turned Herleif into a bear by day and a man by night. And I wasn't supposed to look at his face, but I did, and now he's been spirited away by a magical wind, and I think it's taken him to Kjemper."

Her brothers were both staring at her open-mouthed by the end of this rushed speech.

"What in the kingdom are you talking about?" Felman demanded.

Adrienne made an impatient gesture. "I told you it was too much to explain." She turned to her mother. "Mamma, I have to go after him. The giant queen is going to force him to marry her daughter, and I can't let that happen. For the sake of Frossenland as well as my own. We can't have a giant as queen!"

"Are you saying that technically *you're* queen?" Felman demanded. He exchanged a look with his brother. "Adrienne, I think this Bjørn is playing on your gullibility."

"He's not," Adrienne assured him, not blaming her brother for his skepticism. "We've been living in the abandoned castle all this time, Felman, and I've seen him transform from bear to man and back again with my own eyes. But there's no time to get into all that. I have to go to Kjemper."

"You can't go into the giants' land," said Felman firmly. "Even if you could get over Battlement Wall—which you can't—it's much too dangerous!"

Adrienne met his eyes unflinchingly. "I have to find a way. I'm his wife—I'm the only one with the right to challenge the marriage he's about to be forced into. I won't abandon him." Her voice turned fierce. "I won't surrender him."

"What can we do to help?" Kettil asked.

Adrienne looked up at him, the calm question surprising her.

He shrugged. "I don't really understand what's going on, but it's clear you need our help, and that's what family is for. I don't need all the answers."

"Thank you, Kettil," said Adrienne, her throat tight. "I won't ask any of you to come into Kjemper with me. But there's something else that needs to happen."

"Enough of this nonsense about going into Kjemper," frowned Felman. "That's not an option."

Adrienne ignored him, her eyes still on the younger of her brothers. "Someone needs to inform the queen regent and Princess Runa that their son and brother is alive. And has been taken by the giants." She bit her lip. "I don't fully understand why Herleif kept his survival a secret from his family. I have no doubt he had his reasons, but I'm fairly certain everything's changed now. Whatever magic kept him silent seems to have lifted, because he told me about the giants. I think he would have explained everything if there was time. But there wasn't."

"You want me to go to Sunniva and tell the queen that her son is still alive?" Kettil asked doubtfully. "There's no way she'd believe me. There's no way I'd even get an audience."

"This might help," said Adrienne, pulling the circlet from the pocket of her cloak. "Surely it will be enough to at least get you before the queen." She tried to sound more confident than she felt. She knew nothing of castles and royals and how these things worked. Her own castle, her own royal, had been an altogether different experience.

Everyone stared at the crown, jarringly out of place on the simple scrubbed wooden table. The gold was skillfully wrought to look like a thin branch curving around on itself, the hint of leaves appearing at the point the two ends met and crossed over. It was a beautiful item, more costly than anything any of them had seen before. Adrienne could see in Felman's eyes that he was starting to wonder for the first time whether her story could be true.

"That's a good plan," her mother said firmly. "Felman, Kettil, you'll both go. It will be safer to travel together than alone. And we have enough to cover the journey for you both."

"I'm sorry for the trouble I've brought on you," said Adrienne remorsefully, at this mention of the coins it would cost for her brothers to undertake her errand.

"Nonsense." Her mother's voice was brisk. "Without your husband's intervention, we wouldn't have any of the excess we have."

"But what are you going to do?" Felman demanded. He narrowed his eyes. "You don't really think you can get into Kjemper, do you, Adrienne?"

"Never mind what we'll do, get on with your own task," his mother told him.

She chivvied her sons toward their shared room, organizing them in impressive form. Within a quarter of an hour, they were out the door, the circlet wrapped in linen and tucked carefully in Kettil's rucksack as they went to secure transport.

"Now." Adrienne's mother turned to her. "How will we get into Kjemper? Do you have a plan?"

Adrienne shook her head firmly. "You're not coming, Mamma. There's no way I'd let you take that risk."

"I did this, Adrienne," her mother said firmly. "I told you

what that elf said, and I gave you the candle. It was probably a trap all along, and I played right into it."

"I already told you, Mamma," said Adrienne gently. "It was my decision, and I bear the full responsibility for it. You didn't make me do anything." She drew a breath. "If you want to help me, then help me figure out how to get over Battlement Wall."

Her mother shook her head slowly. "It's supposed to be impassable—from both sides, although that can't be true if a giant managed to get across to curse the prince." She frowned. "I don't think you're going to be able to cross it without magic, Adrienne."

"But I don't have access to that kind of magic," Adrienne said desperately. "Even if I had the training, there's barely anything in the ground here. And there's no time for me to go south to find more and figure out how to harness it. If I do that, I'll surely get there too late or never! They could be trying to marry Herleif off today for all I know!" She frowned as she thought it over. "We have to get magic from somewhere nearby."

"What are you suggesting, Adrienne?" Her mother's voice was wary as she studied Adrienne's face.

Adrienne shifted to fully face her. "The elf who gave you the message. He can't be too far away. And he might have a whole store of mined magic available."

Her mother's brow was creased in a scowl. "No. He's not an option for assistance. At best, he was completely wrong. At worst—and more likely—he was setting a trap for you. In which case, he'd probably welcome the opportunity to do you an injury."

"It's a risk I have to take," said Adrienne, standing. "There simply isn't enough magic in the ground. And elves are too scarce up here to go hunting for others who might be more friendly. I have to at least try."

Her mother stood as well, biting her lip as she thought it over. "I don't like it."

"I know," said Adrienne. "Neither do I, honestly. But I have no other ideas. Do you know where I might find this elf?"

Her mother shook her head. "I don't, but I know someone who might. He got directions in town for where to find us. The shopkeeper sent him here. He might have more information."

Adrienne was halfway to the door when her mother's voice stopped her.

"Wait a minute." The older woman hurried into her room, and Adrienne could see her through the doorway, rifling through her things. When she returned, she was clutching a small golden item, which she held out to Adrienne.

Adrienne took it, staring at the decorative apple in confusion. "What's this? I know times are better than they were, but I wouldn't have guessed you were into expensive decorations now, Mamma."

Her mother snorted. "Hardly. I wasn't intending to keep it. I sold a few piglets from the sow's litter at the last market, and this was part of the payment. I believe it's real gold. I was going to trade it next time I need something substantial, but it occurs to me that the shopkeeper might want payment for any information he has."

"Thank you, Mamma," Adrienne said, her hand closing over the gold. It was cold and solid in her fist. She pulled her cloak around her as she turned again toward the door. "Let's go."

CHAPTER TWENTY-TWO

Herleif

P ain rippled across Herleif's senses, but the progress of
the wind was too violent for him to take proper stock of
whatever injuries were causing it. It wasn't the crushing
agony of the triggered curse returning, that much he knew.
Probably just the effects of being thrown bodily from the
window.

The wind—undeniably magical in nature—carried him up
into the air, the height terrifying in itself. In the darkness, he
could see very little below him, but he knew he'd left the castle
far behind. There was nothing natural about the way the wind
carried him, supporting him like a solid force as it sent him
catapulting northward.

He'd lasted almost six years, but the disaster he'd fought so
hard to avoid had finally befallen him. It was over. And yet,
grave as his situation was, he couldn't seem to focus on what was
coming. All his thoughts were consumed by what he'd left
behind.

Adrienne.

Adrienne in his arms, Adrienne suffering from his curse.

Adrienne pressing her lips to his, waking him with a kiss they should never have shared but which not all of him regretted.

The look in Adrienne's eyes when he'd told her he loved her.

Why hadn't he told her months ago? There was so much he hadn't been allowed to say, but expressing what he felt had never been barred to him. He'd just been too cowardly—he'd never learned the art of baring his heart to a woman. Of course, his guilt over the sham of a marriage he'd trapped her into hadn't helped him to find his words.

And now there was no time left to spend together. How would he bear the separation? Memories of Adrienne, of the feel of her lips on his, would be all that would sustain him in whatever horrors lay ahead.

He continued to climb in height, and it soon became clear why. He was moving at such a speed that it couldn't have been more than fifteen minutes before Battlement Wall loomed into view ahead of him. Dawn wasn't far off now, and in the gray light he could see the enormous stone barrier. It truly was an impressive feat of his ancestors, one for which he had no explanation. The wall stretched upward to many times the height of a normal human wall, and even with his increased altitude, the wind still had to pull him up further in order to clear it.

As he rose in the air, Herleif cast a glance behind him. Dawn was lighting the eastern horizon, and he could see the continent of Providore stretched out behind him. Away to the east, across the channel, he even thought he could catch a glimpse of the Reviled Lands.

Then he crossed the wall, and his eyes turned forward. Kjemper was below him, sinister and barren in the low light. A frozen wasteland, with jagged mountains of ice and vast empty plains.

Herleif frowned. That's what he had expected, at any rate, but there was more to the vista below him. He squinted as he tried to make sense of the huge structures he could see dotting the flat expanse below. He even thought he could see movement, perhaps figures scurrying around the structures, and hear the faint sounds of industry. But it was too dark and too far below him to make out anything for certain. And the next moment the wind had roared into fresh life, throwing him forward without mercy as he continued to travel northward.

As the light grew gradually, he realized that he was heading straight for a city. A huge building rose up in the center of it, hewn stone glinting with ice. It must be the capital of Kjemper, where the castle of the giant monarchs stood. As far as Herleif knew, no human had seen it in living memory. Probably much longer. And yet, he felt no great interest. Everything was blank emptiness ahead, without Adrienne's presence to bring hope to his days.

Dawn was breaking over the eastern cliffs when the wind began to decline. They hadn't gone far north. The wall was visible to the south, just at the edge of what the eye could see.

Whoever was controlling the wind did so clumsily, or perhaps Herleif's sudden, terrifying drops were intentional, aimed at making him feel helpless and afraid. Each time the wind rose again to cushion him, barely giving him time to catch his breath before he was again sent plummeting.

In this haphazard way, he reached the ground, dropped for the last time from about a half dozen feet above a courtyard of rough, dark stone. He fell hard, not quite managing to get his feet under him before he hit the ground. Pushing quickly up to a standing position, he steeled himself to face whatever was waiting.

Framed by the light of the rising sun, perched atop the steps up into the huge stone castle, stood Queen Grograna. Her golden crown glinted in her dark hair, and her expression was unbearably smug.

"I see you have yielded, little king," she said derisively. "It took longer than I thought, but not so long after all. So much for all your determination."

Herleif just glared at her. His father's murderer wasn't worthy of the dignity of a response.

"Nothing to say for yourself?" She raised one eyebrow, her yellow eyes especially unnerving against her gray skin. "Very well. There will be time enough for speech."

She clicked her massive fingers, and at once a line of six guards emerged from the castle doors. They split into two groups of three, moving around Herleif to cover each side. The numbers were overkill, given the sheer size of them. Herleif was honest enough to acknowledge to himself that any one of them could beat him alone in terms of raw strength.

He didn't resist as two of them seized him by the arms, dragging him toward the steps where Grograna waited. It was no time for foolish aggression. With clever blade-work he might be able to take down two or three giants. But he could hardly take on all of Kjemper.

Grograna turned and walked into the castle with a step too heavy for grace, the guards dragging Herleif in her wake. When they entered the building, Herleif found himself squinting, dazzled by the gold that glinted at him from all sides. Every furnishing, every tapestry...everything was gold. Iver hadn't exaggerated with his warning all those years ago. What had he said?

Giants are drawn to three things—magic, gold, and crowns.

He'd been more right than Herleif could possibly have imagined.

Herleif had no doubt that the furnishings pilfered from his own castle could be found somewhere within Grograna's, but he didn't care about that. He had no interest in where the giants had sourced so much gold. What did confuse and concern him was the evidence of magic all around him. He couldn't sense it like a singer would, but there were signs even he could spot. Like the way the doors opened to let Grograna into the throne room, without a guard or servant so much as laying a hand on them.

But Providore's northern lands were barren and frozen, with barely any magic to be found. From what he'd seen when he flew over Kjemper, the giants' land was no exception—if anything, it was even more of a wasteland than the part of Frossenland situated just south of the wall.

Besides which, there were no singers among giants. Everyone knew that. They had no way to channel magic, and they didn't know how to mine it like the elves did. That practice was exclusive to the diminutive creatures, and elves reviled giants even more than humans did.

So where had all the magic come from?

Herleif had no leisure to consider these mysteries. The two giants who gripped him dragged him the length of the throne room—the dark stone walls so high he couldn't see the ceiling without craning his neck—and threw him roughly forward. Once again he found himself on his knees, and once again he struggled up. He didn't attain his feet this time, however. One of the guards gripped the back of his neck, forcing him back down like a disobedient dog.

"Well, well, well."

Grograna's tone was indulgent, and Herleif's anger simmered as he raised his face to see her standing in state in front of the enormous throne. It looked like it was made of ice, but that couldn't be so. Glass, perhaps. He had to admit it was impressive. So far Kjemper was certainly not as primitive as he'd expected.

"So it seems you found yourself a wife in spite of all odds," she said, one thick eyebrow raised. "You are smarter than you look, it seems. Or rather, wilier than I expect from a human."

She descended the steps dramatically, the thud of her enormous feet shaking the stone floor.

"It seems time was shorter than I realized. Only a few months from being free, weren't you?"

Herleif said nothing, but inside he was uneasy. He didn't like this evidence of how well-informed Grograna was concerning his marriage.

"You're fortunate I didn't come and kill you outright when the rumors reached me of the giant white bear on the loose with a human girl riding on his back. I won't deny I lost my temper." Her angry expression twisted into a sneer. "Reports were that the girl is very beautiful, but we all know how meaningless that is. Human concepts of beauty are laughably vile."

There were a few nasty snickers from around the room, and Herleif followed the sound with his eyes, realizing for the first time that they had an audience. The giants were hanging back between the pillars, the gray of their skin blending with the stone. None of them were dressed with the decadence of Grograna, whose gown fell in massive waves of—predictably— golden material.

"My wife," Herleif ground out through clenched teeth, "is more beautiful, more pure of heart, and in every other imaginable way superior to your pathetic daughter, whose mother had to resort to murder and curses to find her a husband."

He had the satisfaction of hearing a collective gasp go around the room, and Grograna's face transformed with fury. She lumbered down the last few steps, abandoning the dignified posture she'd been adopting so far. Her yellow eyes were shooting sparks as she lowered her face close to his, and as she spoke, Herleif was sprayed with her spit.

"You will hold your tongue, or I will rip it out, you sniveling human worm. How dare you speak of a princess of Kjemper like that?" She struck Herleif hard across the face, the force of the blow causing his head to whip violently to the side. His vision spun, and pain blossomed across his cheek. That strike would certainly leave a bruise.

Slowly, he brought his smarting head back around to face Grograna. "I'm not afraid of you," he said steadily.

Grograna's eyes were yellow slits as she searched his face. After a moment, she suddenly grinned, and Herleif shuddered involuntarily. It wasn't just that he was unnerved by her abrupt change in manner. Her teeth were pointed and uneven, and every fighting instinct demanded that he put distance between himself and what were clearly weapons. But he couldn't move, still held down by the enormous guard behind him.

Grograna straightened. "I think you are afraid of me," she said, her coarse voice a purr now. "Or you wouldn't be here. And it's only yourself you insult if you say disparaging things about Princess Mundia. Do you really wish to insult the future queen of your kingdom?"

She turned, beckoning to the shadows to one side of the throne. "Come, Mundia."

With a slow, heavy tread, another giant moved into the light that streamed from high windows down into the center of the throne room. Herleif watched with apprehension as Grograna's daughter walked forward to stand beside her mother. When her form was fully revealed, Herleif's mouth fell open.

Now he understood.

It had made no sense to him that the giant queen would wish for her daughter to marry a human, even a royal one. But one look at Mundia answered that question. She might tower above Herleif, but for a giant, she was tiny. To put it with brutal bluntness, she was a runt.

It wasn't that she was mis-formed—her proportions might

be wrong for a human, but she had the same squarish head and overlong limbs as the other giants. She was just small, somewhere halfway between Herleif's own height and that of her mother. Herleif wasn't sure if no giants would take her due to her size, or if Grograna just didn't want her daughter subject to a husband who would dwarf her. Clearly, she thought that Herleif would provide her daughter with the chance to tower over the man she married. Better to be a queen among humans than a runt among giants.

"Just because I came here doesn't mean I will submit to you," Herleif said steadily. "I will not marry your daughter. I cannot. I am already married."

"You will," said Grograna, her voice dangerous. "Do not think me a fool, little king. You came here willingly, and in doing so, you acknowledged my power over you. You have already yielded, there is no turning back now." She waved a dismissive hand. "As for your paltry human marriage, it means nothing to us. We do not recognize in Kjemper any primitive human ceremonies."

"You might not recognize it, but I do," said Herleif stonily. "I will not be unfaithful to my wife, and no bigamous marriage of mine to your daughter will confer on her the title of Frossenland's queen."

"Be careful what you wish for, little king," Grograna hissed, once again lowering her face to glare at him. "If that is your view, it can swiftly be remedied. I can make you a widower as easily as I made you fatherless."

Grief and fury sizzled through Herleif's bent form as a memory gripped him, the image of Grograna's fist connecting with his father's head as vivid as if it was happening at that moment. It was unendurable that this woman had murdered his father—a king—in cold blood, and faced no consequence whatsoever.

But that wasn't the material point right now. He could do nothing to change the past. But he could protect Adrienne from suffering the same fate. He had to. She was so vulnerable, with no guards, no palace walls to protect her. He doubted she would stay at the abandoned castle alone, and even if she did, the restriction stopping others from entering the area had presumably lifted with the curse.

Hating himself for it, his every muscle straining against the motion, Herleif lowered his head in a gesture of surrender.

"I thought so," said Grograna, unbearably smug. "The wedding will take place in a fortnight."

CHAPTER TWENTY-THREE

Adrienne

Adrienne burst into the shop, her mother at her heels. The walk from their home into town had felt interminable. What was Herleif suffering while she wasted time on practicalities? What were the giants doing to him, or forcing him to do?

The idea of Herleif being bullied into a marriage that might supersede their own gave Adrienne fresh urgency as she stumbled across the room, grabbing the shopkeeper's sleeve.

"The elf!" she demanded. "The one you sent to my mother. Where can we find him?"

"What—?" The shopkeeper turned from where he was placing bottles on a shelf, his gaze bewildered as it passed between Adrienne and her mother. "Estrid? What's going on?"

"Too hard to explain it all," Adrienne's mother said curtly. "But we would be grateful for your assistance. A short while ago an elf came to speak to me about Adrienne. Your wife told me later that it was you who gave him directions as to where he could find me."

The man fidgeted, his expression uneasy. "I meant no harm,

Estrid. The location of your house is common knowledge, surely."

"We're not angry," Adrienne assured him. "We just need to find that elf. Can you tell us where he might be?"

He shook his head, his expression regretful. "I can't."

Adrienne's mother pulled out the golden apple. "We're ready to pay for the information if that's the issue."

A pained look crossed his face. "I'm not trying to extort money from you, Estrid. I truly don't have any clue as to his whereabouts. I'd never seen him before, and I've never seen him since. He came in and asked where to find you, that's all."

Adrienne deflated, turning to her mother. What did they do now? They had no other leads.

"Why do you need to find him?"

The new voice startled her, and she looked around for the speaker. She hadn't even noticed the older woman hovering in a doorway at the back of the room. The shopkeeper's wife moved forward, her expression shrewd.

"Do you need that particular elf, or are you just looking for an elf in general? Is it magical assistance you need?"

"Why?" Adrienne's mother asked cautiously. "Have you started selling talismans yourself?"

"Of course not," tsked the shopkeeper. "We don't want that kind of complication in our lives. Besides," he added frankly, "where would we find the magic for that? The land is barren of it, and elves are correspondingly scarce."

"But not completely absent," his wife chimed in.

Adrienne looked at her in surprise, and the other woman moved fully forward into the room.

"There is another elf who lives in these parts," she said. "She comes in here from time to time, usually under cover of darkness."

"Because she doesn't wish to be bothered by humans, and

she trusts our discretion," the shopkeeper muttered disapprovingly.

His wife disregarded the rebuke. "This is Estrid. She wouldn't be asking for assistance if the situation wasn't dire."

"It is dire," Adrienne said desperately. "More than you can imagine. Please, we'll take whatever magical help we can find."

"Well, I can't promise anything," the shopkeeper's wife said in a cautionary tone. "It's true that she wishes to be left alone. She may be more inclined to be furious at your invasion of her privacy than to help you."

"We'll take the chance," Adrienne said. What else could they do?

With a sigh, the older woman wiped her floury hands on her apron. "Well, she always blows in from the east."

"Blows in?" Adrienne repeated.

"Just my little joke," chuckled the woman. "She tends to look very windswept. Which makes me think she doesn't live in the valley here. If you head east, I reckon you'll find her in the mountains."

"Fross Mountains?" Adrienne asked in dismay, naming the mountain range that separated Frossenland from neighboring Vadolis to the east. It would take days to journey that far.

"No, no, the hills just east of here," the shopkeeper's wife said impatiently. "She comes here for ordinary supplies, so I think we must be the closest town to her home."

"Thank you," said Adrienne fervently. "We'll leave at once."

She looked to her mother, who nodded. "We're grateful for the information," she said, once again offering the golden apple.

"None of that," frowned the shopkeeper's wife. "Not from friends." Her eyes narrowed as she studied the apple. "It's not a bad idea to take it with you, though. The elf might want something in exchange for her assistance, and they do like gold. Good for enchantments, apparently. Wait here."

She disappeared, and Adrienne waited in barely contained impatience as rummaging sounds issued from the other room. The shopkeeper's wife emerged again, holding out a beautiful decorative hair comb.

"You should take this," she said. "It's the only golden item I have that I can easily spare. It might make her more inclined to help you."

"We can't accept this," Estrid protested.

"Yes you can," the other woman said firmly. "So stop wasting time." She glanced at Adrienne. "Your daughter is clearly eager to be off."

It was true, and Adrienne didn't try to deny it. Reluctantly, her mother took the comb, sliding it into her pocket with the golden apple. With a final expression of gratitude, she followed Adrienne out the door.

For her part, Adrienne could scarcely stop herself from running down the street. But if she had to get all the way to the low range of hills outside town, she would do well to pace herself. The two women walked in silence until they left Tove-ham, although Adrienne often felt her mother's eyes on her.

"What are you thinking about?" she asked the older woman at last, unnerved by her mother's serious expression.

"You," her mother said simply. "And this husband of yours. Is he really Crown Prince Herleif?"

"Without a doubt," Adrienne told her.

Her mother drew a long breath. "And are you pursuing him out of duty, or out of love?"

The matter-of-fact question brought a flush to Adrienne's cheeks, but her voice was steady as she replied.

"Both. Equally." She glanced at her mother. "Surely the two aren't always enemies?"

Her mother ran a hand through her hair. "Of course not. They often go hand in hand." She gave her daughter a tight smile. "As you'll discover when you have children of your own."

Adrienne's cheeks heated again, and she said nothing. It was an appealing picture, but it seemed out of reach. She sincerely hoped that if she could extricate Herleif from the mess she'd landed him in, any restrictions regarding their marriage would no longer be in play. But she knew she'd be wise not to build castles in the sky. Not only was the hope of freeing him a slim one, but if she achieved it, he would go back to being the heir to the kingdom. Would Frossenland really accept her as its queen? Would Herleif?

Whatever the giant queen makes me do, whatever she inflicts on Frossenland, you will always be my queen.

Once again Herleif's words rang through her mind, and her cheeks burned fiery hot in the cold air. But a smile curved her lips along with the flush. Yes, Herleif would be true. He didn't have an unfaithful bone in his body.

"Well, then, it seems we've no time to waste," her mother said briskly, as if Adrienne's silent thoughts had been an answer to her comments. "We can't surrender him to the giants, as you said."

Adrienne nodded briskly, and the two women increased their speed. The town soon faded away behind them, the hills that the shopkeeper's wife had generously called mountains looming ahead. They'd been walking for about two hours when Adrienne felt something prickling at her senses.

"There's magic ahead," she said. "I think." She turned her head this way and that, trying to detect the source. "Up in the hills. Hopefully that means we're getting close. Most elves keep a store of talismans, don't they?"

Her mother just shrugged, no more versed in the ways of the diminutive elves than Adrienne was. Nevertheless, they hurried forward with renewed energy as the ground began to slope up under their feet. To Adrienne's surprise, there was a trail, thin but clear, wending its way up the mountain. It branched off from time to time, and on those occasions Adrienne let her senses lead her, following the trail of the magic. After about twenty minutes of climbing, they still hadn't encountered any sign of habitation, and Adrienne wondered if she'd erred. Who would live up here, all alone?

The thought had just crossed her mind when she raised her gaze from the rocky path beneath her feet to see a small figure barring the way ahead.

"Humans." The elf's high voice was clearly disapproving. "Can never stay in your domain, can you? What are you doing up on my mountain?"

Adrienne raised an eyebrow, taking in the elf's long pale hair and bright green eyes. So it was her mountain, was it? She overlooked the generous term for the hills—to someone the elf's size, it wasn't entirely inaccurate.

"We're sorry to intrude," she said politely, figuring it was best not to antagonize their potential source of help. "But we're in desperate need of assistance."

"I don't do assistance," the elf said shortly. "And I definitely don't do desperate."

"Please." Adrienne started forward as the elf turned to leave. "It's not for us that we're seeking help." She paused, honesty compelling her to add, "not just for us." Herleif's rescue was, after all, a matter of crucial importance to her personally. She pulled out the golden apple and comb. "We brought payment, if it helps."

"It doesn't," the elf said, her high voice curt. "I'm in no need of excess gold. All I want is to be left alone."

With the words, she turned and disappeared into a crevice in the rock, one too small even for Adrienne's petite form to enter.

"Please!" Adrienne cried again, rushing forward to place her face against the gap. "The good of the kingdom is at stake."

A snort sounded from the hidden space. "Don't think much of yourself, do you?"

"No, I don't," Adrienne agreed, stubbornly ignoring the elf's sarcasm. "I think very poorly of myself right now, given it's my fault that the rightful king of Frossenland has been taken captive by the giant queen. And I will do a lot more than harass a hermit elf in order to get him back."

A long silence followed these words, then the elf popped her head back through the gap.

"The rightful king? You're talking about Crown Prince Herleif?"

"I am," Adrienne said, jumping eagerly at this sign of interest.

"Taken by Queen Grograna?"

Adrienne hesitated. "I don't know her name," she admitted. "He just told me that the giant queen is the one who put him under a curse, because she's determined he marry her daughter."

"Marry her daughter?" The elf sounded horrified. "Put that violent oaf on Frossenland's throne?" The pointed tips of her ears wiggled slightly in disapproval. "I think it might be time for me to move to Vadolis."

"No giant princess is going to be Herleif's queen," said Adrienne fiercely. "I'm already his wife, and I'm not going to let—"

"You?!" If Adrienne had a more inflated ego, the elf's astonishment would have been insulting. "You're telling me you're married to the rightful king of this kingdom?"

Adrienne's cheeks flushed. "I know it seems unlikely, but it's true." She pulled out the certificate of marriage, smoothing it hastily. "I can prove it."

Her mother stared over her shoulder at the intimidating list of names and titles in Herleif's steady hand. But before she could look too closely, the elf had ripped it from Adrienne's grasp.

She scanned it quickly, her petite brow creasing in displeasure.

"This is all too tawdry for my liking."

"It isn't," Adrienne snapped. "Our marriage might have been…irregular. But there's nothing tawdry about it."

The elf sighed before grumbling to herself. "Why do I let myself get dragged into these things?" She raised her eyes to Adrienne, her voice louder. "Look, girl, in theory you might have the power to stop the prince from being forced to marry the giant princess. But in reality…the barriers are too insurmountable."

"We don't know that unless we try," Adrienne said quickly. "Please, I can't do it without assistance. Won't you help me?"

"You can't do it even with assistance," said the elf brutally. "Even if we could get you over Battlement Wall into Kjemper, you'd never survive the giants. That's even assuming you could find your way through the frozen wasteland on the other side to the castle East of the Sun and West of the Moon, which is unlikely. At least, not before it was too late anyway."

"The castle what?" Adrienne asked blankly.

The elf sighed, her body still inside the cave she'd retreated into, only her head and one arm poking out. "That's what they call their capital. They fancy themselves very mystical and grand, giants. At least since Grograna took the throne."

"How do you know so much about giants and their land?" Adrienne's mother asked suspiciously.

"Never you mind," said the elf crisply. She held out the certificate of marriage. "I don't plan to use up my entire stores of magic for a doomed mission."

Adrienne refused to take the certificate. "It's not doomed," she said fiercely. "I take back what I said before. I *will* get Herleif with *or* without your help. If I have to harness every tiny trace of magic in this barren ground and sing myself there, then that's what I'll do."

"What?" The elf's voice was sharp now. "You're a singer?"

Adrienne nodded.

"Why didn't you say so?" the elf demanded. She looked Adrienne up and down with a measuring gaze. "Well, that changes things. I suppose that's why he married you, is it?"

Adrienne lifted her chin a little. "It's not, actually, but never mind that. Why does me being a singer change things?"

"Because it means that you're not as useless as humans generally are," the elf replied. A skeptical look passed over her face as she once again examined Adrienne. "At least, you *might* not be as useless." She narrowed her eyes. "Even if we could make it work, you would have to go yourself. And there would be no guarantee of your safety, or even your survival."

"I understand," Adrienne said quickly, hope growing inside her at the elf's businesslike manner. "I'm ready to take the risk."

The elf shook her head. "Humans always are," she commented to no one in particular. "Making decisions with their hearts instead of their heads. Foolish, but there you go."

"What do you think are our chances of survival?" Adrienne's mother asked calmly. "If you were to be brutally frank?"

"Our?" Adrienne repeated in alarm. "Mamma, you're not coming with me."

"Of course I am," her mother protested.

Adrienne opened her mouth to argue, but the elf spoke first.

"Are you a singer?"

Adrienne's mother shook her head reluctantly.

"There'd be no sense in you going," the elf told her. "You have neither the magic nor the right that she has thanks to her song and that certificate." The elf jerked her head toward Adrienne. "You'd just be a hindrance, one that would make her more likely to get herself killed trying to protect you."

Adrienne's mother didn't look at all happy with this verdict, but the elf gave an unconcerned shrug.

"You wanted me to be brutally honest."

"I can't let you go alone," the older woman said, turning to Adrienne in distress.

"I understand," Adrienne assured her. "I'm sure I'd feel the same in your position. But Mamma, I'm not a child anymore. I've been married and living my own life for months now. You can't prevent me from doing this, and it makes no sense for you to come with me. You need to go back home, where you're safe. The boys might need your help to corroborate their story to the royals."

Her mother didn't give in quickly. It took half an hour of arguments before she was persuaded to return the way they'd come. Frustrated as she was with the waste of time, Adrienne tried to be patient. Eventually the elf, who'd gotten bored and disappeared into her cave early in the discussion, re-emerged and told Adrienne's mother bluntly that she would help Adrienne and only Adrienne, and if the older woman was determined to stay with her daughter, they could feel free to both go back to wherever they'd sprung from.

Adrienne wished the elf had been a little softer, but she couldn't deny that these strictures had the desired effect. Soon she was watching her mother climb back down the mountain path. She let out a long breath of relief. Whatever happened next, at least her family would live. There was no reason for the giants to come after them if Adrienne was removed from the picture.

Turning back to the elf, Adrienne tried to smile. "Thank you," she said. "For agreeing to help me."

The elf just grunted. "I have magic stored," she said. "But

you'll need to direct it once it's released. It will require some skill. How extensively have you trained in your craft?"

Adrienne shifted uncomfortably. "I haven't had any formal training," she admitted. She saw the elf's disapproval, and hurried to add, "I've studied a bit in the library at the northern castle near here. Mainly in healing magic and in object control."

"Object control?" the elf repeated with interest. "That's a strange one to start with—not exactly a beginner skill. What made you choose that?"

Adrienne gave her a sheepish look. "That and the one on healing magic were the only manuals I found."

"Have you ever done it successfully?" the elf pressed.

"Well..." Adrienne hedged, "yes and no. I did manage to put power into a candle, to gain control of it. And I was able to move it afterward without using additional magic. But I don't know if I'd call it successful, since I was trying to use healing magic at the time."

The elf snorted. "Can you still sense the candle, though?"

"What do you mean?" Adrienne asked, tilting her head to one side.

"The candle." The elf was clearly impatient with her lack of knowledge. "You should be able to sense its location as well as manipulate its movements."

"Oh," said Adrienne. "I didn't know that." She closed her eyes, remembering when she'd made the candle move without touching it. She tried to ignore the pull of the stored magic somewhere in the cave behind the elf, instead focusing on the type of power she pulled from the ground, and which she'd used on the candle. A flicker of awareness entered her mind, pulling her thoughts westward, toward the abandoned castle.

"I think I can sense it," she said thoughtfully. "It's the right direction, anyway."

But the words were barely out of her mouth when she

frowned. *Was* that the candle she was feeling? The same sensation, although fainter, also tugged her mind toward the north, which made no sense. Maybe it wasn't working after all.

"Well, that's something," said the elf, sounding heartened. "If you're able to pull off object control, however unintentionally and however imperfectly, you must have some potential. Who knows? Perhaps you'll be a strong singer."

"I'm not strong," Adrienne said quickly, feeling it was best to be honest up front. "Or skilled. I'm afraid my ability to harness power is weak."

"It might be," the elf agreed curtly. "But then again it might not. If you've lived in the north all your life, you can't possibly know. The magic in the ground is too scarce to allow for your craft to be explored to its full capacity. Especially without training."

She gave a long-suffering sigh. "Well, if I have to basically start from scratch, I suppose we'd better begin right away." Adrienne expected her to go back into her cave, but instead she turned, starting up the path that led higher, toward the peak. "Come on, then."

Adrienne hurried after her, wondering as she did whether the elf was right about her potential for strength. She'd never expected to be anything more than a mediocre singer.

"Why are you helping me?" she blurted out, her eyes on the elf's back in front of her. "I'm grateful that you are," she added quickly. "Incredibly grateful. But you seemed set against it, and then you changed your mind. And from the little I know of elves, I expected you to barter an exchange, at the very least. But you've asked for nothing."

The elf shrugged. "Just because you give me nothing doesn't mean I gain nothing. Whether it's worth it for the slim hope of absolution..." She trailed off with a sigh. They'd reached the top of a rise, and she turned to Adrienne, her voice now brisk.

"Enough wasting time. We have a lot to cover if you're going to master your songcraft enough to pull this off before it's too late. I hope you've come ready to work, because I'm not going to go easy on you."

"I have," Adrienne assured her.

The elf tutted. "Even so, there's no way of knowing whether we'll be too late by the time you're ready."

Steeling herself, Adrienne pushed down her exhaustion. Herleif's face swam before her vision, his voice low and intense as he bared his heart in the moments before he was whisked away. For him, she would do whatever it took, pay whatever price.

"Then what are we waiting for?"

CHAPTER TWENTY-FOUR

Adrienne

"Are you sure about this?" Adrienne's elf mentor sounded just as disgruntled as she had the last five times she'd asked the question. "You're really determined to waste your precious time this way? For the record, I advise against it."

"That's already been recorded," Adrienne replied, trying not to smile. "Metaphorically speaking," she added quickly.

She'd been with the elf for a week, honing her craft as much as the limited time would allow, and she'd gleaned a little about the infamously literal elf culture. She'd be wise not to offer the elf information she knew to be false.

"And yes, I'm sure," she added for good measure. "Of course I don't want to waste time, but…"

She paused, thinking again of the week that had already elapsed since Herleif was ripped from her, and picturing her husband exchanging vows with the giant princess. Panic threatened to rise in her, but she forced it down. She'd made the mistake once before of thinking it was her right to put Herleif's well-being before that of the kingdom he served. And although no curse had been unleashed on Frossenland, she'd still been horribly wrong to take the risk on his behalf, as events had proved.

"But," she tried again, "I've seen the destructive power of these magic winds. I can't justify destroying everything between here and Battlement Wall. It might not be heavily populated, but there are still homes and livelihoods north of here. It will only take a few days to walk to the wall, and I can use the magic to create a wind from there."

The elf shrugged. "It's your funeral," she said skeptically. "Probably quite literally." She sighed as she glanced at the item in her hand. "I hope I'm not wasting the magic in this talisman, though. It represents *years* of mining and careful manipulation."

"I know," Adrienne said, guilt edging into her thoughts at the chastising tone of her companion. "And I'm more grateful than I can—"

"Yes, yes, we've had enough of that." The elf cut her off with an impatient wave of her tiny hand.

She held out the golden item, and Adrienne took it, turning it over. It was large compared to the ornamental apple and decorative comb already in her satchel. The wheel was almost as wide as her torso, and it would be a struggle to fit it into the bag. It was a strange item, like the wheel from a spinning wheel.

"You never explained why you used a wheel," she commented.

"That's because we had time for only the most rudimentary training," said the elf irritably. "You're still only barely ready to manipulate this amount of power in a targeted way. Did you expect to master the lore in a week as well? Suffice it to say that the unbroken line of a circle lends itself to magic, as do the qualities of gold." Her eyes strayed to Adrienne's satchel. "Whether the giants love gold for that reason or for its own sake, I couldn't say. But use those golden items wisely. They'll be more valuable in Kjemper even than they are here."

"Thank you," said Adrienne earnestly. "For everything. I'm greatly indebted to you."

A gleam shot through the elf's eyes, but the apparently instinctive reaction was followed by a groan. "I'm trying to exercise restraint here, child, but you make it impossible."

"Sorry," said Adrienne, wincing. "I forgot. Have I just inadvertently promised to give you my firstborn child or something?"

The elf snorted. "I don't want any human brat disturbing my solitude, thanks. But I think we should set some exchange, to be on the safe side. Then the matter is sealed, and neither of us can succumb—you to your idiocy and me to temptation. Altruism doesn't come naturally to my kind. I have my own reasons for wishing to help you, reasons which have nothing to do with you and everything to do with what you're fighting. But that doesn't mean I find it easy to pass on the opportunity to gain something for myself along the way." She scowled. "And if I do that, I suppose none of my efforts at atonement will count, will they?"

"An exchange is an excellent idea," Adrienne said, her lips twitching. She didn't know what the elf was trying to atone for, or where she'd gotten her notions of altruism. But somehow her irritability was endearing, perhaps because she had to crane her neck back to glower up even at Adrienne's short statue. She doubted her hostess would appreciate her showing any sign of humor, however, so she kept her tone serious. "What do you have in mind?"

"How about you agree that *if* your quest is successful, once your husband is installed on his throne, you will return to me a quantity of magic, conveniently stored in talismans, roughly equivalent to what I've just given you."

"That sounds fair," Adrienne agreed, relieved at the conditional nature of the promise. If she was unsuccessful in freeing Herleif, she'd never be able to repay the magic. But presumably the royal family had stores in the capital, or access to elves or singers who could help them create an appropriate talisman.

"*And*," the elf added quickly, "you agree not to expose my haven here to anyone, or send anyone to bother me with questions about anything. You can leave the payment with the shopkeeper."

"Very well," Adrienne agreed, intrigued by the light that had jumped into the elf's eyes as she thought of this second form of payment. Just what questions did she not want to be asked? Was it to do with her vague hints of seeking absolution?

Adrienne dismissed it from her mind as she took her leave of her reluctant mentor. She had no need or desire to pry into the reclusive elf's secrets.

As she turned down the trail, hefting her rucksack higher up her shoulders, she felt another surge of gratitude for the food and other supplies the elf had given. She knew better than to repeat the thanks she'd already offered, however. At best it would irritate the elf. Equally likely it would lead to a fresh agreement about some kind of exchange. That the elf had her own reasons for helping Adrienne, she had no doubt. She may well never know what they were.

The first day Adrienne made good progress, walking until the light faded with only a few stops for food. She was nervous about finding a place to sleep, but she did as the elf had instructed her, using the few wisps of magic to be found in the ground to turn a shallow cave into a temporary haven. There wasn't enough magic to make the cave properly warm or fully shielded, but it was more secure than being in the open.

The next two days passed in a similarly uneventful way. In

spite of the season, it was increasingly cold the further north she traveled, and Adrienne quickly formed the habit of singing softly while she walked, harnessing the odd trickle of magic to warm her, as she'd practiced doing in the abandoned castle.

The area was only sparsely inhabited, but she passed enough homes to make her glad she'd rejected the elf's suggestion that she harness a magical wind to carry her over the whole area, regardless of the destruction her passage would wreak below. On her final night, she sought shelter in a barn next to the homestead of what must be very hardy folk. She considered knocking on the door to ask to stay in the home itself, but she was too nervous to do it. Who knew what kind of people would choose to live so close to the shadow of Battlement Wall? She'd been able to see it looming ahead for the better part of the day, an unformed mass in the distance, blocking out the sky. It was an eerie reminder of the danger ahead of her.

Adrienne slept little. It was bitterly cold in the darkness, and there was barely any magic in the ground so far north to allow her to warm herself. She shuddered to think what a frozen, magic-less wasteland she would find north of the wall.

Eventually, the sun rose, and with it, Adrienne. She hurried out of the barn at the first sign of light, eager to be gone before the owners discovered her trespass. Another couple of hours of trekking brought her within reach of Battlement Wall.

For a moment, Adrienne just stood and stared at it.

She'd seen the wall close up once before, as a child. It was as impressive and intimidating now as it had been then. The stones—cut to an enormous size—were weathered and rough from generations of exposure to the harsh northern climate, but the wall itself remained strong. Unassailable, she would have said. But the elf had assured her there was enough magic packed into the wheel-like talisman to get her over it.

Looking at the wall, Adrienne could only hope so. It was taller even than the highest spire of the northern castle, and she didn't fancy being dropped from that kind of height if the magic gave out too soon.

Herleif. She was doing this for Herleif. The thought steeled her, and she drew herself up, refusing to give in to her exhaustion.

"You've come this far," she said aloud to herself in a determined voice. "No sense putting it off now you're here."

She fished the golden wheel out of her rucksack, holding it up before her like she was steering a ship. In spite of her bold words, she hovered, hesitating. Deciding to test the area first, she let out a soft, experimental song. Some faint sense of magic stirred deep beneath her feet, but not even a trickle made it up into her, where she could use it. It was the elf's mined magic or nothing. Drawing a deep breath, she sang the words the elf had taught her, the ones that would release the stored power.

Like a tidal wave, magic poured forth from the wheel, wild and unrestrained. Adrienne raised her voice frantically, putting into practice all the training the elf had drilled into her over their week together. It was an overwhelming amount of power, and it was clearly reluctant to bend to Adrienne's will. As she'd been taught, she attempted the minimal amount of control, not trying to form the magic into anything substantial, or to target it to any intricate purpose. It wasn't the time to try to overreach her meager skills.

Slowly, painfully, the magic responded, the raw power funneled into a frenzy of energy-packed air. Once again drawing on the elf's training, Adrienne broadened her song, her words now calling the wind from around her to come to her aid and give form to the magic. As the elf had instructed, Adrienne specifically summoned the north wind, vocalizing her rejection of the south, east, and west winds. Apparently this was supposed to ensure the raw magic she was now trying to manipulate into wind carried her in the correct direction.

Adrienne would have swallowed nervously if she'd dared to stop singing, but there was no time for hesitation. She had to act while she had tenuous control of the huge volume of magic. Under her direction, the magic-laden wind bent back around, lifting Adrienne from her feet and flinging her upward. The sensation was terrifying, but she couldn't scream, couldn't even clamp her mouth shut. If she stopped singing, she would surely drop like a stone to her death.

Because already she'd reached an impossible height. The wall sped past her as she streaked upward, cushioned by the magic-laden wind. It was hard to judge how far she still had to go, so she was taken by surprise when she abruptly popped clear of it, the vast expanse of Kjemper suddenly appearing below her.

Adrienne would have gasped if her voice was free. As it was, the sight distracted her enough that her song faltered, and she jostled against the top of the wall as she passed over it, wincing as the rough stone scratched her legs. She directed the wind to send her northward, even as her gaze strayed back to the wall she'd just crossed. Her eyes widened at the sight of what butted up against Battlement Wall on the giants' side. It looked like a mountain range, except the mountains appeared to be nothing but ice. Had they been there when the wall was built, or had they accumulated against it in the generations since? Just how frozen was Kjemper?

That question was answered as Adrienne turned her attention northward again. The ground was flying by at a rapid rate, but she could see enough to get the general idea. It was a barren wasteland, all right, frozen and bleak. And yet...she frowned down at the strange towers that dotted the expanse. What was their purpose?

She had no satisfactory answer to that when a sprawling city appeared ahead. The scene was dominated by one huge stone building in the middle, looking like a rougher version of the castle she'd been living in since her marriage. Like the near side of Battlement Wall, it appeared to be coated with ice, although in this case it seemed to be intentional. It was an impressive sight, and Adrienne was so distracted by it, she almost forgot how foolish it would be to let the wind carry her straight into the city. As the walls loomed ahead, she dropped her voice, trying to bend the wind to her will.

But the magic was still strong, plenty of power left for a longer journey should she have wished it. It turned out that causing the wind to die down was much harder than whipping it up. The magic didn't want to disseminate—it wanted to be used. Adrienne's panic rose as the magic-laden wind carried her closer and closer to the city. Desperate, she sang a curt command for it to stop.

That was a mistake. The wind dropped at once, although Adrienne's descent was far from complete. Letting out a strangled yell, she plummeted, the ground rising up with terrifying speed. Dimly, she was aware of the magic dispersing, racing off into the ether without purpose. But the next moment she hit the ground hard, and the splintering crunch of her legs, followed by the excruciating pain that took violent hold of her, drove out all other thoughts.

Adrienne's breath came in frantic gasps as she lay prone on the icy ground. Agony radiated out from both legs, and her feeble attempts to move them yielded no results. They were both broken, and badly.

Tears pooled in Adrienne's eyes, and she struggled not to give in completely to her panic. She wouldn't be reaching

Herleif in her state. She wasn't even sure she could survive these injuries if they were left untreated.

Her mind could barely function through the anguish, but she tried with all her might to remember her study into healing magic in the castle's library. She could remember the basic theory. Her fingers closed over the wheel still clutched in both hands. She opened her mouth intending to sing, but a sob emerged instead. She could feel that it was no use. The object in her hand was no longer a talisman. It was nothing more than a golden keepsake, all its magic spent. Wasted on a mission doomed to failure, like the elf had said.

Despair rose up in Adrienne. The talisman was empty, and there was no hope to be found in the ground beneath her back. If the land just south of Battlement Wall was any indication, the giants' land must be all but devoid of magic.

Still, she had to try.

Raising her voice in a feeble song, Adrienne focused on what she'd read in the library books. Bracing herself against the pain in her legs, she dug her fingers into the hard, frozen ground, willing some trace of magic to respond.

To her astonishment, power rushed up to meet her, coming gladly under her control. Or not up, exactly. It didn't feel precisely like pulling magic from the ground, or quite like accessing the torrent of magic released by the talisman a short time before. It was halfway between the two, which made no sense to Adrienne.

But she didn't stop to question the reprieve. Harnessing the power, she directed it to her legs, her voice growing stronger as she released a simple song of healing. Tears of relief filled her eyes as the pain lessened and then disappeared, the bones re-knitting with an audible crack that sent a shudder over her. Tentatively, she pushed herself to her feet. Her legs were wobbly, but they held. It was an inexpert job, certainly. But she could walk, which meant she could go after Herleif.

Wasting no more time, Adrienne stashed the wheel in her rucksack and stumbled forward, the city walls in sight. She could make no sense of what had just happened. Where had the magic come from? Whatever its source, its volume had been immense. But she could feel the ground beneath her feet. It was barren and lacking in power, just like the northern part of Frossenland.

When Adrienne reached the city gates, she was relieved to find them thrown open. At first glance, she thought the two enormous figures on either side were statues, carved from the same stone as the city wall itself. Surely they were exaggerated for effect. Real giants weren't that large.

Then one of them moved, his head turning toward her, and it was all Adrienne could do not to let out a squeal. Holding her head high, she forced herself forward, trying not to dwell on the creature's yellow eyes, set in a square head, or the huge spear it held in one enormous hand.

"What's an elf doing out here alone?" the giant rumbled, his voice like rocks striking against one another.

Adrienne came to a stop, blinking. Elf? She glanced down at herself, then up at the two hulking figures before her, their arms overlong for their bodies and their exposed teeth as sharp as a dog's. She supposed size was relative. Even humans had often commented that she was small in stature. Compared to a giant, perhaps she really did seem elf-like.

"I, uh...I..." Adrienne could have cursed her own uselessness. All her planning had been focused on what to do once she reached the castle. Why hadn't she come up with a strategy for getting through the city gates? Perhaps she should have flown over the wall after all.

"Got separated from the others, did you?" The second giant

leered at her. "No need to look so terrified, elf. We're not going to eat you."

"Not when we've just had our lunch," agreed the first one with a revolting cackle.

Adrienne winced, but hurried to make use of the opportunity. "That's right," she said, pitching her voice a little higher than usual. "Got lost."

"Well, better hurry, then," the first giant said, already growing bored with the conversation. "Her Majesty won't take kindly to you being where you're not supposed to be."

Adrienne stiffened at this mention of the queen who'd stolen her husband from her. Bowing her head, she hid her emotions as she squeaked an acknowledgment, then scampered through the gates.

It wasn't difficult to find her way to the castle. The broad main street led straight to it. Adrienne expected to be accosted at any moment, but the streets weren't busy, and the giants she passed all ignored her. Instead of being grateful for the unexpected lack of resistance, Adrienne felt uneasy. Why was an elf so welcome in Kjemper? She'd understood that the two types of creatures hated each other, even more passionately than humans hated giants.

When Adrienne reached the castle, her courage almost failed her. Built to the proportions of giants, the building was enormous. The sun had passed its zenith now, and in the clear light of a sunny, albeit freezing, day, the ice-covered walls gleamed menacingly. Every instinct in Adrienne told her this was not a place she should willingly enter. And yet, for Herleif, she forced herself to go on.

She had the sense not to barge in at the front entrance, however. She didn't have a solid enough plan for such a brazen approach. In spite of the confusing words from the giants at the gate, she didn't see any other elves wandering the streets. She certainly didn't see any humans. Instead of entering through the guarded castle door, she walked straight past it, skirting the fence that surrounded the imposing structure. It wasn't a solid wall—it was a fence of railings, the narrow metal poles mainly just straight and practical, but occasionally forming decorative patterns. It would be enough to keep out a giant, even most humans. Herleif certainly couldn't have squeezed through it. But eyeing the gaps as she walked, Adrienne thought she might.

She walked far enough around to be well out of sight of the guards at the castle's entrance. The afternoon was wearing on, and she debated waiting for darkness. But the thought of loitering in the city unnerved her as much as the fear of being caught in the attempt, so as soon as a pair of passersby turned a nearby corner, she sprung into action. She turned her head sideways, slipping it between two bars and pulling her shoulders after it. Once they were through, she breathed a sigh of relief. The rest of her would follow. It was a bit of a squeeze at her hips, but she made it, half falling into the shrubbery on the other side just as voices floated through the air toward her from the street outside. Adrienne waited until the unknown giants had passed, then moved stealthily through the garden that surrounded the giants' castle.

It seemed impossible for any plants to survive in this frozen wasteland, but the faint taste on the wind provided an answer. Somehow magic was at work in this garden, little sense as it made. Even the air was slightly warmer, reminding Adrienne of her own trick in trying to keep away the bitter cold with her song. Adrienne crept through the garden, staying in the foliage as much as possible, her eyes on the castle. She could see a number of balconies above her, all currently empty. And along the ground level, there were several doors leading out to the gardens where she was crouched.

She was just hovering in a particularly leafy bush,

wondering what entrance would be best to try, when the loud slamming of a door announced the arrival of someone on one of the balconies.

Adrienne froze, her eyes darting up to the balcony in question. The woman who stood there was much smaller than the guards at the gate, but she must be a giant, given her proportions and her grayish skin. Adrienne saw with growing alarm that a gaudy golden crown sat on top of the giant's square head. Was this Queen Grograna? Or perhaps her daughter, whom Herleif was supposed to marry? Whoever she was, she appeared to be in a very ill humor. Sulky was the word that sprang to Adrienne's mind as she studied the giant's face.

Adrienne tried to draw back further into the bush, but that was a mistake. Her subtle movement drew the giant's eyes with surprising speed.

"Who are you?" she demanded, her petulant voice supporting Adrienne's assessment of her as sulky.

Adrienne moved forward, smoothing her hair nervously over her very human ears and dipping into a curtsy. "I apologize for interrupting your rest, Your...Highness." She took a stab, and her guess proved correct.

"You should be," the princess grumbled. She narrowed her eyes. "What's an elf doing down there in the garden, anyway?"

"Just...just getting some fresh air, Your Highness," Adrienne said lamely. She had no idea what excuse would be credible. How much freedom were elves allowed in the giants' capital?

"And you're not even going to ask me what's wrong?" The giant flicked her dark braid over her shoulder, her thick gray lips settling into a pout. "You must see I'm upset."

"Uh..." Adrienne tried not to stare, taken aback by this childish demand for attention. From her own—admittedly limited—experience, human royals held themselves to a very different standard of behavior. "I'm sorry to hear that you're upset, Your Highness," she said carefully. "Is there anything I can do to assist?"

"An elf offering to assist for nothing?" The giant princess snorted. "I'm not such a fool as to fall into that trap." Her eyebrows drew together in a scowl. "And of course I'm upset. Who wouldn't be upset that their own husband refuses to so much as kiss them?"

CHAPTER TWENTY-FIVE

Adrienne

Adrienne froze, something colder than the icy air washing over her. And it wasn't just because the giant's words hit a nerve in terms of her own experience of marriage.

"Husband?" she repeated, her voice coming out in a squeak that was plenty high enough to be passable for an elf. Was she already too late, then?

"All right, betrothed," the giant said, rolling her eyes. "He'll be my husband soon enough, what difference does it make?"

Adrienne breathed again, some of the tension draining out of her. There was still time.

"It's not like I *want* him to kiss me," said the giant petulantly. "He's repulsive. But how dare he act like *I'm* the one who's unappealing?"

Warmth spread through Adrienne. It was no surprise to learn that Herleif was being true to their vows, even under pressure, but it still sent a pang of longing through her. Where was he? He must be close if he'd offended this princess in the recent past. Somewhere in the castle no doubt. Guest room or dungeon? What exactly was the status of the human whom Queen Grograna was forcing to marry her daughter?

Adrienne's mind whirled, trying to think of how to turn this unexpected encounter to her purposes.

"Perhaps I could help you," she said carefully. "In exchange for your favor."

"My favor?" The princess straightened, her eyes narrowing. "What do you mean?"

"Well, you're obviously someone with a great deal of power here in the castle," Adrienne said. The princess gave the strong impression that she'd be susceptible to flattery.

"Naturally," the giant said as if in confirmation of Adrienne's thoughts, tossing her braid again. "So you want me to put in a good word for you with my mother, do you?" she went on. "Seeking more notice?" She snorted as she looked down at Adrienne, who was intentionally skulking in the bushes, trying to make herself look smaller. "You might regret that. Cleary you haven't spent much time with her."

Adrienne was silent, unsure how to safely respond to this open criticism of the princess's mother.

"How could you help me?" the giant asked suspiciously.

"Well," Adrienne hedged, trying to get her idea clear in her mind. She knew in a vague sense that bargains with elves were bound by strict laws of magic, but of course they wouldn't apply to her, since she wasn't really an elf. She should be safe enough to pretend. "You know we elves can do all kinds of things with mined magic. There are ways to compel a person to cooperate. If I could get access to your betrothed, perhaps I could work some magic on him that would make him susceptible to your instructions."

The giant thought for a moment. "Mother wouldn't approve," she mused. "But I would like to see him stop disrespecting me in front of the guards."

"Is the queen too fastidious to allow you to use magic?" Adrienne pressed, trying to layer just the right amount of polite skepticism into her voice. "And you're not frustrated by such restrictions, Your Highness?"

Her attempt at manipulation didn't quite hit the mark. The princess snorted yet again. It was an abrasive sound.

"I don't think anyone would call her fastidious. She has no objection to magic, as you must be aware. But she would think it was weak of me to use magic to get my husband to cooperate. She thinks I should just force him to do what I want." The princess let out a gusty sigh. "But I've tried that, and it's not working."

A shudder went over Adrienne as she remembered the elf who'd trained her referring to the giant princess as a "violent oaf". What had this childish, self-pitying excuse for a woman been putting Herleif through?

"When something isn't working," she said as smoothly as she could, "it's only sensible to try something else."

The giant considered her words for a moment. "I would only give my favor if you were successful in your enchantment."

"Agreed," Adrienne said quickly.

The princess apparently still wasn't satisfied, her gaze raking over Adrienne, who tried not to fidget.

"It's not a fair exchange," the giant sniffed at last. "My favor is worth more than a paltry kiss from an ugly human, or whatever other cooperation you can compel."

Adrienne had expected bartering. After all, the giant thought she was dealing with an elf. Reaching into her satchel, Adrienne pulled out the ornamental apple.

"How about I add this?" she offered. "It's real gold."

The princess straightened, greed visible on her face. "Real gold? Throw it up here."

"Do we have a deal?" Adrienne asked, trying to look confident. The giant would think she was treating with an elf—she would believe herself bound.

"Yes, yes, all right," said the princess. "If you wait here until after dark, I'll let you in the side entrance and you can take your magic to the human." She said the last word with scathing disdain. "You can have one night with him to work your craft," the giant warned. "One night only."

"Agreed," said Adrienne, relief flooding through her. One night would be enough. Once she and Herleif had the chance to communicate, she was sure they could find a way out together. She threw the apple up, watching as the princess's meaty hand shot out to grab it from the air.

"I'll meet you back here after dark," the princess said. "Just you, all right?"

Adrienne nodded, and the giant disappeared back into the castle. She probably expected Adrienne to go about her business in the meantime, but of course Adrienne had nowhere else to be. So she found a large weeping willow in the garden and hid herself under it to wait for darkness.

As the hours passed agonizingly slowly, her anxiety grew. There were so many things that might go wrong with this plan. The princess didn't seem especially bright, but even so, Adrienne's deception was clumsy at best. When the giant saw her close up, rather than looking down on her from the balcony, would it be obvious that she was too big to be an elf? What about the guards and other giants they would presumably pass in their journey through the castle to wherever Herleif was being kept?

But as it happened, the latter fear was unnecessary. By the time the princess finally reappeared, at least three hours after darkness had fallen, Adrienne was chilled to the bone, and ready to take any risk if it meant moving from her hiding place. The castle which had seemed so intimidating on arrival now looked like a warm haven compared to the frigid gardens. And she could only imagine that the rest of the city, outside whatever magical influence kept the garden alive, would be even colder.

She emerged readily at the princess's call, ensuring her hair covered her ears as she pulled her purple cloak tightly around her.

"I'm here," she said, her tones much quieter and more cautious than the princess's.

"Come on, then," said the giant, beckoning in a gesture that seemed clumsy to Adrienne's human eyes.

Warily, Adrienne followed the giant through a doorway onto the ground floor of the castle. It was just an ordinary door, not a grand entrance, but the lintel still towered above Adrienne's petite form. She hunched a little as she walked, trying to make herself smaller and more elf-like. Fortunately the princess didn't watch her, walking ahead and focusing on their route. Adrienne was soon hopelessly lost as she followed the giant through winding corridors and up stairs. She wasn't sure whether to be relieved or uneasy that they didn't pass another soul.

When the giant stopped at the end of one long corridor and gestured Adrienne forward, she hesitated, trying to keep to the shadows of an alcove so as to prevent the princess from getting a good look at her.

"Where is everyone?" she asked, pitching her voice higher than usual.

"They're all still feasting in the great hall," said the princess. She flicked her enormous rope of dark hair over her shoulder in a vain gesture. "Celebrating my upcoming nuptials."

Adrienne raised an eyebrow. "Even all the guards?"

The giant let out a huff of impatience. "Of course not the guards. I told you I don't want my mother to learn of this, didn't I? Do you imagine she would remain ignorant of it if a dozen guards saw you go in there? I dealt with them—did you think I have no power in my own castle?"

Realizing that she'd bruised the princess's ego, Adrienne hastened to disclaim. She turned to the corridor her guide had indicated. "Which door do I..." She trailed off as she got a good look at the sight before her. There were no doors. A number of rooms certainly opened off the corridor, but rather than solid wall with a door set into it, each was lined with rows of metal bars. But Adrienne was sure they'd gone up the staircase, not down.

"Is this the dungeon?" she asked.

"Of course not," said the princess, once again sounding offended. "This is the guest wing. The second tier of it, anyway. The dungeons are below." She gestured carelessly at an empty room, and Adrienne saw through the bars that it was arranged with comfortable, giant-sized furniture. "And they certainly don't have these luxuries."

Adrienne stared up at her. "But...this is where you put *guests*?"

The giant nodded, clearly impatient.

Adrienne's eyes traveled down the corridor again, hardening at the sight of light spilling from one of the barred rooms. "So you pretend he's an honored guest, but you have him locked in like a prisoner?"

The princess narrowed her eyes. "What do you care? Are you some kind of human-lover or something?"

"It just makes my task more difficult," Adrienne said quickly, trying to cover her slip. "If he's angry about being restrained, he'll be less amenable to the enchantment."

The giant rolled her eyes. "If he was amenable, I wouldn't need magic to bring him around. Did you expect him to be in one of the top tier suites, with the freedom of a local? Those are reserved for guests of the highest importance. We would never put a *human* in there."

Adrienne had no response, so she just moved forward toward the indicated room. Her breath caught in her throat at the sight of Herleif, stretched out on a decently comfortable looking bed, apparently fast asleep.

"How long do you need?" the princess called after her. "Will it take all night? I can't stop the guards on the next shift coming at dawn, not without drawing a lot of attention."

"Until dawn will be enough time," Adrienne said. She spoke quietly, not wanting to wake Herleif before the giant left. What if his reaction inadvertently gave her away? To her relief, the giant princess sauntered away, no doubt off to return to the festivities.

"Herleif!" Adrienne called as soon as the coast was clear.

He didn't stir.

"Herleif, wake up, it's me!" Adrienne didn't dare raise her voice too loud, in case the princess was wrong about all the guards being dealt with.

Still no response.

Adrienne bit her lip, considering the bars on Herleif's guest-suite-turned-cell. They were certainly too close together for a giant to fit through. Even Herleif wouldn't be able to squeeze his excessively broad shoulders through the gaps. But Adrienne was petite, after all. Enough to pass for an elf to an inexperienced giant.

Removing her rucksack, she turned sideways, aligning her head with her shoulders as she tried to edge through. It was tight, but by sucking in her breath, she was able to squeeze in. She dropped her rucksack, rushing to Herleif's side.

"Herleif!" she cried again, shaking his shoulder. She could barely believe her husband was before her, his face gloriously visible in the light of the lantern he must have left on before falling asleep.

But to her frustration, he still didn't wake.

"Herleif, come on," she moaned. "This is our one chance." She shook his shoulder more vigorously, causing his arm to slide off the edge of the bed, where it hung limply.

Alarm trickled in to replace her frustration. What was wrong with him? She leaned close, reassured by the warmth of his steady breaths on her cheek. He was certainly alive, but it didn't seem he was in a natural sleep.

Anguish raced over her as she tried vainly to think of what to do. The giant princess was gone by now, and even if Adrienne had known where to find her, she wouldn't have dared to approach her in the company of all the other giants present for the feast. She had the impression that the queen was much sharper than her daughter, and would likely recognize Adrienne's imposture at once.

Putting solutions aside for a moment, Adrienne knelt beside Herleif's bed, searching his face hungrily. He was as she remembered, his pale, shoulder length hair unkempt and his jaw a little square. She ran a hand gently along his cheek, lifting a strand of hair that had flopped over his eyes. With a hiss of indrawn breath, she saw the bruise blossoming around one eye, and the scratch along the side of his jaw. His prospective giant bride appeared to have tried to subdue him through more primitive means, as she'd said. Strong as he was, Herleif was no match for a giant in strength. Adrienne had to get him out.

But no matter what she tried, nothing worked. She sloshed water over him from a nearby pitcher, she slapped his face gently, she clapped right next to his ear, she shook him with all her strength. He remained unresponsive. Adrienne even tried singing, commanding him to wake, harnessing whatever magic she could grab. Nothing had any effect.

As hours trickled by, despair began to wash over her, intensified by the exhaustion of her journey and the late hour. Eventually, she sank down on the bed beside him, defeated and out of ideas. She reminded herself that she had to leave before dawn, but she had no fight left. Barely aware of deciding to do so, she curled up next to her husband. She couldn't help but be comforted by his nearness after the days of anxious separation, even if his unresponsiveness was unpleasantly reminiscent of the nights she'd lain beside him in their huge bed at the castle, wishing he wasn't so cold and distant. She would only lie there for a few minutes, she told herself. Just ten minutes.

Adrienne woke suddenly, the sound of hurrying footsteps loud in the dim light of pre-dawn. For a moment, she had no clue where she was. Then she turned her head and saw Herleif's face inches from her own. Longing shot through her at his nearness and inaccessibility, even as she hastened into a sitting position. She could still hear the footsteps, louder now. Someone was approaching. Had she left it too late? Was she about to be arrested by the guards?

But it was the princess's face which appeared suddenly between the bars. Her eyes narrowed as they took in Adrienne's position, sitting on the bed beside the still-unconscious Herleif.

"So you *are* still here!" she hissed. "It's a good thing I decided to check. You should be finished by now. Get out of there, before you alert the whole guard to our bargain!"

Reluctantly, Adrienne moved forward, recognizing that open defiance wouldn't serve now. The night's events had given her a painful reminder of her own powerlessness in the situation.

She squeezed through the bars, watched with open disapproval by the princess, then followed the giant down the corridor. Neither of them spoke until they'd left by the same door they entered through all those hours before, emerging back into the gardens. The princess turned on Adrienne the moment they were clear of the building.

"How did you go?" she asked eagerly.

"Why was he unconscious?" Adrienne demanded by way of answer.

"It was night time," the princess said airily. "He was sleeping."

"He wasn't sleeping, he was unconscious," Adrienne said curtly. "There's a difference."

The giant sniffed. "I told you, I don't want this arrangement known. If you think I trust him to keep his mouth shut, you're a fool. Besides," she cast a disparaging look down at Adrienne, "even as a puny human, he'd snap you like a twig if he chose. Did you expect him to just let you work magic on him?"

"I wasn't going to tell him what I was doing," Adrienne improvised. "I would have told him I was there to clean the room, and then worked the enchantment when he was distracted."

"Huh." The princess considered this. "That's smart." She gave her head a shake. "But I don't see what it really matters. I still made it easier for you."

"So you did drug him," Adrienne said, unimpressed. "You didn't make it easier. The enchantment won't work unless he's awake."

The giant scowled. "You didn't say that before."

"I didn't know you were planning to drug him!" Adrienne protested.

"Very well." The princess let out a sigh. "I suppose you'll have to go back again tonight."

"Why can't I go now?" Adrienne asked desperately.

The giant shook her head. "Impossible. The next shift is

starting now, and the whole wing will be carefully guarded all day."

And the castle would be teeming with giants, no doubt, Adrienne added silently. It was frustrating, but not a total disaster. She still had provisions she'd brought with her from Frossenland. She could hide out in the gardens for the day if she had to.

The princess recaptured her attention, her voice lofty. "In light of the need for me to take further risks to give you another opportunity, I feel that further payment is owed me."

Adrienne ground her teeth together, but didn't argue. It occurred to her to wonder if this was the real reason the princess had drugged Herleif. Was she hoping to string it out, guessing that Adrienne had more gold? If what her mentor had said was true, it was often favored by elves for enchantments.

"How about this?" she suggested dryly, pulling the decorative comb from her satchel.

She knew from the light that sprang into the princess's eyes that she had her. The giant was only too ready to agree to another attempt that night in exchange for the golden comb. By the lopsided way she lumbered back into the building, Adrienne suspected the princess hadn't even sought her bed since the evening's festivities began. Not that she had any great desire to know what went on when the giants were up to their merrymaking.

The day passed slowly once again, Adrienne spending much of it dozing beneath the tree. Hopefully she'd need her strength for an escape that night. Fortunately the garden seemed little used. Whether it was because giants had no interest in the beauties of nature, or whether everyone was still sleeping off the effects of the previous night's revelries, Adrienne didn't know.

During her waking hours, her thoughts were all with Herleif. Knowing he was so near, but out of her reach, was maddening. His presence called to her, in a way so targeted and potent, it almost felt like magic. When she closed her eyes, she could feel him, his location in the nearby building tugging at her awareness.

These thoughts, while not exactly unpleasant, didn't make the hours pass more quickly. By the time the princess once again came to get Adrienne, she was ready. They moved through the castle as unobserved as the previous night, the princess's confident swagger easing Adrienne's fears a little. Whatever method she'd used to remove the guards, she felt secure in it. And the sounds of distant carousing told Adrienne that the celebrations were once again in full swing.

"How many nights of feasting is there before a wedding?" she asked curiously, as they approached the "guest wing" where Herleif was being held prisoner.

"For a royal wedding, a whole week," the princess said smugly.

"And is it customary for these feasts to occur without the groom?" Adrienne asked, the dry question slipping out before she could stop it.

Predictably, her companion's expression turned petulant. "It's not exactly *customary* for any giant to marry a human, let alone a member of giant royalty."

"But surely you're supposed to be present at the feast," Adrienne asked, regretting her snide comment and redirecting the conversation. "Won't anyone notice you slipping away for the second night in a row?"

The princess gave an unpleasant laugh. "By now, most are in no state to notice what I'm doing." The grin she sent Adrienne was unnerving, her teeth pointed and uneven.

They'd reached the relevant corridor by now, and the princess hung back while Adrienne hurried ahead. Before Adrienne even reached the right cell—which boasted no lit lantern this time—her guide had retreated back the way they'd come. Adrienne thought nothing of it until she slipped between the bars once again and approached the bed where Herleif was laid out. He was illuminated only dimly by the moonlight that slanted through a narrow, barred window well above their heads.

"Herleif?" she asked, suspicion washing over her at how still he was lying.

There was no reply.

It took only a minute to ascertain that he was in the same state as the night before, but it was long enough for the princess to be out of Adrienne's reach.

Adrienne could have screamed with frustration. She'd been tricked. She realized, thinking back over their conversation, that the princess had never actually promised not to drug Herleif this time. She'd just offered Adrienne another opportunity. Adrienne could only shake her head at her own folly. A real elf would have known better than to be so exploited.

The thought drew her up, caution overtaking her anger. Had it been a test that she'd failed? Did the princess realize she wasn't an elf? Had she just walked—or rather squeezed—her way into a trap? Should she flee?

But without any imminent danger, she couldn't bring herself to leave Herleif's side. Not without at least trying to rouse him. She didn't know if she could find her way back through the castle alone, and if she was going to be caught and killed, she'd rather spend the last of her time with her husband, however unaware of her presence he might be.

She tried all the same things she'd attempted the night before, unsurprised to achieve the same result. She quickly gave up on conventional methods of waking him, settling beside him and raising her voice in a forlorn melody. She didn't know how to sing so as to lift whatever drug was keeping him unconscious, and she soon found herself singing instead about their time together, the improvised words by turns joyful and sorrowful, full of hopeless longing and sweet, heartfelt love.

Again she didn't plan it, but again she fell asleep. And again, she was woken by the princess, appearing just before dawn in an even worse state than she had been the morning before.

"What are you still doing here?" the giant asked groggily. "Do you want me to get the wrong idea, with you sleeping in the room with my husband?"

"He's not your husband yet, Your Highness," Adrienne said, the respectful title passing bitterly over her lips. "And I think you know nothing went on. You drugged him again."

The giant exposed her jagged teeth in a grin that looked almost savage. "Outsmarted an elf, didn't I?" she leered drunkenly. "And my mother says I have no brains in my head."

Adrienne scowled, half inclined to take a stand then and there. But dawn was approaching, and the guards would surely be back soon. Reluctantly, she responded to the princess's imperious gesture, squeezing back through the bars and following her through the castle once again.

As soon as they reached the relative safety of the garden, she turned on the giant.

"Why lie to me?" she demanded. "Don't you want me to work the enchantment *you* asked for?"

"Of course I do," slurred the princess. "I'm just not in a hurry, and there's something else I want first."

"What?" demanded Adrienne, nonplussed.

The princess nodded toward Adrienne's satchel. "Do you think I'm a fool? You realize it's not normal for elves working here to carry their belongings around the castle, don't you? That's the behavior of someone protecting something. You've got more gold in there."

It wasn't a question, and the greed in her eyes was unmistakable.

Adrienne let out a breath. Nerves passed over her as she reached into her satchel. This was her last golden item, her last chance. She couldn't afford to blow it.

When she drew out the wheel, the princess's face lit up further. It was the largest of the items, and apparently the most receptive to magic, if that made any difference.

"This is the last bit of gold I have," Adrienne said. "Which means this is my last chance to work my enchantment and gain the advantage you promised me as part of our bargain. And the magic truly won't work if he's asleep. If I give it to you, I want you to swear that you won't drug him this time."

"Agreed," said the princess, barely seeming to listen to her as she snatched the golden wheel. "It's so bright," she muttered. "And so...round."

She didn't seem to be speaking to Adrienne, so Adrienne considered herself safe to start backing away. "Same time tonight?" she asked.

The princess gave a distracted nod, still focused on the golden wheel. Without looking up, she turned and strode unevenly back into the castle, no doubt to collapse on her bed for most of the day.

Adrienne watched her go, checking there were no witnesses before she once again concealed herself in the protective cave formed by the willow. She had barely enough supplies left to sustain her through the day to come. In more ways than one, the following night would be her last opportunity. She couldn't fail.

CHAPTER TWENTY-SIX

Herleif

Herleif sat up slowly, rubbing his head. It ached as if he'd just received one of Princess Mundia's ringing blows, but that couldn't be the case. He was alone in his room—or rather, his luxurious cell—and the runty giant was nowhere to be seen. It had been the same the day before. Twice in a row now he'd woken much later than normal, his head pounding painfully and his mind extremely confused.

He dropped his head into his hands, resting his elbows on his knees and trying to recapture the dream he'd been having. It had been pleasant. Much more pleasant than his waking reality, although that wasn't a high standard to match.

Pushing the miseries of his true situation aside, he tried again to snatch at the retreating sensations of his dreams. He'd dreamed about Adrienne, that much was certain. But that was nothing notable. He'd dreamed about her every night of their separation, not to mention many of the nights when she'd been lying beside him back at the northern castle.

This one had been different, though. He looked at the empty bed behind him, almost able to imagine her curled up against his side, as she had been on those cold nights when she'd unknowingly crept across the mattress during her hours of slumber. Her warmth was like a memory his heart knew but his mind couldn't quite grasp.

And her song. He sat up straighter, gripped by a sudden certainty. That had definitely been part of the dream. He remembered it now, and it was an unusual feature. Her sweet voice, raised in a melody so heartfelt and haunting it made his chest ache.

"Adrienne," he murmured aloud. The sound of her name in the stillness was like physical pain. Where was she now? Was she safe? Would he ever see her again?

Guilt ripped through him as he remembered the agony in her eyes after the curse had been triggered. First the agony of the physical pain it unleashed on her, then the anguish caused by his decision to leave. But he'd had no other choice. Allowing Adrienne to die for his curse was unthinkable.

He reminded himself of that truth over again, as a different source of guilt sent a shudder down his spine. He'd been given an impossible choice—sacrifice the woman he loved, or bring disaster on the kingdom he served. He couldn't let Mundia become Frossenland's queen. But if he didn't yield, he had no doubt Grograna would readily murder Adrienne, out of spite if nothing else.

He would abdicate. That was the best solution he'd come up with. Once Grograna released him to return to his own kingdom —no doubt with his petulant, violent giant of a false wife in tow —he would abdicate the throne to his sister. Poor Runa would likely not thank him, but she'd been living in the expectation of becoming queen one day for almost six years now. And she would be a better queen than Mundia, that much was certain.

Of course it was imperative that he didn't let Grograna learn his intention until the sham of a wedding was over and he'd been released. Otherwise she'd never let him go freely back to

Frossenland. Even once he was no longer in the line of succession, in his own kingdom he'd have the capacity to protect Adrienne. He had no doubt Mundia would take out her rage on him when she realized she'd been fooled, but that didn't trouble him.

The sound of heavy footsteps approaching caused Herleif to shoot to his feet. He'd been in his cell almost two weeks, and was familiar enough with the guard rotations to know that no change should be happening now. The two posted at the end of the corridor would be there for hours yet. But other than the single meal Mundia provided him with each night—usually served with a generous helping of both physical and verbal blows—he'd never had a visitor before.

Except in his dreams, perhaps.

He allowed his distaste to show openly on his face as the form of his so-called betrothed came into view. Even if she hadn't been a giant, Mundia's habitually sour expression was enough to make her unpleasant to look at. He'd yet to be in the same room as her without hearing her complain.

"What do you want?" he demanded, when she came to a stop outside his bars.

Her brows drew together in a scowl. "That's no way to talk to me, little worm."

"Your mother may be able to use threats and violence to win you an unwilling husband," Herleif said cuttingly, "but she can't make him like you."

A growling hiss passed between Mundia's clenched teeth. Now Herleif looked at her, she wasn't in a very good state. She looked like she'd imbibed much too freely the night before, and had probably slept little. Why was she up and visiting him, when it was barely noon?

"When we're married," Mundia promised him, "you will

have no bars to protect you. I will make you regret it every time you think to insult me."

"I doubt it," said Herleif blandly. "Now what brings you to my humble abode?" The sooner she left, the sooner he had privacy to resume his utterly fruitless pining over Adrienne, after all.

"I come with an invitation," Mundia said sulkily. It was her habitual tone. "Tomorrow is our wedding day."

Herleif just stared impassively back at her. Did she think he'd forgotten?

"And as such, you'll join us for a celebratory banquet tonight."

"A banquet?" Herleif repeated. That was a surprise. And Mundia didn't look any happier about it than he did.

"Those are her instructions," Mundia said. "I will collect you at the appointed time."

With a flounce, she turned away, loping up the hall with the long-legged gait of the giants and leaving Herleif alone with his thoughts.

They were conflicted. On the one hand, he would welcome a change, after so many days locked in one room. On the other, he didn't like the idea of being an oddity on display in front of Grograna's court. But of course, he had no choice in the matter, so there was little point in deciding what he preferred.

The day passed slowly, Herleif's thoughts, as always, on Adrienne. He couldn't banish from his mind the almost-memory of her song from his dream. It seemed significant somehow, like she'd been trying to tell him something. It made him almost eager to sleep again, for the slim hope of encountering her in his slumber.

But that was foolish. He needed to be fully awake, with his wits about him for whatever the evening would bring.

When Mundia came to fetch him, he didn't even waste energy on insulting her. He would save it for Grograna. Mundia gripped his upper arm in one enormous fist, marching him all the way from his room to the dining hall, making it very clear that he would be given no opportunity to escape. But Herleif had made his decision, little as he relished it. Even if there was a way to make a run for it, he wouldn't do it. That would be a death sentence for Adrienne.

He was dragged into the dining hall to such a chorus of jeers and boos that Herleif was momentarily too distracted to take in his surroundings. But as he was thrust onto a seat that he would barely be able to climb onto if unassisted, he couldn't help his gaze from passing in amazement over the opulence of the space. The decorations were lavish, and the food even more so. And little love as he had for giants, he had to admit that the general impression of excess was amplified by the sheer size of everything. The table was huge—the rough expanse of wood stretching all the way down the long room—and covered in food. All kinds of delicacies were piled high, and the knives and forks were made of what appeared to be gold. The giants seated along the table were dressed fairly simply, but Grograna was dressed in her habitual golden garb, and even Mundia wore a festive sash that Herleif hadn't noticed before. Presumably it marked her as bride.

A shudder rocked Herleif's frame.

Grograna rose, cutting off the jeers with a wave of her hand. Her smirk suggested she wasn't going to chastise any of her guests, however. One of the giants across the table from Herleif even went as far as to spit at him, leaning across the bowls of food to do so. The globule of saliva spattered Herleif's entire face, but he refused to flinch. Whatever these creatures thought of him, it couldn't be worse than his opinion of them.

The giant queen spoke at some length, the focus less on celebrating a wedding and more on how the giants of Kjemper would soon lord it over the puny human kingdom of Frossenland. Herleif sat through it all in stony-faced silence, projecting Adrienne's face before his mind anytime he was tempted to rise up and defy them all. Finally, Grograna finished gloating and sat, and the feast commenced. Herleif was hungry enough to devour a boar, but he watched in revulsion as the giants shoved entire handfuls of meat or vegetables into their mouths. It took him a few minutes of observation to realize that although their speed and eagerness were boorish by human standards—not to mention the unashamed way they elbowed their neighbors if they thought their preferred food was in danger of being taken—they were actually very neat. There was no mess of smeared food, or juice dripping down their chins. According to their own customs, they were probably on their formal behavior.

"Well, daughter, tomorrow you'll be married." Grograna was seated directly across from Herleif and Mundia, and her unemotional comment, although not private, wasn't loud enough to carry down the whole table. "It will be a relief to have you accounted for."

Mundia responded to this unflattering comment with her usual glower. "Don't think you'll be rid of me, Mother. I'll be making regular visits."

The queen gave a guffaw. "What will you do, fly over the wall? Do you think the Frossians have enough magic in their barren land to send you back and forth whenever you please?"

Herleif frowned in displeasure at this slight to his kingdom. Kjemper was even more barren than the northern region of Frossenland. He'd seen it himself.

Grograna was still shaking her head as she took a generous gulp of what appeared to be mead. "You may have beauty, girl, but your brains are as small as your head." She looked wisely at her closest neighbor. "It's the size, of course. The smaller the creature, the less intelligence they have. We see it with humans like this one." She jerked a thumb toward Herleif.

He wanted to roll his eyes. He wasn't sure what was more absurd. Grograna's insistence that her daughter was a beauty, or her ridiculous theory about intelligence being linked to size. One needed only to spend five minutes in Adrienne's company to see that was false. Not to mention the elves.

"That's not true, Mother, look at the elves," Mundia said, unexpectedly echoing Herleif's thoughts. "Everyone says they're very devious, and the ones in the castle haven't seemed lacking in intelligence to me. Certainly not as stupid as humans, even though they're smaller."

Herleif frowned up at the giant princess beside him. Elves in the castle? In Kjemper? Surely not. The creatures hated each other, and there could no more be elves wandering freely through the giants' castle than humans. He certainly hadn't seen any.

"Mundia!" Grograna's sharp rebuke only increased Herleif's suspicion. Mundia fell silent at once, and Grograna's eyes definitely flicked to Herleif. The queen wasn't pleased that he'd overheard her daughter's comment. What exactly were they hiding?

"Here," said Mundia, shoving a goblet toward Herleif. "Drink."

Herleif pushed it away, uninterested in mead. He had a strong head usually, but who knew how potent the giants' drinks might be? He'd be wise to keep his focus clear.

"I said, drink," Mundia said, her voice rising angrily as it always did if she didn't instantly get her way.

With exaggerated movements, Herleif pulled a glass of water toward him, holding Mundia's eyes as he tipped it up and took a long draft.

She let out a scream of frustration. "Not that one! This one!"

Her manner was so insistent, it caught Herleif's attention. A quick glance showed him that Grograna's eyes were also on her daughter, slightly narrowed.

"Why that one?" he asked cautiously, a suspicion stirring in his mind.

"Because I said so, that's why." Without a moment's warning, Mundia backhanded him across the face. Ears ringing, Herleif took a moment to regain his equilibrium, then turned back to face her, ignoring the guffaws that sounded from all sides at the human's humiliation.

He took the goblet, but he didn't immediately drink. He studied his prospective bride carefully, his thoughts circling around the previous two mornings, when he'd woken with a raging headache. Mundia had brought him wine both of the preceding nights, and he didn't remember her doing so any other time.

Suddenly his mind was full of the memory of his unusually potent dream, and the ghostly echo of Adrienne's song. He couldn't put any of his thoughts or suspicions into words, but he was increasingly convinced something was going on. Something not even Grograna knew about.

Cautiously, acting as though he was afraid of further violence, he raised the goblet to his lips. Moving his throat, he pretended to swallow down a large gulp. Mundia turned away, a triumphant smile curling her lips. Herleif took another false sip, aware of Grograna's eyes still on him. At the first opportunity, he emptied his goblet into that of the giant on his other side, who was already so drunk he would be unlikely to notice.

Following his instinct, Herleif began to fake signs of weariness. After his head had drooped forward three separate times, Mundia confirmed his guess. With a smug grin, she grasped the hair on top of his head, yanking his face up and letting out a harsh laugh.

"Of course his tiny frame can't hold his drink." Her taunt came across a little too studied, but the other giants didn't seem to notice. They jeered and slapped their thighs, continuing to eat and drink at a dizzying pace.

"Come on, little king," Mundia said mockingly. "Back to bed for you."

Still feigning drowsiness, Herleif didn't resist as she pulled him to his feet and marched him out into the corridor. Mundia was muttering in annoyance under her breath most of the way back, but she didn't speak to Herleif. She practically threw him into his cell, locking the door and disappearing again immediately.

Completely bemused, Herleif dropped the sleepy act. The strangest thing of the whole affair was that they'd passed no guards at the entrance to his corridor. What exactly was Mundia up to? He didn't light the lantern, opting to wait in darkness for events to unfold. Barely fifteen minutes had passed when he heard the princess's heavy steps approaching again, and he quickly draped himself over his bed, as if he'd collapsed there in a stupor. Hopefully he was about to find out what she was trying to orchestrate.

The footsteps stopped before they reached his room, and to his confusion, another pair of quieter ones continued. He held himself tensely, waiting in feigned sleep as the softer steps came to a halt just outside his bars, and the heavier ones retreated hastily. A shuffling noise began that he could make no sense of, then, impossibly, someone seemed to be approaching inside the room.

Herleif was so taut now, anyone looking closely would surely realize he wasn't unconscious. But he couldn't make himself relax. It went against every instinct to continue to lie prone and unarmed while an unknown enemy snuck up on him.

Then a soft voice spoke into the darkness, its familiarity shocking him into true immobility.

"That slimy snake! She lied to my face! Oh, Herleif, please wake up."

"Adrienne?" The sound of his name in that voice had unlocked Herleif from his stupor, and he shot upright, hardly able to believe the evidence of his eyes as he took in the moonlit figure standing before him. "Adrienne!"

He lurched forward, enfolding her into his arms as fierce joy vied with terror in his heart. What was she doing in his prison? How would he protect her now?

"Herleif!" Adrienne's choking cry came out muffled, since her face was now pressed into his chest. "Herleif, you're awake at last!"

Herleif pulled back at that, trying to search her face in the dim light. "At last? What does that mean?"

"This is the third night I've been here," Adrienne told him, her voice coming out rapidly, as if she feared they had only moments. "I made a deal with the princess to get access to you, but she tricked me, and drugged you so that I couldn't wake you the previous two nights."

Herleif stared at her in soundless shock, not sure which part to focus on. She'd been right here in his room twice without him knowing? Was that the reason for his dreams?

"She tried to drug me again tonight," he said stupidly. "But this time I guessed."

Adrienne made a disapproving noise with her tongue. "No doubt she thought she could extort more gold from me. Or get out of her end of the bargain and not have to follow up later."

"You made a deal with Mundia?" Herleif asked hollowly, dismissing the incomprehensible details and focusing on the imminent threat Adrienne faced.

"Is that the princess?" Adrienne asked. "I didn't even know

her name. But I could tell who she was from the crown. Ostentatious, these giants, aren't they?"

"Adrienne, why would you do that?" Herleif demanded, disregarding her question.

"Why do you think?" Adrienne asked crisply. Seeming disgruntled by the question, she tried to pull back, but Herleif held fast, refusing to let her go now he had her in his arms at last. Her voice softened as she went on. "I was trying to save you, of course. Did you think I'd just leave you to your fate?"

Herleif let out a low groan, but his arms pulled her closer. "You should have. I came here to keep you alive, and if Grograna finds out you're here, she'll kill you for certain." She would probably make it slow and painful, and do it in front of Herleif's powerless sight just for spite, he reflected, but he didn't add that thought aloud.

"Well, that's why we need to get out of here before she finds out," Adrienne said matter-of-factly. She gave him a look. "I didn't come here to attend the wedding, Herleif. I came here to find a way to free you."

Herleif released her at last, stepping back slightly as he ran one hand through his hair. "First of all," he said absently, "there's no wedding. Tomorrow's ceremony could never be anything more than a sham. I'm already married, if you remember."

"I do remember," Adrienne said, and in the darkness he could hear the smile in her voice. "It was a very memorable incident in my life."

Herleif smiled as well, warmth flaring in his heart. He was still terrified of the outcome, but he couldn't help his joy at learning that Adrienne had come for him. He moved to the lantern set on a nearby table, lighting it and turning back to survey his true wife. She smiled up at him, every bit as beautiful and dear as he remembered. More so. His imagination had never been able to do her justice.

"I've missed you," she told him, her voice little more than a whisper.

Herleif moved forward, cupping her cheek with one hand. "Adrienne," he said, not sure how to put the intensity of his thoughts and emotions into words. "I thought I knew loneliness in my years of exile. But I didn't know until I lost you how alone I could truly be."

"You didn't lose me," Adrienne said, leaning her face against his hand and closing her eyes for a moment. "I took a vow, Herleif—I'm yours as long as I live."

It took everything Herleif had not to crush her against him, but he restrained himself. The joy of being together didn't remove the danger Adrienne was in. He needed a clear head if they were going to get out of this mess.

"Adrienne, why did you make a deal with Mundia?" he asked anxiously. "Why would she let you in here? Why would she let you *live* if she knows you're in Kjemper? Is it possible it's a trap?"

"I don't think it is," Adrienne said thoughtfully, opening her eyes and lifting her head. "And she doesn't know who I am, of course. She thinks I'm an elf, and that we made a binding bargain for me to use magic on you to make you more malleable in exchange for her favor."

Herleif stared at her. "She thinks you're an elf?" He cast his eyes over his petite wife, letting out a laugh that was half groan. "You're not *that* small. But I suppose Mundia isn't the brightest star in the sky." He frowned. "Why would you want her favor?"

"That's not entirely clear," Adrienne admitted. "But there are definitely elves working with the giants, and she thinks I'm one of them."

Herleif's frown deepened. He would have denied it a short

while ago, but remembering the comment Mundia had let slip at dinner—and Grograna's rebuke for it—he wasn't so sure.

"Do you have a plan for getting us out of here?" he asked, putting the question of the elves aside for another time.

Adrienne bit her lip, drawing Herleif's eyes irresistibly to the feature. "Not a very developed one. There is a way, if it comes to it, but I'm not confident in my ability to..." She broke off, not finishing the thought. "I was hoping that instead of anything complicated, we could just leave the way we both came—on magic-laden wind. But we have to get out of the castle first." She glanced behind her. "I can slip through those bars, but I'm guessing you can't."

"We can't all be elf-like," he told her dryly.

Adrienne searched his face. "Why are you staying here, Herleif? Was it impossible to escape, or did you choose to stay?"

He ran his hand through her hair, pulling the loose strands back from her face. "I chose, love. Not because I want to be here, of course. But she had me in a corner."

"Well, it's time to get out of that corner," Adrienne told him bluntly. Her smile was a little shy as she stepped forward to meet him, laying a hand on his chest. His muscles jumped under her touch. "I haven't liked sleeping alone these last couple of weeks. I'd be glad never to do so again."

"Adrienne." Herleif's voice caught in his throat, her name coming out in a choke. "Adrienne, I want nothing more than to be your husband for the rest of our lives. But I can't protect you here. I hate to admit it, but in Kjemper, we're in Grograna's power."

Adrienne frowned at that. "I still don't understand it at all," she said. "Why does she want you here? Why did she curse you in the first place?"

"She wants me to marry her daughter," Herleif said. "So Mundia will be a queen among humans, lording it over all

Frossenland, instead of staying in Kjemper, where her runt-like size shames Grograna."

"So the purpose of the curse was to punish you for refusing to marry her daughter?" Adrienne asked.

"To punish, yes," Herleif confirmed. "And to make me yield. She wanted to ensure I was bitterly lonely. Lonely enough to be driven to take her offer and escape the bear form altogether. The terms of the magic were that no one could see my human face, and I couldn't tell anyone a single detail of my curse. If I failed in either of those restrictions, the magic would kill me slowly and painfully, with the only remedy found in me yielding and letting myself be brought here. I didn't dare even to contact my family. How could I tell them I was alive without telling them a single detail of the curse? How could I prevent them from looking at my face? And if I'd let my guard down, or made a mistake, it wasn't just me who'd suffer. Frossenland would have a giant queen—no doubt a puppet to Queen Grograna and her malice—forced upon it."

"But how?" Adrienne demanded. "How did she manage it? I thought giants couldn't sing like some humans can, or mine magic like elves."

"They can't," said Herleif, raising his hands hopelessly.

"So how did she curse you?"

"She used talismans," Herleif said. "Incredibly powerful ones. And she didn't just unleash the magic blindly, she directed it somehow. It made no sense to me at the time—it still makes very little sense. Like you said, giants aren't supposed to have access to any magic, let alone be able to wield it." He ran a hand through his hair, glancing around him, his thoughts on the unexpected opulence of the castle. "I know that it's theoretically possible to create talismans sophisticated enough to allow the person activating them to have some say in how the magic operates, and that's my best guess as to what happened. Of course, the creation of such talismans is regulated very closely, as you can imagine. It's almost like giving a non-singer the ability to harness magic. But to tell the truth, the regulations are rarely needed."

"Why?" Adrienne demanded. "Wouldn't everyone want to get their hands on talismans like that if they could?"

"No doubt," Herleif agreed. "But they can't. That's the point."

"Why not?"

"Because they require not only the highest level of skill from the elves creating the talismans, but also a truly breathtaking amount of magic. In crude terms—which is the only level to which I understand it—the elves have to put innumerable strands of magic into the talisman, anticipating almost every conceivable direction the caster might wish to take the magic, and providing the power to enable it. Very few elves would have access to that much magic in their lifetimes, and for those who did, a thousand simpler talismans could be made with the same amount of magic. And given how the human crowns regulate those sophisticated talismans, selling a thousand simpler ones would be much safer and more lucrative."

"So how could Grograna possibly have gotten her hands on one?" Adrienne asked, alarmed.

Herleif shook his head slowly. "It was more than one. And I have no idea. It's clear from the state of this castle that the giants have access to some kind of magic, and I can only assume she'd been gathering her resources for years in order to pull off what was a planned and targeted attack on my father and me. But even so..." He trailed off, then shook his head again. "There are more questions than answers, to say the least. I would never have dreamed that giants could get their hands either on that much magic or on elves skilled enough to manipulate it."

For a moment there was silence, neither of them able to

explain the unsettling mystery. Adrienne rested her head in her hands for a moment, thinking.

"So it was me looking at your face which triggered the magic?" she asked at last, looking back up at him. The mood instantly shifted as the focus turned away from speculation about the broader mysteries and back to their own, intimate dilemma.

Herleif bit his lip. "That began the process, I think. I felt the pain while I was still sleeping. But then..." He met her gaze, letting the heat that rose inside him at the memory show in his own eyes. "But then you kissed me, and that changed the course of the magic."

"What do you mean?" Adrienne asked, her voice delightfully breathless. She seemed mesmerized, her breaths coming unsteadily.

"When she realized Iver had weakened the curse, and I wouldn't be a bear all the time, Grograna wanted to make sure I didn't find solace in marrying a human wife and thereby foil her plan to make me yield," Herleif explained. "She added another layer to the curse. As it was, I would have had to last twenty years—fifteen more than I already had. But if I married, the time would drop to a single year. Except the restrictions were extended. In addition to those regarding my face, and telling anyone about the curse, I had to lie beside my wife every single night without ever sharing so much as a kiss."

He spoke calmly, and his gaze didn't waver from her face, but inside he wasn't so tranquil. Could she sense how much was within his words, how much he wasn't saying? Her eyes suggested that, like his own, her emotions were too convoluted to decipher, let alone put into words.

"Well, that certainly explains some bizarre aspects of our marriage," Adrienne said at last. She smiled. "Like your odd behavior the first night, when we were walking back to the castle after our vows."

Herleif gave a reluctant laugh. "I felt an utter fool. But I didn't know whether that night would count, and I wasn't willing to take any chances." He shifted forward, taking both of Adrienne's hands gently in his. "I wanted so desperately to tell you everything, Adrienne, but I couldn't. I was too afraid even to *tell* you that I couldn't, for fear that would count as telling you a detail of the curse, and would trigger the magic."

"And in the end I triggered it anyway," Adrienne said hollowly. "Because I didn't trust you enough to do as you asked. I broke my word. I'm so sorry, Herleif."

Herleif shook his head, fierceness entering his voice. "No, Adrienne. You can't blame yourself. It was absurd of me to expect you to keep those restrictions without any explanation. What wife isn't allowed to see her husband's face?"

"I like seeing it now," she offered, lifting one hand to touch her thumb to his cheek. "I still can't get over the wonder of being allowed to look right at you."

Herleif once again ran his hand through her hair, this time letting it tangle in her tresses and stay there rather than pulling it free.

"I didn't mean to betray you," Adrienne assured him. "My mother gave me the candle, but she didn't mean any harm, either. She'd been told that you were the prince, and that you'd taken a curse from a giant meant for the kingdom. That if anyone saw your face, the magic would be unleashed on Frossenland. And if no one saw your face for six years, you'd die." Her expression turned pleading. "I thought I was saving you, Herleif, not condemning you. It seemed just like you to give your life for the kingdom, but we had reason to hope that enough time had elapsed that the curse would be weak, and would do minimal damage to Frossenland even if released." She hung her head. "I had no right to make that decision, and I acknowledge it."

"It was a clever strategy by Grograna," Herleif said, unnerved by how accurately the giant queen had read from afar the likely response of Herleif's wife to that rumor. Had she guessed that Adrienne cared for him, or had she just assumed his bride would wish to ensure her husband lived to make her queen? A thought occurred to him, and he added sharply, "Who told your mother that?"

Adrienne gave him a meaningful look. "An elf."

Herleif let out a long breath. There could be no doubt that elves were mixed up with the giants somehow. He brought his gaze back to Adrienne and realized she still looked miserable.

"This isn't your fault, Adrienne," he told her again, bringing his other hand up so that he cupped her face from both sides. "From the beginning, our marriage was forged in secrets that weren't of your choosing. I don't blame you for what you did. You did try to ask the truth of me, and I told you nothing."

"Those secrets weren't of your choosing, either," Adrienne reminded him firmly. "Now I understand the curse you were under, I don't hold you responsible for any of it."

"You're too generous," said Herleif, far less inclined to be lenient with himself. "You knew nothing of the curse, but I did. It was unconscionable of me to trap you into this marriage knowing the risk it placed you under."

"Unconscionable?" Adrienne repeated incredulously. "Herleif, you're the most honorable man I've ever known. You did nothing to be ashamed of. And even knowing everything, I would a thousand times rather be your wife than be married to that man from the tavern." She lowered her eyes, her cheeks coloring once again. "I would a thousand times rather be your wife than safely unmarried back at my family's home, as well."

She snuck a look back up, and her cheeks reddened further.

She must have seen the heat blaze into Herleif's eyes at her declaration.

"I still feel guilty about the reason you married me, though," she added, once again shy. "You did it for my sake, even though it was only ever going to make your life harder."

"Harder?" Herleif repeated the word incredulously, his hands tightening where they still cupped her face. "Adrienne, are you mad? You think having you in my life was harder than my isolation?" His eyes searched hers. "When you came to me, I felt like I was alive again. In every possible way, you made my life better. I would rather go on forever as we were—secrets, distance and all—than spend a single day married to anyone else. I love you, Adrienne."

The words were barely out when Adrienne catapulted herself forward and up, her arms traveling up to meet behind his neck. Herleif responded immediately, pulling her closer and lowering his head to meet hers.

He kissed her with all the passion he had, and she responded in kind, her lips moving eagerly under his. His hands moved from her cheeks to encircle her, pulling her so tightly against him that she was lifted bodily from her feet to bring her face up to his. This was no hasty kiss of goodbye, guiltily stolen while Adrienne was suffering the pain of Grograna's curse. This was the way a husband kissed the wife he loved, fearing nothing, holding nothing back. Except it was all the sweeter and more potent because it contained months' worth of longing. How many times had Herleif dreamed of this moment? And yet, as Adrienne's lips moved against his, deepening the kiss, he acknowledged to himself that the reality exceeded every dream he'd ever had. With Adrienne pressed against him, one of her hands dangling over his shoulder and the other sliding down to rest on his chest, Herleif could feel the pain of their previous enforced distance melting away.

His heart protested as Adrienne broke off the kiss, but he forced his arms to loosen as he responded to her movement, lowering her to her feet and drawing back. When she made no move to pull away further, he rested his forehead against hers, breathing heavily. He would have preferred this moment to happen in their own castle, not the giants', but in that moment he wasn't likely to complain about anything.

The thought triggered a memory, which sent a rumbling chuckle through him. "I seem to recall thinking once that if we were ever free of the curse I'd miss the physical closeness we enjoyed when I was in my bear form, and you didn't hesitate to get close to me." He smiled. "I was a fool."

Adrienne laughed as well, the sound a little unsteady. "I didn't mind you as a bear," she said. "But I like this," she pressed a hand into his chest, "much better."

Herleif gave a contented grunt, breathing in the familiar scent of her.

"I love you, Herleif," Adrienne said, the simple words sending flame roaring through Herleif. "I won't let anything keep us apart now."

"Adrienne." Herleif's voice became urgent, his mind clearing, "I know it might seem like the curse is over, but you're not out of danger yet. If Grograna finds out you're here, she'll kill you. She killed my father for no other reason than to make me king, so that I could make her daughter queen. Do you think she'll hesitate to kill you for the same end?"

"I'm not leaving," said Adrienne fiercely. "Not without you. There's magic here, Herleif. I don't understand exactly where it's coming from, but if we can just harness it, we can—"

She cut herself off abruptly, and Herleif didn't have to ask why. He heard the heavy footsteps as well, approaching up the corridor. He cast his eyes around the room in panic, throwing off the last of the haze caused by their kiss as he tried to decide on the best way to protect Adrienne. It was too late for her to slip back through the bars. Whoever was approaching up the corridor would see her. Should she hide? There wasn't anywhere promising inside the room. And if she was found attempting to hide, she would most certainly be killed.

The footsteps were close now—they were out of time. Herleif drew back from Adrienne, throwing himself hastily into a sitting position on the bed, his eyes widened in warning.

"Try to look small," he murmured.

Adrienne blinked rapidly, then nodded, moving half behind an armchair and slumping down a little. Herleif watched critically as she smoothed her hair over her clearly human ears. He couldn't see how anyone could mistake his ravishingly beautiful human wife for a diminutive elf, but he could only hope she looked different to the eyes of a giant.

Two giants.

The unwelcome forms of both Grograna and Mundia loomed into view on the other side of the bars, the former looking furious while the latter hovered nervously behind her.

"What," demanded Grograna, her eyes shooting sparks, "is going on?"

CHAPTER TWENTY-SEVEN

Adrienne

Panic clouded Adrienne's mind, no clever way out occurring to her, but Herleif seemed ready for the question.

"No idea," he said, his tone insolent. He gestured at Adrienne. "From what this elf has told me, you should be asking your daughter that."

"Elf?" screeched Grograna.

Her eyes passed between the two humans, and Adrienne noticed that their gaze was a little unfocused. The two giants had clearly come from the feast, and Grograna's mind wasn't as sharp as it would have been a few hours ago. A tiny bubble of hope inflated inside her. Perhaps they could pull this off after all.

"She's no elf!" Grograna protested. "She's a human!"

"No, Mother," Mundia said, sounding aghast at the idea. "She truly is an elf. Look how small she is!"

Adrienne did her best to look confused that it was in doubt, tucking the hand that boasted her wedding band out of sight behind her skirts for good measure.

"Look at them side by side!" Grograna roared. "Are you a

fool, girl?" She turned to her daughter, cuffing her solidly over the side of the head. "She's not *that* small!"

"Look at her features, Mother," Grograna insisted. "And her pale hair. She might be tall for her kind, but she's an elf."

"If she's *not* an elf, why is she here?" Herleif asked, his cold tone so convincing, Adrienne told herself to improve her own performance.

As the giant queen responded angrily to the insolence in Herleif's tone, Adrienne cast her gaze subtly around the room, searching for anything that could help them. She needed to think of some explanation for her presence that would satisfy Queen Grograna before she dug too deep into Adrienne's story. If the giant caught a good look at her eyes, for example, she'd realize they were blue rather than the normal elven green.

Those same eyes revealed nothing of use, but it occurred to Adrienne that she had other senses. If there was some way to harness the strange magic to be found in Kjemper, this would be a great time to discover it. Adrienne reached out with her extra sense—the one only singers had—testing the space. The first thing she noticed was that some kind of latent magic seemed to be hidden on Queen Grograna's person. A talisman perhaps? A powerful one, judging by the way the power throbbed out from it. But Adrienne didn't know how to access that magic—it was unlikely Grograna would let her do so without a fight, and they couldn't match her for strength.

Her questing senses found something else as well. To her surprise, some kind of magic seemed to be leaking from Herleif. Adrienne focused on it, losing track of whatever malicious exchange was going on between Herleif and Grograna. He was stalling for time, and Adrienne couldn't waste it. She narrowed her eyes, trying to make sense of the power that seemed to form a thin connection between Herleif and her mind. Surely he had no talisman on him—it would have been confiscated by the giants long ago.

Staring intently at her husband, Adrienne tried to narrow her focus further. He was still in the clothes he'd worn to bed the night she'd stolen a look at his face. There likely weren't any spare clothes in Kjemper to fit him. Adrienne's eyes passed over the rumpled tunic, no longer white and crisp like it had once been. The moment they fell on the messy splotches that marred his chest, her magic awareness caught up with her visual observation, and all at once she understood. The magic was coming not from Herleif, but from his tunic. Specifically, from the wax that had been spilled onto it when he'd pulled her against him back at the castle, moments before he'd been whisked away by the wind.

In lighter circumstances, she could have laughed at the absurdity of it. The enchantment she'd unintentionally cast, giving her object control over that ill-fated candle, apparently included the wax it had spilled as well as the rest of the stick back at the castle. She'd thought it would be no use to her, but perhaps she could turn it to good account.

An idea was only half-formed in her mind when the verbal confrontation between Herleif and Queen Grograna reached a head. Before Adrienne knew what the giant queen was about, she'd reached a long arm through the bars and grasped hold of Herleif's leg, yanking him bodily from the bed where he sat so that he crashed painfully to the stone floor.

"Hey!" Adrienne yelled unthinkingly. The giant queen's yellow eyes turned to hers, and Adrienne hastened to cover her slip. Thinking of the elf who'd mentored her, she furrowed her brow in irritation, making her voice both higher and more curt. "I don't want part in any conflict. I'm here by Her Highness's order, and I'll not take the blame for it."

Princess Mundia looked predictably enraged, and Adrienne

sent her a look, attempting to communicate caution to her hot-headed conspirator.

"So he's claimed," growled Grograna, sounding unconvinced. She turned on her daughter, wobbling slightly on her feet. "Why would you send an elf here—if she really is an elf?"

"As preparation for the wedding, obviously, Your Majesty," Adrienne interrupted bluntly. For the sake of her imposture, she hoped the somewhat abrasive manners of the one elf she knew were indicative of the ways of their kind. "Her Highness was seeking someone to make the bridegroom more presentable for the ceremony, and I volunteered because I have a talisman with just the right sort of cleaning magic." She nodded at Princess Mundia. "Her Highness was to pay me in gold."

Grograna let out a screech of derisive laughter. "Then you've been fooled by a bad bargain, elf! My daughter has no gold of her own save her crown, and you must have known she couldn't barter that."

Adrienne furrowed her brow in feigned confusion. Inside she was thinking that this information went a long way to explaining the rashness of the giant princess's greed when she realized she could barter for Adrienne's gold.

The giant queen looked from Adrienne's apparent consternation to Herleif, who'd seated himself out of reach of the bars now, and the smug smile slipped away.

"It sounds like nonsense to me. How would you make *him* more presentable? You can't change his form."

"I understood it was his clothes that needed attention, not his shape," Adrienne supplied, her eyes lingering on the wax. Even now she could feel it with her magic, calling to her, willing to respond to any prompt. "I don't have anything strong enough to change his form."

"Of course not," the giant queen scoffed. "That takes immense power, more than a puny elf could comprehend." She narrowed her eyes at her daughter. "Why do you care about his clothing, Mundia? Are you so pathetic as to try to curry favor from a *human*?"

"I don't care about currying his favor!" Mundia protested, clearly outraged by the suggestion. Adrienne could have knocked her head against the wall. She'd offered the princess such a simple way to avoid revealing her attempted bargain to her mother, and Mundia was too defensive to take it. Adrienne cleared her throat, and Mundia's yellow eyes flew to her. She blinked, some trickle of comprehension making it through her mead-soaked mind. "He's already enough of an embarrassment as a bridegroom without soiled clothing," the princess added in a belated attempt to go along with Adrienne's story. "There are no other clothes to fit him here."

"Hm." Grograna looked between the three of them with narrowed eyes, clearly not fully convinced by their charade. If she decided that Adrienne was indeed human, she would surely guess who she must be. And then all would be lost for certain.

"Well, then, work your magic," she told Adrienne, her tone making it an insult. "Let's see this special cleaning power."

Adrienne was about to comply, then she remembered she was supposed to be an elf. "What of our bargain?" she asked suspiciously, her eyes flying to Mundia.

"Never mind your bargain," growled Grograna. "If you want to live to see the dawn, prove to me that you're here for the purpose you say."

Adrienne pretended to hesitate for a moment, then turned to Herleif, making sure her back was to the giants.

"What are you doing?" he murmured, under cover of the snide remark Grograna was aiming at her daughter.

"Trust me," Adrienne replied, her words barely more than a breath.

Herleif still looked confused, but he relaxed at once, his eyes on her face as she focused on the wax. She made a show of pretending to pull something out of her satchel, keeping the bag in front of her so the giants couldn't see that she had nothing in her hand. Then, without singing a word, she focused on the wax, instructing it to lift from the fabric. It responded at once, peeling away from the tunic and rising impossibly in the air. After pretending to shove the imaginary talisman back into her satchel, Adrienne held out her hand to receive the wax, closing her fist around it so that the warmth of her hand turned all the bits into a single sizable lump.

She looked up to see Herleif watching her in amazement, and although she was sure it was his true reaction, his impressed demeanor was also entirely convincing for the part he was playing.

"Huh." Far from being impressed herself, Grograna sounded irritated that the so-called elf had demonstrated the truth of her claim, thus denying the queen the pleasure of a summary execution. "Get out of here, then. Back to your own part of the castle." Her eyes narrowed as they rested on Herleif. "We have business with this scum."

Adrienne hesitated, afraid of what they'd do to Herleif if she left him alone with them. But one glance at his face revealed his opinion on the matter. His eyes told her to go as clearly as words, and she realized that if she were to stay, it would be as great a danger to him as to herself. It wasn't as though the giants would hesitate to abuse him if she was there, anyway.

Reluctantly, she turned away, waiting for the giant queen to open the door of the cell rather than slipping through the bars. She could only be grateful that no one seemed to be paying close attention to her as she fled. She had no idea which part of the castle the queen had intended as her destination, and she considered herself lucky that she was able to find her way back to the garden.

But when she was safely hidden beneath the willow again, she felt no sense of relief. She was full of nervous tension, the elation of the kiss she and Herleif had shared driven away by her fear of what the dawn would bring. Herleif and Mundia were supposed to marry the next day, and her last attempt to simply spirit Herleif away first had failed. She would have to rely on the other strategy her mentor elf had suggested, and she was far from confident in her ability to pull it off.

She knew nothing of the wedding plans, but judging by Mundia's state, she guessed that it wasn't to be held first thing in the morning. When the sun finally rose, and she caught the sounds of bustle from the castle, she emerged cautiously. If she wanted to stop the wedding, she would have to actually be present, regardless of the risks.

She got a few strange looks as she moved through the castle, but no one actually stopped her. She kept to the edges of rooms, skulking under furniture, hovering in alcoves, and generally trying to look as small and inconspicuous as possible. It didn't take her long to learn that the wedding was to be held two hours past noon, in the throne room. She retreated to her hiding place to wait out the remaining hours, trying to ignore both her exhaustion and her hunger.

The change in the atmosphere of the castle was unmistakable as the wedding hour approached. At the first opportunity, Adrienne inched in behind a group of bustling servants, making her way into the throne room and hiding herself behind a giant-sized stone plinth.

She'd been lucky to enter the room without being accosted. She'd hoped to see other elves to blend in with, but in spite of all the mentions of their kind, she saw no glimpse of any coming to attend the wedding. Perhaps it was for the best. Next to a real elf, she would have a hard time arguing that she was just a tall member of the same species.

She felt dwarfed in the enormous room. The walls were of a dark stone, and the ceiling was impossibly high above the head of even the tallest giants. Building the castle must have been quite a feat. Golden furnishings were to be seen everywhere, and the throne itself, located behind the bride on a raised dais, was made of glass. An icy throne for a frozen kingdom.

In spite of the heaviness of the walls, the room was far from dark. The afternoon was advancing, and sunshine streamed through high windows on all four sides of the room, filling the space with light and causing the golden furnishings to glow. If circumstances were different, Adrienne might have been quite enchanted by the sight.

But circumstances weren't different. She was here on a rescue mission, out of which she was unlikely to emerge alive, and she couldn't afford to forget it. Her heart hammering in her chest, she waited for the room to fill. Giants thronged in, all of them dressed with great neatness, but none in robes of the resplendent type she'd seen Queen Grograna wearing the night before. When the queen arrived, she once again wore gold. Even the bride, who arrived shortly after her mother and was soon positioned at the front of the throne room, wasn't dressed with as much magnificence. Adrienne began to suspect that the somber hues worn by the other giants were the result of a royal order. Apparently Grograna didn't want to be outshone by anyone on any occasion, even her daughter's wedding.

Adrienne noticed a number of the guests eyeing the golden furnishings with expressions somewhere between greed and longing. She would hazard a guess that no one but the queen was allowed to possess this much gold. Perhaps, given the volume of magic lingering impossibly in Kjemper, the gold was even protected by enchantments so that no one else could touch it. She'd heard with her own ears that even Princess Mundia wasn't allowed to own any gold. If so, Grograna had successfully created the impression that the city overflowed with gold, when in actual fact, it may be the case that little to no other gold existed outside the walls of the castle.

Considering the queen critically, Adrienne realized that she was on the taller side even for her kind. No wonder she was ashamed of her abnormally short daughter, given giants seemed to value size so highly. The queen was accompanied by a man of similar height to her, dressed in expensive-looking clothing which was still nowhere near as eye-catching as the queen's. Adrienne was no expert at judging giants' age, but the man looked too young to be Grograna's husband.

A moment later, music filled the air, and everyone present fell silent. Adrienne peered out from behind her hiding place, surprised by the sweetness of the melody. The music came from an enormous harp on the far side of the room. A female giant was seated at the instrument, manipulating the strings with true skill. The sound seemed out of place in the setting. Despite the opulence of the throne room, the mood wasn't what she'd call festive. In the sudden hush, the doors were thrown open, and two guards dragged in a stony-faced Herleif.

Adrienne's breath caught in her throat at the sight of him. In spite of his relatively clean tunic, he looked very much the worse for wear. He had a new bruise on the side of his neck, and his hair was considerably tousled. Adrienne's hand was in her pocket, and as she curled it into a fist in an inadequate outlet of her anger, it closed around the lump of wax she'd removed from his shirt. She'd forgotten she even slipped it into her pocket.

The wedding was the most surreal event she'd ever witnessed. Herleif's face remained impassive as he was half-dragged up the long aisle of the throne room, the harp continuing to play in the background, although it was mainly drowned out by the jeers of the watching crowd. Adrienne heard many disparaging cries of *human*, and some of the giants even spat at

Herleif as he passed. Others aimed kicks at him, although thankfully the aisle was too wide to allow many to make contact.

All the while, Mundia stood on the dais, smirking at her betrothed as if his humiliation somehow reflected well on her. Adrienne couldn't imagine what was in the princess's mind.

When Herleif was deposited none too gently on the dais beside Mundia, another giant stood up behind them, clearing his throat. Adrienne was expecting a long and ceremonious speech, but the giant got straight to the point. His brief words of welcome and explanation jolted Adrienne into action. She hadn't anticipated needing to be ready so soon after the ceremony began.

Under cover of the giant's booming voice, she shuffled through the few items left in her rucksack. Pulling her certificate of marriage out with shaking hands, she cleared her throat. Singing was the last thing she felt like doing, but this wasn't like the wax, into which she'd previously poured object-controlling magic, however unintentionally. This time she would have to work new magic.

All the magic you need is here, the elf back in Frossenland had assured her, slapping a tiny hand on the document. *And it will be stronger with your husband in the room, and both of your wedding bands present.*

The elf had made it sound simple, but from where Adrienne was sitting, it felt anything but. She'd tried to get a look at Herleif's hands as he was pulled into the room, and from what she'd seen, he wasn't even wearing his ring anymore. No doubt Grograna had taken it, since it was made of gold. Adrienne pushed aside her anger at the thought of the giant queen stealing her husband's wedding band, focusing instead on the task of the moment. Hopefully the magic would still work without Herleif's ring.

She reached out with her extra sense, trying to identify the magic that was supposedly sitting dormant in these items. Again, she could feel the pull of whatever powerful talismans Grograna carried on her person, but nothing from the certificate or her ring. She would just have to try, and hope for the best. There were no other options now.

Softly, Adrienne began to sing. Her voice came out wavering, but she forced herself to keep going, using the words the elf had taught her. She sang of that night in the tavern and of the months that had followed, invoking the vow she and Herleif had made. Tuning out the officiating giants' words and the general hum of the crowd, she focused on the harp still playing in the background, molding her song to its melody. Coming up with tunes had never been a great talent of hers.

The elf in Frossenland had told her that volume wasn't important for the magic to work, so she tried to keep her voice quiet. But bolstered by the harp's music, her song grew in strength enough that those standing closest to her had just started turning to locate the source of the noise when she felt it.

Something subtle but powerful flared to life, a force that was connected to the document in her hand and the ring on her finger, even to Herleif standing on the dais, but which didn't originate from them. It had its own life, one that had sprung into being the night they took an oath to bind themselves together. Adrienne could feel it, like a living thing that twined around both her and Herleif, drawing its power from them in a way that had nothing to do with her being a singer.

It felt like no other magic she'd ever encountered, but she didn't stop to explore its nature. Instead, she seized hold of it just as she would grasp magic she'd channeled up from the ground, sending it out in an invisible net that encompassed both her and Herleif.

She'd been too focused on her own battle to follow the wedding ceremony, but she realized now that Mundia was speaking formal words of marriage in response to the officiating giant's prompt. As Adrienne watched, the giant princess received a quill—the feather dyed gold, of course—and bent to write on a document the giant had produced. Adrienne couldn't help noting that unlike her own certificate of marriage, this one was crisp and fresh. But although Mundia lowered the point of the quill to the parchment, she didn't write.

The princess's brow furrowed in confusion, her hand still on the page for so long that her mother became impatient.

"Hurry up, girl, write! What are you waiting for?"

"I can't," Mundia said, turning to her mother. "It just...won't write."

"What are you talking about?" Queen Grograna raged. "Stop stalling, Mundia. It's past time to get this over with."

"I'm not stalling," the bride protested, her usual petulant expression clear on her face. "I tell you, it won't write. It's like something invisible is stopping my hand."

The drama on the dais had momentarily distracted those standing closest to Adrienne, but in the hush that followed Mundia's words, her song was finally exposed to them. Several large, square heads turned toward her, and one giant let out a shout.

"There! There's a tiny girl singing there!"

"Singing?" Grograna swiveled rapidly, her yellow eyes narrowed in anger as they searched for the giant who'd spoken.

Adrienne swallowed. There was no hope of continuing her deception now. Elves could only access magic by mining it from the ground. They didn't sing. And Grograna would be furious when she realized she'd been lied to.

"Behind that plinth!" another giant yelled, leaning sideways to get a better look at Adrienne. He moved forward in two huge strides, grabbing Adrienne's arm roughly and yanking her out from her hiding place.

Adrienne's voice faltered, but although her song died, she could still feel the magical protection she'd created remaining powerfully in place. No, she realized, that wasn't quite accurate. She hadn't created the protection. It had already existed—she'd simply activated it.

Still clutching the certificate, Adrienne was dragged before the queen, who'd mounted onto the dais to stand beside her daughter.

"You!" the giant hissed. "You *are* a human! And a singer!"

"Adrienne." Herleif's strangled groan cut Adrienne to the heart. "What are you doing here?"

Grograna's gaze sharpened, comprehension leaping into her eyes. "This is her? This is the human girl?" She bared her teeth in a singularly unnerving laugh. "You would prefer this puny stripling to *my* daughter?"

"A thousand times over," Herleif said. His voice was calm now, and although he spoke to Grograna, his eyes remained fixed on Adrienne's. She could see the determination behind his anguish. Adrienne could almost read his thoughts. He knew they would wish to kill her and leave him alive, and he would die defending her before he let that happen. He'd rather die together than watch them kill her.

"You insolent pup," roared Grograna. She looked like she was about to strike him when she suddenly remembered the initial cause of complaint. Her eyes narrowed again as they focused back on Adrienne. "What did you do? Why can't my daughter sign her marriage documents?"

"Because her bridegroom is already married," Adrienne said, proud that her voice didn't waver. "I am his wife, and I invoke our marriage vows."

"Do you, little runt?" The queen laughed again, the sound unhinged. "Let's solve one problem at a time."

Before Adrienne realized her intention, her hand had shot

out. Herleif let out a cry, but the queen didn't strike Adrienne. Instead, she snatched the certificate of marriage from her hand. It was Adrienne's turn to cry out, but Grograna's attempt to rip it in two had no effect. With a scream of rage, the giant tried again, to no avail. Adrienne could feel that strange magic still wrapped around the parchment—it was as though the rumpled, fragile paper had become as hard as diamond.

"Fine," Grograna growled, her breath coming in pants now. "We'll have to end your flimsy human marriage the simpler way. Guards, execute her."

"NO!"

The cry came from Herleif, but it was Grograna's upheld hand that halted the progress of the guards who'd sprung forward at her command. One of them paused, spear already lowered with its point toward Adrienne, his eyes fixed inquisitively on his sovereign.

"I've changed my mind, I want to do it myself," Grograna said, snatching the spear from him. She'd taken one menacing step toward Adrienne, who was powerless to escape the grip of the giant who still held her, when something flew into the queen's side. In his desperation, Herleif had wrenched himself free from the guard who held him, trying to throw his body between Adrienne and danger. Instead of tackling her around the waist, he hooked both arms around one of her trunk-like legs and tugged with all his strength.

"Herleif!" Adrienne cried, as the force of Herleif's unexpected assault sent Grograna toppling. At her cry, the giant who held her slapped his hand over Adrienne's mouth, presumably to stop her from assisting her husband through songcraft.

Herleif and Grograna went down with a crash, and Adrienne fought vainly against the iron grip around her. Grograna might want Herleif alive, but it would be too easy for her to accidentally kill him with the huge spear very much mixed up in the tangle of limbs. Watching with her heart in her mouth, Adrienne realized that the two of them were fighting over the weapon.

After a moment of confusion, Grograna emerged victorious, winding Herleif with a blow to his stomach and wrenching the spear free with her superior strength.

"I'll deal with you later," she hissed at Herleif, who was curled on the floor, temporarily stunned into immobility. Grograna turned to Adrienne, saying nothing, just letting out a feral snarl as she raised the spear once again.

For a moment, Adrienne's mind was blank, no thought in her head but her impending death. But as her gaze flicked to Herleif, whose eyes were wide and terrified as he struggled to regain control of his body, she knew she couldn't just give up. She'd taken a vow, and now her life and death affected someone beyond herself.

But what could she do? She had no weapon, and no freedom to wield it even if there had been one. She couldn't move her arms, and the hand of the unknown giant was even silencing her voice. She didn't see how the mysterious magic of her marriage vows could help protect her now, and she couldn't think of any way to access any fresh magic.

Any fresh magic.

Adrienne stilled as she remembered what was in her pocket. Straightening her back, she faced Grograna, willing her to open her mouth and speak. The queen certainly seemed the type to want to taunt her victims rather than just kill them dispassionately.

Grograna didn't disappoint her. As she drew her arm back for the killing thrust, her lips curled in a grin. "Once I've taken your life, you puny worm, I'll take your husband and your kingdo—"

She never finished the word. As soon as she'd begun to

speak, Adrienne had seized her opening. Without attempting to move either her mouth or her hands, she'd reached out to the magic she'd previously stored in the far away candlestick. Whether the candle back in Frossenland was now soaring bizarrely through the air, she didn't know. But the wax in her pocket had responded at once. Under her direction, it edged its way out past the fabric of her gown, then zipped through the air and straight into Grograna's mouth. Adrienne narrowed her eyes in focus as she forced it in further, so that it became wedged in Grograna's throat.

With a gurgling wheeze, the giant dropped the spear, both hands flying up to clutch her throat. Shocked cries rang out around the space, and the guards started forward in confusion, but Herleif was faster. Springing to his feet, in one fluid motion he seized the spear from the stone floor and plunged it straight into Grograna's chest.

Pandemonium erupted around them as the giant queen toppled to the floor. The random wedding guest who was gripping Adrienne released her in shock, and she leaped forward. She reached Herleif's side in time to hear his calm, quiet words to the dying giant before him.

"You killed my father and threatened my wife. You'll never harm anyone again."

Grograna's eyes were widened in disbelief for one moment more, then the comprehension disappeared as her body slumped, lifeless, across the steps of the dais. The guards were almost on them, and Adrienne knew they had moments at most. Desperately, she lunged past Herleif, one hand seizing their certificate of marriage from where it lay at Grograna's side, the other digging into the queen's robes, following the direction of Adrienne's extra sense.

Her hand closed around something hard and cold just as a guard grabbed her and ripped her backward. Herleif had been similarly swarmed, and Adrienne knew if she didn't act quickly, it would be too late. She barely glanced at the talisman in her hand, noting only that it was made of gold. The magic it held was alarmingly potent given her lack of training, but she didn't have the luxury of doubt. Raising her voice, she pulled on the concentrated power, releasing it in an unformed surge, giving as little direction as possible to that first burst.

The wind that suddenly tore around the throne room was so intense, even the giants cowered under it. Figures ran in all directions, arms thrown up over their faces as they knocked one another to the ground in their panic.

"Adrienne!" Herleif's cry brought Adrienne's focus back where it needed to be.

"Grab hold of me!" she screamed above the melee. Trusting him to do as she'd asked, she raised her voice in song, trying her best to channel the overwhelming force she'd unleashed.

Herleif came launching out of nowhere into her line of sight. Taking her instructions a step further, he threw his arms around her, enfolding her form completely inside his larger one. Chaos continued to rage outside, and Adrienne's shaking voice still grappled with the out-of-control torrent of power, but within the circle of his arms, everything felt calm and as it should be. Even though she knew they weren't out of danger yet, Adrienne felt safe, down to her very core.

Her song rose triumphant, and the next moment, the winds swept under them, lifting their feet from the stones below and sending them hurtling straight upward.

CHAPTER TWENTY-EIGHT

Herleif

Herleif tightened his hold around Adrienne, burying his face in her hair in an effort to shield them both from the wind. The sheer power of it was terrifying. It was every bit as strong as the one that had carried him to Kjemper in the first place. How was Adrienne controlling it?

Controlling might be generous, of course. They wheeled wildly through the air, doing two circuits around the ceiling of the throne room before the wind sent them bursting through one of the tall windows. Glass smashed around them, several points of sharp pain telling Herleif he'd been cut by the shards. With any luck, Adrienne was safe from the glass inside his arms. It seemed likely, given how completely he was wrapped around her petite form.

He could hear the screams of shock and rage below them, but within seconds they were impossibly high in the air, out of reach of the giants' retribution. Herleif barely felt anything when he thought of Grograna's death. He'd imagined seeking his revenge many times since the giant queen killed his father. On those occasions, he'd assumed that he would feel a savage victory, but he didn't. His main reaction was relief that he'd managed to keep Adrienne safe from her violence. That had been his primary concern. He could only hope his actions didn't lead to all-out war between Kjemper and Frossenland.

But he would worry about that later. For now, his focus remained on the ground speeding past far below them as Adrienne sent them reeling drunkenly southward. He could feel the tension in her lithe frame as she continued to sing, and sensed that it took all her energy to direct the tidal wave of power that seemed to be fueling the wind. He didn't distract her, just clinging to her for dear life as they continued to fly toward Battlement Wall. When they passed over it, he felt himself relax slightly. They might still plummet to their deaths, but at least they'd die on Frossian soil.

Looking down, he could still see the trail of destruction Grograna's winds had left when they'd carried him northward. Adrienne struggled a little in his arms, and he loosened his grip enough for her to peer down as well. Her song took on an anxious note, and the wind changed course a little, sending them over a forest and away from a nearby town. He didn't know if Adrienne was unwilling to lower them to the ground or unable. He'd guess the latter. They were still soaring at a terrifying height, and her control seemed shaky.

They continued to follow the path left by his previous passage, and about a quarter of an hour passed before the wind began to slow. It seemed the magic was running out. Just as they began to dip, Herleif let out a cry. Adrienne followed his gaze, and he could tell from her sharp intake of breath that she'd seen it, too. The ruined wall of the castle—their castle—looming ahead through the decimated treetops.

"We're almost home." Adrienne's song faltered as she whispered the words, every syllable communicating utter exhaustion. They plummeted downward, and Adrienne resumed her song with a frantic edge. She must be weary indeed to forget that she had to keep singing for them to stay airborne.

When the clearing was almost below them, Adrienne's voice dropped again, whether on purpose or by design, Herleif couldn't tell. Given the way she drooped in his arms, he wouldn't be surprised if she was at the end of her strength. She managed to let out another catch of song as they neared the ground, however, pulling them up in time to slow their inevitable crash.

Herleif once again wrapped himself tightly around his wife, his much larger body taking the brunt of the fall as they collided with the grassy ground. He felt the last of the wind disperse, and suddenly they were still, alone in the clearing in the slanting light of late afternoon.

"Adrienne," he gasped, unfurling himself and pulling her onto his lap on the grass. "Are you all right?"

She rested her head limply against him, giving a slow nod. "I'm all right," she murmured. "Just very tired. That was more magic than I can really manage, if I'm honest. Much more."

"You were amazing," Herleif said, his voice choked. "You saved us both. I still don't fully understand how you did it, but I know I'd be lost without you."

"It was this as much as me," Adrienne said.

She lifted a crumpled parchment, and Herleif took the certificate of marriage gently from her hand, a smile curling his lips. Soiled, scrunched, and slightly ripped, it was the most precious document in the world.

"And my ring helped, I think," Adrienne added, lifting her left hand. "I tried to use yours as well, but I guess they took it from you."

Herleif shook his head. "They didn't, actually. Releasing her for a moment, he pulled off his boot and produced his ring from inside it. "I knew Grograna would take it if she caught a whiff of the gold, so I hid it at the first opportunity." His smile softened as his eyes searched Adrienne's weary but triumphant face. "I wasn't about to let anyone get it off me when I fully intend to keep it on my person for the rest of my life."

With gentle fingers, Adrienne took the ring from him, smiling at it for a moment. She dropped the other item she clutched—some kind of small ornamental golden urn—and took Herleif's hand. Caressing his fingers, she slipped the ring back onto its rightful spot, her eyes shy as she looked up at him.

Holding her gaze, Herleif pushed his hand upward so that their palms were pressed together and their fingers interlinked.

"Are you sure, Herleif?" Adrienne asked, her voice constricted. "I mean...I'm sure I'm not the wife you imagined taking. Or your family imagined, for that matter."

"You're right," Herleif said evenly. "I could never have imagined anyone as perfect as you, Adrienne. I'm not that creative. And as for my family, they'll love you if they have a grain of sense. Otherwise they'll suffer my wrath." He gave her a swift grin, lightening the jesting words. "I intend to be as tyrannical a ruler as Grograna, you see."

Adrienne didn't laugh, lowering her gaze to her lap. "I'm serious, Herleif. You weren't exactly filling your rightful position at the time of our marriage. I'd understand if you—"

"If I what?" Herleif interrupted, indignant. "If I forsake my vows? I wouldn't understand that. Do you think I have no honor?"

Adrienne didn't answer, her head still bent as she huddled in his lap. Herleif considered her face for a moment, then placed one hand under her chin, lifting her face gently but firmly to his.

"Adrienne, you said once that you married me of your own

will. That however unfortunate the circumstances, you made your own choice. Do you still feel that way?"

She nodded solemnly, surprise in her eyes.

Herleif felt his features soften in the slightest of smiles. Her response sent relief coursing through him, washing away any lingering hint of doubt as to the right thing to do.

"I feel the same way," he told her seriously. "I did from the very beginning. Can you believe that?"

Tremulously, Adrienne nodded again.

"In one sense I acted in the heat of the moment," he acknowledged, "but I knew what I was doing. I meant what I said, and I've never regretted our marriage." He slid his hand up from her chin, his thumb moving in a circle over the soft skin of her cheek. "It's true that honor demands I stay true to the vows I made to you. But even if it didn't, it would change nothing for me. I love you, Adrienne, with all my heart. I didn't love you when we married— I didn't know you. But I fell in love with you so quickly. Much more quickly than I even admitted to myself. As soon as I came to know you, I couldn't help it. You're the kindest, most generous-hearted, most cheerful and selfless woman I've ever met."

He flashed her a smile, his eyes roving over her as he added, "It doesn't hurt that you're astoundingly beautiful either." Her cheeks colored delightfully, and Herleif gave the back of her head a gentle squeeze as he added more seriously, "Adrienne, you're the only wife I want, as long as I live. I can only hope that by some unlikely chance, I'm lucky enough for you to feel the same, now we're free of all the danger and all the secrets."

"I do," Adrienne said, her eyes shining with moisture as she lifted them to his. "I love you, Herleif. I never dreamed any husband could be as true and kind and honorable as you are. There could never be anyone for me but you."

Herleif needed no more encouragement. Pulling her against

him with the hand now tangled in her hair and sweeping his other arm around her, he pressed his lips to hers. Adrienne kissed him back with complete abandon, her hands finding their way up to his chest and fisting in his tunic as she attempted to pull him even closer. At last, at last, they were free to fully belong to each other, free of the danger of the giants, with nothing and no one to come between them for as long as they—

"HERLEIF!"

The frantic cry made them pull hastily apart, gasping in air as they turned to see who had shouted. Herleif's eyes widened at the sight of his mother sprinting across the grass, hair loose and tears streaming down her cheeks.

"Mother!" He sprang to his feet in time to receive the older woman, who barreled into his arms with a sob.

"Herleif, it's true! You're alive! I didn't dare to believe it, but I had to know for sure, then when we got here and saw the damage, I feared the worst, and I—"

"Herleif?" A second, shyer voice interrupted this barely comprehensible flow of words. Keeping one arm around his mother, Herleif turned to see a slender girl staring up at him in amazed delight.

"Runa!" he cried, kneeling down to embrace his sister. He could hardly believe this girl on the brink of being a young woman was his Runa. She'd been a sweet six-year-old when he and his father left the capital to ride out for their ill-fated visit to the northern castle. "You've grown so much!"

"Oh, Herleif, I'm so happy you're alive!" Runa cried, throwing her arms around him. "Now we can all be happy again. *And* I don't have to be queen," she added naively.

Herleif let out a rumbling laugh, joy so powerful it was painful sweeping through him. Without warning, a stab of grief cut through it, and he rose to his feet to once again face his mother.

"I wish Father was here, too."

She smiled sadly, laying one bracing hand on his cheek. "I know. So do I. We have much to discuss, but not now."

Her eyes strayed past Herleif, and he turned as well, to see Adrienne brushing grass off her skirts, her cheeks fiery red at having been caught in a passionate embrace with the uncrowned king of Frossenland.

"Mother, Runa," Herleif said, moving swiftly to Adrienne's side and taking her hand in his, "this is Adrienne. My wife."

He expected his mother to be shocked, but she surprised him. "So I've been told," she said, her eyes thoughtful as they rested on Adrienne's countenance.

"Your Majesty," said Adrienne, dipping into a curtsy that wasn't very steady. Herleif slid his arm around her, supporting her weight. She would have to sleep soon, or she'd simply collapse. "I'm honored to meet you."

"Adrienne!" Two new figures joined the scene, Adrienne's brothers emerging from the contingent of guards currently standing to attention behind the dowager queen and princess.

"Adrienne, you made it back," one of the brothers said, relief evident in his voice. "When you were gone so long, we were frantic."

"I'm sorry to worry you all," Adrienne said remorsefully. "If there'd been a safer way, of course I would have taken it. But I had to be there in person for it to work."

"You have nothing to apologize for," Herleif told her firmly. He raised his face to their audience. "Adrienne saved my life, quite literally. She breached the stronghold of the giants' castle and used her magic—and sheer bravery—to break me out, right from under the giants' noses."

Adrienne made a soft noise of protest, which he silenced with a look.

"Don't deny it, it's the plain truth."

"Then you have my eternal gratitude," his mother declared, her eyes on Adrienne. "And although I'll be honest that it's not what I would have chosen for Herleif, I can certainly appreciate—"

"Mother," Herleif cut her off firmly. "I completely understand you will need time to adjust to my change in circumstances, but I want you to know that I won't tolerate any insult to Adrienne. Not only is she my wife with the full force of the law, but I love her unreservedly. I have complete confidence that she will be a wise and just queen for Frossenland, and the best and truest support I could have in my role as ruler."

Adrienne pressed more closely against his side. He got the sense she was both overwhelmed and pleased by his praise. He gave her a squeeze, trying to communicate that he'd meant every word.

"I didn't mean to offend either of you," his mother said quickly. "Or to disparage Adrienne. My comments were a reflection on the fact that she's a singer. Have you forgotten that royalty do not generally marry singers, Herleif?"

Herleif frowned, nonplussed. "Don't they?" He lifted one hand to scratch the back of his head. "It rings a bell now you mention it. I can't say I paid much attention to these matters before the curse. Matrimony was far from my mind."

His mother smiled, giving her head a little shake. "You were only eighteen," she said. Her eyes passed back to Adrienne. "Well, it is what it is. Frossenland is to enter a new era, it seems. After all, Prince Farrin of Medulle has just married a singer, even if it is a little different, given she's foreign royalty herself." She nodded as if in decision. "We must take what comes, and trust we do not become like the Reviled Lands."

Adrienne looked at Herleif, clearly confused, and he frowned again as he tried to remember his history lessons. He didn't recall much focus being given to the island east of Vadolis, which no one had visited for generations.

"What does marrying singers have to do with the Reviled Lands?" he asked. "Surely we're not in any danger of being cut off from the other kingdoms like they are."

"I'm sure we're not," his mother said briskly. "And I won't let vague traditions prevent me from welcoming my new daughter-in-law into the family."

She smiled at Adrienne, and although the expression was reserved, Herleif knew his mother well enough to recognize that she was genuinely committed to welcoming Adrienne as befitting both her station and the nearness of relationship. His heart swelled with gratitude. He would do everything he could to smooth Adrienne's path as she was catapulted into royal life, but having the former queen in her camp would be at least as valuable.

"I gather that your wedding itself was not precisely what one might desire for the reigning monarchs of our kingdom," his mother added briskly.

Herleif and Adrienne exchanged a private smile as Runa piped up.

"Herleif," she said, her voice awed, "is it true you won her in a dice game in a tawdry tavern?"

"Runa!" Her mother's shocked rebuke made Runa jump guiltily.

"That's what Felman told me," she said, her tone defensive.

Herleif sent a conspiratorial smile at the older of his brothers-in-law, who was squirming under the queen's quelling gaze. Felman had plenty of experience as a big brother himself. It was no surprise he'd taken pity on the twelve-year-old's curious questions on their journey north.

"The details are immaterial," Herleif's mother said with dignity. "What we can know with confidence is that your brother acted at all times according to the integrity with which he was raised."

"That's certainly true," Adrienne chimed in. "I can attest to that."

Queen Sylvi nodded in gracious acceptance of this tribute to her son. "As for the wedding..." Her voice trailed off as she considered them. "The circumstances being what they are, I'm sure we could hold a belated wedding, with all the proper ceremony due to your status, Herleif."

Herleif frowned, not taken with the idea. He looked down at Adrienne, a questioning lift to his brow. "Is that what you want, Adrienne? A big, fancy state wedding?"

"Well..." Adrienne hesitated. "I don't mean to be difficult. But I don't feel any need for it," she said simply. She leaned down and picked up the crumpled parchment which Herleif had dropped when he so naively thought he was finally free to passionately kiss his wife without interruption. "As far as I'm concerned, we have all the legitimacy we need right here."

"I feel the same way," Herleif said, his face softened in the smile that was only for her.

His mother let out a sigh. "Well, it would be little irregular, anyway," she said, conceding defeat. "I suppose we could still hold a celebration of some kind, to welcome Adrienne formally to her new role. In a few months' time, when things have settled down."

"If we wait a few months, then it can be a celebration of our first anniversary," Herleif said approvingly. "I like that idea."

Adrienne made a faint noise of agreement beside him, and his eyes strayed down to her.

"You need to sleep," he said firmly. "As soon as possible."

She met his gaze, her eyes telling him more clearly than

words that she also was thinking of their conversation back in his cell in Kjemper. What had she said?

I haven't liked sleeping alone these last couple of weeks. I'd be glad never to do so again.

Warmth roared to life inside him, and he gave her another squeeze. Their future held so much promise, so much joy to explore. Not least of which was the ease of sleeping beside Adrienne without a hood covering his face, he thought dryly.

"There are multiple rooms in readiness," his mother said, cutting into their moment. "We've been here for a few days, trying to decide what's best to do. The room I gather you used as a bedroom during your years here has been blown open, but there are plenty of others where Adrienne can sleep."

She turned to a servant who'd appeared beside her as if on cue.

"Prepare one of the rooms for Queen Adrienne. She's weary from her travels and in need of immediate rest."

Herleif felt Adrienne's start of surprise at the new title, and he looked down, keeping his eyes on her face until she met his gaze. He sent her a reassuring smile, placing one fist over his heart.

Her eyes followed the gesture, and she relaxed into a smile of her own. He was fairly certain she understood his silent message. A lot of things were about to change, and dramatically. They could never return to their strange but beautiful life of isolation here in the northern castle. But some things wouldn't change, in the weeks ahead or all the years to come.

Now and always, Herleif's heart would beat for his wife. He had so many reasons to be grateful to Adrienne—she'd stripped away his loneliness, broken his curse, saved his life, and extricated his kingdom from danger. But none of that was why he looked forward with such eagerness to a life together. It wasn't gratitude that fueled their marriage.

The simple, beautiful truth was that while he might have taken a wife in haste, he'd come to love her more deeply with every day that had passed since. And, miraculously, she'd somehow come to love his surly, uncommunicative, bear-formed self in return.

What more could he want than a life by her side?

EPILOGUE

Adrienne

Four months later...

Adrienne leaned her elbows against the railing of the balcony, gazing out at the beautiful rose garden below. Most of the blooms were gone, but a few still added their bright colors to the late summer scene, their scent wafting up to her lavish suite.

It was still hard to believe it could really be her suite. The beautifully furnished receiving room connected to an even more extravagant bedchamber which she shared with Herleif, and then his own receiving room was beyond. And of course a host of servants tended to their every need, while guards stood outside the doors at all hours of the day and night. It was a far cry from a few rooms reclaimed in a dusty, abandoned castle in the woods.

There were parts of her new life that were still utterly overwhelming, but there were other aspects Adrienne greatly enjoyed. Such as the sumptuous food, and the fact that it was always a pleasant temperature in the castle. And, most importantly, being with Herleif. Being able to see his face every day, share a bed with him at night, and kiss him whenever opportunity presented.

"Adrienne?"

She turned back toward the suite, a smile lighting her face as the subject of her thoughts approached.

"I'm here."

"Are you ready for tonight?" Herleif asked, joining her at the balcony. He nudged her shoulder with his elbow. "Your Majesty."

Adrienne shook her head, a wry smile on her face as she wrinkled her nose at him. "I can't get used to that."

"You'd better," Herleif told her. "It's about to be made official."

Adrienne shook her head again. Being queen was truly the strangest thing about her new life. The celebration that evening, where their anniversary would be marked and she would be formally crowned, didn't really change anything. She'd had the title since the moment they arrived in Sunniva.

What a day that had been.

Adrienne still felt dizzy when she thought about her arrival at the capital. It had been a whirlwind, to say the least. From what she could tell, everyone had been sincerely delighted at the return of the prince who'd been believed dead. But not everyone was as pleased to have him arrive already married to an unknown village girl. Herleif had been quick to send a message to anyone who dared to cast doubt on Adrienne's right to her position, but she tried not to hide behind him. She knew she had to win people over in her own right if the mutters were ever going to die down completely.

It would likely be a long process.

But for all the detractors, there were many more who'd

welcomed her without question, including Runa, a sweet girl whom Adrienne found very easy to love.

"I'm sorry I've been so occupied all day," Herleif said, studying her face. "How was your session with the tutor?"

"It was good," Adrienne said brightly. She cast her mind back to her hour with the professor Herleif had hired from the Academy of Song to train her privately at the palace. "I think I'm getting the hang of healing enchantments. They're so much more nuanced than I realized when I first tried to perform one. Honestly, I'm incredibly lucky I didn't end up with permanent damage in my legs from my inexpert healing of them. I suppose the sheer volume of magic involved was my saving grace."

Herleif pursed his lips, obviously not relishing the reminder that Adrienne had broken both of her legs in the course of rescuing him. He'd been unmanageably agitated when she'd told him about it, only settling down once the limbs in question had been thoroughly examined by a physician.

Adrienne smiled up into his troubled face. "And you don't need to apologize about today. A king has many demands on his time."

Herleif sighed, gripping the railing with his strong hands. He was a little too tall to make it practical to lean on it with his elbows. "Too many, and often not the ones I'd choose," he agreed. His face settled into a frown. "I had to postpone my meeting with the new Selvanan ambassador, unfortunately. The council regarding the situation with the giants took most of the day in the end."

"Really?" Adrienne turned to fully face him. "Not bad news, I hope. Don't tell me the giants have declared war at last?"

Herleif shook his head quickly. "Thankfully not. We received a message from the new monarch. It was carefully worded, not quite accusing me of killing a foreign monarch, and not quite offering any acknowledgment of her murder of my father. It was effective in its message, which was to distance the new regime from Grograna. I don't think an attack is imminent, but we'd be wise to continue to monitor the border closely."

Adrienne raised an eyebrow. "I suppose advisors must have written the missive. I doubt Mundia has that level of subtlety."

"No, it's not her," said Herleif, surprised. "Didn't you know? She has an older brother, and he's the new king of the giants. That's why Mundia was to be sent away to rule Frossenland. She was never going to rule Kjemper."

"I didn't realize that," Adrienne said. So that had been the well-dressed younger giant with Grograna at the wedding. "So Grograna's son has taken over from her."

Herleif nodded. "And I don't think he intends to avenge his mother's death, at least not openly." His voice turned dry. "From the little I witnessed during my time in Kjemper, I suspect he's privately delighted with me for clearing the way for him to ascend the throne much earlier than hoped. Although of course he can't say that."

Adrienne was no stranger to unhappy family relationships, but even she shuddered at the thought of such an attitude. She could only be grateful the human royal family of Frossenland were nothing like that.

"Well, I'm glad there's no sign of war," she said. "So why did the meeting take all day?"

Herleif ran a hand over his chin. "The elves are still insisting that it's impossible that any of their kind could be assisting the giants in any way."

Adrienne snorted. "Impossible? We witnessed it with our own eyes!"

"But that's just the trouble," Herleif answered. "We didn't, did we? We heard them make cryptic comments, and we drew conclusions from the way they responded to you when they thought you were an elf. But we didn't actually see any elves."

"What about the sophistication of the talismans Grograna used against you?" Adrienne demanded. "They must have been made by powerful elves, surely!"

"If I'm right about where her power came from," Herleif said. "Obviously I think I am, and our experts haven't been able to suggest any more credible explanation, but I can't deny that a lot of my conclusions are guesswork. And there are no other living witnesses to what happened." He scowled. "To tell the truth, I think many of my advisors suspect me of exaggerating or misunderstanding exactly what happened that day."

An outraged retort rose to Adrienne's lips, but Herleif didn't seem to feel the need to be defended.

"It doesn't matter what they think, of course," he went on. "It matters that we find out exactly what access the giants have to magic, and how. The reality is, even if we could prove that Grograna's talismans were made by elves, we couldn't prove that those elves willingly cooperated with her. Maybe they were forced, or maybe she stole the talismans."

"It is possible," Adrienne said reluctantly, thinking of the deceased giant queen.

"So we're at an impasse," Herleif said. "The elves who attended the council today declared it unthinkable that any elf would help a giant."

"What about the one who fed that tale to my mother?" Adrienne challenged. "Surely he was acting on Queen Grograna's orders."

"I assume so," Herleif agreed. "But again, we have nothing but our own speculations to support that idea."

Adrienne frowned. "Or the one who sent me after you. She didn't want to help at first, then when she learned how high the stakes were, she seemed torn. I think she was involved somehow, or at least knew of it, and she helped me because she felt guilty and wanted to make it right. She said something about absolution." She thought for a moment. "I really think she must have known what's happening in Kjemper, Herleif. She seemed to be trying—clumsily, I might add—to do something altruistic to help, and thereby make atonement. She even said her reasons for helping me weren't to do with me, but to do with what I was fighting. For it to be enough that an *elf* considered making amends of value in place of a normal bargain, then whatever she felt guilty about must have been bad."

Herleif thought this over. "Another instance where it's only speculation, but maybe it's worth us sending someone to find out. We could send an investigator with the messenger who's going to take her the talisman when it's finished. Where exactly does she live?"

"I can't tell you," Adrienne admitted reluctantly. "Part of our bargain was that I wouldn't send anyone to bother her with questions, or expose where she lives to anyone at all. We're supposed to leave the replacement talisman with the shopkeeper in Toveham. Come to think of it, I suspect she made that bargain because she foresaw us following exactly this train of thought."

"That's too bad," said Herleif regretfully. "But we certainly won't breach your bargain. Now you're queen, these things will carry extra weight. It would pay to be cautious."

Adrienne nodded her agreement, not even feeling relief that he hadn't pressed her. She knew he wouldn't. Herleif didn't have a demanding or manipulative bone in his body.

"But we will keep looking for answers," he assured her. "This isn't over, not by a long shot. I fully intend to figure out the truth about the elves, but that's not my primary concern. Even without understanding how the elves are mixed up in it, no one denies that there's something going on in Kjemper, something big and dangerous. I know I'll have to proceed cautiously, but I don't intend to just let it sit. A fight of some kind is coming, and we'll face it standing up."

Adrienne leaned against him for a moment, somehow managing to be both anxious at the prospect of the conflict that would surely come and still comforted by his strength and confidence.

"And we'll face it together," she said softly.

"Always," Herleif agreed, putting an arm around her.

She closed her eyes, breathing in his scent, and grounding herself in the feel of being encircled by him. They would face whatever came, and they would prevail. She knew it deep within her core.

"Oh, I almost forgot," Herleif said, breaking the silence that had fallen after his words. "I ran into Kettil in the courtyard. He asked me to pass on a message. Your mother, Felman, and your sister and her family have arrived. They've all taken rooms in the inn where Kettil's working."

"I'm so glad they're here in time for tonight's celebration!" Adrienne said, straightening. She was only too glad to let the somber mood fall away, and return her attention to the more immediate future, which was about celebration not conflict. "They were supposed to be here yesterday, they must have been delayed on the road." She sighed. "I wish they would accept rooms in the castle like we offered them."

"Give them time, love," Herleif said comfortably. "Once they have the chance to see your life here, they'll adjust. And they're coming for the private luncheon with us tomorrow, so we'll have the opportunity to show them around."

"Do you really think they'll all eventually decide to move to Sunniva, like Kettil has?" Adrienne asked him anxiously. "I would be so glad to see them in a better situation."

"Only time will tell for sure, but I really think they will," Herleif told her. He reached out, pulling her back into his arms and resting his head on top of hers. "Change takes time to get used to, even good change. And none of them are used to the idea of receiving anything they haven't worked hard for, so it's only natural it makes them uncomfortable at first."

"That's certainly true," Adrienne sighed. "At least we know they're well provided for in the meantime." She laid her head against Herleif's chest, relaxing as another thought occurred to her. "And if we're really going to reinstitute regular visits to the northern castle, that will provide opportunities to see them."

"Precisely," Herleif said. "Now, as much as I enjoy talking about your family, I have more important matters to attend to."

"What?" Adrienne asked, raising her head to look at him in confusion.

"You," Herleif informed her solemnly, his eyes intense as they rested on hers.

Even after months without the curse's restrictions, Adrienne's heart still raced when he gave her that look. A smile curving her lips, she pushed up on her toes, turning her face up invitingly.

As she'd known he would, Herleif took the bait, lowering his lips to hers and pulling her close. But she'd barely had the chance to respond when a sharp rap at the door caused them to pull apart.

Herleif let out a comical groan, earning a grin from Adrienne. "Are we never to have a minute alone?"

"You should have thought of that before reclaiming your title," she scolded him as she crossed the room to the door. "You could have pretended to still be a bear, and we could have kept living in our abandoned castle."

"That was an option?" Herleif demanded in mock outrage. "Why did no one inform me?"

Adrienne laughed, her hand on the doorknob. "This will be the maids ready to make me presentable for tonight—yes, it takes this many hours, apparently. So I suggest you make yourself scarce unless you want to get pulled into it."

Herleif needed no further warning, slipping through the doorway into their bedchamber and presumably on to his own receiving room beyond. Adrienne watched him go fondly, a smile still on her lips as she opened the door to receive a veritable army of attendants. After all, he was worth all the hassle that came with his title.

That conviction buoyed Adrienne a few hours later, as she tried to catch her breath in front of the enormous crowd that had gathered in the throne room to watch her formal coronation. Seeing her family beaming at her from the front helped, as did remembering the throne room in the castle at Kjemper. Compared to that, life in the castle in Sunniva was a delightful dream.

But even these comforts paled into insignificance when she felt the pressure of Herleif's hand in hers, and turned to find him watching her with his love and joy on full display as the crown was lowered onto her head.

She could never have predicted her marriage, and she'd certainly never seen Herleif coming. But somehow, without intending any of it, she'd found herself living a life more joyful than she'd ever dared to hope for, with a husband who put every other man in Frossenland to shame. Being queen of Frossenland was enormous, but being Herleif's queen was neither too much nor too little. Standing at his side, having his love...it was everything.

And she had the rest of her life to love him back. Which was precisely what she intended to do.

NOTE FROM THE AUTHOR

Thank you for reading *Song of Winds*. I hope you enjoyed returning to the world of Providore. I would be so grateful if you would consider leaving a review on Amazon—it would really make a difference!

If you want to learn more about the magic of Providore, and find out what's going on with Emmett (the brother of Farrin from *Song of Ebony* and *Song of the Sea*), check out *Song of Moonrise*, the next installment of *The Singer Tales*. You'll find more adventure, fantasy, mystery, and hard-won happily ever afters!

Join up to my mailing list at deborah gracewhite.com to be kept up to date on new releases, specials, and giveaways, such as bonus chapters. You'll receive some great freebies, too, including *An Expectation of Magic*, a novella which is a prequel to my completed YA fantasy series *The Vazula Chronicles*.

Plus, you'll receive *Dragon's Sight*, an 8,000 word prequel to my completed YA fantasy trilogy *The Kyona Chronicles*.

Again, thanks for entering the world of Providore! I hope to see you back again.

ALSO BY DEBORAH GRACE WHITE

The Kyona Chronicles: YA Fantasy

The Kyona Legacy: YA Fantasy

The Vazula Chronicles: YA Fantasy

The Kingdom Tales: Fairy Tale Retellings

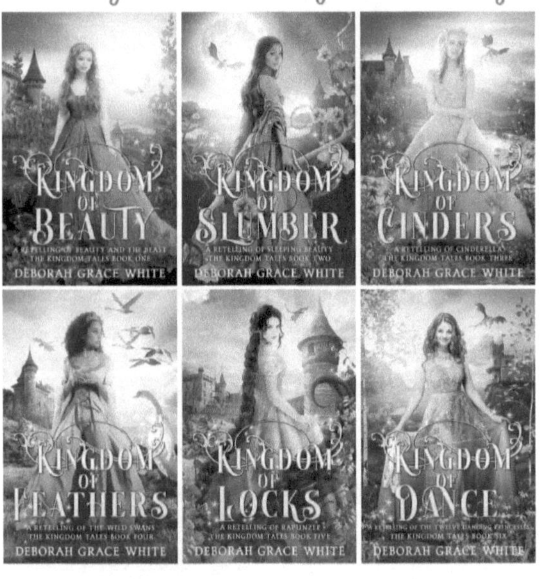

The Singer Tales: Fairy Tale Retellings
(releasing throughout 2023)

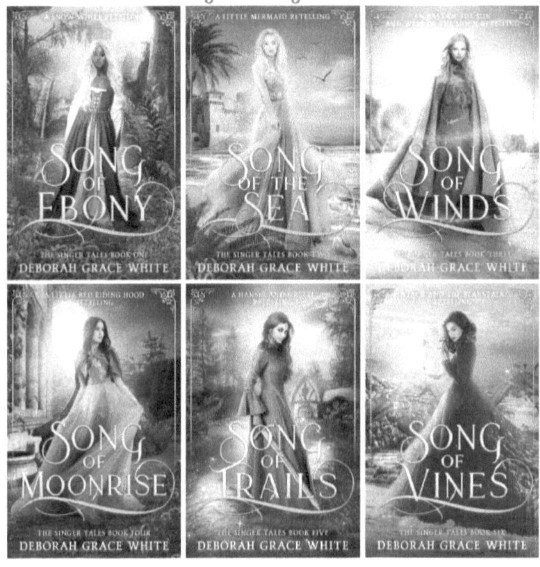

ACKNOWLEDGMENTS

I want to give a big thanks to all the usual suspects for their help with turning *Song of Winds* from a rough draft into a publishable story.

Ray, my patient husband and first reader, for your good listening and great feedback. My betas for being so constructive and so encouraging: Dad, Mel W, Adrian, and Mum. Thanks also to Shae for the excellent job proofreading. Any remaining errors are of course my own.

Thanks to Karri for this fantastic cover that so perfectly captures Adrienne's petiteness and elven features, and to Becca for the gorgeous map that continues to bring Providore to life.

To you, the reader, thank you for giving me the privilege of being an author.

And most importantly, to God, who is the only one we can always and completely trust.

ABOUT THE AUTHOR

I've been a reader since I can remember, growing up on a wide range of books, from classic literature to light-hearted romps. The love of reading has traveled with me unchanged across multiple continents, and carried me from my own childhood all the way to having children of my own.

But if reading is like looking through a window into a magical and beautiful world, beginning to write my own stories was like discovering that I could open that window and climb right out into fantasyland.

I cannot believe how privileged I am to actually be living that childhood dream and publishing my own novels. I do so from my hometown of Adelaide, Australia, where I live with my husband and our three little ones.

I've never outgrown my love of young adult stories, so the genre of young adult fantasy was always going to be my niche. Feel free to email me at deborah@deborahgracewhite.com and introduce yourself! Or subscribe to my mailing list at deborah gracewhite.com for free giveaways, sales, and updates.